T0246148

SANCTUARY

SANCTUARY

Valentina Cano Repetto

A NOVEL

CamCat
Books

CamCat Publishing, LLC
Fort Collins, Colorado 80524
camcatpublishing.com

Hardcover ISBN 9780744309461
Paperback ISBN 9780744309485
Large-Print Paperback ISBN 9780744309539
eBook ISBN 9780744309508
Audiobook ISBN 9780744309560

Library of Congress Control Number: 2023942333

Book and cover design by Maryann Appel
Artwork by Diana Kovach, Ksana Gribakina, Terriana, Weasley99

5   3   1   2   4

For C and L

MADDALENA
1596

DIPPED THE SILVER SPOON INTO the steaming dark liquid and filled it with death.

The dusky blue of the soup plate's painted lilies gleamed through beef and broth, flakes of chopped herbs swirling around the rim of the majolica. I could almost see the enameled figure at the bottom, the maiden always bent of knee, the unicorn's head heavy on her lap. The empty forest around them as if the world had come to a hush.

I doubted I'd manage to reach the maiden with breath left in my body.

I took the first sip of the weak stew. There was a trace of bitterness, a tail end of it, but the rosemary and the basil had disguised it, faithful friends they always were. Even now, the herbs spoke to me, whispering warnings in their earth-soaked language that I blinked away as the liquid scorched my throat. I knew all too well what I was doing.

"It's too hot," Francesco said, his large eyes squinting at the steam.

I forced myself to smile. "Blow on it for a few seconds. Gently," I added as his cheeks puffed up with air.

I looked down the stone table at my other children, eating in silence, my eyes and mind attempting to fly over the empty seat and falling like shot birds. At the end of the table, Florindo sat staring at the walnut backrest of that same empty chair, conjuring up the same tendrils of golden hair that I could still feel under my fingers. His spoon hovered over the plate.

"Eat, *sposo*," I said.

He blinked and the tears fell but he did as he was told. A good husband and father. A good man.

I followed my own instructions and drank more broth, the vital part, my jaw too tight to chew through beef. The only sounds were the tapping of spoons against majolica and the roar of the torrent behind the mill. But under layers upon layers of the noises that had filled my days since it had happened, there was that one sound. That crack. It ricocheted through me still.

A twist of nausea made me bite the inside of my lips. I looked up at one of the etched cornices that encircled the *sala,* focusing on a gold-leaf curlicue as I breathed and swallowed the bile down. If I became ill now, so soon, none of this would work. They would all stop and they must not.

How I wished we'd never left Genova. That we'd never come to this place.

I did what I could to ignore the bite of sudden hot pain in my stomach and dipped my spoon back in the stew. My hand trembled. Candlelight contracted like a pupil.

Please let this be over quickly.

SIBILLA
1933

THE CAR ROLLED OVER YET another stone, the thin and worn leather seat doing little to cushion the steel knobs and joints that had been knocking against me for the past half hour. My hands flew to my stomach to cover the small mound that still didn't require many adjustments to my waistlines, the mound that was the first and last thing I thought about each day. All this movement couldn't be good for him, for the boy I knew I carried. I felt his maleness like a bone ache. It hadn't felt like that before, not in the other two pregnancies. With care, I smoothed out my skirt, eyes sliding down to look for snags in the rayon stockings I'd bought especially for this trip. They were pristine.

The driver jerked the steering wheel, and the car rattled as if it were considering spread-wheeled collapse as it swerved to avoid half a tree trunk. I winced and shifted again.

We'd had the option of a better car at the station in Ovada, one with seats so cushioned and oiled they looked like sofas in those well-to-do clubs that peppered Torino, but Giovanni had insisted on this one. He had to have his reasons, of course, but it couldn't have cost very much more than hiring this rickety contraption, and we had the money now. Habits of the middle class, I supposed.

Yes, out of which his clever mind has lifted us.

Because we now owned a home, a villa, and not just that but a mill and hectares upon hectares of land.

The thought was like a sip of brandy.

With a smile, I slid my hand off the mound and slipped my arm through Giovanni's. I peered past the driver's head. "Do you think there's much more to go?"

"Why?"

I didn't need more than that to know I'd said the wrong thing. Not an unusual occurrence in our five years of marriage, but it still managed to yank me off-center when it happened.

"I was just wondering, that's all," I said, and forced a smile into my voice.

He smoothed out a crease on a trouser leg with a hand that I could have sworn had a small tremble in it. "You're sure you weren't thinking this is too far flung a place to be convenient? That perhaps I've made the wrong choice?"

How had he gathered all of that from my simple question? It was true, he hadn't consulted me before purchasing the property, placing the deeds on our kitchen table just three days before we were meant to take the train down here, but what good would my opinion have been in these matters? I knew nothing of mills or of purchasing land. Besides, he had bought it all with the money from his invention, his patent, money that was his and not mine. He didn't need to consult with me on its use.

The car gave another jostle and I pressed a hand to my stomach once more, as if that alone could keep the child safe. A gust of cold worry swept through me. I didn't know what I'd do if I felt the cramps now, the red loss soaking into my rayon stockings.

"This is strategically smart, Sibilla."

"Yes, of course," I said, blinking, though I didn't know what he meant. "What do you see?"

"I-I don't—"

He gestured outward. "Look, then."

I swallowed, brought my mind to heel, and did what he said, though there wasn't much to see. Out the window smudged with fingertips, I saw a crude road with stones tumbling in all directions, as if a fleeting river had swept over them in the past hour or so, and trees packed so tightly together their limbs grew intertwined under canopies of needles. Felling one would have brought knots of them crashing.

I had no idea what answer he wanted, so it would have to be the truth.

"I don't see anything but trees."

"Exactly," he said. "No competing mills, no real neighbors. Up on the mountain behind the villa, we have hectares of oak trees that have sat untouched for generations and that we can transform into our fortune. You have to look at it with its potential in mind. Use a bit of imagination." He sighed at my silence and flicked his dark eyes to me. "I would have thought you would understand what an opportunity this is for us, whether or not the mill is a bit distant from the hair salons and picture shows."

His words stung like nettle, forcing me to look away from him and into the trees as I blinked back sudden tears. A tightness took hold of my chest even as I chided myself for being so silly. Much too sensitive.

Because I couldn't blame Giovanni for his words. I knew he couldn't help being irritable. Someone who was accustomed to working with fellow engineers, discussing ideas I could barely pronounce let alone understand, would not have found me amusing company today. Until he'd snapped his newspaper open, all I'd managed to talk about during the train ride from Torino had been the child. A man who had found a way to improve the efficiency of sawmills without any assistance but that of his own mind had had to listen to hours of female nesting chatter.

Well, I'd not bother him until we reached the mill. I wouldn't ruin this for us. I'd keep my mouth tightly shut.

⌒⋉⌒

THE DRIVER HAD JUST URGED the car onto another road, this one narrower and without a single signpost, mostly mud and rocks, when I first glimpsed our new home. A roof of toothlike tiles made of red clay had sprouted a hat of green ivy leaves. I sat up and tried to peer through the trees, but it was impossible.

It was like attempting to read in the dark.

"This isn't the original road," Giovanni said, gesturing around us. "This one will take us to the mill, but there's supposed to be another, larger one that leads right up to the villa."

"With respect, *Signore* Fenoglio," the driver said, "this is the original road. Because the mill was here first, you see, two or three decades before the Caparalia family had the villa built."

Giovanni cleared his throat roughly. "Indeed? That is not what I was told."

"Well, signore, I can't speak to what you were told, but that is the truth. And for now, this is the only path to the property, I'm afraid. The larger road you mentioned has been underwater for, oh . . . I suppose it's been . . . yes, almost four centuries. Because of the broken dam."

"You live in these parts?"

"My entire family, Signore Fenoglio. For generations. They've been—"

"It's *ingegnere*."

I winced.

"Pardon?" the driver said, half turning.

"I'm an engineer. It's not signore but Ingegnere Fenoglio."

After a beat of silence, the driver gave Giovanni a nod and turned back to the road, hands tightening on the steering wheel.

My cheeks felt as if they'd caught fire. I restrained my impulse to offer a word of apology to the man.

"In any case," my husband said, turning to me as if the driver had never spoken, "we'll fix that main road when we rebuild the original dam and divert the torrent's water again toward the wheel. We can't have guests arriving at our villa by this path. It's unseemly."

I nodded even if I wasn't entirely sure what guests he meant, other than perhaps my father and his wife if I could pry him away from my two half brothers and his sweets shop for long enough to come down from Torino. Giovanni had no family of his own left, and though he did have business acquaintances, I couldn't imagine that any of them would be willing to leave the city for a *cena*.

It was then, all at once and as if it had shoved its way through the trees, that the mill rose in front of us. My thoughts scattered in all directions— guests, meals, hair salons and picture shows, civilization itself forgotten before the size of a building made of stones so ancient they were black with days. A vertical rectangle of at least three stories and pockmarked with holes where the rocks had shifted or fallen under the pressure of the years, it pushed against the shores of a dried up millrace. Its wooden wheel rested like a weapon at its side.

This was not what I'd caught sight of before, the clay roof and pretty ivy leaves. The mill's structure was made only of those dark stones. Not a hint of green, nor of any color besides black and gray, had laid claim to it. Nothing grew in its crevices.

It was difficult to look away from the dark shape of the mill. Even its splintered wood and iron door tugged at me.

"Hello," I whispered, just a puff of air.

The driver took a turn and the car jerked off the rough road onto even rougher terrain. We passed the mill on the left and that was when the villa itself appeared, down to our right, drenched in sunlight.

The perfectly square villa sat on what looked like a grass-covered dais, with a containment wall of mossy stone encircling the front. Now this was what I'd seen earlier, clay and ivy in harmonious matrimony on the roof. But the ivy was a fickle thing, for I now saw it clung to everything: it had sent its tendrils across the villa's facade, latching on to the stairs and twining around the balustrades that led up to the entrance colonnade, had grasped on to five of the eight rectangular windows visible from our position, and had even slid into the four brick chimneys. Parts of the roof had buckled in. That was visible, too, despite all those plants, and there were obvious water stains along the edge of where the clay tiles met the stucco.

Under and past all that green and all those water marks, though, I could see what the villa had been. Chantilly walls and golden accents. Its past glory trembled like a soap bubble against the present, but it was there.

I decided it then.

Villa Caparalia was the most beautiful place I'd ever seen.

I'd lived my life surrounded by beauty in Torino, palaces and museums and even cafés festooned in gold leaf and Rococo moldings, but none of them compared to this place. Because this one was mine.

The car stopped with a jerk, the driver yanking on the hand brake until I thought he'd tear it right off. Giovanni flung his door open and stepped out without a word, stopping only to smooth his smoke-colored vest and tug on his jacket before starting off for the mill.

I smiled at his enthusiasm, even if it did mean I had to find a way out of this car on my own. He could have been any boy hearing the midnight chimes on the eve of *Natale*.

Well, all right then, nothing to it but to begin. I gathered my purse, adjusted my gloves, and pulled on the metal handle. The door swung out with more force than I'd expected, and before I could shift, it had slammed back into place. With a sigh, I leaned into it to begin again.

"*Signora,* let me help," the driver said.

"Oh, there's no need, signore. I'm sure I can manage."

But he had already stepped out and had come to my side, one hand holding the door open and the other offering me assistance in rising. Despite the renewed warmth in my cheeks, I smiled and took his hand.

"*Grazie,* signore," I said once my heels were on the squelching ground of my new home. "Most kind of you."

He nodded in acknowledgment before turning to the car to start unloading some of the trunks we'd brought. Mainly clothes, some kitchen utensils. Our furniture would arrive later, on the tractor and cart Giovanni had hired to fetch it all from the station.

"Would you like me to take them up to the house, signora?"

I hesitated. That wasn't part of what we'd paid him to do and I didn't have a single *centesimo* to give him for the extra work. But I also couldn't carry the trunks on my own and disliked to leave them sinking into the mud.

I opened my purse and looked inside for my smaller money bag, though I knew well enough it was empty. Giovanni did not approve of married women carrying money if it could be avoided.

"I'm afraid I don't have anything to give you," I said.

"It's no trouble, signora."

"Perhaps my husband . . ."

He shook his head and grabbed the first trunk. "*Va bene,* signora. You should not have to carry these up yourself."

He led the way up the incline toward the villa and I followed, wincing at the mud that was already spattering my fawn-colored skirt and my stockings, seeming to swallow up my heels a bit more with each step. At least I'd been smart enough not to wear the new kidskin boots Giovanni had bought me to celebrate the sale of his patent.

This would be one of the first things that I'd turn my husband's attention to: laying down a stone walkway from the road up to the house to avoid splattered shoes.

The driver had already placed the first two trunks by the entrance and had started down for the rest by the time I reached the top of the stairs, the row of waistline buttons pinching my sides, and walked through the ivy-clad colonnade toward the front door. It was a massive wooden creature under an arch made of black iron cast so thinly it could have been spun sugar. At its center was a knocker featuring a face, perhaps an angel, puffed of cheek as if it were about to blow a tempest into being, a motif echoed in the door handle. It would be a trick to fit the key into the tight opening inside that mouth.

"Oh, the key!" I said and hurried to the smallest trunk.

"Pardon, signora?"

I waved the words away. "Nothing at all. Just me talking to myself."

Like I've been told not to do dozens of times. It's not seemly.

My hand closed around the heavy skeleton key, one of two, and a shiver ran down my spine. I was about to enter my own home.

"That's the last of them," the driver said, placing two more trunks on the landing and smacking a mud spot on his trousers with his cap. "Is there anything else you require, Signora Fenoglio?"

"No, thank you . . . I'm sorry, I just realized I don't know your name."

"Piero, signora."

I smiled. "Thank you, Piero. You've been very kind."

He nodded and made to turn, but stopped himself at the last moment, his hands worrying at his cap.

"Yes?"

"*Scusatemi,* signora. I hope you won't think I'm overstepping, but I just wanted to say that should you require anything, me and my family live a little ways up the valley. On the other side of the river. It'll be lonely up here come winter and, if you'll pardon me, a woman in your condition should know in which direction help can be found."

I blinked. I was certain I wasn't showing yet. "How did you know?"

Piero smiled and nodded to my midsection. "You are so very careful."

I realized then I'd pressed the hand not holding the key against my stomach without knowing it, both barrier and cradle for the life beneath it.

"Oh," I said.

"There's no doctor closer than the one in Ovada, but my wife has had three of her own and can help when the time comes, signora. And, of course, if I'm around, my car is always at your service."

"I, uh, I'm very grateful, Piero. I'll keep that in mind."

He did place his cap on his head now and turned to the stairs with a nod but without another word. What a peculiar man. He should have said all of that to Giovanni, because I was no good at remembering those kinds of things. A mind like a sieve, he always told me.

I turned back to the door.

Besides, Piero made it sound as if I'd be in the house all alone, when that would certainly not be the case. The two or three maids that Giovanni promised me, and Giovanni himself, would be more than enough to ensure there were no complications with the birth, winter or not.

I slid the key into the space between the lips of the blowing angel and turned it, the mechanism engaging with a scrape of metal but no other complaint. The door itself opened with relative ease, too, requiring only a slight push of the shoulder before it dislodged itself from the frame.

Darkness was what I expected. I'd imagined blindly pulling ivy from the windows before being able to catch sight of a room's contours. Instead, ribbons of light unfurled past the curtains of vines and over a courtyard that was already visible through the arch leading from the marble entrance hall. I had been right about the water, though. A rather large pool of it gleamed in front of me. At least it made me feel just a bit less like a muddy-heeled desecrater as I stepped into the house. My house.

My footsteps distorted in all that space, the high ceilings stealing the sound and returning it slightly off rhythm, so that by the time I reached that internal covered courtyard, I no longer recognized my own steps. Not that I cared one jot for that when I finally looked up.

A fresco spanned the entire expanse of the vaulted ceiling. It was divided into connecting panels, the unmistakable scintillating blue of a cinquecento sky the perfect background on which golden-winged figures could frolic. The tops of trees in kaleidoscopic greens provided a border, as if the viewer were looking up at the sky from the center of an immense forest. The fresco shone with gold leaf that was flaking in places, and there were some spots of faded blue, but it retained most of its crispness. It was dizzying to think that I could come and look at it whenever I wanted, for as long as I wanted.

The courtyard opened into four different vestibules and corridors, a cross of passages, and I took the first one to the left now, which led up into what, from its size, could only be the sala where the Caparalia had to have done their dining and entertaining. The damage was extensive here. Water had wiped whatever had been on the walls and had cracked the plaster from the ceiling. Some pieces still rippled with damp. Chunks of it lay scattered on the peach marble tiles that made up the floor, along with cracked glass and, *Santissima Madre*, rat droppings.

I stepped carefully through the mess and started down toward the center of the room. There had perhaps been gold leaf on the walls, for the sun did catch stray flakes that glittered in the cornices, setting them aflame for a moment before the shadow of an ivy covered them again. In its youth, the room must have shimmered.

At the far end, near the fireplace that spanned most of the wall and where the shadows were thickest, stood a table.

How strange that no one had taken it. So far, I'd seen no hint of so much as a three-legged chair.

But the moment I walked over to it, I saw why it was still here. It was made of one giant slab of stone that didn't look as if it'd fit through the door. Its heft was obviously meant to be the focus, for its only ornamentation were four carved rosettes, one at each corner. Even its legs, black with mold now, were bare and simple.

I brushed my fingertips over its surface. It was much smoother than I'd thought it'd be, almost like nacre or polished quartz, and cold. Now that I was closer, I could see it had a vein the color of rose gold and as thin as a thread running down its center. I followed its path down the length of the table with my finger, from rosette to rosette. They looked just like the cream-filled chocolates my mother used to make for Father's shop, the ones women in fine silk dresses bought. She would have loved these.

No question the table was beautiful. The finest piece of furniture I'd ever owned.

Yes, but I don't want to touch it anymore.

I frowned at my thought before realizing my fingers were aching with cold. And it wasn't just my fingers, for my teeth were clicking lightly together and I had a vague idea they had been for a while. There was a trace of something in the room now, too, an odor that I hadn't smelled when I'd walked in, like meat about to turn.

I took a step back.

"Sibilla!"

I gasped, clapping a hand over my mouth to keep from yelping.

"Where are you? Sibilla!"

Sudden relief swept through me, leaving me slightly weak of knee. It was just Giovanni.

Well, of course—who else would it have been?

"I'm in here!" I called out, shaking my head at myself as I walked toward the sala's door.

Madre di Dio, what a silly thing I was. Frightening myself in my own home because a table was cold and the room smelled a bit of mold. Giovanni was right; I always allowed my head to run off following some emotion or other, all feelings and no sense.

"Didn't you hear me calling?" Giovanni said, appearing at the doorway.

"No, I'm sorry. There's so much room, sound gets lost." I hurried to smile. "It's all so beautiful."

"Yes, I suppose so." He peered past me, into the sala. "That's a minor disaster, though. It'll likely need to be completely replastered, practically torn down to its foundations to get all the humidity out."

I nodded. "I wonder what it must have looked like when the Caparalia lived here."

"Expensive. That's what it looked like."

Giovanni grasped a corner of plaster and peeled a hand-sized piece off the wall with ease, letting it crumble and fall like wet sand to the marble floor. I had the ridiculous impulse to offer some kind gesture to the wall, a bit of comfort, a promise that we'd soon resolve its problems.

"After we get the mill running, we'll begin the work in the villa," Giovanni said with a grimace as he drew out a handkerchief and wiped his hands. "For now, look through the rooms and see which ones won't collapse around us and we'll make do with those."

I frowned. "I thought the repairs would happen at the same time."

That was what he'd said when he'd told me about the purchase of the property, what a bargain it'd been because of the condition it was in. That we'd be able to afford to fix it all up.

"There aren't enough men in the area to do both and, apart from wiring some of the rooms for electricity so that we don't have to sit in the dark and installing a telephone. The mill is the crucial thing."

"Oh." A telephone. I hadn't realized that was a priority. The expense of that . . .

I hesitated, a hand going to my midsection. "But the child? I'm just concerned about the damp."

He waved my words away and walked out into the corridor. "There is still time until its birth. I have some of the men coming tomorrow to begin the repairs and in a couple of months, if that, we'll have the mill working and be making our fortune."

He bent, frowning, to peer at a crack on the floor in which his entire hand could have fit. It was one of many.

It was true, I supposed. The baby wouldn't be born for five more months, and we didn't need to have the entire villa ready by then, just a few rooms free of mold and humidity. And the courtyard had no real damage, so the house must have many other places that were perfectly suitable. More than suitable.

Yes, by the time he was born—

If he doesn't follow the fate of my last two.

—I'd make sure he had the loveliest nursery waiting for him, all light and warmth.

I nodded to myself as I reached to close the sala's heavy door. I could start doing some things, too.

When the help arrived, they could assist me to light the fire in all the fireplaces I could find to try and dry out the place a bit. That alone would make a difference.

Having a plan, even one that small, eased a knot in my chest.

"I'm looking forward to seeing the mill running," I said. "Will you show me how the part you invented works once you install it?"

Giovanni glanced up at me before returning his gaze to the cracked tiles. "The repairs will need to be done first and then the addition of reciprocal power to the existing rotary system, but yes, after that I can show you the new crankshaft." He stood. "But never mind all of that, I had something brought for you from Ovada to celebrate."

My eyebrows shot up, both at his words and at the sudden sunlight in his voice. "Really? What is it?"

"Guess."

I smiled. "I don't know, Giovanni."

"All right, a hint, then." He drew closer. "What made you first look at me that day in your father's shop?"

And as if he'd pulled me down the years, I could see him then, all of twenty-three, at the wooden counter behind which my mother and I stood. He held a bowler hat so worn its brim shone, but he had bought a dozen of the *dolcetti di marzapane* that Mother had spent the dawn making. Once he'd paid for them, he'd held the bag over the counter and offered me one. For the next week and a half, until he'd asked permission to call on me, he'd done the exact same thing. I'd gone to sleep each night with the taste of almonds in my mouth and his smile in my eyes.

Much later, once we were promised to one another, he'd told me that very first day was the day he'd been made the director of engineering at the sawmill in which his own father still worked as a laborer. He'd decided to finally approach the chestnut-haired girl who lived among sweets and whom he caught sight of every day on his way to work.

After one bite of marzapane, I'd fallen in love with him. And that hadn't changed.

Except—

I smiled despite the sudden tightness in my chest and shook my head. "Do you know, I don't entirely remember how we met. So many young men were coming in and out of the sweets shop that it's all a bit of a blur."

"Is it? What a shame. Then perhaps you won't want the bag of marzapane waiting in the kitchen." He started forward. "I'll just go and toss it before it attracts rats."

I tugged on his sleeve and brought him closer so that I could reach up and place a kiss on his lips. "Thank you. But, you know, you're late." I gestured to the droppings scattered around us. "We already have rats."

It was only when he laughed that I realized how long it'd been since I'd heard him do so. Even after the sale of his patent almost six months ago, he'd not been quite himself, as if he found no real reason to celebrate. But things would change now. With the baby, and the mill, and this villa. I could feel it.

This was an auspicious beginning.

"Come on, I know the way," he said, offering me his arm and that same smile from that very first day.

Yes, everything would be fine now.

I twined my arm through his and he led us down the corridor, in what I assumed was the direction of the kitchen.

"I sent word to have a few more things delivered from Ovada for our cena, nothing very extravagant, but tomorrow we'll have to get one of the workers to show us where to buy what we need," he said. "We'll have to think about buying a car of some sort as well. Anything with wheels and a motor."

He kicked a piece of fallen plaster out of the way and took us down another corridor.

Tomorrow, then, if I could get some help cleaning up the kitchen, I could prepare a proper meal. The new gas stove he'd promised me would have to wait a bit, of course, but I could manage with a woodstove for now. And though leaving our refrigerator behind in Torino had been almost painful, we had our old ice box. We'd survive.

"Do you think it'll be possible to ask about two or three maids tomorrow morning too?" I said. "I'm sure the workers must know a few women in need of work."

"No, we'd better wait. I don't want any more expenses than are absolutely necessary."

I almost stopped walking. "Giovanni, I can't take care of this entire house on my own."

"You don't have to, just the rooms we choose to live in for now. Then, when we can, we'll hire a woman or two." He flicked his eyes to me. "I thought you understood that the mill comes first."

"Yes, of course I do, but perhaps you can hire one fewer worker and pay that salary to a maid. A girl without experience won't cost much. Less even than a worker. Or perhaps leave the telephone installation for later."

"We can't run a proper sawmill without a telephone, Sibilla. I've already made the decision."

All of the light had disappeared from his voice and I knew I should stop talking, but I just didn't understand. He was the one who had mentioned the help back in Torino, telling me I'd need to be ready to take charge of an entire army of them. Well, I wasn't asking for an army. One would do for the moment.

"Just airing out the rooms we use will take a lot of work and you'll be too busy with the mill to help me. Look at the size of this place!" *Stop talking.* "We likely won't have radiators for the winter in place yet and I can't bring up all of the wood necessary to keep the fireplaces lit on my own, not with the baby—"

Giovanni exhaled sharply, shaking his head "Always the baby. We always arrive at the same place, don't we?"

He tugged his arm from my grip and stalked off around the corner, his shoulder nudging me just enough that I felt the soles of my wet heels lose their purchase on the tiles. With a gasp, I grasped at the nearest wall, digging fingernails into the soft plaster to remain upright. A flurry of it rained down into my hair.

My heart thundered. A tourniquet tightened around my chest, cutting off my breath.

Not now.

But yes, now, and I could only clutch at the crumbling wall as a thick wave of red fell over my vision. I knew that red. I knew the confusion it hid in its folds.

"You can't imagine how lovely it is to see you."

A whimper escaped my lips.

"Here, have some of mine."

Stop it. Please.

I squeezed my eyes so tightly the red bleached into white, and I held on to that, as I always did, dividing it, transforming it into worn ivory keys. And now I dropped in spots of ink that elongated and clicked into place, exactly where they belonged, their smooth surfaces under my fingertips as my hands sped across them. Melody burst like a wineglass shattering. The sound smothered the world into silence. As it always did.

Over and over, I played that melody, that waltz, on the perfectly captured image of my mother's piano.

When the pressure in my chest finally eased, I took a shuddering breath and released the music, feeling as if my bones had turned to aspic. My hands trembled when I placed them on my stomach.

I had to stop doing this to myself and to the baby. This was exactly what Giovanni and the doctor always warned me about—my emotions getting the better of my head, filling in the holes in my memory with anything I could grab hold of. Because I didn't actually know what had happened that night. No one did.

Those two snatches of conversation were the only things my mind could dredge up from the night our last child had died in my womb.

And I didn't even know who had uttered them or why they snapped at my heels like growling dogs.

MADDALENA
1596

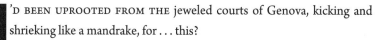

'D BEEN UPROOTED FROM THE jeweled courts of Genova, kicking and shrieking like a mandrake, for . . . this?

It was an ocean of mud.

I turned my head just enough to see my husband, who watched me with a smile that dimpled his perfectly round cheeks.

"Come now, *sposa*. This is the ideal location. We have hectares of prime fields for our wheat and you have a magnificent villa."

"Yes, the villa is nice enough. But Florindo, how do you expect me to get to it without drowning? Is there a barge you've purchased? A gondola, perhaps?"

His face crinkled an instant before he boomed with laughter. The sound seemed to shake the treetops, ruffling needles and rattling cones before easing down my spine. No matter how many years passed, I didn't think I'd ever tire of that sensation.

"If you'll permit me, *Mona* Maddalena," Giusto said, stepping away from one of the carriages. The tutor still clutched the Latin grammar book he'd been trying to get the children to focus on throughout the journey, to no avail. "We could have some planks of wood laid down so that you could cross with ease."

I waved his words away. "I'm not so frail a thing as that. If it must be done, it must be done, though I can assure you I will not enjoy it."

I bent and grasped the embroidered red and cream trim of my gown, holding it out to the side until the heels of my shoes were visible. They'd be ruined, of course.

They were meant for marble floors, at the most for a manicured garden, not for the savagery of the countryside.

And neither was I.

"*Messer* Ugo!" Giusto cried.

I turned just in time to see my youngest child darting past me. Before I had time to open my mouth, he'd leaped into the largest, muddiest puddle he could find and was flopping onto his stomach. It only took an instant for the blue hose and the linen tunic I'd had especially made for this trip to earn their place in the rag heap.

Santa Maria, every day it was some new mischief with this child. No matter how many lemon balm, lavender, and balmony infusions I made for him, calling on every herb of tranquility, patience, and clear thinking I knew, he continued to behave like a feral creature. There was no domesticating him.

I sighed. "Ugo, come here at once."

"*Mamma.*"

I pointed to the ground right in front of me. "At once."

Every bit of him dripped water as he stood. A streak of mud crossed one cheek, which he only made worse when he tried to wipe it off with an equally dirty fist.

Behind me, there was a trickle of smothered childish laughter and a hiss from Giusto.

"Will you please explain to me what could have possibly possessed you to do something like that?" I said when Ugo had come to a squelching stop where I'd directed him. "You are almost six years of age, much too old to be acting in this manner."

Ugo smoothed out his soaked tunic as if he were about to give evidence before the *podestà* and looked up at me.

"Answer me, child."

"It was hot in the carriage, Mamma."

"So you thought it entirely appropriate to roll in a puddle like a farm pig?"

He frowned. "Yes, I suppose so. I'm not hot anymore."

Another spate of laughter trailed by a hiss.

"I see." I bent so that I could meet his eyes. "Here is what's going to happen. You will first turn and apologize to your father for thinking only of yourself and ruining your clothes."

"Maddalena, there's—"

I stopped my husband's words with a glance.

"And then you will take them to the laundress this afternoon, on your own, so that you can explain why they need to be washed and made into rags. Understood?"

He looked down at his feet and nodded.

"With words, if you please."

"Yes, Mamma."

I straightened and motioned toward Florindo. "Go on, then."

He turned on his heels and gave his father a rapid look before slightly bowing his head. "Scusatemi, Papà."

Florindo cleared his throat and nodded. "Yes, yes, that's all right. Try to be more careful next time and we'll not mention this again."

The man was useless with children. And he wasn't the only one.

"A sharper eye, Giusto," I said, half turning. "We cannot have the children run wild."

He bowed his head at once, his face turning an alarming shade of pink.

"All right," I said and clapped my hands. "Let's not dawdle anymore, there are things to be done."

"Do you require me for anything, or might I inspect the mill and the dam?" Florindo said. "I'd like to begin reinforcing it as soon as possible."

"When have I ever required you for household management, sposo? Off with you." Without waiting, I started forward, trying not to grimace at the tragedy brought upon my shoes as I waded a path through the mud and toward the villa. I could have been sitting in the Palazzo Ducale, perfectly dry, sipping *vin santo* from the finest crystal and eating candied fruit from porcelain bowls. What would my father, at one point in time one of the wealthiest spice merchants in Genova, have said at seeing his daughter fighting not to lose her shoes to the earth?

Behind me, my five children groaned or squealed at the novelty of such muck.

There was nothing for it, though, but to continue.

Shaking my dress's skirt free of mud splatters and avoiding all glances at my feet lest I begin weeping, I started up the stairs to the colonnade. A group of men who were not part of my household waited at the top, near the entrance, and I beckoned to them.

"There is a trunk in the second carriage that I need brought up with the utmost care," I said. "Fetch it and between two or three of you, bring it up to the small kitchen beside my chambers. Ask one of my servants for directions."

"Yes, *madonna*," one of them said.

"Oh, and there are some pots with herbs that I need carried inside as well."

The rapid exchange of glances between two of the men—workers my husband had hired, I supposed—didn't escape me and I lifted an eyebrow in question. They bowed their heads and started off to do as I said.

"The utmost care," I repeated. "I don't want a single chip on the glass flasks."

Truth be told, I wasn't entirely sure the journey hadn't reduced all of my late father's alchemical tools to glittering powder. I'd wrapped everything in cotton and linen, but the alembic had always been fragile. It had been

one of the many reasons why I'd never had the same fascination with alchemical experiments as Father, or really as all of Genovese society, for
some days it seemed as if it was all that anyone of note talked about. Recipes
for hair tonics, youthful elixirs, antidotes for poisons, all of dubious efficacy
and all exchanged like currency among my acquaintances. But how could
one enjoy working with tools that could shatter from too sharp a glance?
No, I much preferred my iron mortar and pestle and my herbs.

From somewhere past the villa came the screams of goats.

I sighed. Not that there was much choice in the matter now, in any case.
Even if I wanted to, where would I possibly get the ingredients necessary to
follow one of the alchemical experiments of the great Caterina Sforza? We
had goats and mud, but no apothecaries nearby.

A flurry of activity surrounded us the moment my children, their tutor, and I entered the villa. Exactly as it should have been. The household
servants had had their orders when I'd sent them ahead of our carriage, but
it was always gratifying to know your instructions were followed.

Servants swept the marble floors in the entrance hall, or rolled out
gold-flecked tapestries, or ensured candelabras were firmly in place, each of
them bowing their heads as we passed. One of the younger women waited,
eyes on the floor, until we'd stepped through the vestibule before beginning
to wipe the marks our feet left.

"Magnificent," Giusto said, staring up as we came to the internal courtyard.

I glanced above me, though I had been the one to choose the fresco's
motif and knew well what it would look like. Pleasant enough, but I'd seen
grander.

"Wait for me here," I said to Giusto and the children. "I don't want
any of you running off yet, do you hear? The villa is large and I don't fancy
spending my afternoon searching for you and undoing all the work the
servants have done."

My children nodded, though I knew only Marcellina could be trusted.
The four boys might disappear the moment I was out of sight, tutor or no

tutor. I left them to their fate and walked into the sala, where the servants were placing dining chairs around the stone table that had been carved right where it sat.

I swept my eyes around the room, taking in the two *credenze*, one already gleaming with silver platters, while the other one was still awaiting the salads and cheeses that would make up part of our late dinner. The figured velvet drapes had been hung, excellent, and our head steward was busy counting out the wax candles necessary to light all the chandeliers.

We might have a civilized meal today, after all.

My gaze snagged on movement by the fireplace. A young man, someone who had to be newly hired for I could not recall him, was maneuvering a large copper cauldron onto a hook, its great belly blazing in the sun. No, that would not do.

I walked to the hearth. "Your name, if you please."

The young man, a boy, really, looked up and made the slightest inclination of his head. "Antonio, madonna. One of the kitchen steward's assistants."

"Antonio, remove that cauldron. I have no use for it in this room."

His eyebrows shot up. "It's a custom here to have one in the main hearth, madonna."

Yes, and apparently another custom was questioning your mistress's wishes. "If I require your advice, I will ask for it. Do as I say."

I turned without waiting for him to move and almost collided with one of the men to whom I'd given orders on the stairs. He carried my wooden crate full of pots in various sizes, each one a home for a different herb.

"Madonna, where would you like these placed?"

"Most of these will go up to join the trunk you took to the kitchen on the second story, but let me see . . ." I shifted the pots about, waiting for that peculiar susurration that I didn't so much hear as feel. An essence that vibrated against me, communicating what it needed without words.

Yes, there. And of course, it was the hyssop, already drooping from the lack of light and demanding water after so many hours in a carriage. Oh, and the mint had soft complaints because somehow the parsley pot had shifted in the journey and was much too close. I should have been more careful.

It always amused me when people expounded on the gentleness of plants, how calming, how peaceful sitting among them could be. Because plants had their violent quarrels. They could be as vicious as wolves, twisting their roots tight enough to smother or starve neighbors they didn't care for, draining the soil and gorging themselves while nearby plants crackled with thirst. They bullied. They hated. They even killed. They were complicated beings and it was no more peaceful to sit among them than to sit amid the finely dressed gossips of a Genovese *palazzo*.

That rich complexity and their willingness to share their secrets with anyone who was quiet enough to listen were just a couple of the reasons I reveled in their company and had done so since I could remember.

I took the mint, cradling it against my hip like an infant, and was readying to grab the hyssop pot when I saw the red patches at the top of the worker's hands. Large marks. The skin was flaking off and there were abrasions where the man had likely scratched at the inflammation. Swelling had made the knuckles of his fingers disappear.

I recognized the condition. I'd seen milder versions of it in Genova last winter season, on a few women who had bought marten fur cuffs that had not been treated in the correct manner. The furrier had had to present himself before the podestà for the havoc he'd wreaked on noblewomen's soft wrist skin, and the afflicted had hurried to find me for whatever unguent I could concoct. It'd been a simple enough blend.

"I can give you something for that," I said.

"Madonna?"

"For your hands. I have a formula that can resolve it in a day and a charm to prevent it from happening again." I just had to find the dried persimmon leaves and sorrel roots that were in my herb chest. "I'll prepare it for you before you leave."

The man's eyes widened and he shook his head. "No, madonna. Thank you but no."

"It's no trouble at all if—"

"No." He dropped his gaze to the floor. "It's not necessary."

"But why? They obviously pain you."

"I don't need special formulas, madonna. Or charms."

Frowning at the firmness edging much too close to impertinence in his voice, I took the hyssop pot and walked past him, back out to the courtyard. I flung one last look behind me as sharp words came to my lips and caught the man crossing himself, crate in one hand.

My feet stopped of their own accord.

I'd made a mistake.

Despite everything, I'd forgotten for a heartbeat that this was not Genova. Alchemy, herbalism, cartomancy, all those founts of knowledge and guidance and, yes, entertainment, that were so popular in the city, could only be seen as suspicious here. As ungodly.

Perhaps as something even darker.

My skin prickled because I knew that slip of mine, slight as it was, would have consequences. I could only pray they'd not be too costly.

The sound of shattering glass flinched me out of my stillness. An explosive wail raced through the courtyard. I was grabbing at my skirts and breaking into a run before my mind had time to put a name to the voice my very bones had already recognized.

I shoved the herb pots against a passing servant's chest, who scrambled to hold on to them, and I kept running, right out the front door.

"Francesco!"

Another wail of pain.

My wet heels slipped on the colonnade's marble, but I gripped the balustrade and hurried down to where the sounds had come from.

Francesco sat in a field of glass shards that winked in the sun as pages of Giusto's grammar book sank into the mud around him. The man himself knelt beside my second-born son, whose face gleamed with tears, and was removing glass from his tunic.

"What happened?" I gasped.

"He fell, Mona Maddalena."

"And all of that glass? Where did it come from?"

Giusto sat back on his heels, shaking his head. "He saw one of the women bringing down refreshments for Messer Florindo and insisted on helping. I warned him it was dangerous but he'd not listen."

I pressed a hand to my pounding chest. These children would be the end of me.

The boy whimpered and attempted to stand, but Giusto halted him. "One moment, Messer Francesco. There are still glass pieces on your sleeves."

Shaking my head, I started down the stairs toward my herd of children. They had been shocked into silence, at least for the moment, Giacomo holding Marcellina's hand as I always urged him to do when she was frightened, and even Ugo pressed against my eldest's leg. Vincenzo just watched his twin cry and fuss in the mud.

"All right, let me see," I said, stepping into all that wetness once again and kneeling beside Francesco. There was little point in worrying about my gown now, for it appeared my children would not be content until all of them had had a mud baptism. I would have to apologize to the laundress myself, later.

I took stock of my son. The boy had scraped the left leg of his hose open in the fall and the knob of his knee peered through, as red and raw as the worker's hands had been. A thread of blood had started to surface, but nothing else seemed to be amiss.

"Come now, child," I said, wiping at his tears. "It's not as bad as that. We'll clean that scrape, and I'll prepare something for the pain, va bene?"

He sniffed, nodding, and I offered my hand to help him up.

I glanced up at Giusto, lips full of orders, and I saw the mill for the first time.

When I was eight years old, my cousin came to stay at our estate for the summer. The moment I saw her, hurrying through the garden toward me with a cloth and porcelain doll in her hand, I'd erupted into the kind of tears nothing could quench. No one knew their cause, not even I. For her entire visit, I'd felt as if hands wrung my chest. I'd wake at night with the certainty that she had died and only hurrying to her bedside and listening for her breath would calm me.

A week after she returned home, she drowned.

My mother forbade me from mentioning what I'd felt to anyone, including Father. He could understand the mathematical formulas to create *acqua celeste*, the temperature fluctuations in his alembic that could calcify mercury, and the exact point of distillation in which scorpion venom could transform into an antidote for numerous poisons, but there was no reason to that certainty I'd felt and therefore no merit. It was as impossible to depend on a feeling as it was to quantify it. For him, the best thing one could do was ignore it.

Numerous times throughout the years, I'd had that same sensation: when my mother sickened, when plague came to the city aboard a Barbary pirate ship and took my brother, and when bandits stole last year's wheat harvest on its way to Genova, but also the first time Florindo smiled at me and the day after Giacomo's conception. Confused warnings that I'd stumbled onto my fate.

And I felt it now.

The stone structure of the mill rose black against the twining background of sky and pines. It stood angled away from the villa, as if scowling at it, its wheel turning and turning and creaking like bones. Despite the workers coming in and out of it, all the noise and activity, there was an emptiness to the building that made it seem as if it had been abandoned for a long time.

I took a step back, toward the villa's stairs.

"Mamma," Francesco said as he lurched forward.

"Oh, I'm sorry, *amore*," I said. I pulled him a little closer, when what I wanted to do was clasp all five of them to me, turn, and flee. My hand scrambled to find the small cross, silver coral branch, and wolf's tooth hanging around Francesco's neck.

"Do you all have your charms?"

"Yes, Mamma."

Giusto stood. "Mona Maddalena, is everything all right?"

I nodded and tore my gaze from the mill. "I want to see them, if you please."

One by one, the children tugged out identical charms from under their tunics. From the moment they were born, they'd had these nearby to shield them from the ravages of *il malocchio* and other ungodly influences. Not a one of them had succumbed to a single bout of pox.

Whatever it was that I'd felt, I hoped it would get lost in the reflective surface of those charms. I murmured a quick *Padre Nostro* and breathed deeply to dislodge the stone of worry in my chest.

"Madonna, is there anything else?"

I looked up to find a worker at the top of the stairs, the very man with the hand condition. His eyes traveled to the charm I still touched and to all my children's necks.

"No, I don't require you anymore," I said, my jaw tight. "You may join my husband at the dam."

Something tugged at my sleeve.

"Mamma, look," Francesco said.

I followed his finger to the pool of blood that had dribbled from his leg and was settling like oil on the mud.

This had not been the most auspicious of beginnings.

SIBILLA

1933

"ALL RIGHT, BRING THAT BEAM over here," Giovanni said.

Two of the workers did as he said and pulled at the rope wrapped around both ends of a thick piece of wood that could easily have been a ridge for a roof. They dragged it through the muddy bank of the torrent toward the wide mouth of what was left of the original dam.

It wasn't much. Just a few beams that were not too ravaged by the water and the years, and a structure on which they leaned that looked like the crates of sugar that came to the sweets shop every other day, one stacked on top of the other. Giovanni and the workers had spent most of the morning replacing these with new ones. The river still roared down the wrong tributary, though, leaving the mill's wheel untouched.

"Hold it there!" Giovanni said, climbing over the planks they'd laid down across the banks to be able to work safely.

I dug my nails into my nearly raw palms. No matter how many planks they laid down, this was not safe. He helped shift the beam against the others, pulling until he was able to tighten the rope around the wood already in place. He motioned to one of the men, who leaped up to the space next to him, hammer and iron nails thicker than my wrist in his hand.

Rushing water foamed at their ankles now that the weight of two bodies bore down on the wooden board. I turned away and started walking downriver, toward the villa. I should have stayed inside, washing floors, listening to the chatter of the men festooning the four rooms we'd chosen for our current use with the stiff garlands of electric cables instead of coming out here to suffocate on my own fear. I was no good in these situations.

A sudden scream shattered the morning.

Its piercing violence froze every muscle in my body, bringing me to a stop with a gasp.

It seemed to come from the sky itself, and it tore across the valley, swiping at the treetops, a sound that had to have ripped open the throat it'd burst from. A gust of frozen air pushed me back a step.

A snap and a rough male yell chased after it, this time coming from behind me, and I whipped around in time to see the wood splintering and cracking, water and rocks smashing through the morning's work.

The torrent roiled wild.

Giovanni jumped off the plank in an instant, but the worker was slower and the water ripped the wood from under his feet. It took him with it. The rocks slammed into him, knocking him backward and dragging him under the fierce current.

The other men ran down the bank, shouting.

"No!" Giovanni said to two of them who were gauging the distance to the protruding rocks near the center of the river. "It's too far!"

The fallen worker shot up from the water with a gasp, already far downriver, hands scrabbling for purchase, before disappearing again under its coils.

"A rope, grab a rope!" a voice said. "He's right there!"

A young woman was racing toward the torrent from up by the villa. Her feet slid in the wet earth, but she kept moving down the incline, dragging piles of drenched leaves and twigs down in her wake. She motioned in my direction toward a coil of rope just a few meters from me. With a gasp, I took one end and hurried downstream while attempting not to lose my own footing. But I didn't know where the man was. I couldn't see more than froth from this angle.

In a moment, the young woman had ripped the rope from my hands and had run ahead. She didn't hesitate to step into the water despite the way it shoved at her legs, drenching her oversized trousers, wading in up to her calves even as she tossed the rope into the current.

The man came up gasping again and lurched for the rope, releasing his hold on the rock he seemed to have been clutching. Trembling hands gripped the cord.

"Help me!" he yelled, his voice full of water.

"What do you think we're doing?" the young woman said. "Playing a hand of *Scopa*?"

The men careened into us an instant later and pushed us aside, Giovanni directing them as they wrapped the rope around their forearms and began to retrieve their fellow worker from the river's jaws, one pull at a time.

Stepping back, I pressed my hands to my midsection, heart still racing, and watched as the danger passed. Only then did I notice a strange ringing in my ears, like I'd heard something terribly loud and—

The scream. That first one that seemed to come from the sky.

What could possibly have screamed so loudly? Had it been one of the men? Or perhaps the young woman calling a warning? But no, it hadn't felt like that. There'd been pure terror in that sound.

"You don't feel any cramping, right?"

I blinked and turned to the young woman, or girl, really, since she had to be no more than seventeen. "Pardon?"

She nodded to my stomach. "Any sharp pains? Sudden backache?"

"No."

"Then you can stop fussing, the child is fine. A little bit of exercise won't hurt it. My mother worked in the fields until the day she birthed me and I was as hale as a farm beast."

I frowned.

She smacked at the dirt on her trousers and wiped a hand across her forehead before fixing her brown eyes on me. "I'm not much, I know, but I'm here."

"Yes, and you're late," Giovanni said, rolling his sleeves down as he walked toward us. "I said dawn."

"And I've been walking since before dawn but I couldn't find the property. I don't know this area." She glanced past us. "But I do know a troublesome river when I see one, and that one won't grant you any favors."

I followed her eyes to the group of workers, the unfortunate man in the middle, soaked and shivering in the nip of the September morning.

"Yes, well, that is not your concern," Giovanni said. "Your tasks will have nothing to do with the torrent."

I turned to look at him, not daring to hope but hoping.

"Yes, she's your new maid," Giovanni said.

"Really?"

He nodded, a smile tucked into the corner of his lips.

"Oh, thank you!"

"She's not served in a proper house a day in her life, so perhaps thanking me is premature."

"No, I'm sure she'll be wonderful." I found myself bouncing on the tips of my toes like a child and stopped at once. No signora with a villa would do such a thing. I looked at her. "What's your name?"

"Buona."

"Buona, Signora Fenoglio," Giovanni said. "And I'm Ingegnere Fenoglio. You will address us correctly."

The girl's lips twitched but she nodded.

"All right. As you can see, I have plenty to keep me occupied here," he said, motioning to the dam, which looked worse now than when we'd first arrived. "Go on to the house."

"And that poor man?" I said.

"We'll get him inside and warm."

With a nod, I looked at Buona. "Come, then; we have plenty to do as well."

We picked our way through the sludge of leaves, or rather I did, for the girl was as sure-footed as if she possessed hooves. She was small, all knobs and angles, and dirt clung to her like a second skin.

"How old are you?"

"Eighteen, signora."

I'd been about right, then. "And you do not live around here?"

"On the other side of Ovada, beyond the old bridge, signora. Neighbors told me your husband was looking for a maid, and here I am."

I didn't know the area well, not enough to know what bridge she meant, but I did remember the trail we'd taken from the town to the mill. Most of it was through the woods. "You walked all this way on your own?"

She flicked her eyes to me and for a second, I thought I caught the glint of something sharp in them. "Yes, signora. Why?"

"You weren't afraid? I would have been if I'd had to walk alone in the near dark and through the forest."

Buona shrugged. "What would I need to be afraid of? I know how to scare off wolves, and the rest is just trees, signora."

"Oh, you don't need to keep calling me that when we're on our own." It would drive me mad to have that word wedging its formality into every sentence. "Just remember to do it when my husband is in the room."

"What should I call you, then?"

"Sibilla will be fine."

We left the mud and took what held traces of having been a pebbled path up to the villa.

I'd hurried from room to room this morning, hand on the mound, flinging open the windows and doors not covered in ivy to drive out the worst of the chill, and the house gaped open now, as if in surprise.

Buona bent to grab a patched-up sack from the ground, swinging it over her shoulder. She must have dropped it when she heard the commotion coming from the dam.

Which reminded me.

"Was it you who screamed?" I said, starting up the stairs to the colonnade.

"When do you mean?"

"As the man fell in the water." No, that wasn't right. "Actually, I think it happened right before the dam broke and he fell."

"I only called for the rope."

I paused on the stairs. "But you did hear it? Was that what brought you to the dam?"

"It was the men shouting that did it."

I frowned. "You really heard no other scream, earlier?"

She shook her head.

I searched her face for a lie, though I couldn't imagine why she *would* lie about that. Perhaps the scream hadn't reached up here despite its fierceness. Or maybe it'd been a distortion of some other sound, something giving way in the dam that I'd misheard.

But it had seemed so very much like a scream.

I led the way inside, through the vestibule, and pointed to one of the branches leading off the courtyard. "What used to be the servants' quarters is through there, but since it's just you for now it might be too much work to clear up an entire wing. We can put you in one of the rooms near us."

Buona readjusted the bag. "I'll sleep anywhere, dirty, clean, wet, dry, outdoors, indoors. It's all the same to me."

"Well, it'll certainly be indoors," I said and tapped the tip of my shoe into a puddle, "but I can't promise it'll be dry."

She smiled for the first time and I did the same, oddly at ease already with this sure-footed, angular girl.

I NUDGED THE RADIO AGAIN, coaxing it out of its crackle. Throughout the entire morning we'd not been able to get a single tune out of it that wasn't riddled with static. Perhaps once the men finished the puzzle of electricity and we managed to plug it into the wall and get all the antennas in place, we'd have better luck with the reception.

With a sigh, I sat back on my heels and wiped my hands on the apron that had been white when I'd put in on this morning. It was tinged gray and black with ashes and soot now.

The kitchen hearth looked a bit better, though, the stones and bricks visible once again after centuries of caked-on dirt. We'd not really have much use for it once the gas kitchen stove was in place, but it could help with the worst of the cold if the radiators hadn't been installed yet by the time winter came.

It was a shame that the pile of ashes in the wooden bucket next to me was too old to use in the garden plot behind the kitchen. Not that anything but weeds and stinging nettle was growing there at the moment, but I would like to clear a patch of soil and try my hand at tomatoes, perhaps peppers, and a few herbs.

Giovanni hadn't taken to the idea of plants in the house, and with no garden, I'd never been able to grow anything in Torino, so I didn't know if I had the aptitude for it or if I'd wilt everything I so much as looked at. But I was willing to try.

With a swing of a hip, Buona pushed open the door leading out into the garden, a bucket of water in each hand.

"They used to keep birds," she said. "There's a dovecote out back."

"That must have been nice, to hear the cooing through the day."

Buona eased the buckets down. "I don't know, birds are messy things. Besides, they likely just kept them for food."

She was probably right.

I'd seen a chicken coop past the well, too, so perhaps I could convince Giovanni to let me have a few. I doubted the signora of the Caparalia household would have considered fetching the eggs herself, but it'd be pleasant to get up each morning and gather them with my son.

"When will the baby be born?" Buona said.

I frowned at her words until I realized my hands were pressed yet again against my stomach.

"Oh, in five months."

"A winter's child, then." She plunged a rag into the water. "My mother always said that they were the most pleasant, that the darkness of the days soothed them."

She tossed the rag to the floor and knelt beside it. Her hands were a bright pink from the cold well water.

"Your mother's gone, then?" I said.

"Yes. She's not dead, mind, she just left us years ago." A quick flick of her eyes. "My father and me."

I felt my cheeks warm. "I'm sorry. I shouldn't have mentioned it."

"I've made my peace with it. I was a summer child, see, full of fire, so maybe that was the problem."

She said it simply, as if the words were part of a well-worn prayer.

The radio yodeled between two stations, and I tapped it back to coherence.

"You live with your father?"

She nodded. "But he hires himself off to farms throughout the region most of the year, so I hardly see him." She scrubbed fiercely at a blotch covering half a stone tile. "And you won't find me complaining. You know how difficult everything is with a man in the house. Things must be done *just so*, but see if he isn't the first to leave the room when it needs doing."

She surprised a laugh out of me.

It'd been so long since I'd had female company that I'd forgotten this kind of banter. I'd heard plenty of it from my mother's friends, even from the woman my father wed after her death, but once I married and had to stop working at the sweets shop, I'd not had much opportunity for chatting. At least not this sort of chatting. For the past year, most of what I'd heard around our dining table was about Giovanni's invention.

"It's a good thing, too, that he isn't around," she said, "because my father wouldn't have let me come work here."

I frowned. "Why not?"

"Well, see, both my grandfather and uncle died in these parts. A hunting accident."

"How terrible!"

"It was before I was born, but my father has unpleasant ideas about the place." She shrugged. "All nonsense. It might mean, though, that when he returns in late December, I'll have to absent myself for a few days. Just until he leaves again."

It didn't seem like the kindest thing to do, to lie to a parent in that manner, but it wasn't my right to lecture her.

"This blasted mark is stubborn," she hissed, dropping the rag back in the water.

"I think there's a wirehaired brush in the pantry." I grabbed hold of the kitchen table and stood. "I'll get it."

But Buona had already leaped up and was halfway to the door.

I winced at a twinge and pressed a hand to my lower back. The girl was practically a bundle of bones in shirt and trousers, but she had enough energy for the both of us.

The room felt too close around me all at once, probably from all the dust and ash we'd whipped up, so I opened the kitchen door and stepped outside.

The chill of the early fall air swiped at me, bringing with it the chirpings and rustlings of the small creatures that went about their lives, unseen. I passed the well and saw the leaning dovecote, twisting ivy a leafed serpent holding it captive.

"Sibilla," Buona called from behind me. "Someone is knocking at the door."

I turned and made to head back before realizing that this was not my cramped house in Torino anymore and I didn't have to do everything myself. This was a proper villa, even if it was a bit sodden, and I had a proper maid to help me. The thought sent a shiver of delight through me.

"You can answer, Buona," I said.

The girl's eyes went round as almond *pignoli*.

"Really?"

"Yes, go on. And if it's someone calling on me, lead them to one of the *sale*." I waved a hand in the boneless manner of the silk-clad, pearl-draped ladies who came to the sweets shop.

"The one black with mold, or the one with water that reaches your ankles?" Buona said, smiling.

"Either one is perfectly suitable."

Chuckling, she hurried to do as I said. I had no doubt she could manage whatever the knock involved, including shoving guests into crumbling rooms.

I tilted my head back and breathed in the pine-scented air. It was even colder here, at the edge between garden and forest, the trees having extended their branches in a tangle of limbs over the stone wall that divided the tame from the wild—had divided, at least, for sections of the wall had collapsed. Nettle and elderflower patches had spilled through those gaps into the darkness of the woods. A darkness that looked enticing.

Well, why not? Buona's father might fear this land, but I didn't have to. Stepping over all that green, I walked into the wild.

It was a forest dense with pines, a carpet of their cones making my progress less calming and more of a balancing act than I'd imagined. Needles brushed my cheeks as I ducked under heavy branches. The sun did what it could to weave through the latticed canopy, but the ground was damp with darkness. A few early mushrooms had already raised their umbrella heads.

I'd only made it a few steps when a snort stopped me.

The tusks of the *cinghiale* flashed through my mind, accelerating my pulse, but only for an instant because no, this had been the sound of an animal even larger than a boar. But what? A deer, perhaps? Did bears roam this side of the Alps?

With no clue as to what I'd do if it was a bear, I remained as still as I could and listened.

Another snort. This one a bit closer.

My heart thudded in my temples.

The high neigh a beat later made me exhale with relief. I rolled my eyes at myself because, truly, what a goose I was. It was a horse, of course. Whoever had come to the villa had likely done so on a horse and buggy, not a car, and its sound had echoed back here.

"Mystery solved," I murmured, "by a woman with a mostly functioning brain." I was only thankful that Giovanni hadn't been here to catch me in another exemplary instance of weak-mindedness.

"A bear, indeed."

I turned to start back for the house.

The sudden thunder of racing hoofbeats filled the woods, rooting me in place. Branches snapped as another neigh swept like a gust through the trees behind me.

There was someone in the forest on horseback, then, not a buggy, there had to be, one of the workers or someone from nearby who didn't know we'd bought the—

I yelped at the screeching whinny that came from just a few meters away this time, and I leaped out of the way of the charging, crashing animal. I felt it speed by me, its momentum lifting the hem of my housedress. Panting, I spun around, hands blocking the soft mound of my stomach.

But there was nothing.

Just the afternoon shadows draped around trees and needle-heavy branches shifting in the breeze.

"What are you doing all the way back here?"

"Santissima Madre," I hissed. Giovanni really had to stop stealing up on me like this. I swallowed the dry fear in my throat. "Did you see it?"

"See what?"

"The horse."

Giovanni frowned. "Sibilla, what are you talking about?"

"There was a horse, right here. It came galloping at me."

He looked past me, deeper into the forest. "You saw it?"

I hesitated. "No. I-I just heard it."

He sighed, his thin lips becoming thinner as he pressed them together. He motioned me forward with his arm. "Come on, let's go back to the house."

"I did hear it, Giovanni."

"It was probably a deer. The forest is packed with them."

Perhaps he was right. It could have been a deer, couldn't it? I'd never heard one whinny in that manner, but it wasn't as if I had had many encounters with them. My presence could have frightened it, and it could have taken off in the wrong direction, toward instead of away from me. They were notoriously foolish animals.

Like me.

Yes, it was possible. More likely than a horse racing through the middle of the forest, in any case.

I followed Giovanni.

"I came to tell you that we have the dam mostly fixed," he said, pushing aside a branch and ushering me into the garden. "The water still doesn't flow into the millrace because—I think—there's an obstruction of some kind, but at least it is going into the right tributary."

"That's wonderful." See, now here was sense. Logic. Order. "Can I go see it?"

"If you'd like."

Buona shoved open the kitchen door and started toward us. "Ingegnere," she called out, and I could have sworn she leaned into the word a bit more than she needed to.

"Is the yelling necessary?" Giovanni said.

"Scusatemi, ingegnere, but I ran to the dam and back looking for you. This letter came."

A letter, already?

If it surprised Giovanni, he didn't show it. He snatched it from her hand and slid it into one of his pockets without a glance.

"Do you know who it's from?" I said.

"I'm sure it's not important."

That made little sense. How could he know it wasn't important if he'd not so much as looked at it? But the slight pursing of his lips told me not to ask again. Perhaps it was just my impression, or the vestiges of a long day's labors, but I thought a slight flush had come into his face.

"I'll leave you two to your work," he said, sweeping past me as he started for the house.

"But I thought you were going to show me the repairs to the dam."

"I don't have time right now." He waved my presence off like he would a bothersome child. "Find something else to amuse yourself with."

In a moment he had disappeared into the house.

It was my turn now to feel a flush rising to my cheeks. It was one thing to dismiss me when we were alone, which, though unpleasant, was something I could shoulder and most of the time even understand, for I knew I possessed no scintillating genius. It was quite another to do so in front of someone who was supposed to respect and obey me.

I looked at Buona, but she had her gaze fixed on her hands.

No matter how much I pretended to be a signora, nothing would ever make any difference when my own husband still treated me like I was a child.

Buona sniffed. "The postman said the letter was marked as urgent." She glanced up at me, that sharpness I'd seen earlier turning her eyes into hard caramel.

For the length of a heartbeat, I hesitated. But no more than that. "You didn't happen to see whom it was from."

"I wouldn't have known what I was looking at. I don't know how to read."

No, of course not. I should have realized it before making her admit it.

"I did, however," she said, lowering her voice to a murmur, "see a strange marking on the envelope. Like a large stamp. Fancy."

I met her gaze and held it, waiting.

"It had a wolf on it."

Dottore Lupponi. The urgent letter was from Giovanni's lawyer.

MADDALENA
1596

PULLED AT A FOLD OF Florindo's lace neck ruff, which wasn't as starched as I would have preferred. Even the wires that held it up had trouble keeping the structure fanned to its full width. The damage was done for tonight, his golden silk doublet only just managing to draw the eye from the drooping neckline, but I'd have to have a word with the servants about it.

"Sposa, you'll end up ripping the lace. Leave it be."

"All of the work I've done, just to be thwarted by a ruff," I hissed.

He chuckled. "Thwarted? Amore, this night is already a success. The villa looks exquisite and so do you." He glanced about the courtyard and quickly placed a kiss on the tip of my nose. "You are by far the loveliest woman present."

I frowned more markedly to try and hide my rising smile, but I knew I'd fail. He always found the precise words to unlace my sternness like a gown. "You really think the house looks as it should?"

"Better. But I'm not entirely surprised, with the expenses I've written down in my *ricordanza*." He cleared his throat and pursed his lips in his own best attempt at seriousness. "They were substantial. We'll have to tighten the purse strings a bit for the remainder of the year."

"It's the first time all these people meet us, Florindo. The expenses were necessary and you know it as well as I do."

He shrugged, the movement flattening his ruff again. "Perhaps. Though I can't imagine all those new tapestries were crucial to our position in the region."

"They were if I say they were. You want people to have confidence in what we're doing, so we need to look successful."

I widened my smile at the woman in the blue brocade gown with rather disappointing gray embroidered sleeves who had started toward us. I'd never have chosen those with that overdress and certainly not for the evening. Not so much as a lone pearl on them! Nothing gleamed. Nothing caught the eye and held it. Genova might own this region once again, but its sartorial influence had not reached it yet.

"Yes, but the sugar sculptures. What shall we do with all of them when the evening is over?"

"Hush, sposo," I said, casting about for the woman's name. What had it been?

Ah, yes. I had it now.

"Messer Caparalia, Madonna Caparalia," she said, with a fold of her knees.

I did the same, Florindo bowing his head. "Madonna Rosso."

"I wanted to offer my congratulations on the villa," she said, her smile a pinched, tepid thing. "The frescoes are some of the loveliest I've seen."

"They are my wife's own designs," Florindo said, as he'd done the entire evening whenever anyone even glanced in their direction.

"Alas, not my own executions," I said. "My talents do not lie with a brush and paint, at least not those that I do not apply to my face."

Her laugh was as brittle as early frost, and she made no attempt to continue the banter. I could think of at least four different things to say that would have charmed a hostess, amused her enough to have earned myself a place at her side for the remainder of the night. Madre di Dio, this woman wouldn't have lasted more than a day at a Genovese court with these rather weak attempts at flattery.

Madonna Rosso's smile drooped more with each beat of silence that passed, because now that she had run out of things to say, she also didn't seem to know how to extricate herself from our presence. That was one of the first things my mother had taught me before plunging me into society: never begin a conversation without knowing how to end it.

The sound of the bugle made Madonna Rosso almost exhale with relief.

"If you'll pardon me," she said with another tight curtsy. "I must find my husband."

"Of course."

I waited until she'd disappeared to groan lightly. "This is going to be a very long evening if they all put as little effort into conversation. So far none of the women I've spoken with have exactly glinted with wit."

Florindo lifted his arm and I rested my hand on his. "You can't expect all of them to be as clever as you, Maddalena."

"I expect what I am used to."

"This is not Genova, sposa."

"Clearly."

I adjusted my white cuff so that the threads of silver caught the court-yard's candlelight and then I nodded to him to begin. To lead us into the sala.

I couldn't help smiling at the beauty of the room. As I'd instructed, the servants had lit all the candles, dozens of them catching the gold leaf of the cornices and of the silk-thread tapestries I'd purchased. The candle-glow swept across the red beaded birds on my full sleeves as I stepped inside, setting them aflame against the black silk and velvet brocade. Exactly as I'd intended.

Florindo guided us down the length of the room to the stone table decked in unadorned white linen. The silver on the tables echoed the silver in the credenze, light bouncing from one to the other as the candles flickered. I'd had two more tables brought in and placed perpendicularly to the main one, all of them crowned with a sugar sculpture of a griffin at each end, along with a dais I'd had placed at the center for the lute and the viola da gamba players. The hand bowls filled with rose water at each place setting released their soft perfume into the glowing room.

I took my seat to my husband's right, leaving a seat empty between us for our guest of honor, Dottore Cestarello, the chancellor of the region. His wife, a woman who had donned a rather fetching set of sleeves featuring embroidered stalks of wheat, took the seat to my right.

Walking silently into the room with their instruments, the three players stepped up to the dais.

The head steward's eyes were fixed on me from the corner of the room leading out into the servant's passage so that I only had to give him the slightest of nods to launch him into the beginning of the cena. He, in turn, motioned to the wine steward, and the entire affair began.

"This is perfection," Madonna Cestarello said, watching the synchronicity of the men, one for each table, pouring wine in rhythm with the music. "You've truly outdone yourself, Madonna Caparalia."

"Thank you, but please, call me Maddalena."

She smiled. "And I am Silvia."

"I agree with my wife," the chancellor said. "It's not at all what we're used to here, but it should be."

"That is most kind. It really is all a matter of planning."

"With respect, Maddalena," the chancellor said, motioning to the near dance occurring in front of us, "there is real artistry in this."

My cheeks seemed to glow as much as the room did as I bowed my head in acknowledgment. Now that was how one flattered a hostess.

The light clearing of a throat shifted my attention farther down the table to the newly appointed *massaro*, Messer Alessandro Scappi, and his wife. She was inspecting the silverware, her lips pursed as if she had found water marks I knew were not there, but he was watching me. He tipped his head in my direction. I returned the gesture.

"And how was the journey here?" the chancellor said, lifting his wine-glass. "Did you have any trouble with the bandits?"

Florindo shook his head. "Not at all, Salvatore. But we did have escorts through most of the trail, because my wife wouldn't have stepped foot in a carriage with our children if there'd been the slightest chance of danger."

"Entirely reasonable."

Yes, I'd thought so, too. If I had to trek through all of Liguria with the five most precious things I possessed, falling victim to the banditry that had been spreading across the entire region for years could not be a possibility.

"And we've already had our share of trouble with them," I said.

"Oh?"

I nodded, watching the servers bring the first two cold dishes from the *credenza*, a pear *crostata* with dried prunes, and fried cow's udders dressed in cinnamon and a dollop of a sauce made of carrots. Exactly on time.

"Yes, we had one of our shipments of wheat stolen on the road to Genova last year," I said. "It was . . . unpleasant."

Words were weak to describe the anguish of those days. The loss had come on the heels of the previous season's poor harvest, the supplier we'd bought from having delivered chaff with mere aspirations of being wheat. That was when we'd had to resort to the first loan.

"Is that why you decided to begin your own wheat production?" Chancellor Cestarello said.

"Partly, yes," Florindo said, wiping sauce from his chin. "In truth, I've always wanted to have my own hectares to ensure the quality of the grain is up to my own personal standards. And those of Maddalena, of course, which are even harsher."

I smiled and wished I could squeeze my husband's hand. Because the truth was infinitely more complicated.

After the poor harvest and then the robbery, we'd known we'd not make it through another year if we did not attempt to take our fate back from other people's hands. Our fortune would have disappeared on the backs of bank loans. We spent entire nights scratching numbers on ledgers, adding and subtracting expenses until they did not tip sharply into the negative, days spent fawning over investors. The braided scarlet bracelets I made us wear and that I'd dipped in a mixture of ginger, frankincense, and boiled mercury to transform fortune into a docile thing turned our skin raw with boils.

But it'd worked. We'd found our solution, unpleasant as it was for my Genovese soul.

I'd plunged my dowry into the villa, knowing well that if something were to happen to Florindo I'd be left without recourse. We'd sold our home in Genova and our small mill on its outskirts to buy this mud-swamped one that my husband had found for less than it was worth, and we'd even managed to charm an advance on this year's flour from one single investor, allowing us the possibility of seeding thirty hectares of wheat fields. Every *scudo* we had was here.

None of it had been easy. And it wouldn't begin to be until this year's wheat poured golden into the mill. We would still have one more loan to pay back, but the worst of it would be over. Our future would be in our hands and in our fields.

"Have you had many instances of bandits in the area?" I said, turning away from my anxious thoughts and toward the massaro and his wife. "We're here chattering away when you surely have the most experience."

Messer Scappi waited for the server to place the platter of quails stuffed with sausages on the table before looking over at me.

"Not in this region, thankfully, Madonna Caparalia. I've set guards on the roads, but they've had no encounters."

"That is reassuring. There is no danger in me allowing the children to play about the property, then?"

"Not from bandits, no."

That was a strangely oblique answer. I felt a flutter of something, the hairs on the back of my neck rising.

"Where are the children now?" Silvia said. "I would have so liked to have met them."

Santa Madre preserve us from such an event. There would have been pieces of sugar griffins embedded in the frescoes. "They are with their tutor, Giusto, and if the stars have been kind, already asleep."

Silvia smiled into her wineglass.

I almost asked if she had any children herself, but an internal pulse, like a plucking of strings, stopped me.

It was a sensation I had learned to heed.

I took a bite of the quail and waited.

"I've not been fortunate enough to have children, yet," Silvia said, lowering her voice. "It is something I have always longed for."

"You are still very young," I said. "There is no reason why it should not occur."

She looked down at her plate, her light hair coppering in the candleglow. For the first time, I noticed how pale she was. "Yes, I suppose so."

"Perhaps you can create one of your tonics for her. Or give her a charm of some kind."

I turned to Madonna Scappi, swallowing down a needle of irritation. She'd been listening to what she had to have realized was a private conversation. Hadn't she heard the softer tone, seen the lowered head? In Genova, this intrusion would have been met with a wall of silken retreating backs.

"Madonna?" I said.

"It is true, isn't it, that you are known in Genova for your potions and your charms? Everyone in Ovada says so." She cut into a slice of salami and apple *pasticcio*. "Do you read fortunes, as well?"

A seat away from me, Florindo boomed with laughter at something the chancellor had said.

"Cartomancy is not my specialty, alas," I said, "but yes, I have provided many of the ladies in Genova with various powders and tinctures. Though I wouldn't call them potions, as such. That has an undertone of something darker, wouldn't you say?"

"I'm sure I don't know. I don't meddle in such things."

I smiled away the strong words I wanted to say because this was not the place for them. But how rapidly the gossip had spread! In this respect, if in nothing else, the countryside was not so very different from the city.

"Do you truly believe that charms and potions can influence what our *Dio* has intended for us?" Her voice was light, no trace of threat in it, but there didn't need to be to make this conversation a precarious one.

I had to tread with care.

Placing my fork down, I turned fully toward Madonna Scappi. "I believe our Dio offers chances of changing the course of our lives, yes. He quite often sends us warnings and signs to guide us, so why wouldn't He be open to the adjustments in our fates that the heeding of those warnings would bring? We have to be alert to what He and the world tell us and act accordingly. Those charms can aid us in that. They are tools, nothing more and nothing less."

"There are those who would find that blasphemous."

"Then they would have misunderstood me."

A trace of amusement shaped the slight lift of her eyebrows.

"Mona Maddalena," the chancellor said, to my really rather strong relief, "you must convince your husband to consider selling the lumber on the property."

I blinked. "The lumber?"

"The hectares of oak trees on your mountain, mona. I've not been to see them in months, but the trees grow there like the heads of the Hydra."

I looked past him at Florindo, who shrugged lightly. I'd known the property was large, but not that anything worth our attention was on the mountain itself. It really wasn't at all a bad idea. Oak lumber could help us cut into the debts we had while also allowing us to increase our influence in the region.

"I have to warn you, it is somewhat complicated to bring the wood down from the mountain, for the passage giving access to the oak forest is quite narrow," the chancellor continued, "but consider it, Mona Maddalena. I have no doubt your husband will listen to you."

Florindo chuckled. "I never have much choice in the matter, Salvatore. Once she decides, it might as well be law."

It would require a small investment, then, into equipment, more horses than the one we had, though that would be a necessity regardless, more men, but it could be worthwhile. It would bear some thinking about and some more nights with our abacus and ledgers. It may not be feasible until after the harvest, but it was an appealing notion.

I glanced up to say exactly this and my eyes met those of one of the men on the table to our left. I had the impression he'd been staring for some time. He lifted his wineglass in my direction and I nodded at him, trying not to focus too much on the white scar that marred his right cheek.

As was my custom whenever someone's eyes lingered too long on me or my children, I went to tap the silver horned hand I always carried.

It wasn't there. I'd forgotten to tie it into the neckline of my chemise when I changed for the evening.

Of all nights for that to happen.

I breathed out the knot of sudden tension. It couldn't be helped now. I would have to wait until the cena was over.

Amid a fog of simple chatter, course after course came and went: shrimp in vinegar, veal bones cooked in lemon, roasted pigeons from our own dovecote, and even a *pasticcio all'inglese*. Wine flowed from the decanters, music gurgled from the dais.

I dipped my fingers in the bowl of rose water the moment my last dish had been cleared and motioned to the servers to begin the preparation of the sweets. With the speed and care that I'd demanded of them when they stepped into my service, they removed the tablecloths and the protective leather layers beneath them to reveal a second cloth. At the other two tables, this meant linen with fine embroidered borders of ivy, but at our table, it was my grandmother's masterpiece that they now uncovered.

A silk and linen tablecloth that had been part of her trousseau, she had spent years of her childhood embroidering delicate blue and silver flower bouquets at random across its surface. Lace panels draped down its sides in gossamer folds, brushing the marble floors as lightly as seafoam. Through all of the banquets I'd attended since I'd been of age, in all of the stately homes in Genova, I'd never seen its like.

Silvia pressed a hand to her chest and leaned to look at the flowers, and even Madonna Scappi murmured her appreciation of the lacework.

Feeling satisfaction down to the center of my bones, I nodded to the servers to begin the last course.

It was well upward of midnight when the dancing finished and guests crossed the courtyard toward the front door.

In all, the cena had been a success. Even the sapphire earring in my hand, which had dripped from a woman's earlobe to the floor and for which four of my servants had had to scour the sala, had no marks or chipping on it.

Now if I could only find the woman, I could wind down the evening.

I eased along the wall of the courtyard to avoid the worst of the skirts and doublets, searching for the burgundy velvet sleeves that, from the elbow fading that not even the added beading could hide, had been worn too often. What kind of headdress did she have? A headband or a snood?

There. That was her.

I slipped past two men in animated conversation and started toward a group of women, one wearing a sole earring.

"—her dress. Who wears black silk in that fashion?"

"The Genovese, it seems."

My legs stopped moving.

Their laughter tried to scrape paint off the frescoes.

"And Santa Maria! Thinking the griffin sugar sculptures would be the right choice. In this region! With the new taxes Genova has imposed on us, I had to restrain my husband more than once from knocking those horrid things off the table."

My cheeks burned as if they might catch flames. I could feel each beat of my heart in the tips of my fingers.

Madonna Scappi, for now I saw that she was part of the group, leaned forward. "I, for one, want nothing to do with someone of her kind. There's something perverse about flaunting her defiance of our Dio in the way she does."

"What we heard is true, then?"

"Entirely. She is ungodly."

"That would explain why her children are said to be little *diavoli*," the woman missing an earring said, setting off another bout of laughter.

If I truly had been what they professed me to be, their skin would have melted off their bones.

I could stand criticism to myself and my home, even from peasants dressed in airs and last year's gowns, but I'd not have allowed talk of my children from the Prince of Melfi himself.

Clenching the earring in my hand until I thought I'd snap the sapphire off its setting, I walked toward the group.

Madonna Scappi saw me first and signaled to her companions with her eyes.

"It is unfortunate that your lack of breeding made it difficult for you to enjoy the evening, because it was a rather lovely one," I said, handing the earring to its owner. "Be sure to have a close look at the courtyard before you leave, for none of you will step foot in my home again."

I turned without allowing them to so much as open their mouths and walked back to where Florindo stood, seeing off the chancellor and Silvia.

I should have felt some satisfaction from the confrontation, but all I wanted was to race up the stairs and embrace my children. Florindo seemed to sense my uneasiness, for he drew closer, his arm brushing mine, as he nodded to another couple.

I stood straighter and pulled my mind from those women's words. It would be giving their opinion too much importance to allow them to tinge the entire evening with failure.

And yet, I felt a tightness in my chest, the rising pressure of the kind of tears I never knew if I'd be able to quench. It was a sensation I recognized all too well.

IN THE MORNING, A SCREAM I'd half anticipated dragged me out of sleep and propelled me down the main stairwell to the mud-spattered vestibule. On our doorstep, slashed to ribbons and dripping with blood, was my grandmother's embroidered tablecloth.

SIBILLA

1933

THE BUZZ OF ELECTRICITY MADE the hairs on my arms stand up as I lifted the coffee cup to my lips. We'd had electric light in Torino for years now and I'd never felt the like. It vibrated against my teeth.

"Is this normal, do you think?" I said.

"What?" Giovanni glanced up from his newspaper.

I pointed to the cables on the wall in front of us, the nest of colors that the men had wrestled into service.

He sat back in his chair. "It is a bit distracting, isn't it? They should have done a better job of it, considering what I paid them." He shook his head. "A fortune for people without proper titles. I'll have to speak with them and see if they can improve it."

"They weren't real electricians?"

"Of course not, Sibilla. We can't afford that."

I bit my lips because . . . couldn't we? Wasn't a bit of expense better than the danger of an electrical fire burning the house down to ashes? I sipped more coffee. I would have thought that was more important than the telephone he was having installed in his study this week. It wasn't as if he had any clients to speak of yet, and his lawyer obviously knew where to find him, so what could possibly be the urgency?

I blinked as the answer came to me with the force of a slap. Of course. What a ninny I was.

The urgency was the child we were awaiting. He'd want to make sure he could call a doctor at once.

Buona stepped into the room and started toward us, the house shoes I'd given her hitting the tiles as she tried to keep them from slipping off her thin feet. When Giovanni bought a car or when he asked to borrow a buggy from a neighbor, I'd try to convince him to take us into town. The girl needed clothes and shoes and, despite myself, I would have liked to purchase a new set of curlers. My old ones had somehow been misplaced in the move from Torino and though I knew how to make them out of aluminum and paper, it seemed like unnecessary work. Surely Giovanni would allow me that small luxury.

"You've boiled it, I presume?" he said as the girl filled his glass with water from a decanter, her lips pursed in concentration.

"Yes, ingegnere. As you've told me to do."

He nodded and picked up a slice of toasted bread from the plate resting between us. I'd done what I could to scrape the burnt layers off their undersides, but he was bound to notice. He liked the bread crisp and golden, without a hint of singeing, and the girl still hadn't quite managed it. Tomorrow morning, I'd help her with the toaster myself. It was a fussy thing that required as much monitoring as the radio now seemed to need.

"Even if you're washing dishes, the water should still be boiled," Giovanni said, smoothing a thin slice of butter onto the bread.

"But it's well water we're using," I said. "Isn't that safe?"

He flicked his eyes up at me. "I've not checked the state of the well yet. Have you?"

"No, of course not." I reached for the bowl of peach jam. "I wouldn't know what I was looking at."

"Precisely, so just do as I say and boil the water."

He took a bite and almost immediately grimaced. With a sigh, he turned the slice of bread over, the evidence of Buona's distraction making him shake his head.

Yes, tomorrow I'd have it resolved. I cleared my throat and shifted to place the bowl back within his reach in case today he decided to try a bit of it along with the butter. As I moved, my stomach pressed against the stone table and I flinched at the shock of cold it sent through me.

"Sibi—signora?" Buona said. "Is everything all right?"

"Yes, I'm fine." I placed a hand over my midsection, where the fabric still retained the chill. "I brushed against the stone and it's frigid."

Giovanni frowned, placing a hand on the table. "It's a perfectly normal temperature."

Perhaps it was just on this side, then, facing away from the bit of sun coming in through the window. I shrugged, smiling lightly. "It's really not important. I'm being silly."

He watched me for a second more, the frown remaining in place even as he lifted a napkin to his lips and dabbed at nonexistent crumbs. "Right," he said and stood. "Well, the men will be here soon and I want to take some measurements before they do."

"Oh, could I come to the mill with you?" I said, setting down my untouched slice of bread. "You haven't shown me the repairs you've made yet, and I would like to see them."

"I suppose." He reached for the coat he'd laid across an empty chair. "But that actually reminds me, I wanted to ask if either one of you has heard or seen anyone walking about the property. Other than the workers, of course."

I frowned. "I don't remember seeing anyone. Buona, do you?"

"No, signora."

I stood, pulling my cardigan a bit closer around me. "Why do you ask?"

"I found some fresh footprints yesterday morning, in the mud on the other side of the river, and I've not had any of my men working there." He shook his head, his jaw tight. "I don't like the thought of people walking where they have no business doing so."

And perhaps not just walking.

"Do you remember the horse I told you I heard in the woods a few days ago? Maybe someone is just used to passing through here and is not aware it's no longer appropriate. The land has been abandoned for a very long time, after all."

He tugged on his coat, straightening it. "Yes, well, that will have to stop. I won't allow it. Come on."

I followed him out, hurrying to keep up with his steps as we crossed the courtyard. I glanced up and felt the same ripple of pleasure from the first day.

It was mine.

"Isn't it incredible?" I said.

"What?"

"The fresco."

His gaze rested on the beauty above him for only a moment, his feet already moving again. "It's damaged."

My smile wavered. "Just a little discolored."

But his thoughts were already on something else and he turned, leading us through the vestibule and to the front door.

The morning light revealed a tightness in his face. Preoccupation. I'd noticed it more often these past few days, ever since Dottore Lupponi's letter had arrived.

I started down the steps with care.

Giovanni hadn't even mentioned the letter again, and although I was sure he had good reason, I couldn't help wanting to know. I'd not really had a chance to ask him about it, either, for he was always at the mill, giving orders to workers, or slipping into sleep the moment his head touched the pillow. Even at mealtimes, his forehead was furrowed in thoughts that appeared too weighty for me to shift aside for long enough to get his attention.

But now, perhaps . . .

My blood bubbled with nerves as I looked down at my feet, already sinking in mud. I had to be careful with the words I chose, the tone I used. Giovanni was sensitive to all of that.

"Have you had any interesting news from Torino?" I said, my voice all light, like glinting crystal.

"Why would I have heard anything from Torino?"

I swallowed. "Because you got that letter a few days ago. I just assumed it was from acquaintances there, that's all."

"It wasn't."

I bit the inside of my lip. I knew I shouldn't ask, I could feel it. "Was it about the mill, then?"

He looked at me. "I've already told you, it was nothing important."

"But you've seemed preoccupied and I just—"

"Enough, Sibilla."

He walked ahead, leaving me to manage through the mud on my own. I sighed. So much for that.

An apology on my lips, I stepped into the mill but all words dried to dust on at the sight of Giovanni rooted in place. And at what lay beyond him.

It was impossible.

The new wooden beams Giovanni had fetched from the station two days ago were smashed to splinters, the large metal cogs warped out of all recognizable shape, the scaffolding to reach the topmost mill cranks reduced to firewood. Everything my husband and the workers had spent repairing, undone.

I shook my head, as if a negation of what was in front of us was enough to clear it away.

Giovanni slammed a fist into a plank, making me flinch. "This is preposterous!"

I swallowed, dragging my voice up from where it hid. "I don't understand. Did something fall and break?"

But no. If it'd been only some of the wooden parts and structures, then perhaps it could have been an accident, something tipping over in the night and crashing its way down, but there was no manner in which the iron cogs could have been twisted out of shape in error.

"Someone did this," Giovanni.

"But who?" I touched the twisted metal. "How could they have done this?"

How could anyone have managed to do all this damage in just a few hours and without any of us hearing it? It was true that sound moved strangely through the property, but we would have heard all of this crashing, wouldn't we?

We had to report it to the *carabinieri*.

"I should have known they'd do something like this," he said.

My eyes widened. "What are you talking about?"

He shook his head.

"Who would have done something like this?" I asked.

He waved my words away. "The—the people in the region."

Giovanni ran a shaking hand through his dark hair. He practically vibrated with anger. "I'll need to go buy more parts. I'll walk to find Manfredo and see if he'll lend me his buggy."

"But he'll be here in an hour or so, and besides, don't we need the carabinieri—"

"I'm going now, Sibilla." He bit the words out more than said them. "Two of the parts are made in Alessandria, so I need to get to the post office as soon as possible to send a message to the provider. You, who are always going on about why I could possibly need a telephone, see? This is what I need it for. So I can behave in a civilized manner and not beg favors off subordinates."

Oh. Yes, of course. I should have realized. How many times had he told me that to be powerful, one had to first look powerful?

He stalked across the floor toward the cave-like opening that allowed a glimpse of the water wheel, which remained as silent and still as it had been for centuries.

The fixed dam hadn't yet made a difference.

I placed my hands around my mound and held my breath, waiting for another frustrated yell as Giovanni leaned into the opening and took stock.

But it didn't come.

"The wheel appears intact," he said. "Whoever did this limited their destruction to this area."

I exhaled. Something to be grateful for, then.

A sudden silvered ringing sound pealed through the room. It quivered about me and faded.

"What was that?" I said.

Giovanni frowned, stepping from the edge of the opening. He paused to listen. And there it was again, the chiming of what sounded like a bell, coming from right above us.

His face cleared. "It's one of the dansil's bells," he said. "Probably a rat or something is moving it and—"

But the sound of two more bells stopped his words.

We listened to what was rapidly becoming a frantic, dissonant ringing for an instant more before Giovanni launched into action and hurried to the steep, narrow stairs leading up to the floor above us.

I followed, sensible heels that were still not very sensible for this property clicking against the wooden floorboard.

The ringing grew more desperate with each step I climbed, the sound multiplying as more bells joined in.

It was a cacophony by the time I reached the top.

I'd been up here only once, on the day of our arrival, but now that some of the workers had pried the wood that had boarded up the windows, I could see more than silhouettes. Shattered remnants of fifteen large circular containers, like barrels, that had once held grain, lay scattered, the wooden funnels above them in various stages of decay. The only trace of one was a ring of black iron from which the funnel had hung and that only a single nail held up. Attached in some form to what was left of each of these contraptions was a small golden bell. And each one of those bells was ringing to call down the heavens.

"Why are they doing that?" I called over the noise. All I knew of milling was what I'd learned from Giovanni, and since I'd met him, he'd only worked in sawmills.

He shook his head. "I-I don't know. That is, the bells are only supposed to ring when there's no more grain to send to the millstones. It's a warning that gives the miller a few seconds to bring the mechanism to a stop before the stones grind together, create a spark, and light up the flour dust. The smallest spark could cause an explosion that'd destroy the entire building." He motioned to the broken containers. "But the mechanisms are not working at all now. How could they be? Entire sections are missing!"

I drew closer to one of the furiously ringing bells and saw that, of course, Giovanni was right. This one wasn't even attached to anything more than a drooping frayed cord, and still it chimed. I reached out to stop it and yanked my hand back immediately.

It boiled.

"Giovanni, it burns like it's been under a flame."

He touched the one nearest to him and hissed, shaking the burn off his fingertips. "This one, too."

We moved from bell to bell, allowing our hands to hover near the metal to confirm what we really already knew: they were all scalding hot.

And then, midring and without warning, they stopped as if they were one.

Silence flooded the room.

"What is happening here?" he said.

The high whinnying of a horse jerked my head up from the bells.

"Did you hear that?"

"What?" he said.

"The horse. I heard it again."

Frowning, Giovanni walked to one of the windows and looked out to see if anyone approached, but the sound seemed to come from behind the mill and be heading toward the villa. Even as I thought that, though, it changed direction with all the speed of a panicked animal.

"I think it's in the woods," I said. "It's the same thing I heard the other afternoon."

"That must be them," Giovanni said, racing to the stairs.

"Who?"

"The people responsible for all of this!"

I blinked, my mouth filling with questions, but he was already gone, bounding after the sound like a hunting dog. Leaving me to work my own way down steps so narrow I had to turn my foot sideways to keep from slipping, hands pressed against my stomach, elbows out to scrape the walls in lieu of the support a banister would offer. I knew my heels made me much too slow and cumbersome for Giovanni's quick mind, but sometimes I did wish he'd offer to help me.

Rapid movement from the floor I'd just left drew my eyes for a moment, bringing me to a stop again. I stepped back up and peered at the bells and the rotten wooden containers. Had it been this dark up here just a moment ago? I could have sworn . . .

"Don't start with nonsense, Sibilla," I murmured. "They're just shadows."

I made myself turn away.

I eased down the stairs and reached the ground floor just as another whinny echoed across the length of the forest.

Giovanni shouted from outside, but I couldn't make out what he said.

I hurried out of the mill and cast my eyes about for my husband, finding him at the edge of the woods. My feet squelching with every step, I started toward him.

"*Bastardi*!" he shouted.

"Did you see them?"

"I didn't need to. They were here, I know they were, and they got away. They have to be the ones who destroyed all of the repairs. They must have somehow rigged those bells, too, as a distraction. A bait we easily took." His hands clenched into fists. "They're sabotaging us."

"But why?"

"What do you mean, *why*? To harm us."

I frowned. All this damage? To what purpose? I'd heard of some of the less reputable businesses sabotaging others, burning their stock or stealing it outright. It had happened among sweet shops when I was a child, forcing my father to sit with a pistol in his lap for a few nights. But here, in this case, sabotage wouldn't benefit anyone.

"Giovanni, I don't understand. You told me yourself there aren't any competing mills in the area. We don't have neighbors. Who could possibly want to harm us when we've practically just arrived?"

He turned away from the road and looked at me. His eyes took me in with one sweeping glance, from muddy heels to undefined curls.

I thought there could be nothing worse than the casual irritation that many times I saw on his face when he glanced at me. Annoyance at something silly I'd said or done that would fade when I quieted or sat down. What I saw in his face now made my breath lock in my chest.

It was a flare of dislike.

"You're so simple sometimes," he said, as if he were telling me what time it was, and walked away.

His words were glass shards that lodged into my skin. He'd said them easily, without hesitating. Like he'd thought them many times before and this time articulated them. If he'd thrown the words at me in anger, I might have been able to set them aside, but in this manner, the simple stating of a fact, it was impossible.

I felt a sudden tightening in my midsection, the squeezing of a vital part, that dislodged a gasp. I closed my eyes against the galloping of my heart, tears trailing down my cheeks.

"Sibilla," Buona called from the villa's front door.

I bit my lips to keep the sob compressed, as if that alone would make the fear that was rising like water stop. My shaking hands went to the mound. I could see it, the loss, the blood, I could smell the sharp hospital scent, feel the rough and overstarched white sheets.

"What's the matter? Are you ill?"

Despite my best efforts, the sob found its way out.

The girl ran down the villa's steps and hurried toward me, coming close enough I could smell the carbolic acid she'd been using for the washing. I hesitated. I felt the need to speak with her, with someone who would listen without telling me I was imagining things or being silly or hysterical, but was it the right thing to do?

What did she care about my problems?

"Sibilla, I probably can't do much to help," she said, coming closer, "but my father always tells me I'm a good listener, if you want to talk. Or not. We could just go inside and have tea in one of the sale."

She placed a hand on my arm.

"Chat with the mold a bit, strike up a conversation with a rat, perfectly normal ladylike activities."

That pried a small smile out of me.

I breathed in deeply and decided.

"It's just . . . I've already lost two pregnancies," I murmured. "And I'm so frightened for this one that I don't know how I'll get through the next five months."

She gave my arm a light squeeze but waited as I gathered the words I needed to say.

"The first," I began, "happened when I'd been pregnant four months. This was three years ago, come November. It was a very difficult time for us. Giovanni had had a serious argument with one of his superiors and there had been threats of him being let go from the sawmill. As you can imagine, the baby was inopportune. I was just very nervous all the time, crying for no reason at all, and Giovanni wasn't in the most pleasant of moods either. The doctor said it was those bouts of nerves that caused the miscarriage." I swallowed. "The second pregnancy was different, though. The issues at the sawmill were resolved by then and Giovanni had even been given a higher salary. We were both very happy. Probably happier than we've ever been, save for our honeymoon."

My fingernails dug into my palms.

"I had the miscarriage at six months, that time." I blinked back new tears. "I was in the hospital for three weeks afterward, recovering from whatever caused it."

"You don't know?"

I shook my head. "The doctor said that I fell but I can't recall anything substantial from that night. He told me that the memory loss pointed to a brain lesion and that it would heal with time, but it's been a year already and it's still no better. I think it might actually be worse, because I get overwhelmed with the *feeling* of the memory without being able to sift through what actually occurred. It puts me in such a state of panic that I fear for the child I carry now. I could lose it just like that first one."

"And your husband? He doesn't know what happened either?"

"He wasn't there. He was at the sawmill, working late into the night on his invention. The one that allowed us to buy this place."

I could still see his face when I regained consciousness in the hospital. There had been such grief in it, his eyes swollen from crying, and even his suit, which he was always fastidious about, had been wrinkled, tie undone. He'd not left my side for days.

"Have you told your husband about your fears? Perhaps he could get a doctor to visit every couple of weeks or so, to put you at ease."

"He's got too many worries already, with the mill, the dam, and now with what happened."

"Something did happen, then?"

I nodded, wiping at my eyes. "Someone destroyed all of the repairs he and the workers have done."

She sucked in a breath.

"Sometime last night, it seems. All of those new parts are broken. And we didn't hear anything while it happened, when we really should have. Did you?"

"No."

I turned at the speed of her response, catching the rapid tightening of her jaw. "Nothing at all?"

She shook her head. "You're sure that someone did it? That something didn't just break or fall and cause the damage?"

"I'm not sure of anything. Giovanni thinks someone is sabotaging us, someone from the region, and I suppose that's the most logical explanation, but he also doesn't want to fetch the carabinieri."

"It—it may be better not to," Buona said. She looked down at her hands. "They'll delay the repairs and get underfoot, and, really, it won't bring the parts back in functioning shape." She shrugged. "It's not even as if they can truly do anything now if you didn't see who did the damage."

I sighed. "Maybe not, but it could frighten the culprits into not doing it again."

"There's no reason to think that it'll happen again. Maybe it was just a bit of mischief. Who wants to put all that effort into doing something like that more than once?"

I hoped she was right.

"In any case, I don't want to add any more weight to Giovanni's shoulders with my nonsense."

Buona nodded, eyebrow lifted. "Yes, the superior sex always seems to have difficulties carrying more than one bucket at a time. I dread to think what would happen if they had to worry about children and housework."

I chuckled. "I'm not sure I could manage what Giovanni does, either."

"You've never been given a chance, though, have you? Sometimes I wonder if men are just afraid we'll be better at their jobs than they are, and that's why they've trapped us in heels and skirts and told us our minds are too frail."

She was speaking in jest, I knew that, but her voice had a tightness to it that made me want to talk about something else.

"We'll never know, I suppose," I said.

"No, likely not." She offered me her arm to help me through the worst of the mud. "Did you ask him about what was in that letter from the lawyer?"

I frowned at the abrupt change in topic. "Uh, yes, well, I tried. He told me not to worry about it, that it wasn't anything of importance."

She bit at her bottom lip, her eyes fixed on the dirt as if she were reading something off it. "I think he burned it."

"Oh." That was unusual. He kept all his letters.

"If another one comes, I could bring it to you first," she said, flicking her gaze at me. "If you'd like. We could say it was opened in error."

The meaning of her words settled on me, heavy, but my hesitation was heavier still. I should have immediately refused to entertain her idea, even for an instant, maybe even rebuked her for her forwardness. Instead, my mind rolled the suggestion about like hard toffee.

But why? Giovanni had never done anything to garner such suspicion and disloyalty from me. Even deciding to purchase this property without consulting me had been for the best. If he told me it was nothing, then that was what it was. I trusted him. I'd not betray him in this manner.

I felt my own slight flare of irritation. It wasn't seemly for her to be questioning her employer in this manner.

"Thank you, but there's no need," I said. "If there's something of importance in the letter, he'll surely tell me."

Buona recognized the chilled finality in my voice and nodded, lips pressed together as if to keep stray words from leaping out.

We started for the house just as Giovanni raced right out of it, pushing a hat on his head. Off to buy more parts, I imaged. Hopefully ones that would not meet the same dreadful fate as their predecessors.

MADDALENA
1596

❦

"**O**NE MOMENT," I SAID.

The workers tugged the horses to a stop, and I stepped onto the field, nearing the beasts just enough to tie the sprigs of wheat and the medals of Sant'Ansovino onto their harnesses. Four identical bundles for four powerful plow horses. I knotted them in place with a prayer for a bountiful harvest, unstoppered a flask, and spilled a splash of pig's blood onto the fertile field.

I knew the workers were exchanging glances at what they imagined was superstition reserved for peasants, but I'd not be cowed. After the desecration of my grandmother's tablecloth, I'd not take any chances. Anyone who could do something of that sort had enough malice in them to corrupt our entire harvest without protective measures in place.

I stepped out of the way of the beasts and nodded the workers forward.

For days after the loss of the tablecloth, I'd been a river of tears. I'd had the laundress try every trick she knew for removing bloodstains to at least allow me to keep ribbons of it with my linens, but there'd been no saving it. It'd been too fragile and had unthreaded after a few washes. I had suspicions as to who was responsible, of course, but there was no proving it. And the culprit or culprits had not settled for just that act of destruction. They'd already begun a finely woven process of slandering my family and me. Purchasing these horses alone had been quite an affair, since word of what had occurred at our cena had spread across the region, rootlike.

It resonated in every conversation and every look directed at me or at my husband. Only one farmer, a man with a field bordering one of ours, had bent under the weight of the *scudi* we offered and risked offending Madonna Scappi and the rest of the women I'd rebuked by selling us the horses, their collars and yokes, and an extra plow. Hopefully he would not be made to suffer for it.

"We'll start over there," Florindo said and urged his own horse forward. He directed the workers down to the first field.

If it'd been up to me, I would have put that great, useless beast to work alongside his brethren, but Florindo would have sooner placed the yoke around his own neck than around Spuma's.

"Perhaps that's for the better," I murmured as I watched my husband yank on the reins to keep the white horse from rearing back at the first loud call from the workers.

The blasted thing had always been a nervous, finicky creature, and too smart for its own good, but the move from Genova had been as distressful for it as it had been for me. Its latest compulsion was to kick the rather rudimentary stable door open at night. For the past two mornings, the stablemaster had woken to find Spuma wandering the grounds. This night, it would battle a padlock.

It was my turn to give in to my nervous compulsions now, and so I glanced up at the sky as I'd done for days. It was the glazed blue of majolica and there wasn't a single scuff of a cloud as far as I could see. A fine day for beginnings.

And it needed to remain this way for a bit because I could already see that it would take a few days to get the fields ready. The progress was slow and uneven. The horses were pure muscle, but the plow we'd bought before leaving Genova was larger and of a better quality than the one we'd acquired from the farmer. That was to be expected, of course, for the man only had a small field of barley to tend to, but now that both plows were working beside each other, the difference was vast. If the fields were not as soft as they were from the years they had spent underwater before the dam diverted the torrent, this smaller plow would be useless. We'd have to invest in a better one next year.

The rumble of wheels made me turn toward the road. A carriage was approaching.

A gloved hand appearing at the window in greeting as it drew closer.

I squinted to try and make out who it was, but it was impossible to wipe the sky's glare from my eyes.

"Maddalena!"

It took only a moment to recognize the voice. Silvia, the chancellor's wife.

I raised my hand in cautious greeting and started toward the carriage with a sharp exhale. Nerves bubbled in my stomach as if it were full of *vino spumante* and I almost stopped to laugh at myself. I'd dined with dukes and princes in Genovese palaces and here I was, worried about what reprimands I might receive for my conduct in my own home.

Nonsense. Besides, Silvia had given me the impression of kindness and simplicity, and that wasn't something I encountered often.

I straightened my spine and walked on.

"Forgive me for intruding like this, without so much as a message," Silvia said, smiling. "I was never any good at all the rules that need to be followed when meeting an acquaintance. I'm much too impatient."

"It's no intrusion, Silvia. You are most welcome. Oh, and what beautiful gloves you have," I said, drawing closer to the carriage window.

They truly were, with embroidered and beaded blackberries and rose hips on a cinnamon background. The beauty of summer giving way to the richness of autumn.

"That is so kind. My husband considers them a bit extravagant, so I don't wear them often, but I thought you would appreciate them." She glanced behind me. "But I've caught you at such a busy moment."

"Not at all. Not much is required of me except to stand about and look supportive."

Silvia laughed, a bright sound. "I'm not sure I believe that for a moment, Maddalena. I rather think you are the one directing the entire endeavor. No one who prepared that cena in the manner in which you did could just relinquish command of any situation."

I smiled. "Perhaps not."

"And I hope you won't find me too forward in saying this, but I admired the way you dealt with all that . . . boorishness. I'd not have been able to do such a thing." She leaned forward in her seat and lowered her voice, as if we were in the middle of a gowned throng. "I, for one, think that it was past time someone put those madonne in their proper place."

I didn't allow myself to show the surprise I felt. Taking the side of a newcomer instead of rallying with the old guard was not usually a successful strategy in societal skirmishes.

"You are the only one who seems to think so."

"To *say* so, perhaps. They don't want to fall from their good graces, such as they are, especially with the wife of the massaro. It's understandable."

I nodded. "And you?"

"I'm the chancellor's wife," Silvia said, tossing her head and lifting her chin in what I was sure she intended to pass for haughtiness. "And if I weren't such a consummate coward, they'd have heard from me long ago."

I chuckled.

"But never mind all that nonsense. I wanted to ask you something rather delicate."

"Of course." I motioned up to the villa in the distance. "We can sit and have some tea."

"I wouldn't dream of imposing on you like that when you are so busy. No, no." She opened the door of the carriage and tapped the velvet seat next to her. "Please, this is more intimate anyway. Much more in keeping with my woefully misguided longings for intrigue."

"You're certain? It really wouldn't be much trouble."

She waved my words away and shifted down the seat with a hiss of linen against velvet.

The driver made to get down from his seat to assist me, but I stopped him with a hand and a nod and reached to grab hold of my skirts. I scraped my boots on the foot iron before stepping up and easing onto the seat beside Silvia.

Despite the lightness in her voice just a minute ago, I could feel her nerves racing along my skin, the flutter of them as she turned to look at me. There was a flush to her cheeks that only heightened the paleness in the rest of her face.

She appeared to physically gather her words, picking them like flowers for a bouquet.

"I know," she began, "I just said I didn't want to talk about everything that happened at the cena, but I did want to ask you about something that Madonna Scappi said that night. About your affinity for preparing tonics and tinctures." She clutched her hands together. "I was wondering, have you ever helped a woman conceive?"

There was such hope tucked into her voice that I felt a surge of sympathy for her. I'd not had trouble conceiving or birthing my five children after I'd stopped the pennyroyal infusions that had granted me ten years of childless freedom after Florindo and I married, but I had seen the anguish other women had gone through in Genova. It ate at them, the need to create life.

I also knew I had to be cautious with my words. Misplaced hope could be as dangerous as hopelessness. Sometimes more so.

"I have, yes."

"I mentioned that night that I'd had difficulties in that respect." She lowered her eyes to her beautiful gloves. "My husband is too kind to say so, but I know he is disappointed every month. We've been married three years already and there hasn't even been a prospect. The doctors don't know how to help me, and I don't really know how to talk to them about it, especially when all they speak of is womb nervousness and unbalanced humors. They've given me all manner of things to counteract what they say is my overly sanguine nature."

I scoffed. "I assume those doctors bleed you."

"Yes, every few weeks." Her face was an entire wrinkle of concern. "Is that not right?"

Those barbarians were still in the Dark Ages, leading women to their deaths with their blades and ceramic bowls. It was no wonder Silvia was as pale as watered milk.

Taking a deep breath to keep my anger from singeing everything I touched, I shook my head. "No, it is not. There is nothing wrong with your humors, sanguine or not, and those so-called doctors are doing more harm than good."

Her hands tightened together. "What should I do?"

"The first thing is to tell your husband you've had enough of blood-letting."

"I-I can't just tell him that. He won't heed my thoughts over those of the doctors."

No, of course not. I kept forgetting most women did not have someone like Florindo at their side.

Most women found themselves unequal to their husbands, a tier below, requiring masculine permission even to their own bodies. I couldn't imagine my husband so much as thinking such a thing.

"Then, if you must submit to the bloodletting," I said with a sigh, "you need to make some changes to your diet. Add more fish and stinging nettle. Drink juices made of every fruit you can find, and have your cook use the best olive oil available."

She nodded, her eyes fixed on me as if she were afraid of missing a single syllable.

I took her hands. "The tonics I make for conception are not pleasant. They will give you nausea and even cramps for the first two or three days you take them. Some of the women I've helped have felt palpitations for days at a time and one had hives break out throughout her body. You may not be able to leave your home because of the necessity to use the latrine at all hours, and there are no guarantees. It could happen immediately or it could take weeks. The pregnancy may not even last very long the first time and we'd have to try again. Is that something you are willing to go through?"

"But the women you helped did conceive?"

"Yes. In the end."

"And they had healthy children?"

"All but one. She lost the child during her confinement."

She paused and that moment, that silent, honest consideration, was what made me certain that despite her gentleness and her self-purported cowardice, there was iron in her. She could do this.

"Yes," she finally said. "If you'll help me, I'm willing."

I squeezed her hands and smiled. "Then I'll be glad to do so, Silvia. I'll prepare the first tonic and send it to you tomorrow."

The sudden glint in her eyes made her look like a child who had just been promised a gift.

"All of today, I want you to drink a substantial amount of water and to have some milk tomorrow morning to prepare a base in your stomach. When will the next bloodletting be?"

"In about two weeks."

That didn't give me as much time to strengthen her against that idiocy as I would like, but if she followed my instructions perhaps it wouldn't weaken her system too much.

"From tonight onward, I want you to drink a glass of red wine fortified with cinnamon and honey after your meals. As soon as the doctor departs on the day of the bloodletting, have your cook prepare you a bowl of boiled nettles and a glass of wine, no matter what time of day it is."

She nodded.

"You'll know your husband better than I, of course, but it may be wise not to mention any of this to him. If he becomes concerned with any effects the tonics have on you, tell him you ate something that didn't agree with you."

Her cheeks reddened once again as she lowered her voice. "And my relations with my husband? Is there anything . . . different that I need to do when I submit to him?"

Poor child. To think of the act as only a submission. "Continue as you have. The tonics will do their work. And if you have any concerns at all, about any of this, have a servant fetch me at once."

Before I'd realized what she was doing, Silvia had leaned forward and wrapped her arms around me.

"Thank you," she said.

If I'd needed any other reminder that this wasn't Genova, this embrace would have been it. No madonna in her right mind would have shown this kind of softness in front of someone they'd only met twice. In the city, Silvia would have been a doe among wolves. I could have torn her into bits with a few sentences.

As if she had sensed my thoughts, she pulled away. "Just look at me, ready to weep at a touch of female kindness." She sniffed. "It's just so rare among these parts."

Among all parts, really. "It's quite all right. I'm glad to be of help."

I stepped out of the carriage and closed the door.

"Oh, please send me a note with the expenses for the tonics," Silvia said.

"I wouldn't dream of it."

"At least for the ingredients!"

I shook my head. "Everything I need is already in jars and flasks up in my *cucinetta*, just waiting to be put to good use. The satisfaction I get for assisting someone as kind as you is plenty."

There really was the sheen of tears in her eyes now, even as she smiled. "I'm so glad you're here, Maddalena."

Although I couldn't in all honesty say the same thing, I bowed my head in acknowledgment and stepped out of the way of the carriage.

"And please don't worry too much about these madonne and what they've been saying," she called out over the crunch of the wheels. "I'm sure it will all be resolved soon."

I waved and watched the carriage, knowing very well she was wrong. I knew how these things went, and they didn't resolve quickly. If they ever did at all.

⁘

"NOT SO FAST, UGO, AMORE," I said. "Do you want your mother to fall?"

"No, Mamma."

But he didn't slow down as he led us to the kitchen, his hand small and hot as it clutched mine. His siblings' laughter trickled down from up ahead and he pushed his legs to move faster and catch up.

Perhaps it hadn't been such a wise idea to ask them all to join me while I gathered herbs in the woods. All the fresh air they'd received today had been like a shock of sweets to their systems.

Well, at least Giusto would get a much-needed bit of rest. He had looked rather haggard after hours of running after them ensuring they were well away from horse hooves and plows.

We raced into the kitchen, my wicker basket swinging, and almost slammed into Octavia, who was carrying two freshly baked loaves of bread.

"Scusatemi, Octavia," I called out as my youngest, fiercest child plunged us through the kitchen. The women stirring the cauldron at the hearth smiled and curtsied, as did one of the cuoco's assistants, who stood by a kneading table, splashed with flour, holding a copper rolling pin. Even that new servant, Antonio, halted on his way to the cellar to watch us pass.

The door leading out to the garden gaped open and I could see my children skirting the well and the chicken coop in their race to reach the gate leading out to the woods.

"All right," I yelled. "Do not step foot into the forest on your own."

Like I'd yanked on reins, my voice brought the four of them to a stop.

Even Ugo finally slowed. Giacomo, Francesco, Vincenzo, and Marcellina turned to look at me, their impatience written into every part of their bodies while they waited for the two of us to catch up.

"You all know better than to go into the forest alone," I said when I'd reached them at the gate.

"But, Mamma, you were right there," Giacomo said.

"That makes no difference. I could get distracted and not see where you go. It is too easy to lose your way in a forest, children, and you never know what could be there waiting."

My eldest raised his eyes to the sky with a sigh, in a way that made him look just like a fourteen-year-old version of myself. I bit back a smile.

"Will you look so bored when a boar decides to chase after you? Or when *un lupo* howls its hunger and snaps its fangs into your heels?"

"Mamma, *per favore*," Giacomo said, the quick flick of his gaze behind him, into the trees, belying the exasperation in his voice.

Perhaps some mothers would have thought it unnecessary, even cruel, to frighten their children in that manner, but I'd rather they be frightened than dead.

I walked past them and opened the gate leading out of the garden. "Come now. With care and always minding where each of us is, let's find some herbs."

As soon as I stepped into the forest, I felt the whisper of the plants, a tapestry of not-quite-voices vying for attention. There would be plenty to find, I could already hear that.

"Please remember not to put anything in your mouth. Not the juiciest of berries or the most colorful of flowers." They knew this well, having heard me say it in every outing we'd ever made, even in domesticated gardens, but it cost me nothing to repeat the warning.

The four boys started off together, their attentions already lost to things other than herbs. It had taken Francesco and Vincenzo mere seconds to find sticks suitable enough to function as swords.

Marcellina, however, shifted to my side. Just as I'd expected.

Even in Genova, I'd seen her interest in my pots growing. More than once I'd found her in the room I'd reserved for my work, standing on the tips of her toes to smell the herbs or turning the pages of my herbarium with exquisite care.

I'd always left her to it, knowing how important it was for her to decide on her own if it was something that she needed. If she didn't, she'd bore of it with or without my intrusion.

She'd shown no signs of being able to hear the herbs yet, but she was only eight. I'd been well into my eleventh year when I heard the birdlike chirp of the lemongrass in my mother's kitchen for the first time. A simple request for water had begun my endless conversation with them all.

A steeple of powdered blue caught my eye among the grass. I smiled.

"Look, Marcellina."

I motioned her to follow me to the first bugleherb, standing like a sentinel before a small crowd of its peers. It had a mild voice, like a breeze on a summer's day.

"This is a marvelous find," I said and knelt beside the cluster of small flowers stacked on fuzzy leaves. "It's called bugleherb, and it is a light sedative, excellent for people of nervous constitutions."

"Like Giusto," she said.

I swallowed a chuckle. How could I tell Marcellina that the only cure for her tutor was for her brothers to behave less ferally? Even now, the noises coming from a bit farther up ahead made it sound like they were destroying the entire forest. "Quite so. It is also good for alleviating pain and can make a good tea for sore throats."

I reached for the silver scissors hanging on the chatelaine around my waist and placed the blades near the base of the herb.

"When you harvest herbs for your use, you must leave the roots intact. If you want to take the whole plant to place it in a pot, you never yank it up, because that pains them. Instead, you want to dig a little and scoop them up, gently. Since bugleherb tends to languish in pots, I'm just going to take a bit of it."

I snipped the stem and allowed the blue tower of flowers to fall into my palm. "Always thank the herbs when you harvest them, and never take more than you need, for there are other creatures who have use of them."

After following my own instructions and offering my gratitude to the plant, I unhooked the scissors and handed them to Marcellina.

"Go on. Fetch me ten or so more so that I can dry them."

She got to work at once.

I stood and peered through the trees until I could clearly see the boys. Four sets of limbs intact, no blood. All was well.

Wiping the sheen of sweat from my forehead, I watched Marcellina wielding the scissors as if she'd done so for years. She possessed the patience for herb work, taking care to look for the best specimens, the ones I would have chosen, inspecting leaves and flowers for qualities that only someone with an innate affinity could intuit.

Her soft words of thanks as she cut the herbs and the gentleness with which she placed them in my basket brought on an urge to embrace her tightly enough that she'd become part of my body once more. But I let her be. I'd not interrupt.

"Very well done, amore," I said when she'd brought me the basket. I took the scissors as she turned toward the crashing sounds of her siblings. "You can go play with them, if you like. You've already been a great help."

But she shook her head.

"All right. Let's go up ahead, then."

Wrangling the boys with my voice, I led all of us farther into the woods, trying not to wince at the clamor. Birds flapped into the sky with indignant cries and creatures scurried away, unseen in the weeds and tall grass. Woven through everything was the smell of pine trees and wet earth.

The familiar vibration of voices, as warm and welcoming as a parent's, pulled my attention to a large patch of feathery leaves and lacy white flowers sitting on thin, branched stalks streaked with purple. Now here was a chance to teach Marcellina something important.

"Let's get some cow parsley," I said, nodding my daughter forward.

The patch of herbs was much larger than it had first appeared, with flowers shoving each other to feed on the rays of sun that made it through the canopy of needles. Some of the stems rose higher than my daughter's head so that she had to peer up at the small star-shaped flowers.

"Listen carefully now. Cow parsley is wonderful for stomach complaints and can be useful for headaches, but it is important that you . . ." I frowned, losing the thread of words as another sound pulled at me. A low, smoke-filled voice that made me hold my breath.

I'd only heard it once before, years ago, but there was no forgetting it.

I'd truly not expected to find it here. So easily.

"Stay right where you are and don't touch anything."

"Mamma?"

I motioned her to stillness and eased around the edges of the patch of cow parsley, following that low voice. I peered at the plants, tracing their stems, until I found what I was searching for. The very object of the lesson I'd wanted to offer Marcellina.

Hidden among the friendly cow parsley, like a viper under fall leaves, was poison hemlock.

It quieted now that I'd seen it and I bowed my head in gratitude at its warning. I would have noticed it, but my child would not have.

Swallowing the dryness in my throat, I waved Marcellina closer and called to the boys. They should learn this as well.

They heard the tightness in my voice, for the clatter of sticks stopped at once and they were at my side in an instant. Five pair of eyes watched me as I parted two stalks of cow parsley so that they could see what death dressed in green and white looked like.

"This is poison hemlock," I said. "It is one of the reasons I always warn you not to put anything you find in the woods in your mouth. It will kill you very quickly if you eat any part of it, even a tiny bit. What do you notice about it?"

Giacomo opened his mouth but hesitated. His sister did not.

"It looks the same as the cow parsley," Marcellina said.

"Well done. That is exactly right. If you do not know what to look for, it appears identical. Fortunately, a few subtle differences exist." I knelt and pointed to the stem. "No hairs on the hemlock, see? While cow parsley's stalk is covered in fine ones that you can see or at the very least feel when you touch it. And, of course, the purple marks."

I bent one of the cow parsleys over until they could see the solid streaks of it that ran up from the ground. I did the same with the hemlock, gently moving it with my sleeve.

"Do you see the marks on this one? They're like splashes of color, uneven, like someone's paintbrush splattered it."

They nodded, almost as one.

"Most of the time, what you see will be cow parsley because it grows like a weed, but hemlock loves to grow beside it. Never pick it if you are not ready to wage your life on your choice."

I watched their faces, making sure that they had heard me before I stood up.

"We'll leave these be for now. Come."

I'd return for the cow parsley without the children, so I could concentrate fully on what I was doing when I harvested it. I couldn't depend just on hearing the herb, not with the threat of hemlock nearby.

The boys ran off without another glance, but Marcellina gazed at the two plants for a beat longer before returning to my side. We set off together.

The wooden whacks of stick against stick had already begun again. How could they still have such energy?

"Mamma," Marcellina said after we'd walked for a bit.

"Yes, child?"

She drew a little closer to me. "The herbs speak to you, don't they?"

I almost stopped walking.

This, I'd not been ready for yet.

No one had ever asked me the question in such a forthright manner, without skirting around it. Not even Florindo. He knew some of it, of course—it was difficult not to notice your wife nodding at the pots of rosemary or speaking about the feud between the parsley and the mint at the breakfast table with all the exasperation of a mother. He trusted that I was tuned as tightly as a harp string to the world around me and that the slightest vibration, good or ill, would ring through me. He never doubted, but he had never really asked either.

There were lies I could give Marcellina to delay this conversation until she was at least a bit older.

Until I had an answer prepared.

But why? If she had taken notice of my affinity and had formulated the right question to ask me at the right moment, she deserved the truth.

"Yes," I said. "They do. Though it's not a conversation like you and I are having. There are no real words as we speak them, they're more like . . . well, I always call them vibrations."

She frowned. "Like music?"

"Yes, somewhat."

"And the herbs tell you what they need like that?"

I nodded, shifting a pine branch out of the way. "But it's not always a request for something. Many times, like people, they just want to say hello."

"Is that what happened with that plant, the hemlock? It warned you it was there?"

"Yes. And it would have done the same with anyone else, it's just that very few take the time to listen."

Ugo let out a shriek of laughter, the sound turning my head just as Vincenzo began a strategic attack with small and still-green pinecones. Giacomo and Francesco ran to the nearest tree in search of ammunition.

"Your brothers, for example," I said, "will likely never be quiet enough to hear the herbs. They can barely hear each other."

Her lips pursed. "But I can't hear them either."

I grasped her hand, giving it a quick squeeze. "You're still very young, Marcellina, and though I can't guarantee that you'll be able to do so, I can tell you already possess the most important criteria for working with herbs as I do: the ability to listen."

I waited for more questions, but she was quiet, her brow lightly furrowed in thoughts I didn't want to interrupt. We walked on in silence while the boys crashed about behind us.

The corner of my eye caught a blur of movement the instant before a man stepped onto our path. I did stop walking now, biting back a gasp and tightening my grip on Marcellina's hand.

What was this, now?

Three more men walked out from behind a group of trees to join him, all of them in ragged tunics and breeches, their wide-brimmed hats flinging shadows on their features. They stood, staring at the two of us, making no attempt to explain their presence in our woods.

Standing up straighter, I fixed my eyes on the first man I'd seen. "Scusatemi, but you are on my land."

They remained silent. My jaws clenched.

"Are you workers my husband hired? If you are, the worksite is at the mill, not here."

The men looked at one another and smiled as if I'd said something amusing. One of them took a step closer.

The air began to pulse with a warning.

A knot in my stomach tightened, a cold splash of fear beginning to battle for dominance with my mounting anger. They knew they shouldn't be here and they didn't appear to care. I wanted to order them out. I knew it was within my right to do so, but I couldn't find the words because what I *also* knew was that Florindo and the workers were too far away to hear us.

Fear won.

"Children," I called, my voice echoing through the forest, and pressed Marcellina closer to my side. Once I could clutch them all to me, we'd leave. Head back to the house.

It felt like endless minutes of feeling my heart beating in my temples before I heard my eldest's familiar footsteps nearing us.

"What now, Mamma? We're not—" Giacomo crunched to a stop. "Who are you?"

Still, the men said nothing.

"Madre?"

"I don't know," I said. "They've refused to speak."

There was an edge of anger in Giacomo's movements as he came to stand next to me. He bristled with energy.

"I asked you a question," he said. "This is our land, so who are you and what are you doing here?"

I touched my son's arm.

"Leave. This instant," I said.

One of the men chuckled, and I tightened my grip on Giacomo, trying to tamp down the fire that he'd inherited from me. The situation could not escalate enough to pit four grown men against a boy of fourteen. And it would if he didn't heed me. I could feel it.

The man nearest to us turned his head just slightly and spat onto the dirt close enough to my feet that I could see the spume sink into the ground before he started off deeper into the woods. Two of the others followed him, chuckling. The last man touched the brim of his hat in an acknowledgment that dripped with mockery and left, slipping through the trees. None of them had said a single word.

I didn't wait so much as the length of a heartbeat before moving. "Let's go. Back to the house."

I pulled on Giacomo and Marcellina, my basket of herbs swinging from the crook of my elbow as I hurried us toward the rest of my children. They were still flinging pinecones and laughing, having entirely missed what had happened. Later, I would deal with them not obeying my beckon, but now I needed to get us all out of the woods.

"Playing is over for today," I said, clapping my hands. "Come now."

Ugo groaned and Vincenzo opened his mouth in the beginning of a protest, but Giacomo shook his head once, stopping him. A wise choice.

Together, the six of us retraced our path.

As we walked, my mind fought to make sense of what had occurred, trying to calm the fear I felt by somehow rationalizing the presence of the men. But no logic could drown out what the racing of my heart and the roaring of my blood warned me of.

This was not over. We'd see those men again, and it would all be much worse than today.

I felt it with the same certainty with which I'd felt my cousin's life running out all those years ago.

SIBILLA

1933

THE SOUND OF MY OWN name pulled me up from layers and layers of hot sleep. I gasped awake.

The sun was already the yolk yellow of late morning as it poured into my bedroom and slipped into my bed, letting me know with one glance that I'd overslept. Substantially.

"Sibilla," Buona said, tugging on the bedcovers. "You should get up."

Sweat pressed my slip to my back as I sat up, blinking. Everything ached. Every movement as heavy as if I were trying to make it underwater. It'd been this way for days now, the pregnancy feeling as if it'd deepened, the child seeming to triple in size overnight, which I knew was not possible but which still sent me looking at my profile in the mirror every few hours.

I wiped at my forehead. "What time is it?"

"Past eleven," she said.

I winced. Giovanni had eaten his breakfast alone then. "You shouldn't have let me sleep that long, Buona."

"I didn't want to, but your husband told me to leave you be."

I smiled, quick relief dissolving the tightness that had already come into my shoulders. That had been kind of him. I knew how much he frowned on lounging in bed.

Buona offered her hands to help me up and I took them, though I should not have needed the assistance yet. If this was how I felt now, at not quite five months, what would I do at nine? I'd need a wheelchair.

"Where is Giovanni?"

"That's why I woke you. He's with the lawyer, that Dottore Lupponi."

I blinked, trying to make sense of what she'd said with a mind still slippery with sleep. "He's here?"

"Yes." The girl fixed her eyes on mine. "He arrived a bit over an hour ago. I think that's why your husband didn't mind you sleeping longer than usual."

I looked away. "That's nonsense, Buona."

"The moment the man stepped into the house, I made to wake you and your husband told me not to. He then immediately sent me to town for flour, milk, and eggs, knowing it would take me a while to return. Today's Tuesday, Sibilla. The grocer is making his delivery this afternoon, like always." She pulled open my armoire. "Your husband didn't want me to come and let you know."

The words of rebuke that had come to my lips crumbled under the first bite of doubt.

Because we still had plenty of eggs. I'd checked on that myself last night before preparing the list for the grocer to take with him. And when had Giovanni ever paid any real mind to the contents of our pantry?

"I've only just returned," she continued, "and they are still in the study with the door closed."

I allowed her to slide one of my two oversized woolen dresses over my head. Had he really gotten her out of the way so she wouldn't wake me? But why would—

Oh, but all of this intrigue and plotting was tiresome. My mind was not made for suspicion. There was surely a reasonable explanation for the letter and the visit, and it was likely so dull Giovanni had not mentioned it for fear of boring me to pieces. I'd go down there and greet Dottore Lupponi before he left, chat with him for a bit, and see what all this was about, and that would be enough to settle this entire mystery Buona kept insisting existed.

I motioned for her to help me into the heels I'd been forgoing most of these days as I pulled the bedcap from my head and reached for my brush to see what I could manage with my fuzzy curls. I didn't even know if I had any molding gel left.

But all I saw of Dottore Lupponi when we headed toward the courtyard a few minutes later was his tweed-clad back and his leather case as he stomped out of the villa. The door's slam resounded throughout the otherwise silent house.

I stopped walking.

His car's engine rumbled to life.

I'd had many an occasion to be in the man's presence, and I'd never seen him like that. He was the kind of person who always had a smile pressing against his rather full cheeks, a clever quip, or sometimes even a riddle at the ready to lighten the seriousness of any room. If he could think of nothing else, a dance hall tune was enough. It made him an oddity in his profession. Until now, I wouldn't have guessed he could ever be in a disagreeable enough mood to slam doors.

What could have happened to put him in such a state? And why was Giovanni allowing him to leave like that, when they'd known each other for years?

I glanced up at Buona who was watching me, eyebrows lifted. There was no helping it, then. Taking a deep breath, I turned and started for the room Giovanni had set up as his study. The girl followed.

The door was wide open and no sounds came from inside. I couldn't help hesitating, my already trembling hands going to my midsection, as I tried to think of how to ask what I wanted to know. But my mind was a swath of white nerves.

I forced myself into the room before I gave in to the urge to retreat.

The desk was strewn with papers, like someone had raked their arm across its width. The famed black Bakelite telephone had its handset hanging half off its perch. The lamp my father had gifted Giovanni after our engagement was announced was askew, and the desk chair had been flung back against the wall with enough force that it had brought down a sprinkling of plaster.

My husband stood by the window to the left of the desk with his back to me, his hands fists at his sides. I swallowed.

"What happened?" I said. "Why did Dottore Lupponi leave so angry?"

"We'll talk about it later."

"But Giovanni, why did he come all this way? What did he want?"

His back twitched. "Later, I said."

I almost asked him if it was about the letter before remembering I wasn't supposed to know whom it was from. Pressing my lips together, I stepped closer to the desk. If I could at least see what they'd talked about I might be able to offer Giovanni a few soothing words. He had a tendency to work himself up into a froth of anger and irritation over things that had, at least to me, simple solutions.

Most of the papers that I could see from where I stood had my husband's tight scrawl on them, but others bore what looked to be official stamps.

One was written with Dottore Lupponi's letterhead and had a number of signatures on it, including Giovanni's. Frowning, I reached for it.

"What are you doing?"

I flinched and made to move back, but he crossed the room in two strides and wrapped his hand around my wrist. He yanked me away from the desk, squeezing until it felt as if I'd have an imprint of his fingers burned into my skin forever.

"Ingegnere!" Buona called from the doorway.

Giovanni turned his head, meeting and holding her gaze. The room hummed with tension and a sudden crackle of electricity, all of it filling my mouth with the bitter taste of something burning.

With a scoff, he released me. "I don't have time for this, Sibilla. Get out and take the girl with you. Go back to bed or . . . just go."

Wrapping my arms around myself, I hurried out of the room. The need to get as far from him as I could took control of my limbs. Buona's footsteps rang after me, down corridor after corridor, into the kitchen. My hand had gripped the doorknob before I realized I was doing so.

The sputtering, hissing of the radio clicked into pure transmission as if someone had adjusted the dial.

I stopped.

Music poured out of it now, strings of some kind playing a lilting chamber piece. But it was the noise around the music that really locked me in place, the halo of chatter, the silver ringing of cutlery, the laughter that seemed to sink into me. And one voice, a woman's, like singing crystal rising above the rest.

"There is no danger in me allowing the children to play about the property, then?"

The surging string melody swallowed the answer.

The skin on my arms puckered and it took me only a moment to realize that I was shaking with cold, the kitchen air itself having grown frigid enough to see it as I exhaled. The music rose and I held my breath, the sounds growing louder and louder until I expected the radio to start twitching in place under the force of its own vibrations.

"You need to get out of here."

I jerked back.

"Girl, you have to leave."

My shoulder hit the door as the woman's words scraped against me, so near they seemed to be coming from my own mouth.

"What is this?" I said through clenched, chattering teeth.

But with the wheeze of an exhausted machine, the sound began to falter. The music grew weaker and the background voices muddled, all of it fading, bleaching down into the white emptiness of static.

In a moment, there was nothing left but the crackle of a mistuned radio.

I DIPPED THE STOCKINGS IN the vinegar and water mixture one more time to remove the rest of the soap from their folds. My wrist gave a twinge at the movement, and the feel of Giovanni's hand as it had wrapped around it returned, the force of the squeeze. Each individual finger digging into my skin.

But no, enough. No point in reliving that, of laying blame when we had both been at fault. After all of these years of marriage, I really should have known better than to interfere.

"Do you iron them?" Buona said.

I blinked. "What?"

"The stockings." She carefully shifted the decanter of fresh elderflower and lemon water into the ice box.

"Oh, yes," I said. "Though I haven't done it before, so I can't speak to how complicated it may be."

"They look as flimsy as suds." She gathered the remnants of the lemons into her apron and walked to the waste basket. "I can't imagine they're comfortable."

"They're not, really. But they are the rage."

From the way she glanced at the beige webbing I was trying to keep safe from the edges of my fingernails, she wasn't entirely convinced even of that.

"Do you mind if I turn the radio on?"

I hesitated, the tightness forming in my stomach again just as it had through all of yesterday. The woman's voice had prodded at me for hours, the intimacy of her words urging me to pick them apart, to roll them about my mind. Until I'd come to my senses and had given my mind the same kind of good shaking I gave it now.

Of course, her words had not been directed at me. How self-important I was, thinking that a woman on a radio program could have meant her words for Sibilla Fenoglio listening in her crumbling villa. What a goose. And yet, I'd not managed the courage to turn the radio on this morning.

That would be remedied this very instant. "Please do, Buona. We need a bit of music if we are to make any dent in the pile of chores ahead of us."

The girl nodded and reached to turn the dial, and I couldn't help but hold my breath.

I exhaled at the cheery baritone voice advertising the latest automatic washing machine design that promised to make my days more fruitful. Perfectly normal words said in a perfectly normal manner.

Buona hissed and tugged her hand back, shaking it.

"Are you all right?"

"I think something is off about all of the wiring. Electricity is not supposed to shock you like this, is it? It's happened twice today already, with the ice box and that light fixture there."

I frowned. "Giovanni is going to have to call—"

A shout cut my words off.

"What was that?" Buona said.

It only took another call to help me recognize what I was hearing. I wiped my hands on my apron, heart already racing. "That's Giovanni."

I crossed the kitchen to the door leading out to the garden, my hand flinching back from the handle as a pinch of static surged through it and onto my skin. With a grunt, I pulled my sleeve's cuff down and used it as a barrier, tugging the door open.

"Grab on to it!" Giovanni said, his voice cutting through the distance.

It was the edge of bright panic in it that got me running before I'd realized I'd done so. I took the side path out of the garden, my legs finding more speed as workers' voices rose to join my husband's.

My house shoes skidded in the mud and I gasped, my arms shooting out for balance, but I didn't fall. And I didn't stop either.

I reached the mill door and plunged through it. It was like walking into a winter's day, the cold seeping into my very teeth.

It wasn't the cold, though, that froze my steps.

A black form stood behind my husband. It was tall, thicker and darker than a shadow, as if someone had gouged at the air where it stood and left nothing behind but emptiness. The workers' shouts lost their pull on me as I watched that blackness expand and contract, like it was breathing. It bent forward, toward Giovanni, its movements as stilted as if centuries of pain made each shift an agony. I sucked in a breath and the shape jerked. The black form had nothing that could be thought of as a face, but I didn't need that to know it had seen me see it.

It gave another jerk and disappeared into the shadows of the mill.

"No!" Giovanni yelled, tugging my gaze back to him. He lunged for the rope in front of him.

But it snapped, lashing like a whip at his face, and the wooden axle, the gigantic part that had arrived only yesterday and that hung suspended from a pulley, plummeted.

It hit the side of the new scaffold and shattered it, the strike changing the direction of the fall.

My eyes widened as I saw what was about to happen.

With a splintering crash, the axle slammed into the two men on the ground still holding on to the slack rope. An explosion of screams tore through the day like a pistol shot.

The impulse to run back out of the mill, to let Giovanni deal with the chaos and pain, *with what I just saw,* was powerful enough to make me retreat a step. My blood seemed to have bubbles in it.

I shook my head. I had to be of some use to my husband.

I ran to the nearest man as Buona raced past me to the other one, who lay immobile on the mill floor, the remnants of the wooden part pressed against him. His leg had too many angles.

"We need a doctor, Giovanni!" I said, kneeling as the man in front of me coughed, wheezing and gasping as blood flecked his lips.

I heard my husband hurrying down the ladder, his own soft groan of pain bringing my eyes up to his face. A large cut bloomed red on his left cheek, touching his lips and his eye. Blood had already run down to pool at his shirt collar and he was having trouble keeping the eye open under the swelling that appeared to grow by the second.

"I'll phone the ambulance," I said and made to get to my feet again.

"I'll do it," Giovanni said. "Stay here with the men."

He ran out before I could tell him to sit still and let me at least press my apron to his face and all I could do was kneel beside the worker coughing globs of blood while Buona monitored the breathing of the worker with the mangled leg.

From the lack of screams, it seemed he had lost consciousness.

Even when the ambulance arrived in a blare of horns and the injured men were loaded onto the vehicle, Giovanni waved off the offer of care for his own injury. I followed him back into the mill the moment the men were gone, watching him in silence as he kicked away the broken axle sections, his whole body a knot of tension, as he pulled down the rope that had given way, as he started to sweep bloodstained sawdust from the area of the accident.

The memory of the form I'd seen made me shiver. No, but that couldn't have been real. I'd likely seen a cloud of that same sawdust, shadows thickened by my own fear and nerves. I was always doing that kind of thing, creating mysteries out of nothing. I'd not annoy my husband with nonsense, today of all days.

So I remained quiet because didn't know how to break the silence.

Until I saw him waver, his hand reaching out to grasp part of the wooden structure left standing.

"Giovanni," I said softly. "This can all wait."

He started to shake his head but paused, the tension in his body making his shoulders tremble.

I walked to him and touched his arm. "Will you come to the house? Please. For me?"

He breathed out and his shoulders slumped.

My wrist ached as I shifted to take his hand in mine, pulling on it to get him walking, following me to the villa. Out of this wooden disaster.

The way he clutched at my hand, as if expecting someone to come and rip us apart, made my heart beat a bit faster.

"Please get me the alcohol and some cotton gauze," I said to Buona as we passed the courtyard. "Scissors and tape, too, if you can find them."

The girl nodded and I led us to his study, where he seemed to feel most at ease. I couldn't help glancing at the papers on the desk, but I forced my eyes away before he could follow my gaze. This was not the time to pester him about Dottore Lupponi.

I tugged my hand from his now and made to start unbuttoning his bloodstained shirt, the collar beyond salvaging, but he shook his head and stepped back, wincing as every moment seemed to pull on his injury.

"That's two men lost," he said, sinking into his chair. "Neither of them will return."

"Well, not for a while, at least." One had a punctured lung and the other had a leg that had shattered like porcelain. They would need substantial recovery time, that was certain.

Giovanni shook his head again. "They won't come back at all. Would you, when all the work you do seems to be in vain?"

I frowned, feeling my pulse speed, and dragged the other chair to his side of the desk. "What happened today was an accident."

He sighed. "Can you really think so?"

Buona stepped into the room with the items I'd asked for, and I nodded for her to leave them on the desk.

I popped the cork out of the rubbing alcohol bottle. "I don't understand."

"Sibilla, I checked the pulley rope last night before doing this. I had the men buy it brand new and it didn't have so much as a snag. Did you see the end of the broken pieces?"

I pressed a cotton ball soaked in alcohol to the ridge running down his face. His jaw tightened under the sting. "No, I didn't."

He closed his eyes against the worst of the burn and held his silence for a moment. The blood continued to flow as I washed the cut, revealing how much deeper it was than I'd thought. If he'd had a doctor tend to him, he might have saved himself most of the scar, but with just my inexperience at hand, the memory of this day would remain on his face.

"The rope," he started again. "It'd been burned black. Like someone held an open flame to it." He swallowed, shaking his head and shifting the cotton. "This wasn't an accident. It was the same people who destroyed the other parts."

My temples throbbed as I met his eyes. "I— Are you sure?"

"Who else could it be?"

Not who, but what.

Nonsense. Mere fantasies of a tired, silly mind.

I drew the scissors under the tape and snipped off a piece. "Then we have to call the carabinieri. We have to alert them and let them know what is happening."

"No, we can't do that. I've already told you." He moved away from my hands. "I know you don't trust what I'm doing, but you have—"

"Wait a minute, what?" Something in my chest tightened at his words. "Why would you think that? I've always trusted you, Giovanni. Always." I leaned forward, forcing him to look at me. "I am always on your side; you have to know that. Nothing could ever change that."

He did look at me then, with a sheen of tears in his eyes I hadn't seen since the days after the loss of our last child.

"Oh, Giovanni," I said and drew closer. I wrapped my hands around his. "Things will be all right, I'm certain of it. We're just in a difficult transition, and we always knew getting the mill to work would be stressful, but you're so clever! Look at everything you've done, creating the patent, buying us this beautiful home, getting us here, all on your own."

He nodded, but his lips tightened, as if he were holding back words. I smoothed back a lock of his hair.

"You do know that you can tell me anything, right? I may not be able to help, simple creature I am, but I can listen, and sometimes that's exactly what's needed."

He held my gaze, and for an instant I was certain there was something he wanted to say.

I could see it, like a door creaking open.

He frowned.

"This is about yesterday, isn't it? You want to know about Dottore Lupponi's visit."

And just as easily, the door slammed shut again.

"No, that's not it at all," I said.

He scoffed. "Always the same, Sibilla, always interfering, meddling."

I blinked, trying to shake the words off before they landed their blows. He was tired and in pain, anxious from the loss of the new part and the worry over the injured men. He always said things he didn't really mean when under this kind of stress.

I pressed the last piece of tape to the bandage covering half his cheek and stood. "I'll bring you an aspirin."

He said nothing as I left the room, though I could feel him watching me, probably already thinking of a few neutral words to balance out the cruel ones. It was his way.

I was almost at the kitchen when I remembered he'd not eaten anything since this morning. Buona had likely put something together, but when he was in this state it was better if I cooked what he liked in the way he liked—eggs or perhaps a cut of the meat we had in the ice box, with potatoes. Yes, I'd ask.

I hurried back to the study.

What I saw as I made to pull at the half-opened door stopped me.

Giovanni was slumped over the desk, hands shaking as they clenched a piece of paper so tightly I could see his knuckles.

"What am I going to do?" he whispered.

Holding my breath, I slipped out of sight before he could look up, my back pressed against the wall.

Buona had been right all along.

There was something important he was keeping from me. If it could cause him that much distress, shouldn't he have told me? Why go through that kind of worry alone?

Well, if he didn't want to tell me, I would find out on my own.

Then I would be able to offer him the help he needed while skipping over the part that seemed the most difficult for him: the asking of it.

I GASPED AWAKE, THE NEIGHING of a horse following me into consciousness for an instant before receding.

I placed a hand on my stomach and felt my pulse beating in each of my fingertips, the muscles in my arms clenched so tightly they ached. I realized I was still waiting to hear that sound again.

But it didn't come. Well, naturally, since it'd just been a dream.

I exhaled. Because of course I'd fallen asleep when it was the opposite of what I'd told myself I'd do. Dio, how frustrating even I found myself sometimes.

I took care to make as little noise as possible as I turned to look at Giovanni. I could just about see that the bandage on his face still glowed white. It couldn't have been that long since we'd gone to bed, then, for the wound had still been bleeding with enthusiasm when we'd lain down.

His breathing was deep and steady though.

Am I really going to do this? If he catches me, after—

Yes, I had to. If I wanted to learn the truth, I had to try.

I pulled the covers gently away from me, my eyes on my husband, and sat up. I winced at the creak of the bed, which joined in duet with the floorboards as I shifted my legs and stood. Holding my breath, I waited for movement or for a change in his breathing.

He remained as he was.

The floor was cold as I tapped my foot in search of my bedroom slippers, without success. My mother would have been horrified to hear of me walking about barefoot in my condition, but I couldn't risk making more noise. I'd have to manage.

I pulled my bed jacket over my slip and started toward the door. I moved with care, only just seeing the silhouette of the footstool at the far end of the bed, holding my arms out in front of me to avoid crashing nose-first into the wood.

When I felt the grain of the door against my fingers, I took as steadying a breath as I could manage. For this would be the most difficult part. Giovanni insisted on locking the room each night, and the lock and key were just as rusted as could be expected after so many years of disuse.

My hand closed around the skeleton key and, with a quick appeal to the Santissima Madre, I turned it.

The clank of it would have woken the long-buried. And Giovanni was very much alive.

"Sibilla?"

I swallowed. "I'm here."

"What are you doing?"

"I-I wanted some water. I'm sorry I woke you; go back to sleep."

Only silence from the bed.

"Have the girl fetch it for you," he finally said, his voice losing its focus as sleep drew him down again.

"Yes, of course. I'll just go wake her," I said, pulling the key from the lock and opening the door in one sharp movement. I'd have to be quick now.

There was more light out here in the corridor, so I walked as close to a run as I dared, past Buona's bedroom, and to the study. I tried the handle but it was locked, too, as I'd assumed.

In an instant, the skeleton key fixed that predicament and I was inside the room, the door clicking closed behind me.

I bit the inside of my cheek at the memory of Giovanni's hand tightening on my wrist. It would be so much worse than that if he saw me in here now . . . no, I couldn't let that overwhelm me. I had to know the truth.

But a quick glance was enough to see that Giovanni had taken more precautions than locking the door. The pale moonlight streaming past the curtains he'd forgotten to close revealed a desk empty of everything but the telephone and the lamp. All of the scattered papers I'd seen just this afternoon were gone. I walked around the desk and began pulling open the drawers, one by one, wincing at every screech of parched wood. There wasn't much. A set of ink pens in their velvet pouches, blank papers, a few newspapers from Torino, but none of the documents I'd seen yesterday.

Well, they couldn't just have disappeared. Perhaps he'd placed them—

I frowned. There was a pile of ashes in the fireplace, which wouldn't have been unusual except that Buona and I had left it spotless a few days ago, ready for the winter in case we couldn't manage the expense of radiators yet.

No wood had been cut, no pinecones gathered nor coal ordered, yet there were ashes.

I closed the last drawer and went to the fireplace, kneeling by the hearthstone. I took the iron poker from its stand and began shifting the ashes about.

Had he really done this?

A corner of blackened paper shifting from under that pile of gray was my answer.

And it carried a fierce sting.

None of this was an attempt to spare me from worry, as I'd first thought. No, this was concealment. Lies. If these papers were important enough to burn so that I wouldn't read them, they were important enough for me to know what they'd said. Wasn't my life tied to my husband's, after all? What affected him was bound to affect me.

Did he not realize that, or did he just not care?

I blinked back tears and forced myself to stand because I had to try and get something more than pain out of all of this. Even if it was just a kernel of truth.

Taking the bit of singed paper to the window, I lifted it up to the moonlight, for I dared not turn the lamp on.

The fire had eaten away at most of the writing, warping all legibility from the rest. Except for two words. A name, it seemed.

Squinting, I brought it closer. Yes, it was a name and . . . it was one I knew. Leonardo Pisani, the assistant engineer in the sawmill Giovanni had worked at. What did he have to do with anything? It'd been at least half a year since Giovanni had seen or spoken with him.

A creak made me flinch.

I'd been too long. Giovanni had woken again.

I stuffed the burned paper into the pocket of my bed jacket and darted to the door, taking the skeleton key before opening it and slipping out.

There were footsteps in the corridor, drawing nearer.

My heart pounding in my throat, I tucked myself into the darkest corner I could find, pressed against a wall dusted with black mold. But there was no helping it. If he continued down to the study, he would see me.

I felt a splash of frozen fear. I'd forgotten to lock the door.

It wasn't Giovanni that the moonlight revealed, though. It was Buona, fully dressed, the hem of her trousers dark with mud. She clutched something in her hands, but the light's angle was wrong and I couldn't quite see what it was.

With her head turned toward the corridor leading to our bedroom, her body poised to dart away, she slowly opened her door. She paused and listened.

I was certain she would hear my heart beating like birds' wings in all that silence, but she just slipped into her room, readjusting her grip on what she held as she made to close the door behind her.

A pale beam of light fell upon it now.

How strange. She had a bouquet of plants in her arms, the haze of moonglow settling on greens and purples and blues and whites.

What could she possibly need flowers for in the middle of the night?

MADDALENA
1596

POKED AT THE BURNING WOOD in the hearth, allowing the fire new breath. It flared the red of poppies, in gratitude.

A quick peek into the cauldron told me there was only five or so minutes left before the simmering tonic would be ready. The smooth, warm smell of cinnamon filled my cucinetta, almost masking the bite of the motherwort. Which could mean . . .

I closed my eyes and listened to the voices fluttering against each other, the cinnamon's lute-string ping threatening to smother its softer companion. As I'd thought. It was not quite right, yet.

I walked to my worktable and took another sprig of the dried motherwort, placing it in my iron mortar. I'd have to purchase more soon if Silvia required many more weeks of tonics, though I'd not the least idea if the apothecary in Ovada had the kind of supplies I needed or if I'd have to bring them in from Genova. To think that just a couple of months ago, I could have had the apothecarist himself delivering anything under the sun to my very doorstep!

I'd just touched the pestle to the motherwort when I felt the sharp tug of another voice. It was an unfamiliar one, coming from the glass containers sitting on the shelves on the wall beside me. I turned.

"All right, I'm listening. Which one of you is it?"

Frowning, I looked from container to container, waiting for that coffee-dark voice to reveal itself.

There. The sellenis.

No small wonder I didn't recognize it, for I'd never had much need for these oat-colored berries. They'd been silent for so long I'd thought them mute. Or useless.

Florindo had bought them for me years ago, off a Barbary pirate who had boarded the wrong ship and had ended up commandeering a hold full of spices. And not even the kind of spices that my father would have paid gold for. There'd also been sacks of dried herbs with all manner of names on them, some unpronounceable, and after sharing a glass of wine with the man, Florindo had handed his purse over to purchase them for me. I smiled at the thought of my husband laughing and speaking of his family with a pirate, for he could converse with anyone about anything. He could find common ground with a serpent, if allowed. I'd just been surprised he'd not invited the man to cena.

I took the jar and unstoppered it.

"What is it, then?"

Fixing my eyes on the brick-red vines of ivy I'd had painted on the wall before me, I cocked my head and listened.

It was a matter of seconds before I understood. It wanted to help.

I hesitated. It was not my habit to offer someone anything I wasn't entirely certain about, and I'd no experience whatsoever with these berries. They had never offered themselves before, not for any of the other women I'd assisted in conceiving. Still, I sensed no malice in them, not even the weaving singsong tease of the belladonna.

As I always did with indecisions, I focused on where my instincts were tipping me and followed them.

With a nod, I mixed a few of the dried berries into the mortar and ground them together with the motherwort.

There was a knock on the door.

"Enter," I said, walking back to the cauldron.

"Scusatemi, madonna, but dinner is ready."

I glanced up at the male voice, entirely out of place here. "You should not be on this floor, Antonio."

"I apologize, madonna. I wasn't aware of that."

"Were you not?" If I knew my kitchen stewards, which I did, I knew very well that would have been one of the first things they'd have told him. "But now you are, so I'll expect you to remain on the ground floor."

He bowed his head. "Yes, madonna."

I finished adding the crushed herbs and berries to the tonic and glanced at the servant. "Now go and tell Alba to come up here. I need her to clear up some things in here."

"She's indisposed, madonna. Fever, I think, since last night."

I exhaled sharply. "I should have been told." I grabbed a pouch of willow bark shavings from where it hung on the wall. "Here. Take this down to the kitchen and have one of the women make her a strong tea out of its contents."

He bowed his head again. "Yes, madonna."

"And then, I suppose, tell Maria to come tidy up."

"I could do it, madonna. Since I'm here already, I mean."

As if I'd leave the care of my herbs and of my father's alembic to a boy with hands that were covered in scrapes, that were scuffed and bruised. Even his tunic had something untidy about it, like he flung it off him at night and let it rest where it landed.

"That will not be necessary, Antonio," I said. "Just do as I've told you."

"As you wish, madonna."

I smoothed my skirts and headed for the door.

Out in the corridor, the scent of the stew filled every cranny, rising from the main kitchen in waves, like steam. Such a familiar smell, pulled up from the depths of my childhood, that for the first time in many months the need to embrace my mother was almost painful.

She'd been the daughter of grain merchants, and her household had observed the fall Embertides every year with a week of austerity at the table and extravagance in prayer.

Even when she'd married Father, whose fortune rested on ocean waves and not on golden fields, she continued the tradition, the week culminating in a dinner of vegetable and eel stew that had been slowly boiled for hours, and nothing but prayer for cena. My father had observed with her despite his aversion to eel.

Florindo had no such compunctions and welcomed the yearly stew I, too, had tacked on to my household traditions. Though he did have a tendency to doze after the second or third hour of vigil.

I took the stairs to the first story, running my hand over the banister and checking for granules of dust before descending. Not one.

Excellent.

This year, everything had been more rigorous in the preparation for the fall Embertides. I'd had the house scoured, days and days of cleaning and opening windows to allow the snapping September air full run of the villa. Marcellina had made wreaths of corn husks, bramble, and dried apples, and even the boys had been able to delay pelting each other with pinecones and hazelnuts for long enough to thread a needle through their centers and hang them with silk from the mantle in the sala.

The praying, too, would be more arduous, beginning earlier this year and lasting until midmorning tomorrow. And although the children would not have to spend the night in vigil, they would help us for the first couple of hours. We couldn't afford to offer less than out best. Humbled before our Dio and His seasons, we would raise our devotion, syllable by syllable, to the very gates of heaven.

"Mona Maddalena," Giusto said, stopping on the landing and bowing his head.

"*Buon pomeriggio,* Giusto. Are the children ready?"

"Yes, mona. I was just heading to fetch them. They have all washed and dressed." A spasm of exhaustion swept across his face. "Messer Ugo had complaints about the water being too cold."

I started down the steps to the ground floor. "I gather it wasn't cold when it was brought up from the kitchens."

"No, Mona Maddalena. He was . . . reluctant to wash and allowed it to grow cool."

"Then Ugo only has himself to blame." I glanced back at Giusto. "I'll speak with him."

He bowed his head.

Yes, I'd have to show my youngest how much work went into preparing his bath, perhaps have him carry a brimming bucket up to his bedroom a few times, and maybe then he'd not be so cavalier with his actions.

But that would have to wait until tomorrow.

On my way to the sala, I stopped at the small chapel to see that everything was in place for this afternoon. The polished wood of the prie-dieu glimmered under the light coming in through the stained-glass window, the rosette turning the sun's rays a rich, luxurious red. Behind them, the kneelers for the children had been readied, as well.

Good.

I reached the sala just as Florindo did, his hair still wet from his own wash.

He smiled in that way that always made warmth pool deep in my center and gave me a courtly bow.

I chuckled. "What is all this, then?"

"I am just expressing my admiration for you, that is all. Because each year you surprise me a little more."

With a shake of my head, I drew closer and pressed a kiss on his cheek.

"You are even more beautiful now than when we married," he said.

"Now I know without question that you are addle-minded." I smacked his arm lightly. "There is no comparison between a woman of forty and one of fifteen."

"Oh, that is certain. No girl of fifteen would stride into a room as you do, as if a crown belonged on her head." He pulled me even closer. "I thought you were beautiful the day we met, of course, but now you are exquisite."

There was nothing I could say to that, so I didn't. I kissed him instead.

"All right, enough nonsense," I said, pulling away and clearing my throat. "A servant might see us."

"Heaven forbid a servant see spouses who have had five children together kissing."

Yes, and where were those children? I'd just realized the conspicuous lack of noise and chaos.

As if he'd heard my thoughts, Florindo nodded to the door. "They're in their seats already. I ushered them in while you were, I'm assuming, looking in on the chapel. The silence concerns me, as well, and I can't vouch for Giusto's well-being, but I know they are in there."

Leaning against him, I took a deep breath.

It was time to begin, then.

Together, we walked into the sala and took our places at opposite ends of the stone table. The children *were* in their seats, though Vincenzo and Francesco had switched places. As if I'd not notice. As if I'd not be able to distinguish their very essence, their very smell, when they'd been formed within me.

All it took was one of my lifted eyebrows to set them scrambling for their correct seats. When he'd realized what they'd done, Giusto hissed a warning at them.

The steward brought in my grandmother's clay stew pot and placed it in the center of the bare table. Our bowls, too, were clay, our spoons wooden, luxury struck from the dinner. There wasn't a gleam of silver, not even in the credenza across from us.

Fragrant steam veiled the steward's face as he began ladling stew, which was a sign that the whole thing had been timed correctly. For this recipe, which looked deceptively simple in my grandmother's curling handwriting, was, in fact, a test of organization. It had to be cooked, covered, left at a low, steady fire for ten hours, and it had to be served as soon as it was done, for it lost all its flavor if cooked for too long or if reheated.

That meant a sleepless night for our cuoco, Martino, and one or two other servants if they wanted to be able to serve the stew in its perfect state for our dinner at one.

Martino had done it for the past twenty years, with only one misstep that had required the addition of a last-minute roasted eel to substitute some of the lost flavor. Florindo had had to hold the man up to stop him from falling to his knees as he begged for my forgiveness. It had never happened again, and it looked like this year could be added to his list of successes. I'd have to remember to give him my compliments.

The steward filled every bowl and every water glass and stepped away from the table. I nodded to Florindo.

He stood and opened his father's gilded prayer book to the psalm he read each year while I placed my hand on the gold cross around my neck. I made certain that all my children's heads were bowed before I, too, bowed mine. The words began to twine themselves around us, verse after verse, his strong voice as warm as the steam coming off the stew.

I closed my eyes and breathed. May our labors have pleased our Dio.

"... benedic anima mea, Domine. Amen."

"Amen," we said in unison.

I crossed myself and took up my spoon, the signal the hungry creatures along the table had been waiting for. As if they'd not eaten a full meal in days, they practically dove headfirst into their bowls.

With a smile, I glanced beside me at Giacomo, his eyes wide as he had the first taste of the stew. I saw the years fall away from him for a moment, leaving an infant so precious I'd spent the first few months of his life in a rosy daze. Like a cherub had fallen from the heavens and landed in my arms.

And then the memory of him standing beside me in the forest came, all bristling anger as he spoke to the trespassers. Those men a dozen of our workers had not been able to find trace of.

Anything could have happened that afternoon.

I shoved the memory aside and brought a spoonful of stew to my lips. This was not the time for dark thoughts.

Something lodged into the back of my throat as I tried to swallow. I tasted the metal of blood in the midst of sweet squash an instant before the pain began. I flinched, my spoon clattering to the table.

"What's the matter, sposa?" Florindo said.

I tried to speak but something was pressing against my palate.

"Maddalena." He rose from his seat.

"Mamma?" Giacomo said.

I stopped the room's mounting panic with a hand that, despite myself, I couldn't prevent from shaking, and reached into my mouth. My eyes watered as I took hold of what was embedded in my skin. I pulled.

I recognized what it was before I saw it.

A small feather. Its quill red with my blood.

"Stop eating," I said with a wince, my chair screeching as I stood. I circled the table and reached for the ladle in the clay pot, lifting it full and allowing the liquid to spill out. There was another feather. And another.

"Giusto, stay with the children," I said at the same time that Florindo came to my side.

"Of course, Mona Maddalena."

"And don't let them eat another mouthful."

Florindo followed me out of the sala, down the corridor to the main kitchen, and past the flurry of exclamations when I stormed through the door, toward the hearth.

The extinguished logs still smoked under the cauldron where the remainder of the stew sat. I could feel my heart beating in my throat as I snapped a cloth from a nearby table and used it to lift the searing cauldron lid.

The liquid bubbled lightly. It looked just as it always did.

"The stirrer," I said.

The cuoco stepped forward. "Madonna, is there someth—"

"The stirrer," I said, my voice a whip of sound.

Martino handed it to me with a bow and I plunged it into the stew. A swirl of feathers floated to the surface almost at once but I kept stirring, the truth of what I'd find already biting at me.

Birds' bodies rose past the squash and pumpkin lumps, tender meat sliding off their bones with the movement, leaving behind beaks and ribs and empty skulls. Familiar metal rings encircled the steaming feet of the carcasses.

These were our doves. And they'd been tossed into the cauldron, whole.

"What is this abomination?" I hissed.

Martino hurried to my side and looked in. He pressed a hand to his mouth in an unsuccessful effort to contain his shriek. His knees buckled under him and it was one of the younger stewards who had to move to catch him this time.

I turned until I could see every soul in the kitchen. Florindo, wisely, made no attempt to corral my anger but instead took his place beside me.

"Who is responsible for this?"

All eyes were fixed on the floor.

"Which of you helped with the cooking last night?" I clapped my hands. "Come, I need an answer. I need to know who dared desecrate this sacred day."

Martino found his feet, though he did not straighten himself. "Madonna, I'm responsible for the cooking and—"

"That is not what I asked."

"I helped, madonna," Antonio said, stepping forward. "But I did not do that and neither did Messer Martino. I know it."

"Did you see who did?"

"No, madonna."

"You mean to tell me you were both here the entire night, watching the stew, and saw no one? Heard nothing?" I motioned to the cauldron. "Am I supposed to believe the birds flew themselves into the pot?"

There was a beat of tight silence.

And then Martino let out a half-strangled sob.

"Oh, madonna, I'm so ashamed." He paused, clutching at his hands. "I fell asleep. I slept through the entire night. I've never done such a thing before, I swear to the *Santissima Vergine,* and I knew the moment I woke that I'd shamed the entire household, but I never dreamed that . . . that anyone would . . ."

His voice unthreaded into weeping again.

Now we were getting to the crux. I turned to Antonio.

"Why did you not wake Martino?"

He kept his eyes fixed on the floor. "Because I wanted to leave my post, madonna."

Madre di Gesù, did no one do as they were ordered to do in this house? I exhaled sharply. "Was it pure willfulness or did you have a reason for your disobedience?"

"I went to inquire on Alba, madonna. She had been poorly."

I lifted an eyebrow. "You thought it your responsibility to do so? You felt it appropriate to step foot in the women's quarters?"

"It was just a moment, madonna, and I stood in the corridor. Octavia can vouch for me."

I glanced at the woman, who nodded.

"Most unusual." I held his gaze. "This atrocity could not have been done in that short amount of time, which means you are not telling me everything."

The boy pressed his lips together. For an instant, I could have sworn he was trying to hide a smile.

I shook my head. This was all too much. "The little patience I have is seeping away second by second, so if you have any intention of remaining in service, mine or anyone else's, I urge you to speak."

Florindo did shift beside me now. But if it were up to him, there would never be any consequences for anything, and that was not how the world worked. Nor my household.

"On the way back to the kitchen, madonna," he started, "I stopped by the music room."

I frowned. "Whatever for?"

He wrung his hands together, and for that instant he really looked just like one of my sons in the maelstrom of punishment. Another disobedient boy.

"Speak."

"I wanted to see the clock, madonna. I've heard the girls speaking about it, how it has little figurines in it that move, and I wanted to see it for myself." He bowed his head. "Scusatemi."

Father's Bavarian clock with the dancing peasants. I rubbed a hand against my forehead and swallowed down the sharpest words I wanted to say, for they were not appropriate, even in these circumstances.

"And how long do you gather you were in the music room?" Florindo said.

"Perhaps twenty minutes, messer. I was waiting for the hour to strike so I could see the figures appear."

"Plenty of time for someone to break the necks of the doves in the dovecote, come in through that door, and stuff them in the pot." I shook my head. "How did you not even notice that they were in there? Did you not look at what you were stirring?"

He clenched his hands. "I didn't know if I had to stir the stew, so I didn't, madonna. It was my first time and I didn't want to do the wrong thing."

"And yet, you did not wake Martino or stay at your post." I glanced about me until I caught sight of the head steward. "To make up for this, take the cost of the ingredients for the stew out of Antonio's pay—"

"Oh, madonna, please!" the boy said.

"—and relegate him to menial kitchen duties. I don't want to see him anywhere else in this house. If he makes another error in judgment, you may dismiss him without consulting me."

The steward bowed his head. "Yes, madonna."

"Scusatemi, but I'm to blame," Martino said, still not daring to look up at me. "Please, take the costs out of my pay and dismiss me."

"I've made my decision, Martino. You've served us loyally for twenty years, and I'm not going to punish you for falling asleep. It was not a conscious choice you made to disobey, while Antonio chose, unequivocally, to leave his post. Besides, I know that what has happened is punishment enough for you and that you will never allow it to occur again."

"On my life, I won't, madonna."

I waved to the cauldron behind me. "Remove the stew and scour the pot until every trace of this filth is gone. It is a good thing you managed to sleep some, Martino, because I'm afraid you will have to prepare another meal for our dinner."

The man's face mottled with red.

And still none of this told us who the actual culprit was, for despite everything, I did believe Antonio in that respect. He didn't look the sort to have done something so brutal. So then who could have?

"Maddalena," Florindo said, turning to me, the tightness of his face revealing that his thoughts ran along similar paths as mine. "Didn't we hire a man to care for the doves when we arrived?"

My eyebrows shot up. I'd entirely forgotten about him.

"Why did he not raise the alarm this morning? He would have seen the missing birds first."

"You're entirely right, sposo. We should have known about this earlier." I nodded to the silent cluster of people in front of me. "Someone find him and bring him here."

There was a murmur among the servants as the head steward made rapid inquiries from each of them. Florindo motioned to one of the men before crossing the room and flinging the door to the garden open. The two of them hurried to the dovecote near the forest.

"No one has seen him since last night, madonna," the head steward finally said. "He didn't come to break his fast this morning at the servants' kitchen."

Had the man seen what had happened and hid for fear of being blamed? Because anything else would be nonsensical. What need did he have to do something of this sort? Why make his own position obsolete? He was a local man, someone who would not have many other prospects available, certainly none that would pay as well as this one did.

Florindo returned a minute later, shaking his head. "He's not at his post and his room in the stables is empty. None of the grooms have seen him. It seems he's left."

I exhaled. Had the entire world gone mad?

"The dovecote will need attending to," Florindo said to the steward. "There's . . . uh . . . a lot of feathers and . . . and blood."

My hands clenched to fists at my sides. It was true that we'd always planned the birds to be food, but they deserved better than this vicious, cruel, wasteful end.

I'd have to keep the children away until everything had been cleared. And I'd have to prepare a purifying solution to help remove all that violence from the garden stones. As soon as possible.

The steward was already giving orders to a few of the servants who were arming themselves with water buckets and rags, and even Martino had found enough voice in him to direct three women to the cauldron. They crossed themselves before swinging the iron arm out of the hearth and reaching for the pot.

Florindo came to my side. "We'll have to alert the massaro about all of this. Not just about today, either."

I hesitated. The news would make it all over the region in half a day.

"You know this is about more than the doves, Maddalena."

Yes, of course I did. The very thought of an intruder slipping so easily into our home, even if it had been someone in the fringes of our employ, chilled me. Besides, hadn't I just objected to Florindo's tendency to sidestep consequences? We'd already allowed the incident with my grandmother's tablecloth to go unpunished and perhaps that had emboldened this man to do what he did.

Unless I'd been wrong in my suspicions and he'd been behind the tablecloth too.

I closed my eyes, feeling as if this day had lasted for years, and gave myself permission to lean slightly against my husband's arm. What a disaster this had been. The worst Embertide I'd ever gone through.

Something in my chest squeezed. I felt a flutter of fear.

"I don't like this, sposo."

"I know. I'll send for the massaro and then we'll do the vigil, just as we planned," Florindo said, his voice a caress. "We won't have the stew, but everything else will be the same."

Tears pricked at my eyes. I tried to stop them, but they were waves, pulling me under.

He pressed a kiss to the side of my head. "Our Dio understands and so would your mother. It'll be all right."

How could I explain that it wasn't the stew or my mother's memory or even the fear of divine retribution that left me with a sob locked in my throat? It was the feeling growing second by second that this was an omen no amount of prayers would touch. A carcass-strewn warning for what lay ahead.

THE MASSARO DIDN'T COME. Not that day or the next.

And then the rains began.

Three days after the horror of the Embertide, the blue started to leach from the sky, taking the sun with it. Clouds the color of slate formed and spread as far as we could see from the villa, flattening into a lid over us until there wasn't a single patch of clear sky. The rain that started was almost invisible and so light it hardly shifted the leaves on the trees. At least until that afternoon.

Florindo and I were watching the children race on one leg across the courtyard, the thuds of their hopping syncopating with their laughter, when the first roll of thunder rippled along the walls. The crystal of our wineglasses tinkled.

We hurried to the nearest window and looked out just in time to see a blade-scratch of lightning. Like it had been waiting for just that signal, the threads of drops gave way to a heavy gray curtain of rain.

I glanced at Florindo and he took my hand. "It'll exhaust itself soon," he said.

But it didn't. The rain and lightning continued, indifferent to the sun's setting, to the extinguishing of our candles, to the silence of a house attempting to sleep through what could have been cannon shots.

I stared up at the folds of our bed's canopy as Spuma screamed in the stables, waking the other horses, whipping them up into a froth of panic. Hour after hour.

By the second afternoon, I found myself drifting to windows every few minutes, the knot of nerves growing each time I saw no sign of the storm lifting, until my chest ached with the weight of worry. I gripped my cross and the acorn talisman hanging from my chatelaine and said every prayer I knew.

"The fields can withstand a good amount of rain," Florindo said, coming to stand beside me as we waited for the call to cena.

"But the wheat is so young." I shook my head. "It'll rot in all of this."

"No, no. Not yet. All it'll need is a few days of sun."

I looked at him, at the dark pouches under his eyes and the lines that had appeared around his mouth in what seemed to be just the last couple of days. It all belied his words.

"What will we do if this doesn't stop, Florindo?"

He eased closer, wrapping his arms around me. I hadn't realized how much I'd needed him to do exactly that.

"It'll stop, amore," he said. "I spoke with one of the workers earlier, and he said that this is normal for the region at this time of year. He's lived here his entire life, so he's bound to know."

The words should have eased a bit of the pressure in my chest, but they didn't. The feeling I'd had since the last day of the Embertide, like a pulse in the back of my mind, surged forward.

As if in sympathy, the torrent behind the mill gave a rumble. Its steady stream had turned savage with the rain and pushed against its banks a bit more each hour. The water had to be pouring into the millrace.

"Is the wheel safe?"

"Perfectly."

"What about the dam?" I said. "Will it hold?"

"Oh yes, you do not need to concern yourself with that. I had it reinforced and raised the very first day we got here, remember? It would take something akin to the Great Flood to break through."

I bit my lip but nodded against his chest.

"Would you like me to check on it again?"

The man knew me much too well. I looked up at him. "Would you?"

"Of course, Maddalena." He pressed a kiss to my forehead. "I would swim across the torrent itself to hold the dam in place if you wanted me to."

I lifted an eyebrow and tapped the bulge of his stomach. "And you'd sink right to the bottom."

"It is not my fault that I am substantially built."

"What you are is substantially filled with *crostate*."

His laughter shook the fear off me for an instant, like birds spooked off a tree. It'd be back, I knew that, but for now, I'd just remain as I was, still in the refuge of his arms.

THE CRASH WRENCHED ME OUT of my doze. My eyes flew open at the same time the horses began to shriek.

"Florindo," I said.

He groaned but made no attempt to rise.

I sat up and shook him. "Florindo, wake up."

"What is it?"

"I don't know, but something's wrong."

A roar of surging water drowned the sound of the horses.

For a moment, that rushing, thundering sound was all we could hear. Florindo jerked up, the end of his nightcap thumping me in the nose as he pulled the curtain open. I did the same, shoving my feet into my slippers, snatching my robe from the chair by the bed, and slipping it on as I hurried across the room.

Giusto stepped into the corridor an instant after we did, his own cap askew, blinking in the trembling light of a candle.

"Go to the children," I said as I passed him.

"What is happening, mona?"

"We don't know yet. Keep them calm and inside!"

"Yes, mona."

Florindo and I raced down the main stairwell, just a sliver of moonlight and the horses' screams guiding our way.

Servants in various degrees of disarray began to slip out of their wing of the villa and into the courtyard, the housekeeper and the first steward holding candelabras high, the glow illuminating the fear and confusion in all their faces.

"Men, come with me," Florindo said.

Without hesitation or questions, the men started after us as we left the house and ran down the colonnade and its steps. Stones could have been coming down instead of waterdrops from the force that pelted us the instant we were out from under cover.

Thunder boomed, the vibrations rippling across a pool of water and mud that glimmered in front of the last marble step and Florindo stopped, turning to me.

"I'll carry you. Come."

"I can walk through it, sposo."

"Maddalena, the water is freezing and you have on a pair of bed slippers. Don't be stubborn."

Barely waiting for me to nod in agreement, he tucked an arm under my knees and another against my back and lifted me as if I weighed about as much as his pillow.

I held on to him, feeling more than a little foolish as he stepped into the pool of muddy water. It reached halfway up his calves.

It was when he set me down on the opposite side that I first heard the change in the land. The distance hadn't allowed me to realize from inside the house that the resonances were all wrong.

My teeth chattered with the sudden wave of cold understanding that racked my body.

The river wasn't where it should have been.

"Oh, no. No, no," I murmured and forced my legs to move.

"Maddalena!" Florindo called after me, but I didn't stop.

I broke into a run, moving so quickly the momentum kept me from falling when my feet slid time and time again in the mud. It splashed cold against my robe and seeped into my nightdress, like it was trying to weigh me down. Keep me from seeing.

I ran past the towering mill and across the dirt road, the shrieking horses, the hammering rain, the calls from behind me, none of it managing to drown out my heart or my mind, which roared along with the river.

I slipped as I began climbing the hill overlooking the fields and landed with a shock to my knees. My slippers found no purchase in the wet grass. With a wince, I dug my fingers into the cold earth and started crawling up.

"Please," I said, unable to say the rest.

My knees trembled so much I thought I'd fall again as I began to stand, but I didn't.

And then my own wail rooted me in place until I thought I'd always be there, on that hill, staring down at our fields.

There was just enough moonlight to see the great rippling blackness in front of me.

The dam had broken.

Our wheat lay, drowning, under folds of violent water.

SIBILLA
1933

I PRESSED A HAND TO MY mouth to hide the yawn from a night of missed
sleep. Novels of spies and intrigue had never been part of my reading
fare, but I couldn't even recall any movie in which the protagonist dragged exhaustion behind him as he spent nights breaking codes and chasing
villains. One night of searching through a study and I was ready to collapse.

I considered returning to bed now that Giovanni was at the mill but
pushed the thought aside. What I really wanted was to get out of the house,
clear my head, and see if I could come up with the right way of getting the
truth from my husband. Speaking with him was always the same—like
trying to open a lock with a key you weren't sure would fit.

"Perhaps the forest has the answers that I don't," I said as I crossed the
kitchen and made for the door. "A bit of air will do us both good, in any
case, child."

With a gasp, I pulled my hand back from the handle the instant the
metal met my skin. Santissima Madre, if someone didn't fix the wiring, we'd
all end up sizzling!

I turned, searching for something to use as protection, and frowned.

There was a large stain in the center of the kitchen that I was certain I'd not seen this morning. Had Buona spilled something?

I grabbed the rag on the table and walked over to it. The last thing any of us needed was someone slipping and breaking a limb.

Just one look, however, was enough to realize that the stain was old, so much so that the stones appeared to have absorbed it. But we'd spent days in this kitchen, scrubbing every speck of dirt and dust, every grease stain, from it. This one had not been there. I was certain of it. Its size would have made it difficult to miss.

I bent and brushed it with my hand. It felt slick and slightly warm, and more substantial than I'd expected, almost viscous. When I looked down, I saw that fingers came away gleaming with the red of blood. Even as I watched, it seemed to throb against my skin.

A drop of blood fell on my wrist, then another. Like the air itself was bleeding.

My vision pulled in like a drawstring bag. A pressure began in my head. *All that red.*

My pulse leaped into a race in an instant, beating with fury in my temples. I felt them rising rapidly, those two half-remembered but wholly useless bits of conversation that told me nothing yet could tear at me with such precision.

The cloaked memory smothered me in its thick red folds, allowing me to see nothing but that color, to feel nothing but the crushing panic I must have felt that night.

No, I couldn't allow it to overtake me. I had to protect my child from this. From me.

I forced my legs to start moving. I left the kitchen and ran to one of the rooms off the courtyard, where the one thing sat that was truly mine in this world: the piano that had once been my mother's.

My hands shook so violently that the embossed wooden lid slammed closed twice before I managed to open it fully. The yellow-tinged ivory keys were cool under my fingers, the feel of their smooth surfaces alone already easing the first layer of pressure from my head. I closed my eyes to avoid seeing the streaks of red I left on the keys and began to play.

The melody was a stumbling thing, the dissonance of trembling fingers transforming the light waltz into a lopsided musical aberration, but I didn't stop. I fought through the red of that missing memory, the notes helping me claw my way out of its embrace.

I played the waltz over and over.

And slowly, like an animal's jaws prying open, the pressure eased. My pulse slowed.

The melody regained its shape.

By the time I opened my eyes, Buona was standing at the door with a bucket of water, her sleeves rolled up to her elbows. She watched me go through the melody one more time.

"That's pretty," she said. "You're a real talent at that. I can't imagine how you don't tangle your fingers up."

My lips twitched as I forced myself to smile. A thread of sweat slid down my back.

"You look pale, Sibilla. Do you want me to make you some tea?"

I shook my head. "What I want is to go outside." As I said the words, I realized just how much I needed to get out of the house. Right now. It was like someone was pulling on a leash, urging me forward. "Would you come with me?"

"Of course. If I ever turn down a chance to avoid cleaning, you'll know I'm ill."

This time I didn't have to force the smile.

I stood, hand on my child, but hesitated. "Could you do me a favor first, though? Could you wipe that bloodstain, just so that I don't see it again? It's ghastly."

"What stain?"

"The one in the kitchen. The chicken we bought yesterday for our cena must have dripped on the floor as we prepared it. It's almost in the center of the room, a few paces from the stove. And check the stove, too, because I felt some drops."

She frowned. "I just came from the kitchen and there wasn't a stain of any sort."

"Well, it is there. I touched it. It was even slightly fres—"

What I saw when I looked down stopped my words.

There was no blood on my fingers, on my wrist, no blood on the piano keys. No blood at all.

WE SET OFF INTO THE WOODS, down the same path I'd taken when I'd heard the horse that afternoon, and continued on. I forced my attention to the land around me and away from whatever I'd thought I'd seen in the kitchen.

It was a pleasant enough day. I'd come to realize that Buona was perfect company, at least for me. She didn't chatter but her silence didn't weigh on me either. Whenever I walked with Giovanni, I was as worried about saying the wrong thing as I was about not saying anything. I always ended up letting him talk and just agreeing with whatever he said. It was one of the reasons I'd always enjoyed going to the pictures with him when we were courting. I could sit beside him without worrying about conversation.

The frustration that had verged on anger last night as I knelt in front of the fireplace tried to grab hold of me again, but I swerved around it. I was too tired, too heavy-minded and heavy-bodied, to think on that right now.

We passed the forest of pine trees and kept walking, nearing the mountain's side. We stepped around a collection of rocks that were dressed in moss and, all at once, there was white everywhere. Small white flowers woven together into a carpet that covered the grass and the rocks and the dirt itself. They pressed tightly against each other so that it was difficult to believe that a single petal more could fit.

"How lovely they are," I said.

It was impossible to move without crushing them underfoot. With each step, the forest began to fill with a dark, sharp odor that reminded me of my father's cellar the summer that mice had overtaken it. It was strangely comforting.

I bent to look closer at a cluster of them. "Do you know what these flowers are?" I said.

"My mother called them poison parsley, but I don't know if that's their actual name. We have them near my house." She shrugged. "It could be another plant, though, because I've never seen them spread like this. There's usually just one or two."

I frowned. "Are they actually poisonous?"

"Madre used to slap my hands if I tried to touch them, but it was impossible to tell with her. She was always deep into her cups, no matter the time of day, and couldn't be trusted not to be imagining entire conversations." She snorted. "One morning, she thought the mayor had come to compliment her on her garden, which was dead, mind you, and had been for years. She'd actually been speaking to a fence post. I saw the whole thing and almost choked myself laughing."

Like me and that imaginary bloodstain.

I blinked. I couldn't conceive that. Until my mother had died, she'd been a lighthouse beam for me, guiding me through the darkest of moments.

"Look," Buona said as we drew close enough to touch the steep mountain. She was pointing to a wide opening that had been carved into it, most of it draped with vines of ivy, the carpet of white flowers continuing to unfurl into it. "It looks like a cave."

I vaguely remembered Giovanni mentioning to one of his colleagues back in Torino that there was a passage on the property allowing easy access to the hectares of oak trees on the mountain. This had to be it.

"Should we go in?" Buona said.

I rested my hands on my stomach. "I'd like to see it, but do you think that animals could be in there? I don't think I could climb a tree if a cinghiale comes after me."

"I could go first."

"No, no, you'll not go alone. We'll just, uh . . ." I bent and grabbed the first rock I found. "We'll go in armed. It's not quite Giovanni's pistol, but it might buy us time to run."

With a chuckle, Buona also bent and picked up two rocks, stuffing one into each of her trouser pockets. "We're ready, I think."

"Let's go."

We eased under the vines and stepped into the passage. It was taller than it had looked from the outside, the rock ceiling rising high above me, and now that we were through the ivy-darkened opening, it was easy to see this was indeed a passage leading up the mountain.

Steps wide and deep enough to allow three or four people to walk up side by side had been carved into the cave wall. It would have taken substantial time and effort to build them, but I assumed the woodcutters would have needed to bring tools, maybe carts of some sort, up to the top and this would have been easier than scaling the mountainside and then pulling them up.

It was a clever solution.

Buona hurried ahead and climbed up a couple of steps, stomping on them to check their firmness. Nothing shifted.

"They feel sturdy enough, but I'll go up first and make certain it's safe for you."

It had to be the strains that pregnancy placed on the mind, because that simple sentence squeezed something in my chest. I blinked back sudden tears.

She bounded up the stone staircase until I could hardly see her in the thin light streaming in through the opening at the top.

"It's safe!" she called down.

I started up, grateful for the size of the steps.

And even so, I soon felt like I was lugging a cart up myself, my breath quickly tightening into a pant as I cradled my stomach with one hand and pressed the other against the cold mountain's side.

Above me, Buona was shifting branches and tearing at the vines blocking the opening, and the stone walls amplified her muttered curses at the debris that fell on her hair, allowing them to reach me with ease. At her age, I wouldn't have known half of those words.

Halfway up what had to be at least a hundred steps, my thighs burning, I realized I'd earned every unkind word Giovanni had ever thrown at me. I was an idiot.

I stopped, feeling my heart's thudding vibrate through the liquid that shielded my child.

"Sibilla?" Buona called. "Are you all right?"

The girl already thought me feeble. How could she not? Soon I'd start seeing the same distaste on her face as I'd seen in Giovanni's.

I flinched away from the thought.

"I'm fine," I said. "Just allowing myself a few breaths. You go on up."

Her hesitation rained down on me, and I expected the trail of her footsteps to unwind as she returned to my side.

But they didn't and she didn't.

Both hands around my child, I made myself continue. It felt like ages before I stepped, panting, through the opening at the top.

Oak trees of all sizes covered the mountaintop. Hectares of them. Those same white flowers piled beneath them, their delicate petals in perfect contrast with the jagged flakes of bark.

From the forest below, where the only thing visible was a sheer rock face, it was impossible to see how massive the mountain itself was, how many terraces and mounds and even narrow valleys it had. And all of it brimming with oaks.

Giovanni had told me that no one had touched the trees in the centuries since the Caparalia family had owned the mill, and it showed. Some of the tree trunks were twice the length of my arm span, the ridges in their bark large enough to fit an entire finger, and I could have used just one of their leaves as a fan.

The silence up here was striking too.

Despite the acorns I could feel cracking under my boots, the trees swallowed up the sound of our steps. Even the wind refused to shatter it by ruffling through the leaves.

"Oh, this is so beautiful," I said.

Buona glanced at me, a slight frown on her face, and shrugged. "I suppose."

And Giovanni would be shocked. For I didn't think he had a real idea of the number of trees we had.

When he'd visited the property and decided to purchase it, he'd planned on going around the mountain, to the narrow access path leading up to the oaks on that side. It didn't really belong to us, but since no one else used it and the sellers hadn't known where our entrance was, it'd been the best option. A heavy storm had rushed through a few days before, though, and the rain had brought down rocks, so he'd not been able to pass. He still hadn't. Now that I'd found our entrance, he'd see that just a quarter of the oaks up here would allow him to invest in purchasing more lumber and planting faster growing black locust trees in the fields below. With the influx of the lire these trees would bring, he could start his sawmill in earnest.

Despite myself and last night's frustration, the thought of seeing him smile, of being the cause of that smile, made my heart stumble over a beat.

"I think I see some mushrooms up there," Buona said, bringing my eyes and thoughts down from the trees. She pointed to a slope a bit ahead of where we stood. "I could see if they're edible. The right ones can be good for women in your condition."

I followed her gaze but could see nothing except more of those white flowers. Perhaps a tip of something blue. Were there blue mushrooms?

"It's a bit of a climb, Buona."

She waved my words away. "I'll be back in a moment."

She hurried off toward the slope and didn't hesitate, not even bothering to grasp the nearby oak branches for help. As sure-footed as ever, she pulled herself up until she disappeared over the lip of the hill, decapitating some flowers on her way.

I heard the horse the instant she was gone.

A shock of cold went through my limbs.

It was the same high neighing and the same thundering hooves that I'd heard twice before already. And it was all coming from up here now, on the mountain.

The trespasser.

"Buona," I called, though I knew the galloping animal and my own fear had smothered my voice.

But I needed to do something. I couldn't just stand here.

I spun, searching through the trees for sight of anything moving, following the sound of the horse crashing through the forest first with my eyes and then my feet. I swerved between oaks at a near run as the hoofbeats grew louder, but there was nothing at all. How was that possible?

And where was Buona? Could she not hear this?

When the first ripple of nausea overtook me, I realized something else was rising with the noise, growing stronger with each second. The smell of crushed flowers. The original comfort of the odor was warping into something so suffocating and cloying that I had to cover my mouth and nose. It surged like a wave and shattered against me over and over. I could taste the bitterness of bile.

A whinny climbed to a shriek.

Much too close.

I gasped as something struck my cheek, whip-like, leaving it stinging. Another strike, this one to my neck, was strong enough to jerk me back. My hands flew from my mouth to cover the growing mound of my stomach. What was this? What was hitting me?

The sharp blows doubled, tripled, coming faster, an icy gust of wind snapping the hem of my dress up and bringing with it the pain of a classroom switch against my knees.

"Stop," I hissed, though I could see nothing actually hitting me. For an instant I thought I saw a twisting black form through the trees, but it was gone before I could focus on it.

I heard a resounding dry crunch and then wood splintering and snapping, the thud of a crashing tree shaking the ground.

As suddenly as they'd begun, the blows stopped.

"Buona!" I finally managed to yell. "Someone's up here!"

But I didn't wait for her. I had to be able to tell Giovanni that I'd at least seen the horse of the trespasser.

I followed the still-echoing crash.

The instant I saw the tree, the only one among its brethren that had fallen, I stopped, locked in place.

Half of it sat at the edge of the mountain and the other in the air, a jagged edge of its trunk shooting up from the ground where it had snapped. But it was draped in moss and vines and white flowers, vegetation trapping it in place. The bit of bark I could see was black with age.

This tree had fallen years ago.

No, but it couldn't have. I'd just heard it.

I cast about in search of another tree that could have been the cause of the noise, but they all stood tall, unwavering, solid as the mountain on which they lived. Not so much as a lone branch had fallen from any of them.

"Sibilla," Buona said, suddenly at my side. "What's the matter?"

"The trespasser," I breathed. "He's up here."

The girl searched my face. "The one who broke the mill parts?"

"Yes, riding a horse. I don't know how he was doing it, but he was flinging—" But I stopped myself, for what could I tell her I'd felt? I didn't know how to explain it to her without sounding hysterical, and after the stain nonsense, she'd think me well and truly *pazza*. "Do you hear the horse? Perhaps we could still follow it."

"No, Sibilla."

"But you did hear it when you were up there with the mushrooms?"

She shook her head.

Something about the way she looked down at the ground, her lips thinning, made me frown. I kept my eyes fixed on her face, not wanting to but feeling the first prick of doubt. Because I'd heard the horse the moment

Buona had disappeared. The very instant. I looked at her empty hands. "You didn't manage to gather the mushrooms?"

"No. They weren't the right type." She looked up at me for a beat before motioning back the way we'd come. "Maybe we should return."

"Yes. I suppose so."

"And you should rest when we get back. I'll prepare a cup of tea for you."

She offered me her arm and I drew closer to take it, pushing the residue of suspicion from me. I was being silly, as usual. And that was exactly what Giovanni would say if I told him everything that had happened up here today, so perhaps it would be wiser to limit myself to an abridged version. If he kept things from me, it seemed only fair that I do the same.

"What a morning," I said, shaking my head.

Buona snorted and tugged up a trouser leg in urgent need of hemming. The movement shifted her shirt. From the corner of my eye, I caught a bit of color, something tucked into the piece of twine she'd fashioned into a belt.

I only managed a glance before it disappeared from sight again.

A handful of flowers.

MADDALENA
1596

"**W**HAT ARE OUR OPTIONS?" I said.

Florindo sighed and ran a hand through his shock of un-combed and unpomaded hair. The early morning light did nothing to lighten the darkness under his eyes, and he still had mud splattered over his tunic. I daren't imagine what I might look like.

"We don't have many." He gazed down at the ledger on the table in front of him. There were figures circled and scratched out, numbers written with hands that had shaken with so much grief they were nearly illegible. "We need to pay the investor back, either in the promised flour or in scudi, neither of which we have. That's before even worrying about the bank loan."

"And we don't have enough to purchase the wheat, either."

He shook his head.

Two loans on our shoulders and our only means of paying them off underwater. I was too tired even to weep. I sat back, my eyes snagging on the frieze I'd had made depicting the twelve labors of Ercole. Had he ever had to make gold out of cold autumn air?

I bit my lip, tracing the intricate plaster carvings.

Perhaps we'd not need to make it entirely out of air.

"Could we get another loan? A smaller one?" I said. "Just enough to buy the wheat we need."

"We don't have collateral, Maddalena, and we already have two large debts. No bank will take that risk."

"We do have collateral." I motioned around us. "This beautiful new villa, the mill, the land. They have to be worth something. And we don't have to turn to a bank, we could approach a private lender."

He frowned. "It's dangerous."

"Yes."

He shook his head. "You'd lose your entire dowry."

"It's already at risk, sposo. What do you think will happen when we can't pay the investor back?"

"Yes, but private loans are even less regulated, with higher interest rates. If we forfeited, we could lose everything."

I met his eyes. "I don't see what other option we have. There's jewelry and clothing that we can sell to start paying off the first loan but none of it will be enough for the investor. We need the wheat."

"But how will we pay off that new loan, then?" He tapped the ledger in front of him and lowered his voice. "We don't have much left for our everyday expenses. We'll have to dismiss servants in a few weeks if nothing gets resolved."

"We'll sell one of the fields. Some hectares of land or . . ."

And then it came to me, and I felt like a simpleminded child not to have remembered it sooner.

"The oak trees, Florindo. We have that."

His eyes began to widen. The smallest point of hope, like the tip of a needle, gleamed within them.

"The chancellor said we have hectares of them up on the mountain."

"That they grow like the heads of the Hydra," Florindo said, a smile rising to his lips.

For the first time since I'd seen the flooded fields, I felt I could breathe again. I glanced up at Ercole once more, high above us, and smiled. This might just work. I reached for Florindo's hand and gripped it as tightly as he gripped mine.

We could do this.

A door slammed in the courtyard, making both of us flinch.

Loud voices erupted, and the rhythm of racing footsteps accompanied them. Florindo frowned and rose, starting for the door.

"No, you cannot go in there!"

A dull thud and the door swung open to reveal a crowd of people, soaked with rain, dragging mud and leaves through the corridor and into the room.

"What is the meaning of this?" I said, leaping to my feet. "Who are you? And what possessed you to enter our home, uninvited?"

"It's your fault!" a man yelled, shoving himself forward, until he stood at the head of the crowd.

It took me a couple of seconds to recognize him through the film of rain and mud and rage: it was the man we'd bought the plow horses from.

"You've done this!" He thrust a finger at us "You've destroyed us! My barley field is gone, my house is underwater. And so are all of theirs!"

The crowd began screaming again.

Florindo lifted a hand in an effort to silence them. "I am sorry to hear of your misfortunes, but we've lost our fields, as well. We cannot help you."

"It's your fault!"

That was quite enough. I walked to the fireplace and took hold of the velvet bellpull, giving it a number of sharp tugs.

"Why did you do it?" a young woman said. Neither her voice nor her body held the anger of the others, just a slumping resignation.

It was the only reason I paid her real mind and did not leave the room. For I was not as kindhearted and patient as my husband. I did not acknowledge rabble behavior, and especially not when displayed in my own home.

"Do what?" I said.

"Dismantle parts of the dam. With all the rain that we've had, why do something like that? You had to know the dam wouldn't hold if it wasn't complete."

I shook my head, a frown cutting into my face. "I don't know what you're talking about. We've not dismantled anything." I stopped her next words with a hand. "On the contrary," I continued, "my husband reinforced it the very day we arrived. There is no one at fault here but the deluge."

The servant I'd summoned stepped up to the doorway and halted, his eyes widening as he took in the scene.

"We saw the dam, we walked right up to it," the young woman said and clutched at her hands. "There are entire sections of it resting on the bank, neatly piled. Bags of sand, too, sitting there, useless. Why remove them?"

That was preposterous. "You are mistaken."

"She is not mistaken, you foolish woman," another man spat out. "We all saw it."

That was entirely the wrong thing to say.

Like a great flustered bird, Florindo drew to his full and considerable size and strode to stand in front of the man, blocking his view of me.

"You do not address my wife in such a manner," he said, his voice tight enough to snap, "not ever, but certainly not after barging into her home. You will leave her presence."

The man scoffed. "No, I won't."

"You will, and if I ever see you near our home again, or trespassing in such a brazen way, I'll have the massaro pay you a visit."

The man's lips lifted into a leer. "I'd like to see that."

He was about to say more, but one of his companions halted him with a sharp look. That brief silent exchange made my pulse speed up, though I couldn't have said exactly why.

"Remove him," Florindo said, motioning to the steward and the other servant.

The man tried to shift away from their reach, easing backward, but he bumped into the barley farmer.

The steward grabbed his arm and dragged him forward.

"You've ruined us all," he said, bucking against the grip of the two servants, to no avail. "We have nowhere to go!"

Florindo turned away. He didn't see the man spit in our direction.

"We have nothing left for winter!" he shouted as they shoved him out of the room.

As if he had been the knot holding the rest together, the moment he disappeared from view, his companions started shifting apart, shuffling their feet, exchanging swift glances before lowering their eyes to the floor. The group collapsed.

"I suggest you all leave," I said. "And take my husband's words to heart. Do not step foot on our property again."

"Madonna, what are we supposed to do?" the young woman said. She held her hands out, open in supplication, like she expected my answer alone would solve it all.

I swallowed. "I don't know."

"But the dam was your responsibility."

"And we took it as such, I assure you."

She shook her head, lips pinched. "You've doomed us all, and now you won't even help us."

The realization of what she and the rest of them wanted struck me, then. *Scudi.* Enough to compensate them for what they'd lost.

I almost laughed. If they only knew the condition of our finances!

No, I'd not be bullied in this manner. We'd given them and their disrespect enough of our time.

With a curt motion to the door, I turned away to join Florindo by the table. There was scattered muttering from the group, but I heard the shift of clothing and then their footsteps as they started down the corridor. The voices of puzzled servants followed them.

I waited until the last of the sounds faded.

"We have to go inspect the dam. They surely misinterpreted what they saw, but I'd like to be certain."

Florindo nodded. "I can go alone. No need for you to get soaked again."

"No, sposo. I'll join you."

After the night we'd had, the last thing either one of us needed was to be alone.

He offered me his arm and I took it, the two of us walking quickly down the hall, through the courtyard, and out the front door.

The land that greeted us was a swamp. Wild black locust saplings lay on their sides, roots like fine tangled hair shifting in the wind and not even the stalwart ivy had been safe. Wreaths of it floated in puddles or lay suffocating in mud. They gasped at me, asking for help I couldn't give.

And still the rain fell in the same insistent beat of all the previous days and nights, showing no signs of weakening.

This time, I did shake off Florindo's offer to carry me across puddles, for he looked all of his forty years in the morning light, and we made it, shivering and dripping, but without injury, to the narrow passage to the dam. The first sight of the silent and empty tributary brought the tears I'd thought exhausted to my eyes again. Stones that sheets of river water had covered for decades now gleamed, exposed, and thrashed by the wind. A few small fish rested at the bottom, the raindrops sliding down their scales as if attempting to comfort them. It was too late, of course. No amount of water could save them.

In silence, we walked on and rounded the slight turn to the dam.

There were jagged pieces of wood everywhere. The force of the crashing water had split entire planks down the middle, flinging splinters as thick as my wrist in every direction, spitting bent iron nails even into the trunks of nearby trees.

I narrowed my eyes against the rain and looked across the river. I gripped Florindo's arm.

"Sposo," I murmured, because I couldn't find the rest of my voice.

He followed my gaze up to the opposite bank and I heard his breath catch. I clutched at my horned silver hand until I felt its raised digits digging into my palm.

The young woman had been right.

Piles of planks were carefully stacked on the grass, whole and un-damaged, together with coarse bags of sawdust and sand. At least a dozen of them, still wet but full. All of it set far from the edge of the bank and in clear order. Like one of the men had paused in the midst of work.

Someone had done this on purpose. Someone had sabotaged the dam.

"Who would do such a thing?"

My hands trembled with as much fear as anger. The culprit had planned all of this with care, with precision and purpose. The hate in their actions blared like a clarion call.

Whoever had done this didn't just want us ruined, they wanted us blamed, the whole region turned against us. And if this morning was any indication, they had succeeded.

The memory of those trespassing men in the forest returned, the malice I'd sensed that afternoon. Could they have done it, all of it? Were they connected in some way to the women from the cena, who'd perhaps decided they were not satisfied with destroying my grandmother's tablecloth or ruining of the Embertide stew? Because I was certain this was all related.

It had all started that night. It would even explain why the massaro had ignored our call of help.

Did my words and actions that evening cause this kind of brutal ret-aliation?

I didn't know. And what made it all the more frightening was that I couldn't begin to guess when, or if, someone filled with this much hate would ever be satisfied.

SIBILLA
1933

THE ANNOUNCER'S VOICE DISSOLVED into static.

I allowed my eyes to close, my head aching in a hollow way, as if the skull itself throbbed. I was too tired to fuss with the radio.

I would have liked to ask the local doctor if a mild sedative would be harmful to the child in the sixth month, but Giovanni had never gotten around to calling him, not even to look after his own injury. I wanted nothing too strong, of course, just enough to tamp down the horse's cries so I could sleep.

After the morning up in the oak forest, I seemed to have carried them back with me just as I had the pain from the invisible blows, because I'd heard those cries every night for the past two weeks.

Sometimes the noises would start after midnight and other times not until two or three in the morning. Sometimes they were shrieks and other times they were whinnies. And they went on for hours. I'd woken Giovanni the first two nights, but he'd not heard anything. He'd been so irritable the following days, claiming exhaustion, that I'd not done it again. If there had been more damage in the mill I'd have insisted, but whatever the sounds were, they'd not come nearer.

Not that there were new parts to sabotage. The last order Giovanni had made to Alessandria was taking almost a month longer than it should have. Another source of frustration for him. He'd even dismissed most of the workers for the moment because there was nothing for them to do.

I shifted in the mustard armchair and groaned at the throbbing in my temples.

If I could just manage at least half a night's sleep, I was certain I'd feel more like myself again. It was true that I did take short rests through the day, but none of them seemed to chip away at this coating of fatigue. Buona even refused to give me coffee, plying me instead with teas that she said were better for the child. She was likely right, but a cup of coffee now would have helped my head.

I took the light blanket folded on the armrest and spread it over my legs. The stack of logs that Giovanni had had cut now that we were certain we'd not have radiators this winter was just across the room, ready to replenish the weakening fire, but I didn't relish the idea of getting up. Buona could do it when she came in. Perhaps I could ask her for something for the ache in my limbs, too, since aspirin wasn't budging it. I'd had no bruises from the blows, but the pain was rooted in me. Bone deep.

There was a light knock at the door.

"Yes?"

Buona leaned into the room, streaks of flour across her forehead and on the ridge of her nose. "There's a man come to call. Piero, he said his name was."

I frowned. What was he doing here?

"He said to remind you he was the driver who brought you from the station."

"Yes, I remember him."

I glanced around the room, taking in the coating of dust on the squat walnut table in front of me and the soot marks on the mantle of the fireplace.

The buzz of the electric cables competed with the radio's static for attention. It wasn't the kind of reception room I'd dreamed of when I'd thought about living in a villa, but none of the other ones were much better. Buona could do only so much in the day and lately I had become a useless waddling creature.

"Do I show him in here?" she said, smacking a cloud of flour from her apron.

"It'll have to do, I suppose. Could you put another log in the fire, first? And turn off the blasted radio." I had to at least be able to provide a bit of warmth, if not luxury.

She did as I asked and then left to fetch the man. I smoothed out my still-uncurled hair, folded the blanket out of the way, and gathered as much of my tired mind as I could.

Piero held his wool cap in his hands as he stepped into the room, his head tilting to look at the ceiling, which, though stained in various shades of yellows and browns from water damage, still had carved cornices and friezes on display.

I shifted forward in the armchair and pulled myself to my feet. "How nice to see you, Piero."

He turned to me and frowned. A peculiar reaction.

He tightened his grip on his cap before giving me a nod. "Signora Fenoglio, please forgive the intrusion, but I was on my way to Ovada and thought I'd stop by and see how you and your husband were doing."

"That is very kind." I motioned to the other armchair. "Please, sit."

"No, signora, I couldn't impose."

"It's no imposition at all. You're giving me an opportunity to entertain, which I've not had the chance to do yet." A spell of dizziness made the room lose some of its definition, but I forced myself to smile as I sat back down. "I don't have much in the way of neighbors unless I count the trespassers."

"Trespassers, signora?"

The lack of sleep was truly making me loopy. He had no idea what I was talking about, of course, and I really shouldn't have even mentioned it.

I waved my own words away. "Just a bit of trouble we've had. Nothing at all to worry about."

"Shall I bring tea?" Buona said.

"Yes, please," I said. "That would be exactly the right thing, wouldn't it, Piero?"

He nodded, his eyes on his hands.

"I do apologize for the state of the place," I said once she'd left. "Everything is taking longer than we thought, and with only the girl helping me, it's difficult to keep up with the house's needs."

"Are you happy with Buona?"

"I am, yes." I frowned. "You know her, then?"

He hesitated. "Well, just in passing. It's a small region, signora."

But when she'd announced him, she had given me the impression she'd never seen him before. Like she'd never even heard his name before.

"If you'll permit me the question, how are you, signora?"

"Oh, I'm very well, Piero, thank you. Though I am moving a bit more slowly these days."

He cleared his throat and shifted his cap from hand to hand. "I only ask because, scusatemi, you are looking rather pale. Not quite as well as when I last saw you."

"I've—I've had some trouble sleeping, that's all." I smiled again. "And the sun hasn't cooperated much since we arrived, has it?"

"Perhaps you could ask your husband to go down to Savona, to the seaside, before the child comes. I'd be happy to drive you, signora." He looked up at me and there was an urgency in his eyes that I didn't understand. "Just to get away from the house."

"Perhaps. Though Giovanni is rather busy these days."

He leaned forward, hands tightening on his cap. "I don't think you should stay here, signora. You're not—"

Buona's entrance, all clinking ceramic, stole the rest of his words.

"What do you mean, Piero?" I said. "I'm not what?"

With a rapid glance at the girl, he shook his head.

"Thank you, Buona," I said, frowning, as I took the cup she carefully handed me.

The tea was stronger than usual, and it had a bitter edge to it that was almost unpleasant, a bit like burnt coffee. I glanced up at Piero as he took the first sip and found his eyes on me already. I smiled despite the grainy sourness scratching my palate. Like I had a dusting of sand in my mouth.

I took two cubes of sugar and dropped them in the dark liquid.

We chatted as we drank our tea, mostly about Piero's work driving people to and from Ovada and about the mill, and the bit of energy I'd mustered up for my guest started to fade.

Piero placed his cup on the table. "I really must leave you now, signora. I've taken up so much of your time." He stood and I made to do the same, but he stopped me. "Please, do not trouble yourself. Buona can show me out."

I hesitated, thinking of what Mother would have said if she saw how little effort I was making for my guest. But I felt mired in this headache, this exhaustion that had worsened despite the tea. I nodded and sat back.

"Grazie, signora, for welcoming me into your home."

"Anytime, Piero."

He gave me a small bow of his head and followed Buona out of the room.

I groaned and closed my eyes, trying to part the pain like a veil, get at least an instant of peace, but there was no shifting it. And the armchair's stiff back was offering no help. Perhaps it would be best if I tried to rest in bed, fully prone. The thought of closing the curtains and lying in a dark room, in silence, was enough to get me moving again.

Cradling the mound of my child, I rose and crossed the room to the door. The voices reached me when I neared the bedroom. They came from the courtyard, magnified by the height of the ceilings and the marble lacquer of the villa. Buona and Piero were talking, which would not have been unusual if they'd been speaking in the same moderate manner that they had been until now.

But they weren't.

Even though I couldn't quite make out the words, the agitation and tension of their voices clearly indicated that they were not exchanging the pleasantries of taking leave.

And that was what made me continue past the bedroom door, toward the courtyard and its vestibule. They were having a conversation like they'd known each other for a long time. Which meant that they had both lied.

Why?

I stood as far up on the tips of my toes as I could manage without capsizing and drew closer. I pressed myself against the pillar of one of the arches leading into the corridor, peering out at the two of them. They stood close enough to embrace.

"—plenty of that tea. It is all under control," Buona said. "It won't be a problem."

"You can't be certain of that."

"I'm being very careful, Piero. There's no reason anyone should ever find out."

He shook his head before shoving his hat on it. "It's a mistake and you know it. You have to realize it won't end well."

She said something else as she pulled the door open, but she whispered it and I couldn't hear the words over the sudden rush of blood to my head.

What did she mean? What was under control?

Buona closed the door and leaned her back against it. Her face was creased with irritation, her features pinched in a way that made her look a decade older.

I shifted, ready to slip out from behind the pillar and ask her about what I'd seen, get the truth about this, make her tell me what she meant about the tea, but I halted myself. Because what would that achieve?

I hadn't heard enough to differentiate truth from lie. I had no context. All I'd accomplish would be to put her on the alert, making it more difficult for me to learn what she was doing. I'd realized that much from the matter with Giovanni and his papers.

He would have told me to dismiss her, of course, but I couldn't do that yet. I couldn't risk being left alone now that I was finding it difficult to merely greet guests without collapsing, and I doubted I could drag Giovanni's attention away from the mill for long enough to get him to find me some other help.

No. I'd not let Buona know what I'd heard, and I would not dismiss her. I had to let her continue as she was while taking note of her actions. Once I knew what she was hiding, I'd make a decision.

What I'd not do, however, was drink a drop more of her teas. I was not that simple.

"WHAT DO YOU SEE?" Giovanni called.

I bent as much as the child in my belly allowed and squinted into the dark mouth of the millrace. "I don't see anything. The smell is atrocious, though."

Something had certainly rotted in there.

Giovanni spoke to the worker perched beside him on the bridge over the deep stone opening that allowed the deviated river to flow to the wheel. Only a light stream of muddy water trickled in. The flow was so constricted that Giovanni had had to allow a gap in the dam to give the water somewhere to go.

He took hold of a rope and began tying it to the new iron railing he'd had installed on the bridge.

I straightened. "What are you doing?"

"I need to see what is blocking the passage and I can't do that from up here."

"But you're not going in the millrace."

He gave the rope a sharp tug. "Of course I am. How else do you think I'll be able to fix this?"

"Giovanni, you'll get swept away if the water flows in!"

At the very least he'd crack his head against the bottom of the wheel. How would I help him in my condition? Only one worker was here today, and I wasn't at all certain that he and Buona would be able to fight the current for him. I'd never get to the telephone in time to make a difference.

"That's what the rope is for," he said, wrapping it around his waist. "No need for hysterics."

I leaned against the mill's wall. Buona drew a little closer, lightly taking hold of my arm as we both watched Giovanni climb down the side of the bridge.

My head began its low, simmering throb again.

He landed with a squelch at the bottom of the millrace and at his first breath began to cough. He pressed a hand to his face. I heard the hollow croak of a gag as he stumbled away from the dark mouth, pulling a handkerchief out of his pocket. He shook it open and tied it around his head.

He needed to get out of there. Why couldn't he understand?

Hands on his hips, he took a few deep breaths, facing away from the opening. It could happen at any moment, the current could slam through whatever was blocking its passage and drag him under, and he just stood there.

He turned, squinting as he looked up, and motioned to me. "Hand me the pole."

"I'll do it," Buona said and reached for the metal rod beside me. She knelt and allowed it to slide down the side of the millrace's bank, where Giovanni grabbed it.

The worker crouched on the bridge and looked at me.

"Va bene, signora," he said with a nod, hands tightening around the rope in a way that made me feel just a bit steadier. Although I would have preferred if he'd just started pulling my husband up, fist over fist.

Giovanni walked back to the opening and shoved the pole into the stone tunnel. Once, twice.

"There's definitely something here," he said. "Something rather large."

With a grunt, he tugged the pole back and raised it, sliding it right against the tunnel's top edge with a scrape of metal on stone.

All of that water was going to come rushing through. I could see it.

Giovanni brought his full weight and all of his strength down, leaning into the metal rod as if he were operating an uncooperative lever.

A suctioning, wet sound fell on my ears. A gust of putridity burned into my nose, setting my eyes watering and blurring my vision, so that at first I only saw the silhouettes of what poured out of that opening.

Giovanni exclaimed and leaped back.

I blinked.

And then screamed.

Four horse carcasses oozed out of the opening, their rotten legs tangled around each other, what remained of their black meat dropping off the bones in chunks, their hooves covered in layers of green scum. Their eyeless skulls were all bones and teeth. My stomach contracted and bile rose up my throat. The whinnies I'd heard every night for two weeks filled my head. I couldn't seem to catch my breath.

"Sibilla," Buona said, grabbing my arms.

"Would you stop making such a fuss?" Giovanni said. "They're just dead animals. And there's more of them, so I suggest you leave if you can't manage their sight."

A numbness had come to my lips so that I couldn't feel them move when I spoke. The blows I'd received on the mountain throbbed with the beating of my heart. "Those poor horses."

"What do you mean?" Buona said. "What horses?"

Had she gone daft? I jerked my arm away from her and pointed to all that death at the bottom of the millrace. "Those! Those right th—"

They were deer.

The carcasses I'd seen weren't horses but roe deer. There was even a crown of antlers on one of the skulls.

"No, I saw them," I said. I stepped away from Buona and peered over the edge, scouring the shapes.

My hands and head felt terribly hot while the rest of me was drenched in frozen sweat.

"There's only deer, Sibilla." She took hold of my elbow. "Come away from there; it's not safe."

"Buona, I saw them, I swear it."

She nodded. "You're very tired and you've had a lot of headaches the last few days. Your eyes got confused, that's all." She pointed. "Look, I think the water's coming through."

She was right. Two more deer carcasses slid out of the tunnel with a wet thud, garlands of bare bones adorning them, and a gush of water followed.

I held my breath as Giovanni leaped to the side, clutching his rope, and began climbing up the bank while the current dragged even more bones out of the opening. An entire graveyard of them.

My husband came to stand beside me.

We watched the water crash through the rest of the barrier, cracking skeletons and pushing skulls down with its force. It grew muddier and wilder and continued to pour into the millrace. Another deer carcass appeared, a flap of its hide snapping like a sail in the current.

"It's no wonder the water couldn't come through," Giovanni said. "Some of those bones look old enough to be from the time of the Caparalias, before the dam broke. I suppose they have to be, for there wouldn't have been enough force to have dragged them in there afterward." He bent, peering in at the still meaty carcasses that were rising slowly to the surface. "These are probably from the past few weeks."

"There are so many of them," I said.

"Likely a herd that got spooked by the change in the water, leaped in, and got swept downriver. They're notoriously stupid creatures."

"Poor beasts."

I could see him from the corner of my eye as he turned to me, but I couldn't look away from the lives the torrent had taken, not even to mind Giovanni. Something was pressing against me, an edge of that memory drenched in red. I could almost—

"Sibilla," Giovanni said, "look at the wheel."

I flinched and the memory disappeared. I turned to Giovanni, who was smiling for what I was certain was the first time in weeks. When I met his eyes, though, none of the smile reflected in them as they searched my face. For what?

The creak of long-dormant wood started behind us.

"It's finally working," he said, the wheel pulling his attention entirely from me with that one mewl.

Buona turned, following his gaze.

But I glanced down at the deer again, pieces of them now floating at the top, a flotsam of bones and rotten meat. I prodded at the red memory as one would an aching tooth. Nothing came.

Whatever had been there was now gone. Hidden. Buried.

"At least this one thing has gone right," Giovanni said.

"It's powerful," Buona said. "I've never seen anything like it."

I forced myself to look away from death and up to the wheel, which was turning as if it had been doing so without pause for centuries. Moss that had spent its entire life staring up at the sun now found itself underwater.

"It'll turn even faster," Giovanni said to Buona, who had drawn closer and was peering up at the structure on the tips of her toes, "when I open all the chutes that bring the water up to that trough there." He motioned to another long stone tunnel above the wheel. "The water will fall and fill the buckets on the side of the wheel."

"And that will weigh it down and make it spin faster?" Buona said.

"Exactly. Right now, the wheel is only turning because of the force of the water beneath it."

I couldn't help feeling a pinch of irritation. He'd never taken the time to explain the workings of any mill to me, not even bothering to show me what the function of the part he invented was. Why did she deserve an explanation?

I pressed a hand on my stomach.

Oh, but perhaps I was being unkind. This could be a good sign.

This could be how he would treat our child. How lovely it would be to see our son in his arms, staring up at this same wheel.

"We'll have to drag all those bodies and bones out," Giovanni said, calling up to the worker on the bridge. "We'll start now, but bring two more men tomorrow and I'll call for a tractor to come help us. I don't want any more delays."

"Yes, ingegnere."

He started to turn but hesitated, pausing to look at Buona again. "When the entire mechanism is working, I'll come fetch you so you can see it."

"Well, I'd like to see it, too," I said.

He cleared his throat and shrugged. "Of course, Sibilla. If you wish." He nodded to the bridge. "Now the two of you should head back to the house so we can work without worrying about you."

Buona bounded to my side like a colt and offered her arm to help me walk over some of the rougher terrain.

"No, I-I can do it. I'm fine."

"You're certain?"

There went that needle of irritation again. What was wrong with me today? "Yes, thank you." I made myself smile at her.

"I'll make you some tea, now, and something to eat. Would you like to have it in the music room?"

"Uh, no. I'll have it in my bedroom. I'd like to rest for a bit."

"Of course."

And though it was true, I did want to lie down for an hour or so, what I most wanted from my room was the solitude that would allow me toss the girl's questionable tea out the window to the ivy below.

MADDALENA
1596

T HE TWO FLASKS TINKLED AGAINST each other as I walked down the corridor to the children's room. I glanced down at the dark gray liquid in them, like watered ink, the spiced bite of the pine bark tea arguing with the black pepper and purple loosestrife, while above them the clear voices of Indian holy basil and moonwort rose in perfect balance. I sent yet another prayer up to the Santa Madre.

The moment Florindo and I had seen the black shifting masses of flies on the stagnant water, smelled the rot seeping into the land, we'd known there would be sickness in the region. We just hadn't expected it would be the bloody flux.

Or that it would touch our household.

I took care to knock as softly as I could on the door, and Giusto was just as careful in opening it.

"Vincenzo sleeps," he whispered.

I nodded and stepped into the room. The cloying scent of sickness seemed to cling to the very walls, easily overcoming the cinnamon and clove incense I'd ordered burned every two hours. I laid the flasks down on the table next to Giusto and walked to the chamber pots beside the window.

Pressing a handkerchief bathed in rose water to my nose and mouth, I leaned over them. There was more blood in the watery bowel movements than there'd been last night. I swallowed back fear.

"Mamma?" Francesco said.

I glanced up at my son and motioned for him to be quiet so that he'd not wake up his twin across the room.

It had not been easy to separate them once I'd realized they were both ill. They'd slept next to one another their entire lives, from their conception onward. Most nights in the same bed, legs twined together. Which was why it had been so easy for one to hand the sickness over to the other. If not for the alternating cramps and fevers that had been making it impossible for either of them to rest, I might have allowed them to comfort each other as they'd done in my womb.

Perhaps in a day or two, when they felt better. I skirted firmly away from the hidden *if*.

Taking one of the flasks, I walked over to Francesco and placed the back of my hand against his forehead. He was much too warm.

"My stomach hurts, Mamma," he said. "It won't let me sleep."

"I know, amore. I've made you something to drink that will help." I swirled the flask and tipped half of the contents into the water glass by his bed.

Francesco groaned.

"It looks rather awful, doesn't it?" I said. "It smells pretty terrible too. I'm not sure I'd be brave enough to drink it." I took a large sniff. "No, definitely not. But you've always been much braver than I."

His large brown eyes glistened as he looked from me back to the glass. "And it will help?"

I almost smiled. Even with a mind skidding with fever, he was ready to calculate whether the unpleasantness would be worth it.

"Of course."

I could only wish I were really as sure as all that.

He reached for the glass, and I helped him bring it up to his lips. His hands simmered beneath mine. If the fever didn't retreat soon, I'd have to place him in a cool bath.

Francesco's face scrunched up at the bitterness of the tonic, which I'd not been able to curb with much more than a thread of honey lest it affect the balance of the entire thing. I watched, expecting him to argue, but he kept drinking.

That, alone, told me how ill he felt.

As I'd slowly boiled the tonic last night and into this morning, I'd tried to pry out the source of the illness, but I just couldn't come upon it. How had it insinuated itself in here? Because I'd done everything I could think of to prevent it.

From the moment I'd heard that some of the mill workers had the sickness in their homes, I'd ordered all water boiled, even from our well, all vegetables and fruits cooked. I'd given every servant a large vial of rose water to use before sitting down to eat their own meals and a pouch full of charcoal and the same powdered cinnamon and clove incense I'd made for my children to burn in their rooms. I'd even allowed them half a day off so that they could bathe properly, without having to share the water. And still, the bloody flux was here, in this very room.

Francesco gasped as he finished the tonic and thrust the glass away from himself, toward me.

"How brave you are, amore." I brushed a lock of hair, slick with sweat, from his eyes. "I want you to drink lots of water, and when your brother wakes up, you need to help him with his tonic too. Show him how to be just as strong as you."

He nodded, his lips still pinched with the liquid's bitterness. "And Giacomo, does he have to drink it? Or Marcellina and Ugo?"

"Not yet." Hopefully not at all. "That's why I had them go to another room last night. So that they wouldn't get sick."

"Will they come in to play?"

"As you and Vincenzo start feeling better. Which is why you want to drink your tonics just as wonderfully as you did now and encourage your brother to do the same. Yes?"

"Yes."

I leaned and placed a kiss on his damp forehead. I started to turn but he grasped my hand.

"Do you have to go?"

The words drew blood. I wanted nothing more than to root myself by my twins' sides, pull them both to me, and clutch them until the illness burned itself out, but the potential investor Florindo was courting would be here at any moment.

"I have to help your father with something very important, but then I'll be back. And if you've behaved, both of you, I'll tell you more about that pirate I saw in Genova. Would you like that?"

His eyes widened and he nodded.

"*Bene*. Now Giusto is right here if you need anything, but do your best to rest."

I walked over to their tutor and motioned to the other flask. "When Vincenzo wakes, give him half of it. I'll have a servant come to remove the chamber pots, and I'll be back as soon as I can."

"Yes, mona."

Not for the first time, I was grateful Giusto's father had been a physician and had dragged the poor boy on his calls as his assistant.

I forced myself out of the room. I started for the stairs before the tug of my children's need was too strong to break from, wiping my hands with the handkerchief drenched in rose water as I walked. I could not allow the illness to send its tendrils through the villa. It had to be contained in that one room. In my sons.

Shoving the worry back as far back as I could, at least for the moment, I hurried down the stairs.

Even from here, the land's strange warping of sound made it possible to hear the hammer strikes and worker's voices coming from the dam's site. Now that the rains had finally stopped, the repairs could be tackled. Florindo and I would have preferred if they had been finished before this private lender came to inspect the property, but a substantial number of workers had fallen ill in the past two weeks. Despite the violent words that those of the region flung at us at every opportunity, we *did* understand that the faster the repairs were done, the faster the soaked, sick land could dry, but there was only so much we could do with just a handful of workers.

"Scusatemi, madonna," a servant said when I reached the courtyard, tapping lightly toward me. She bowed her head and held up the silver tray she carried, a single missive resting on it. "This just arrived."

"Thank you," I said and took it. I was about to slide it into one of my overdress's pockets to tend to later when I saw it was from Silvia.

I waved the servant off and broke the seal.

My dearest Maddalena,

If the roads were in better condition and half our grounds were not the consistency of zabaglione, I would be there in person to give you the blessed news: I am with child!

You are the first person I've told now that my physician has confirmed it. Not even Salvatore has the slightest idea, and it'll likely remain that way until at least a few more weeks go by. I know you will keep the news close.

I truly do not know how to thank you for the wonder of your tonics and of you, my dear friend. I send a grateful prayer up to our Dio every night for bringing you here, for placing you in my path. Or perhaps for placing me in yours.

As soon as our driver is able to dislodge the carriage from its mire, I'll be on my way to thank you in person.

Your loving, grateful friend,
Silvia

It was difficult not to smile at the happiness bubbling in every word she'd written. One good thing had happened in the last few weeks, at least. Now we just had to see if the pregnancy would hold.

The sound of a carriage reached me and I tucked the letter into my pocket before starting for the front door again. My right hand went to the red thread around my left wrist, one I'd subjected to the same bath of ginger, frankincense, and boiled mercury that had helped us with the previous investor. The sting of the welts the mercury had already caused reassured me.

"Oh, Maria," I said, stopping one of the women sweeping past me on their way to their various morning tasks, "the chamber pots in the children's room need to be emptied."

"Yes, madonna."

"Use the strongest solution of lye we have to clean them and, once you've finished, be sure to give the laundress your tunic so that she can boil it. Ask her for a spare one."

She bowed her head. "Of course, madonna."

I nodded and continued out the door just as a man in a rather virulent shade of mauve stepped out of the carriage. He lifted an eyebrow at the mud that overtook his boots the moment he touched the ground, and I saw the thought of retreating sweep through this face.

I'd not give him the chance.

"Messer Farris," I said, brightening my voice as I would have when entering a particularly unwelcoming Genovese sala. "You must please forgive the dreadful wetness. As I'm sure my husband mentioned in his correspondence, this has been a difficult season of rain for us."

Never mind that the mud had been here every day since we'd arrived, rain or no rain.

Florindo, who had been waiting for his arrival on the last stair step, walked right into all of the brown muck. "You are very welcome to our home, Messer Farris."

And now the man had no choice.

"Thank you, Messer Caparalia." He merely nodded in my direction, giving me the tersest of glances.

In just that one tight gesture, I knew the kind of man I had before me and what he expected me to be. Certainly not what I was. Florindo would have to take the lead today.

"Would you like to begin in the villa or in the mill?" my husband said, motioning past the carriage.

The man looked behind him, and I could almost hear his sigh of disgust at what he would have to walk through. "The villa, if you would be so kind."

I pasted on a smile and waited for the two of them to start up the steps, allowing them to pass in front of me. Florindo flicked his gaze in my direction as he did so, and I fluttered my eyelashes at him, putting on as accurate an imitation of female foolishness as I could manage. My husband pursed his lips and I saw that he understood.

He led us into the villa.

One benefit of having to act the subservient wife was that I could see every reaction Messer Farris had to what he was seeing. Every twitch was visible, even from a step behind. I could follow his gaze as he turned to look at sculptures or stared up at the fresco above the courtyard, I could see the boredom in the tilt of his head as Florindo expounded on marble and stone selections.

Despite knowing very well this had been my idea, I felt like an animal whose den had been invaded as I watched this boorish but wealthy man inspect my home. A primal need to hiss and growl filled me every time he stepped into a new room. Because I knew that he was transforming everything he saw into scudi. Putting a number on every polished door handle and carved corbel.

And he was thorough, insisting on seeing everything. The only two chambers I'd motioned to Florindo to refuse access to were the children's and my small cucinetta, for I couldn't imagine what he would think if he saw its contents. He did not look the kind to have read Caterina Sforza's Experiments. In truth, he did not look the kind to imagine women could write.

On the way back out, the steward and two of his men came forward at my discreet signal and offered wine, which Messer Farris took, and pear slices, which he did not.

The mill and dam inspection came next, neither of which seemed to cause much excitement. And that concerned me. If the mill, with its size and obvious, though silenced, power could not impress him, we didn't have much more to offer. Florindo's own silence as we walked back out to the carriage indicated he had realized the same thing.

"Messer Caparalia," the man said, coming to a stop, "I'll be as direct as I can be out of respect to you." He sighed. "The mill is not worth much, not in its current condition."

My jaws clenched enough to hurt.

"The land is unusable and the dam is still not repaired."

"But Messer Farris, that is why we've asked you here today, why we would like a loan. So that we can rectify these problems."

The man sniffed. "Yes, but you have to see it through my eyes, messer. There is no delicate way of putting this, so you'll have to forgive me for my harshness." For the first time since the inspection had begun, he looked at me. "Scusatemi, madonna, but this business talk is not appropriate for your ears. Perhaps you'd like to return inside."

I was willing to make a lot of concessions and play the role required of me up to a point, but this, I would not do. "I'm quite all right, messer. But thank you."

He glanced at Florindo, who just lifted his eyebrows in expectation.

Messer Farris cleared his throat, tight lines forming around his mouth. "Well, the reality is that if you were unable to pay back the loan, forfeiting it, I would end up with a property with which I can do very little. Even selling it wouldn't bring me the amount you've requested. I'd lose part of the loan, and that is not something I'm willing to do, especially when I can turn to other prospects instead."

"One moment," Florindo said. "The villa is newly built. Surely it has its worth?"

The man nodded. "The villa is certainly beautiful, and I would gladly offer you a loan with it as collateral, but it can't be for the amount you've asked for."

And that would not be sufficient. What we were requesting was the minimum we needed to buy the grain, maintain our household, and repair the dam.

"What amount did you have in mind, then?" Florindo said.

"Without added collateral, half of what you've asked. Perhaps slightly more."

We couldn't even purchase all of the grain with that.

"You are welcome, of course, to speak with other private lenders before deciding, but I doubt anyone will offer more."

That wasn't even an option, for none of the other lenders Florindo had contacted had bothered to respond.

It was then, facing the reality of our situation, that I made the decision to mention what Florindo and I had planned to keep to ourselves.

I disliked doing it, for I would have objected if my husband had done it to me, but I had no time to waste. Not even to consult with him.

"We have hectares of oak trees up on the mountain," I said.

The man's eyes widened and he turned to look at Florindo. "You have lumber?"

"Uh . . . yes." He cleared his throat, keeping his face clear of any surprise. "An extensive amount."

He scoffed. "Well, that would certainly change matters. Why did you not mention it before?"

"We didn't think it would be necessary," Florindo said.

"Could I see the trees?"

"Of course. Give me a moment to fetch one of the local workers to lead us up the mountain." Florindo did not wait for an answer but strode off toward the dam.

Messer Farris frowned and he was forced to turn to me. "You've not been up there yourselves?"

"No, we've been kept rather busy lately, too busy for mountain expeditions. I'm sure you understand," I said, making myself smile. "But Messer Cestarello, the chancellor of the region, told us all about them. Apparently, there is no other spot quite like it in the area."

It was impossible to miss the hard spark in his eyes.

Florindo returned moments later with one of the workers, a man in his forties who looked as if he continually had one glass of wine too many and whose tunic was dripping with river water.

He nodded his head at each of us, clutching his hat in his hands.

"Ilario has worked in this mill for two decades," Florindo said. "He knows the path to the trees very well."

"I could walk it blind, messer."

"Lead on, then," Florindo said, smiling.

With another deep nod, the worker started off toward the woods, paying no mind to the puddles or to the ground that seemed to give way under his feet, sinking him in muck up to his calves. I skirted the worst of them but still felt the cold wetness reach my hose. Messer Farris didn't bother to mask his groans.

I'd never taken this path into the woods, always slipping in from behind the garden instead, and it was not as easy to navigate. Not with all the pine trees that threatened to poke needles into eyes and other soft spots.

"It's rather a shame that these are not oaks," Messer Farris said, shoving a branch aside. "You would have a true fortune on your hands. Unfortunately, pine trees are rather useless except as firewood."

I bit back all the uses I had for pine bark, needles, and sap. Including the tonic to fight the illness wracking through my twins' insides. What would have been the point in contradicting this kind of man?

Ilario led on minute after minute, until birdsong replaced all sounds of the villa. He twisted to look at us every few steps, like he couldn't hear us stumbling behind him, softly muttering curses as our feet slid over slick pinecones the sun's rays had not reached enough to dry. We couldn't have been walking for more than ten minutes when he came to an abrupt stop.

"What is it?" Florindo said.

"The entrance up the mountain, the cave opening," he said, pointing. "It's behind those."

In front of us, three boulders that would have scraped the villa's ceilings stood pressed against one another, sentinels of stone. A fourth was tipped on its side before them.

They blocked the path. Completely.

"It must have happened in the storm," Florindo said. If I'd not known him since we were fifteen, I would have missed the tremor of dawning despair in his voice.

"Is there no other path up?" I said, turning to Ilario.

"Not that I know, madonna."

Oh, Santa Madre.

Messer Farris sighed behind us. "That is unfortunate."

"We'll get the boulders removed, of course," I said. "The delay will be only a matter of a day or two."

The man nodded, but he was already turning. "When the path has been cleared, send me a note and I'll return to inspect the trees."

My temples pounded. We were going to lose this opportunity. We couldn't afford to wait, not so much as another day.

"I'll be as direct with you as you have been with us, messer," I said, drawing closer to him. "I'm afraid we can't wait that long. Is there no possible way you can grant us the loan, the full loan, without having to see the trees this very moment? Whatever we can promise you, we will." I tilted my head and made myself as innocuous, as sweet, as I could. "We will sign any papers you need."

He looked at me, his lips poised somewhere between a smile and a sneer. I felt his answer before he said it.

"It's impossible, madonna. I sympathize, truly, but it is not my responsibility to correct the mistakes your husband has made with his finances. He shouldn't have allowed matters to get to this desperate point. Perhaps he shouldn't have bought this property."

The need to strike him was so great I clenched my hands to prevent it. This ignorant man, someone who thought me so insignificant he hadn't deigned to greet me, someone who knew nothing at all about us, laying judgment on my husband.

Florindo walked toward me, touching my shoulder with his.

"My original proposal still stands, however," Messer Farris said. "You can sign the paperwork today and get the funds you need. Then, when it is possible to see the oak trees, I can arrange for the rest of the loan."

I looked at my husband.

Little would have pleased me more than ordering this man tossed out of our property, but what choice did we have? It was either this or nothing at all.

I didn't need to do anything but press my lips together for Florindo to understand.

"That will have to do," he said. "We'll accept the loan with the villa as collateral and arrange for the rest in a few days."

"Excellent," Messer Farris said, smiling widely. He motioned to the path we'd forged through the forest. "It'll take me a mere moment to prepare the paperwork."

Florindo sent Ilario ahead of him to keep the man from cracking his head open or sinking into the bog our land had become, both of them quickly disappearing behind curtains of pine needles.

"Forgive me for mentioning the oaks, sposo," I said the instant we were alone. "I know we agreed to keep that to ourselves."

He shook his head. "It was the right thing to do. It still is. Though I'm not at all sure how we'll manage paying the first loan if we utilize the trees for this."

"We'll sell whatever jewelry I still have." Not that they would bring in much, because we'd already sold off the best pieces after the theft of last year's grain. "Gowns, too. I have some lace panels that are exquisite, and I suppose we'll have to reduce the number of servants. The newer ones, at least. Whittle everything down to the minimum."

He didn't need to say it. I knew it still wouldn't be enough to cover all of our debts. I slipped my hand into his as we began the walk back to the house. Worry gnawed at me. But perhaps this concern would be spooked away the moment we climbed up that mountain. Who was to say there weren't enough oak trees to clear each one of our debts?

Our fortune could be up there right now, just out of reach.

SIBILLA

1933

T HE DOOR TO THE STUDY clicked shut behind me. I paused, listening for noises in the house, but there weren't any. Everything was as it should be.

For the first time in weeks, Giovanni had been called out of the villa to fetch the newest mill part that had finally arrived at the station in Ovada, and despite the seemingly unending exhaustion I felt these days, I had latched on to the opportunity. With Buona in the mill sweeping and tidying up as I'd asked, I had the entire house to myself for at least an hour. It would have to be enough for what I needed to do.

I walked past the desk and to the wooden crate stuffed with our old household management folders resting by the window. Giovanni had brought it up yesterday from the room where we'd stored some of our things from Torino, which I'd found strange. Why would he want to have all these old papers at hand?

I'd not even realized he'd bothered to bring them.

"Let's see, then," I said.

My husband had always been meticulous with his correspondence. All of it. I knew somewhere among his papers I would find a neat stack of the letters we'd written each other when we'd been courting. Years ago, when we'd first married, he'd asked me for the ones he'd sent me to file both sides of the conversation together, and I could only imagine he had them arranged in chronological order. It was just his way. Father had been of a similar mind, so it was familiar to me. And his tidiness would make things a bit easier now.

I drew out the first thin folder, *Torino* written in my husband's tight script on the front. It held mostly bills from the past few years. Gas, electricity, water, butcher, and bakery debts I remember seeing him scratch off, his smile tight, when he'd sold the patent. The next folder had my name on it, and I flinched to see that it contained doctors' bills from the loss of the first child, bills from the long hospital stay after the second loss, and even the visit to the last doctor to confirm the current pregnancy. I would have liked to yank that paper out of the folder and away from the death that surrounded it, but Giovanni might notice.

Next were collected letters between one of his cousins to let him know of an uncle's passing, messages from the patent office, and even the messages he'd had in return to his inquiry about this property.

I went through three folders of detailed accounting without finding anything of note. With a sigh, feeling my head begin another bout of its aching, I pulled out the next one.

I almost didn't see it as it slid from between the pages of the deeds to the villa and mill. A telegram, misplaced. But no, because my husband was as likely to misplace paperwork as I was to end up in the movies.

It crinkled as I unfolded it.

It was a collection of wrinkles, like Giovanni had crumpled it in his fist. And more than once, by the look of it. I searched between the creases for the name of the sender and there it was again: Leonardo Pisani, the assistant engineer from the sawmill. But why would he be sending my husband a telegram when they'd worked side by side for two years?

Up until just a few months before we left? How strange.

Walking closer to the window, I smoothed the paper out against my dress as much as I could and raised it to the sunlight.

The postmark was from Milano and it was from eight months ago. All it said was, "I trusted you. How could you do it?"

I frowned. What could he possibly mean? Giovanni had always been more than kind to Leonardo. He'd been the one who'd hired him, fresh out of university and without much experience, entrusting him with many of the responsibilities of the sawmill. We'd even had him and his wife over for dinner.

And when had the man gone to Milano? Surely my husband would have told me if he'd been dismissed or transferred.

But now that I thought about it, I did recall how Giovanni had reacted when I'd asked about inviting the Pisanis over once more before we left the city. How he'd refused without any real reason. I'd found it peculiar then, but I'd been so busy with the preparations that I'd not paid too much mind to it. Whatever falling out they'd had, it had happened by then.

The shrill ring of the telephone made me yelp.

Santissima Madre, the noise could spook paint off the walls. We'd not been able to afford one in our home in Torino, and now I couldn't help but be glad I'd been spared these jolts for so many years.

I walked to the desk but stopped short of answering, fingers touching the smooth black handset. Giovanni would not want me to. He would say I was meddling.

But what if it was him calling, if he'd been in an accident or needed to tell me something urgently?

And what if it's Dottore Lupponi?

Swallowing, I lifted the handset and pressed it to my ear.

"*Pronto,*" I said.

The scream cut into my head, a serrated shriek that shattered everything in its path. A woman, clawing down the sky, the entire world, with sound. My knees and my arms shook with its power, the scream finding every cavity in my body to rattle through, and I knew I needed to pull the telephone away but I couldn't do it. I opened my mouth but found no voice to compete with that roar.

And then the sound shifted, like the woman on the other end had turned her head, and she gasped in a breath.

"Get out!" she shrieked right into my ear, impossibly loud, a throat-tearing sound. "Get out now, girl!"

The line disconnected with a dry click.

The telephone slipped from my hands and landed on the desk with a clatter as I staggered backward, the window frame alone bringing me to a stop as it lodged into my shoulder.

Dio, I'd recognized the voice. It'd been the woman from the radio. She'd given me the same warning, speaking to me as if she were right there, as if she knew me. Like she—

Oh.

I blinked as I spied the truth for the first time.

Hot anger rushed through me as the pieces slotted together.

The trespasser. It had to be, for nothing else made any sense. This was a concerted effort to drive us out of here, destroying Giovanni's work and frightening me in my own home with the radio, this call, the horse. That was their plan. It was so obvious now.

Yes, and it would not stand. They would no—

Sudden movement outside the window drew my attention.

A man was crossing from the side of the villa to the forest.

I leaned closer to the glass and narrowed my eyes to see if it was one of the workers. But no, he was dressed strangely, with a patched-up green wool coat and a drooping blue cap I'd never seen any of them wear. And besides, none of them were supposed to be here today, not with Giovanni being gone. It was just Buona and me.

This was one of the intruders, I was sure of it.

A fresh flare of anger got me moving, cutting through my headache and through my exhaustion, because this was the chance I'd missed up in the oak forest. I could get a look at him, perhaps even follow him so that the carabinieri could finally put an end to this.

I would have to deal with the Pisani message later.

Despite the urgency, I hesitated, considering whether to head for the mill to fetch Buona or not. By the time I waddled over there, though, found her, and the two of us headed for the woods, the man would be gone. And even if the sound didn't distort to absurdity on the property, he'd run off if I called for her. I couldn't allow that. What would Giovanni say if he learned I'd just permitted the trespasser to stroll about unimpeded?

There was nothing for it but to do it myself.

I started walking, moving as quickly as I could toward the courtyard, despite the child and the house slippers that pinched more each day.

I didn't need to get too close. All I needed was to see the man, just enough to describe him, and then we could prevent more damage. Giovanni's mill parts would be safe and the horse would finally be quiet.

The thought of a full night's sleep sped my feet.

I raced out the front door.

There he was, the blue of his cap slipping into the pine trees. Gripping the balustrade with both hands, I took the steps at a near run and followed the path I'd seen him take, walking onto the carpet of dry needles that led into the forest.

It was even more crowded with trees on this side, forcing me to duck under branches and pull on locks of hair that had tangled in pinecones. I cast about for that flick of blue again, but all I saw this time was a flash of it, like a bird's tail, as he headed deeper into the forest. He was probably going to fetch that wretched horse of his.

If there even was a horse. If the trespassers could infiltrate the radio, they could buy a record with the sound of a horse and play it over and over. Surely such a thing was possible these days.

I made to race ahead, but an edge of darkness came into my vision. I grabbed on to the nearest tree to keep from falling. A peculiar emptiness came into my head, like it had separated from the rest of my body. I'd never fainted before, but I knew, with an animal's knowledge, that I was edging on it now.

I tried to shake the feeling away, but it had its teeth in me. Damn it.

"Buona!"

My voice sounded so distant, I didn't know if I was shouting or whispering. But I said her name again and again, the forest closing tighter around me with every breath.

There was a thud next to me and hands on my arms.

"What's the matter?" Buona said. "Is it the baby?"

I shook my head, a mistake, since the trees began a slow carousel spin. "Dizzy," I said.

"Come on, we need to get you inside."

Buona tucked her shoulder under one of my arms and started pulling me forward, groaning under my weight and the inefficiency of my legs. All of me felt like stone. I wanted to tell her about the man, to convince her to run after him, but even my tongue had stiffened, the root of it feeling strained enough to snap off at the first syllable I made.

I clutched at Buona as she led us out of the forest. My feet half dragged behind me, my slippers scooping up mud.

A cramp made me dig my fingers into Buona's arm as I bent over with a hard puff of air.

It was a sensation I'd not been able to describe to my doctor after it had happened the first time, but which my entire body recalled with precision. It was the doorway to pain and loss.

"I think it's happening again," I gasped out. "Am I losing this child?"

"No, you're not. Take a breath, Sibilla. Through your nose, come on." She gave me a swift shake, as if she were trying to rattle the shock out of me. "Listen to my voice, all right? And breathe. You know what my father always says? He says there is nothing better than fresh air. That it can cure any ill. Well, at least he said that until he caught a chill one winter that left a hole in his lung. Sometimes when he breathes, he whistles. And for a few *centessimi*, you can get his lung to serenade you with any tune you like."

I exhaled, trying to grab on to her words.

"What's that song you always play?"

My midsection tightened and I felt a flutter, something shifting.

"What's the song, Sibilla?"

"It's . . . a waltz by Chopin," I said.

We walked past the mill.

"Can you hum a bit? I love hearing it."

I shook my head. I could hardly breathe, how could I possibly hum?

"It starts like this, right? Tell me if I'm getting it." She began the first few measures of the right hand, a shaky melody that became a bit less tuned with each note.

I could feel my fingers on the keys.

A whiff of my mother's scent, burnt sugar and butter with a scraping of vanilla seed, pressed against my nose. I could see her then, sitting next to me on the piano bench, an already purpling bottom lip swollen from Father's knuckles. Her jaw tight. But her hands steady as she played.

My voice was as crackling as French meringue when I joined Buona's, taking over the melody when she ran out of it.

The waltz ended and began again and then we were somehow at the foot of the villa, the tightness in my stomach only now beginning to ease. Not completely, but enough. My fingers started to tingle with sensation again and even my legs seemed to regrow their bones.

Buona must have felt some of the tension fade because she looked at me. "Do you feel somewhat better?"

"A bit, yes." My lips trembled as I gave her a small smile. "You knew just what to do."

"The song calms you. I've seen you play it against your legs when you're nervous." She readjusted her grip on me. "But we have to get the doctor here."

I hesitated only for an instant. Giovanni would likely disapprove, but I needed care. I had to ensure my child was safe. I'd never gotten to this point in a pregnancy before, so I couldn't be sure.

I gripped the balustrade, helping both of us up to the first step.

"Yes, you're right." I leaned against her. "Could you call him? The number is tucked under the telephone and . . . perhaps let Piero know, in case he needs to fetch him in his car. I think he said he lived up the valley and on the other side of the river."

"I know where Piero lives. He has a phone."

Of course. I'd forgotten they knew each other better than they'd told me.

"I'll call them both and then I'll make you some tea to bolster you while we wait."

I looked away from her and down at what I could see of my feet. Why did she insist on the blasted tea? "Thank you."

I allowed her to help me up the rest of the stairs.

She sounded so sincere and she was always so helpful, yet I found it difficult to forget she had lied and had hidden things from me. With such ease, too, that it was impossible to tell when she was doing so again. Just as Giovanni had. I would have liked nothing more than to be able to trust her, but how could I truly do so?

She smiled and pulled the front door open.

"You'll see that you'll feel even better after some tea. It'll soothe the child, too," she said, that hard glint coming into her eyes as she placed a hand lightly on my stomach.

I couldn't shake the feeling that she was just a tad too helpful sometimes. Her kindness, as saccharine as molasses, began lodging in the back of my throat.

"THE CHILD IS PERFECTLY HEALTHY," Dottore Mirenda said, placing the stethoscope back in his bag, "but your wife is underweight. From her color and the irregularities to her heartbeat, I would also add that she has anemia."

"What is that?" Giovanni said.

"A deficiency of iron. It is not uncommon in pregnant women. It can bring on fatigue, headache, dizziness, and a general sense of malaise."

I pulled the zipper up the side of the dress and tried not to exhale too sharply in relief. That explained most of what I'd been feeling lately.

Though not all. Could the anemia explain the stain I'd imagined, the carcasses my eyes had misseen? Because even the trespassers, clever as they were, couldn't have managed to make me see what wasn't there.

The doctor looked past me once again to my husband. "At least it is simple to resolve. Who prepares her meals?"

"Our maid, Buona."

He waved a hand as he snapped his bag closed. "Would you call her?"

"Certainly."

Giovanni left the bedroom.

This was my opportunity. I swallowed, fixing my gaze on my hands as I tried to formulate how to ask what I'd really wanted to know for the past hour.

By the time the doctor had arrived, Giovanni had already returned from the station and had, of course, been present throughout the entire examination, so I'd not had the chance to speak with the man about the other things I'd been experiencing.

"Dottore," I said, but had to stop and clear the nerves from my throat.

For the first time since he'd arrived, he looked at me directly. He frowned as if he'd forgotten I was in the room. "Yes?"

"Well, I was just wondering . . . can my condition affect my eyes? Is it normal for expectant women to see things?"

"See things? Like spots in your vision?"

"No, not—"

"That is perfectly normal, especially when you add anemia to the equation. It's just dizziness and it will fade when your iron levels increase."

He looked away as Giovanni returned with Buona, then picked up his bag and walked toward them. I clenched my hands together. The opportunity had disappeared.

"I want you to listen carefully, now, girl," he said, "because it is essential that you start adding a few things to her diet."

Buona bowed her head, flicking her eyes toward me for a moment before returning them to the doctor.

"She needs to have lots of green vegetables, broccoli and spinach and the like, as well as fish and liver. Nuts and seeds of all sorts too. And make certain that you include a small glass of wine with each meal."

"Yes, dottore."

"Do you need me to write it all down? Can you read?"

"No, dottore, I can't, but I'll remember it."

He looked at Giovanni, who nodded. "I'll remind her if she needs it."

"Excellent. One more thing, ingegnere," the doctor said. "I'd like to know when your wife saw a doctor last, and I'd like to have his name. Whoever it was should have seen the symptoms of anemia and could have prevented today's fright."

I was certain Giovanni wouldn't remember, for I'd gone on my own the last few times in Torino. He's been in the midst of making the arrangements for the sale of the patent and then for our move here.

I waited a few beats, but my husband only offered silence and a frown.

"It was almost three months ago," I said. "In Torino."

Dottore Mirenda's mouth tightened as he looked briefly at me and then back at my husband. "Is that true?"

Giovanni cleared his throat. "I would say it's closer to two months, not three. It's been terribly busy here, with all of the repairs and everything else that needed to be done."

He shook his head. "One cannot be too busy for the welfare of one's wife and child. She needs closer monitoring from now on."

Even from where I sat, I could see Giovanni's jaws clench, a flush rising to his cheeks. My mouth dried. I'd no idea what he would say.

But my husband just gave him a curt nod.

"I'll send you my fee in a few days," the doctor said, walking past him. "And we can arrange for another visit in a couple of weeks."

"Yes, dottore." He looked at Buona. "Would you please see him out?"

In the second before she bowed her head to obey him, I saw their eyes meet. Something in my chest crackled, like ice melting.

That's a familiar look.

I had to remind my body how to breathe.

She followed the doctor out of the room and Giovanni exhaled, turning to look at me the moment the door closed behind her. "You couldn't have waited until I returned from the station? You had to involve that driver, whoever he is, so that now he can tell half the region our business?"

I shook my head lightly. "I was frightened for the child, Giovanni. I thought I was going to lose him, just like the others." I hoisted myself up from the bed. "And the man's name is Piero. He offered to help me if I needed it, and today, I did."

"When did he offer that?"

"When he brought us here." I almost mentioned his previous visit, but swallowed the words before they made it to my lips.

His eyebrows lifted. "Well, I'll have to speak with him about taking such liberties."

I walked closer to him, brushing his arm with my hand. "No, please don't. It's all right. I am sorry, I didn't want to cause any trouble. I won't do it again."

He rubbed his forehead and sighed. "What were you doing in the woods on your own, anyway? In your condition? I don't understand how you can be so foolish."

"I saw a man walking about the property, going into the forest."

"A man?"

"I thought maybe he was responsible for the destroyed mill parts."

His eyes widened. "And your idea was to go after him alone?"

I bit the inside of my lips. I was explaining this all wrong and I hadn't even told him about the telephone call yet. "I wasn't going to get close, Giovanni, I promise. I just wanted to see his face so that I could describe him to the carabinieri and we could put an end to all of this."

"I've already told you I don't want them involved." He shook his head. "How many more times do I have to repeat it?"

"I was trying to help you."

"I don't need your help, Sibilla. And, for the last time, forget the carabinieri."

I turned away from him.

It just wasn't logical to me. I knew he didn't want to waste time with an investigation, but weren't we already doing that when he had to call for a new part and wait for the carpenter in Alessandria to make it and then to ship it here? Not to mention the cost of it all. There had to be something he wasn't telling me, perhaps something connected to the other matter he was keeping from me.

"Well, did you see him, then?"

Behind me, the door clicked open and I heard the clinking of a tray.

"Not his face. Just the strange blue cap he was wearing."

The crash sent a yelp up my throat and pieces of glass bouncing against my leg.

I spun to find Buona, the tray in her hands dangling loosely over a disaster of shattered glasses and red wine, watching me with the unguarded horror of a child.

MADDALENA
1596

THE TWO SERVANTS SWAYED UNDER the weight of the full buckets as they walked the last few steps to the river's edge. I knew they were not amused at having to do this kind of work when they were primarily kitchen servants, but there were gaps in our service now that I'd dismissed all the local help except for the workmen. They would have to be patient for a while longer.

"I heard about it, too," one of them said, setting her bucket of boiled water down. "It's getting troubling. I don't even want to leave the villa anymore."

A wise choice. With the bloody flux gaining the kind of ground it had in the past three days, the best thing anyone could do was stay away from town and from people who might be sick. I only wished I could prevent the workers from going home every night. On my property, I could control the water and food they ate, even how often they washed their hands with rose water, but how could I make certain that they were careful in their own houses?

At least I had managed to contain the illness here. Only the twins had it. And even they were growing stronger with every tonic they drank. With the help of Dio, His Santa Madre, and His plants, the villa would be free of it altogether in a few more days.

"It's even in the chancellor's home," the other woman said. "Everyone says his wife has it."

I sucked in a breath, pivoting to look at them. "Is that idle gossip or is it true? Is Madonna Cestarello ill?"

The two women exchanged a rapid glance before dipping their gazes to the ground. "Madonna, that is what we heard."

Why had I not heard anything? Received no missive from Silvia or from her husband? "When did you learn of this?"

"It must have been one or two days ago, madonna."

It was early still, then. I could help her.

"Good," I said. "Make sure the workers drink from the water in those buckets and not from the river."

The two women made hurried curtsies as I strode away from them.

At a close run, I went to my cucinetta and took two of the flasks full of the tonic I'd prepared yesterday. I hesitated.

I lifted the lid of the cauldron and peered inside. There wasn't much of it left, and I had, perhaps, enough ingredients to make another small batch. I doubted I could provide Silvia with a full treatment, not when my children still needed care.

I exhaled sharply. Some of the tonic was better than none of it, and it would at least take care of the worst of the symptoms. It would give her enough strength to battle the disease on her own.

Slipping the flasks into a leather pouch, I left the room and started for the stairs.

"Is everything all right, amore?" Florindo said behind me. He clicked our bedroom door shut.

"I need to take one of the carriages over to the chancellor's home. Silvia has fallen ill with the flux."

He walked toward me. "I'm sorry to hear that. You wouldn't rather send a servant?"

I shook my head. "She is with child and I need to see what she looks like to know how much of the tonic to give her."

"What you made for her worked, then?"

"Indeed."

Florindo placed a quick kiss on my forehead. "You are a wonder, you know? *Un angelo.*"

I scoffed. "I think a few people in the region would disagree." I looked up at him and tapped his chest. "Any news on the grain shipment?"

"It appears it will get here in two or three days."

"Excellent. I presume by then we should have gotten the rest of the loan?"

He nodded. "The men will be finished with the dam today, and tomorrow morning they'll begin removing the boulders."

"Bene." Standing on the tips of my toes, I kissed his cheek. "I'll go take this to Silvia and then we can go through my jewelry to see if we have anything left worth selling."

A clap of pain crossed his face but he nodded again.

I left him there and made my way to the stables where Spuma was, as usual, being as problematic as possible. The only groom we'd retained held the horse's reins as he tried to brush its mane, and the animal snorted and kicked like it was being branded with a blazing poker. How Florindo had so much love for this mad creature, I would never understand.

"I need to ride to the chancellor's home," I said, my voice barely cutting through Spuma's.

The driver leaped up from his stool and bowed. The poor groom only managed a nod before the animal attempted to nip him.

It was mere moments before the carriage was ready and I could only smile at the efficiency of the men. They could have served at any court in Genova. I'd not left our property since the rains had stopped, and the sight of the damage drew out a sharp gasp from me as I stared out the carriage window. There was stagnant water everywhere. In every field that edged on the tributary that had flooded. The river no longer flowed through here now that the dam was almost completely repaired, but, if anything, that appeared to have just made things worse. Because there was no longer a current to sweep the dozens of rotting animal carcasses away. How had no official taken steps to remove them?

Little wonder the region was boiling with fever.

The roads weren't much better. Here there had been obvious attempts to create canals for the water, with crevasses dug into the sides of the road, but the earth was already saturated with it. The carriage wheels trudged through what felt like porridge.

The chancellor's villa, up on a slight hill, had at least weathered the worst of it without visible damage. There were fallen trees nearby, making the progress up to the entrance a rough, turbulent affair that jolted me all over the carriage, but none of them had touched the property.

The nearer we drew, however, the more I noticed a stillness to the villa that I did not like.

No servants were waiting to help me alight from the carriage and none came to direct the driver to where he should wait. I felt my chest constrict.

Holding on tightly to my leather pouch, I left the carriage, walked to the door, and knocked.

Slow footsteps echoed through the villa too many seconds later and made their way to me. The door creaked open.

The man who greeted me had a tinge of yellow to his skin and the dull, off-centered gaze of missed sleep. I pushed back the urge to clasp my handkerchief to my face.

"Buon giorno," I said. "I would like to see Madonna Cestarello."

"I'm afraid she is indisposed, madonna."

"Yes, I am aware she is ill. Please let her know that Madonna Caparalia is here and that I've brought her something that can help."

The man's gaze found its focus for the first time. He stepped aside, allowing me to walk into the villa. "This way, please, madonna."

I followed his rather unsteady gait into a room crackling with a cheery fire, the gold-threaded brocade of a pair of exquisite blue armchairs shimmering in its light.

"If you would be so kind as to wait here, madonna," the man said.

"Yes, of course."

He bowed and left the room.

Apart from the chatter of the flames, the silence that fell when the man's footsteps faded was like a crystal dome closing over the house. A villa this size should have reverberated with all manner of sounds—doors creaking open as servants went about their tasks, the steward's voice as he gave orders for the preparation of dinner in the sala, even hushed laughter and coarse words echoing in from the servants' quarters. They all made up a living, breathing household.

This villa had the muteness of the grave.

It was a long while before I heard steps approaching.

The chancellor himself walked into the room, thin of lips, with creases on his skin that were much more pronounced than the last time I had seen him. He could have been a decade older than he was.

"Dottore Cestarello, how pleasant to see you even in these difficult times."

"Madonna Caparalia." He made no move to offer me a seat or even a smile. "May I enquire as to the purpose of your visit?"

There was winter in his voice. Something besides sickness had occurred. "I heard that Silvia is ill and I've brought one of my tonics to help her recover. Would it be possible to speak with her?"

"I'm afraid not. Her doctors have forbidden it."

Of course they had. They were probably also getting ready to do the worst thing that anyone could do against the bloody flux: bleed her.

I took a deep breath. If I couldn't see her, I would have to risk the dose, perhaps a little bit more than half a flask. "Since that is the case, could you please administer the tonic I've prepared?"

I reached into the leather pouch and brought out the flasks.

"No, I will not."

My hands clenched around the glass necks as I looked up. "Chancellor?"

"I will not allow a drop more of your concoctions to pass through my wife's lips. I'll not expose her to that kind of danger."

I frowned. "Danger? I don't understand."

"I've had a visit from one of your servants, as I gather most of the region has by now, a young man who told me that you are using unspeakable ingredients for your tonics. Blood and fluids drawn from the womb of a dead sow. Herbs with unpronounceable names." His lips curled up in disgust. "He claims that he has seen you make unholy bargains up in your cucinetta."

A flush rose to my face before quickly morphing into a damp chill. "Who dares spew such lies?"

"That makes no difference. I've forbidden my wife from having anything more to do with you and your family."

"You cannot possibly believe any of that! It's superstitious madness!"

"All I know is that there has been nothing but misfortune since you arrived in our region. The endless rains, the broken dam and the flooding, this disease that is rampaging through the countryside. Look around you, madonna. There aren't enough healthy men to remove the dead animals and more than half of my help is ill, delirious with fever. I expect to fall prey to it myself soon enough. And Silvia . . ." He shook his head. "After what your own servant has said, confirming all of the rumors we've heard for months, it is not too wide a leap to think that you've cursed our land with your presence."

That was enough.

I drew myself up as tall as I could manage and walked toward him. "You may think whatever you please of me, but Silvia needs these tonics. My own children have been drinking them, so I assure you they are perfectly safe."

"As were the last ones you gave her?"

I frowned.

"I found them, despite the attempts my wife made to hide them from me. She spent an entire night in the latrine, vomiting until she lost consciousness. Our Dio knows what that abomination was for, but I will not subject her to it again when she is already so weak."

"She did not tell you, then?"

"Tell me what?"

I held his gaze. "She is with child."

The bit of color he had in his face seeped away.

"Those tonics you found were to help her conceive and she knew exactly what to expect from them. I warned her of the effects they could have on her body and she was still willing to go through the discomfort of the process."

"Discomfort? She was close to death!"

I sighed. "I assure you, she is much closer to it now. As is the child within her."

He clenched his hands together, shifting his stare from me to the floor, as if the truth would be written on the golden mosaic flowers. "The doctors said she would never be able to conceive."

"The doctors don't know anything, especially about female bodies." I held up the flasks. "Salvatore, she needs these."

He looked at the dark liquid inside it, his lips pressed tightly, and I could taste his fear, as metallic as blood.

I held my breath, using every ounce of silent will I possessed to tip him over to his wife's aid.

I saw his eyes snag on the red thread I still wore around my wrist. His jaw clenched.

"No," he said.

"Salvatore—"

"No." His voice boomed above mine. "I will not let her drink whatever horrors you've put in those flasks. I cannot allow it. It goes against our Dio and the learned science of our doctors." He shook his head with violence. "We are not in the Dark Ages anymore, madonna, and I will allow no sorcery in my household."

He could have slapped me and caused less pain.

"I would ask that you do not return to my home or I will have to fetch the massaro, who is busy enough with his own sick child."

My cheeks burned as I slipped the flasks back into my pouch. I harnessed the desire to rush out of the room and try to find Silvia because I knew it would do no good. One dose would do little and her husband wouldn't allow her any more.

The damage here was done.

The chancellor made to reach for the bellpull but I raised my hand. "That is not necessary. I know the way out."

I walked to the door, each step a bit heavier than the last, for I was failing Silvia. Failing myself, too, but I didn't know what to do. "Please, Salvatore, at least do not allow the doctors to bleed her."

"They have already done so, madonna, and I'm certain they will again."

"Then your wife and the child she carries will die."

Before he could say anything else, perhaps even accuse me of threatening him, I left the room, blinking back tears as I made my way out of the villa and back into my carriage.

"Madonna?" the driver said.

"Take me to the massaro's home. It's a five-minute drive or so down this same path." If I couldn't help Silvia, perhaps I could save the Scappis' ill child.

"Yes, madonna."

The carriage started off and I sat back, clutching the pouch to my chest. The chancellor's words were barbs that I couldn't dislodge. He'd believed every single lie someone had conjured up about me despite having met me, having dined with me. How could he have taken the servant's words seriously?

The servant.

It wasn't difficult to suspect Antonio. I had no reason to think that it would have been any of the men who had served me for years in Genova, and of the newer help, only Antonio could be considered a young man. Only he had been problematic from the instant we'd met. If I'd not already dismissed him along with the rest of the locals, he would not have finished the day in my home.

Was that why he'd done it? As retribution?

The open fields that surrounded the massaro's smaller villa made it visible from a distance away and I felt a simmer of nerves. If Antonio had visited the chancellor with his lies, he would have carried them here as well.

Nothing to be done except face them.

The carriage didn't have time to stop before Madonna Scappi lunged through her front door, her husband at her heels.

Collecting myself as best I could, I opened the carriage door and stepped out. Or made to.

"You will not touch a foot to our land," Madonna Scappi said.

I halted, half my body still in the carriage.

"Have you not done enough? Must you impose more wickedness on our family?"

"Madonna Scappi, I've not done anything to you or your family and I don't intend to." I took a breath, ready to continue, to try to explain about Antonio and what he'd made up, but what good would it do? The massaro's wife had branded me the night of the cena and she would not change her mind. In any case, I had not come to clear my name.

I pulled out one of the flasks. "I've brought you something to help your child, that is all."

The massaro stepped closer to his wife. "You truly think we'd let our child drink anything you've made when you're the one responsible for all of this? You've cursed us."

I fought against the growing exhaustion I was beginning to feel. "I would never curse anyone. I've given my children this same tonic and it has helped reduce their fever and halt the blood in their expelled fluids. Please, accept it."

"Leave our home this instant," the massaro said.

I turned away from him and looked directly at his wife, extending the flask toward her. "Help your child, madonna."

She moved so quickly I didn't have time to flinch.

She snatched the tonic from my hand and swung it against the carriage's side, the white screech of shattering glass falling over me before the slivers did.

The driver exclaimed and leaped out of his seat, but I stopped him with a hand.

I was done here as well, it seemed. Everything I said or did would only be seen as an attack.

Without another word, I closed the carriage door and tapped the roof, urging the man to ride off. The lies had spread like the sickness, and I did not have the strength to battle them both.

I PLACED THE WET CLOTH on Vincenzo's forehead and smoothed out the thin wool blanket that covered him. The fever was almost entirely gone but I'd not risk a reemergence. Across from him, Francesco slept soundly, his breathing heavy and steady. I'd had to practically restrain him earlier to keep him from bounding out of bed and running off to find his siblings.

With a stifled groan, I sat back in the chair I'd been perched on for the past two nights. The unpleasantness of this morning tried to crash over me for what felt like the hundredth time since it'd happened, but I pushed it away. I'd thought of Silvia's situation the entire day, turning it over in my mind, recruiting Florindo in my search for a way in which I might help her. But other than sending up fervent prayers, we could do nothing without her husband's consent. She would either improve or she would not.

I shook my head to clear it of some of the worry. At least we'd wrestled one positive thing from the day: the dam was finished. Tomorrow, the men would be able to start removing the boulders blocking the path to the mountain, and when we received the grain, the mill could be set to work.

What I couldn't shake was the persistent feeling that all our plans were too precariously built. They were like the mill's grindstones, waiting for the slightest misstep to set everything ablaze. A horse's neighing rang out. The bang of hooves hitting the stable door.

I sighed. That blasted animal must have gotten out of its stall again. I'd have to speak with the stablemaster about reinforcing it with iron or adding yet another lock.

But it could and would have to wait until morning. I closed my eyes. I had time to sleep a bit before I had to give Vincenzo and Francesco their next dose of tonic.

It was the panic I heard in the next whinny that snapped me back to alertness.

That was not Spuma's usual tone.

I stood and walked to the window, making as little noise as possible as I pulled back the thick curtain to keep from bothering the twins.

I sucked in a breath.

On the hill leading to our drowned fields, the glow of torches brightened the night. Even from here, I could see four figures, their shifting silhouettes pressed against the orange light. And, like the fire cut through the darkness, their radiating hate cut right through the distance, to me.

A warning blared within me.

I ran out of the room, all pounding heart and steps, the horse's cries trailing me like a veil, and flung open our bedroom door hard enough to drag Florindo up from sleep.

"Maddalena?"

"There are people with torches on our property!"

The sheets snapped as he yanked them to the side and I left him to follow me as I continued down the corridor, down the stairs, and out the front door.

The chilled night was sharp and clear as glass, allowing me to see what was occurring on the hill.

The four silhouettes had become five. To a command I couldn't hear, they swung their torches down, joining the flames at the feet of the central figure, and the fire latched on, crawling up and up. There were no screams other than Spuma's. I didn't know what I was seeing but I'd not allow it on my land.

I raced down the colonnade's stairs.

One of the figures shouted as it caught sight of me and they all sprang into movement, the flames they carried flapping like flags when they took off across the hill and toward the forest.

My skirts threatened to topple me and I gripped them in a fist of cloth while I ran past the mill. Imitating that horrid night, I grasped grass and earth and pulled myself up the still slippery, muddy hill to the burning figure. Immobile, it crackled and smoked.

It was a creature of sack and straw and it wore a blue overdress with lace accents that were blackening and curling into themselves. It was one of mine.

"What is happening?" Florindo called from the bottom of the hill.

I could only stare at my overdress, feeling the residue of hate those figures had brought and then lit like oil. My effigy, in flames. But that wasn't what chilled my insides so much that I didn't know if I'd ever be warm again.

It was the thought that they'd been in our bedroom, in my very armoire, without anyone seeing them or stopping them. They could just as easily have slipped into the children's room.

"Maddalena!" Florindo said, puffing up the side of the hill, oil lamp in hand.

"This cannot go on, sposo. It cannot." I pointed at the wide lace collar he himself had purchased for me, already scorched black. "This is a warning."

His face tightened as he recognized what burned before him. "Did you see who they were?"

"No. I saw no faces, just their shapes as they ran off."

"Which way?"

I motioned to the darkness of the woods.

He said nothing but started across the hill toward all that blackness.

"Florindo, stop."

"I'll not stand threats to your life, sposa."

"But you won't find them!"

"I'll at least try."

He sped up and the forest swallowed him in an instant. I looked back toward the villa, but none of the servants had woken, not even Giusto, and I couldn't waste time fetching them. I couldn't leave Florindo on his own.

I ran after him.

I didn't know what he thought the two of us could possibly do against four trespassers. Between us, the most dangerous thing we had were the small scissors hanging from my chatelaine.

"Florindo, this is ridiculous. They could be anywhere in this forest, perhaps not even in it anymore at all."

"But look." He pointed to a drooping branch, one of its edges still smoldering. He pressed his sleeve against it until it stopped. "They've passed through here with their torches. We just have to watch for the traces they've left behind and we'll find them, we'll see who is responsible for all of this destruction, and we'll bring them to justice."

What justice? The massaro had not deigned to help us last time we required him and now the chancellor had deemed me monstrous. How could we achieve justice when we had no assistance from anyone with the least bit of power?

The more we walked, following the lamp's light down an uneven trail of snapped pine branches and burnt needles, the more I began to realize we'd already come this way just a few days ago. It appeared to be the same path Ilario had taken to reach the mountain. But that was irrational. Why would the trespassers choose a passage that offered no escape unless they turned back toward the villa? Did they not realize that a mountain would be blocking their way?

My thoughts snapped in two as something sharp cut through the sole of my shoe and into my foot. I winced and stopped.

"Are you all right?" Florindo said.

I waved his words away, steadying myself against a tree before reaching to pull the thorn or pine needle loose.

But it was porcelain that gleamed under the flame's golden glow.

Holding my breath, I picked it up from the soil, the shape of it familiar between my fingers. A shape I had longed to see as a child, perching on a chair to await the strike of the hour and touching it lightly as it passed.

It was one of the dancing peasants from Father's Bavarian clock.

Its base was cracked and part of it was missing, probably still attached to the rest of the mechanism. The top of the shepherd's crook had snapped off where I'd stepped on it.

"What is it?" Florindo said.

I held the figurine up.

"Is that . . . ?"

I nodded, wiping with fury at the sudden spring of tears in my eyes. Father had loved that clock and so had I. It was the second priceless thing I had lost since we'd come to this place, pieces of my youth, of my life, taken and destroyed.

Florindo drew closer and touched the figure as lightly as my childhood self would have done. He shook his head.

"It has to be that servant who's responsible for this," he said. "He must be one of the trespassers. He would have had access to everything, from the start."

He was right, of course. It would have been nothing at all for Antonio to take my grandmother's tablecloth, my overdress, and now my father's clock. Knowing the lies he'd spread, it would not have surprised me to know that he had been involved in the ruining of the Embertide stew as well.

The question was why. I had reprimanded him the first time we'd met, it was true, but that did not warrant this aggression.

I wanted answers.

"Let's continue, sposo," I said, slipping the porcelain peasant into one of my dress's pockets. "I would like to see that treacherous boy's face one more time. I want the truth."

We hurried on. But we couldn't go much farther. Soon enough, the mountain rose black in front of us and all torches, voices, and movement had been swallowed. The trespassers should have been trapped, but they'd disappeared.

"It's impossible," Florindo said, turning in every direction, the lamplight sending shadows scattering.

It certainly looked impossible, but these were people of flesh and bone. They couldn't have just vanished at will, so the answer was here somewhere.

I walked toward the boulders blocking our path, skirting them in search of an opening large enough for a human to have walked through. They were pressed so tightly together, however, that it was difficult to slip a hand between them, let alone an entire person. Not this way, then.

A murmur turned my head away from the stones. A sound like the ruffling of leaves.

It was coming from a clump of shadows pressed against the mountain's side. On my left. It was not a familiar voice, but it was plucking at me with weary insistence and I never ignored these callings.

Carefully, I stepped closer to the murmur.

It came from a patch of sow thistle, its butter yellow flowers heavy on broken stems, leaves crushed and already wilting.

"You poor thing," I said and knelt before it. "What happened to you?"

I sensed Florindo stepping closer and doing so as quietly as he could manage, for he didn't need to ask with whom I was speaking.

I tilted my head toward the thistle and listened.

It told me about the figures, the stomping boots, the floating fire, and the cold draft it'd felt chilling its uncovered roots. The draft that had come from behind it.

I glanced up at the mountainside in front of me and at the cascade of ivy that covered it. Conveniently.

"Can you raise the lamp, sposo?"

The instant he did so, I saw the lacelike border of singed leaves on one side of all that ivy and a dusty streak of black across the rocks on the other. Grasping a few vines, I pulled as I would a curtain.

A mouth opened up in front of us.

Florindo gasped.

This was where they'd gone: it was a passage carved right into the mountain. Through its center.

I looked down at the ravaged plant again and bowed my head, pressing a hand to my chest. "Thank you," I said. "I am in your debt. Can I do anything for you, to ease the pain?"

I listened to its weakening voice and nodded once before grasping the scissors hanging from my waist and sliding the blades around the few roots still clinging to life.

"I'm sorry," I said and cut through them. The voice stopped.

Florindo took my free hand and squeezed it as I cleared the sadness from my throat. "You are extraordinary, you know?"

Smoothing my dress, I stood and pulled aside more of the ivy, allowing a bit of light into the passage.

"No dawdling, Florindo." I tugged on his hand and pulled him into the passage with me.

It was narrower than it looked, so that we could not walk beside one another. I started forward but he stopped me with a touch.

"I have the lamp and I will not have you walking first into darkness." He shook his head, swiftly anticipating my attempt at objecting that he could simply hand it to me, and took the lead, the light raised high above him.

With a sigh, I followed. It was not my natural state.

Soon, it wasn't enough to walk in a line, but also sideways to fit through the passage. If it narrowed much more, we'd not be able to continue at all.

With an extravagant amount of puffing from my husband, for which he would earn a daily dose of brisk walking from tomorrow onward, we rounded a slight corner.

My eyes widened.

A cavern opened before us, all of it naturally formed, it appeared, except for the more than hundred wide stone stairs that had been built right into the cave wall. My pulse sped as I realized they had to lead up to the top of the mountain.

"I think this is the passage to the trees," I whispered. Still, my voice bounded from wall to wall. "Yes, look." I pointed to a larger entrance to our right. "That must be the path the boulders are blocking."

"But do you really think they went up the mountain?"

"I don't see what other option they'd have," I said. Except for the two openings we'd spotted, everything else was jutting rock.

Florindo lifted the lamp and walked into the cavern, each step revealing a bit more of the wide stairs. Loops of ropes hung down from the opening at the top of the mountain, buckets knotted to the end of a few of them, others tied around pegs wedged into the wall. A pulley system, but for what?

Something clinked at my feet and I looked down to find an empty bottle rolling away from me. Not too far away, a pile of rags lay in a heap that vaguely resembled the shape of a bed, and the stub of a candle sat on the floor beside it. Someone had spent time here.

The lamplight caught a shimmer of red coming from the wall above the rags.

"There's something there," I said.

The color looked familiar.

I didn't need to get very close to it recognize what I was seeing. It was one of my necklaces, one of the few I'd not been able to part with despite our need, the garnets glowing like drops of wine against the stone. Florindo's gift to me when we'd become betrothed to one another. I snatched it from the nail on which it hung.

Florindo met my eyes and I could see the same worry-tinged anger on his face that I felt. At least one person had been freely making use of our land, living right here, and then coming to our home at night to cause damage. With Antonio's help, that person had had full access to every room in the villa.

My hand tightened around the necklace.

Had it all been just to rob us, then? Sabotaging the dam, killing the doves, destroying the tablecloth, tonight's effigy, all to take my father's clock and the few baubles I had left? It was absurd. We had no fortune to steal. Antonio must have realized that the moment he slid his fingers into my jewelry box. They would have had better luck in the chancellor's home or perhaps even in the massaro's.

I tucked the necklace in my pocket alongside the broken figurine.

"Disgraceful," Florindo said, with more disgust in that one word than I'd heard him utter in all the years since I'd met him. "We must report him. He cannot be allowed his freedom."

What I really wanted was to see him.

I strode to the stairs and began making my way up as Florindo hurried to follow. We had little chance of catching up to the trespassers, not with all our delays, but perhaps we could still see the direction in which they'd gone. Anything that provided us with more information.

I realized only now that I didn't even know where Antonio lived.

Even with the help of the steps' width, my sides twinged with the effort of climbing them, my bodice sticking to me with sweat. Florindo's panting filled the cavern.

I clenched my jaw to keep from groaning as I took the last steps up and out onto the mountaintop. I looked up.

My gasp resounded across the hills and valleys of our property.

I'd been wrong. And how!

We did have a fortune to steal and that was exactly what the trespassers had been doing.

"Oh, Dio, no," Florindo said behind me.

There was nothing but the stumps of oak trees all around us.

I shook my head, pressing my hands to my temples as I tried to dislodge this tragedy from my mind and failing and then failing again. We faced a field of decimation, of ruin. The theft as sharp as an axe strike on our future, as those that had felled the hundreds of trees we no longer had.

If all the hectares were like this, we were lost. Santa Madre, even if they weren't, the outstanding debts would crush us.

My breath coming much too rapidly, I started running.

"Wait, Maddalena!"

But I couldn't and didn't, speeding instead through this first field, skirting the stumps, racing toward the far side of the mountain.

All about me, there were chutes of wooden planks, mazelike veins through which our fortune had flowed down the mountain and disappeared into other hands. Ropes coiled around axe heads and empty bottles. Laughter stained the air, and the lingering thuds of metal on wood, steady as a heartbeat, followed me as I careened toward the next field.

I almost fell to my knees with relief at the first sight of the towering trees.

We still had some hectares left. We weren't buried yet.

"Grazie, Dio," I said and crossed myself.

It wasn't everything we needed, but it would at least allow us to buy the rest of the grain.

I tried to catch my breath as I looked out at the darkened army of oaks, taking in the logs that the trespassers had left in the chutes, the tools dropped in proprietary clutter on our land. How had we not heard any of this, any of the trees crashing to the ground?

With shaking hands, I brushed the nearest tree trunk.

We needed to get those boulders out of the way, boulders I was now certain had not fallen into place without a bit of help, and we needed to rip these thieves from our home before they could continue. Because it was obvious they would. Wherever the trespassers had gone now, they'd be back to stealing what was ours if we didn't take measures to defend it.

"But how?" I said, gazing up at the sky. "What can we do to protect ourselves?"

The cold night and stars kept their own counsel, offering me no answer but that of an even colder silence.

SIBILLA

1933

TURNED ON MY SIDE WITH care, cradling the mound of my stomach as I adjusted, and pulled the bedspread up to my chin. Tomorrow night, I'd have to ask Buona about lighting the fireplace in here before turning in, and perhaps bringing in our hot water bottles. The nights were becoming too cold to just slip into bed without heating. Most mornings, a crackling layer of frost now covered everything, the sound of it melting, drop by drop, punctuating each dawn.

I winced at an especially high whinny from the woods.

Waterdrops in the mornings, horse cries through the nights, and the buzz of electricity through the rest of the day.

I didn't know how long the cries had been going on for tonight. An hour? Two? The minutes just folded into one another under the pressure of the noise. I hoped it really was a recording of some kind, otherwise a poor animal was being tortured out there night after night.

Giovanni had to be able to hear it now that he was down in the mill. Despite my worries and my fussing over the mounting cold, I knew he had made the right decision to set up guard through the night at the mill now that the workers had installed the new parts. Even if it was just a one-man vigil. It had seemed to work already, for these parts had been in place, intact, for longer than any of the others: two entire days.

I could see Giovanni's bright smile again when the rumble and creak of that wooden mechanism had begun, the gleam that had come into his eyes as he'd turned to me and pointed to the smoothly moving parts. He'd not even complained about having to drag out a new deer carcass from the millrace.

I tucked my own smile into the bedsheets. It had been a good two days. Perhaps the best we'd had in years, and not only because of the functioning mill. My own exhaustion had loosened its grip on me. Even though I wasn't sleeping more than two or three hours at night, I no longer felt as if I were close to swooning every time I left a chair. I didn't know whether it was the food that the doctor had prescribed or the pool of tossed tea soaking the ivy's roots outside the bedroom window, but I would ensure it continued in this manner. This child and I would remain healthy.

Another horse shriek seemed to light up the night as white as a bolt of lightning. Was the blue-capped man waiting out there for another chance to cause us harm?

It all still made little sense to me. What could possibly be the reason to do this to us? And Giovanni's refusal to talk about any of it or to telephone the carabinieri was equally baffling. Perhaps in a few days, if the mill parts remained intact and, with them, Giovanni's good mood, I'd ask again. Surely the carabinieri could set up just as successful a vigil as my husband's.

At the next whinny, I sighed and sat up. I wouldn't be getting any sleep with all that racket, and spending hours looking up at the ceiling was not a particularly attractive prospect.

"Let's see how your father is doing," I said, patting my stomach and shifting with a grunt. "We can at least keep him a bit of company."

I walked us through the silent house and outside, toward the warm lamplight coming from the mill. We'd still not been able to afford to wire it for electricity, but, although I wouldn't have said it to Giovanni, I almost preferred it as it was. Electric light would have felt off in there. Like an intruder. And it wasn't as if the mill itself needed the electricity to function.

"I hope you like this place," I said, nearing the door. "Maybe one day you'll be the one running it and—"

My voice disappeared as I realized what I was seeing through the window.

The dark form from the day of the accident that had broken parts and bones. Yes, but now it was double the size it'd been, and it had a vaguely human shape I didn't remember from before. It still moved in painful jerks, as if someone had slowed a moving picture's frames, its every shift making the lamplight flicker. And it was moving toward Giovanni, asleep in a chair.

I hadn't imagined it.

My heart pounding, I raced the rest of the way to the door and pulled.

It didn't budge. It couldn't be locked because we had no key for it, we'd never found it. No, that *thing* was doing this, it had to be. But why? What did it want with us?

I could have been filled with ice water and have shivered less as I wrapped both of my hands on the handle and tried again, but the door only groaned.

"Giovanni!" I slammed my fist against the wood. "Something's in there! Giovanni!"

I gasped as the lamplight pouring out of the window disappeared and I forced myself to turn to it, to look at what I didn't want to see.

The figure pressed against the window. As I watched, its hands curled into black claws on the glass and it began scraping at it slowly, the sound making my bones, my teeth, throb.

"Get out," it whispered. The rasping voice of something that'd been screaming for centuries.

"Sibilla?" Giovanni said, his voice muffled. "What's happening?"

But I couldn't shape the words. All I could do was stare at that darkness, even as the shrill ring of furious bells began, tolling as if to warn us that the grindstones, though still, were about to unite in explosive coupling with the flour dust.

"No," Giovanni said.

The form jerked back, out of sight.

A crash resounded through the property, rattling the window, the door, shaking everything within me. Another followed it. And one more.

"No!" Giovanni screamed. "No!"

It was as if my limbs had become packed with snow or straw or something entirely useless, for every move I made to again reach the door was weak and too slow. Images of Giovanni, bleeding, torn, flesh ripped from bone, shuffled through me like a deck of cards as I gripped the handle once more. With a groan, I pulled with every bit of strength I had and the door shifted, creaking open just enough to let me through.

The bells stopped ringing at the same time I stepped inside, like someone had clasped all of them tightly. The black form had disappeared just like the previous time, leaving nothing behind but smoldering destruction.

Pieces of wood were scattered in all directions, some scorched black and others still aflame, acrid clouds of smoke and sawdust scratching at my throat and eyes as I searched through the gloom.

"Giovanni?" I called.

I felt splinters cutting through my slippers and into my feet with every step, but it was a distant pain. Like a memory of it.

"Giovanni, where are you? Are you hurt?"

I shoved aside jagged pieces of wood that blocked my way and headed deeper into the mill. I coughed, pressing a hand to my mouth and nose.

There.

Giovanni knelt by a mass of shattered wood, his back to me, his whole body slumped.

I ran to him, grasping his arms.

Scratches riddled his face, wooden splinters lodged in his skin, soot marks and blood streaked like paint, but that wasn't what worried me. It was the dullness that the stray flickering flames allowed me to see in his eyes.

"Are you hurt?"

"I fell asleep," he said. "They were waiting for that chance to do this."

"No, it was something else. I don't know how to explain it, Giovanni, a creature of some kind, large—"

"What nonsense are you talking now? Do you really think this is the time for it?"

"I saw something in here. I saw it last time, too, with the burned rope, but tonight it looked almost human. It told me to get out."

He made a sound between a laugh and a sob. "They're not even bothering with subtlety anymore. It didn't look 'almost human,' Sibilla, it *was* human. Someone is trying to destroy us—I've told you."

"No, but who would do this? And why?"

"That doesn't matter! Don't you realize? They've managed it, they've won, because we have no more money. These were the last parts I could buy."

I frowned, blinking, the words I was about to say dissolving. Because that couldn't be right. He'd made a substantial amount when he'd sold the patent. It was true, we had spent more than we'd planned to on all of the replacements that had been broken, but it couldn't have been everything we had.

"I don't understand, Giovanni."

He jerked his arms away from my touch and leaped to his feet, the abrupt force of his movement tipping me sideways. I winced at the splinters that cut into the palms of my hands as I tried to keep the ground from hitting my stomach.

"You never understand anything," he said.

With a grunt, I righted myself.

"It's less work to talk to a wall."

"You don't tell me anything, Giovanni. How can I understand or help if you don't let me know what's happening? You can't blame me for that."

He stomped toward me, and all my muscles tightened. I wrapped my arms around my child.

"You want to know what's happening?" he hissed. "Why people are sabotaging the mill? Why we have no money left? Why someone is trying to scare us into leaving?"

Firelight flickered across his face, revealing the twist that rage had brought to his features. There was nothing there that I recognized. He could have been anyone.

"I'll tell you, Sibilla! If only to wipe that cow look off your face." He drew closer and I glanced down, like not meeting his eyes would somehow help me fade away from there. "I stole the plans to the part I patented. I didn't invent anything. I stole it all from my assistant."

The mill swayed lightly around me.

"Leonardo came to me for help with getting the patent, and I instead passed off his work as mine. I even had him sent off to a new mill in Milano to get him out of my way. Are you happy? Does it please you to know the truth? To see what a husband you have?"

He kicked a piece of wood next to me and it splintered. My teeth chattered together.

He had lied about everything.

"When Leonardo realized what I'd done," he continued, stepping away from me, "he made a fuss and I had to involve Dottore Lupponi. I lied to him, too, and he vouched for me. He signed an affidavit claiming he'd seen my plans earlier than he actually had, and then a new witness appeared, with a telegram Leonardo had sent telling him all about my offer to help with the patent. Dated and time-stamped. They had proof and we didn't." His harsh laughter tried to scrape skin off. "I thought by moving here, it'd somehow be over, but no. There's no running from this. I have to return the patent money. I should have done so already, actually, according to the notices I've received, and I have to finish paying off Dottore Lupponi's fees as well as whatever else he demands for vouching for me."

His hands were fists at his sides.

"The only hope we had was this mill, getting it running, and now that is gone. We have nothing."

I closed my eyes.

"Leonardo and his people found us here. They're the ones who have been tormenting us since we arrived. And they're well aware I can't fetch the carabinieri without revealing that I've defaulted on a debt that the court itself has ordered me to pay, so they'll continue doing this. I can't stop them and I can't pay them."

Exhaustion had seeped back into my body, a noxious weight that bent my knees so that I had to reach out for the nearest mill section to keep from falling. I allowed myself to ease down to the floor once again.

Giovanni had turned away from me, his hands clutching at his hair. "They have to be getting help from at least one of the locals, for they know the property better than I do."

The truth began to rise then, breaking through the fog of confusion I'd lived through for far too long now.

A local. And wouldn't it help if that person had regular contact with us? Access to the house?

It was the girl.

She could have done it all, the phone call, the recording of the horse, she could even have fashioned some way to get the radio to speak to me as it had.

But the black form?

I almost laughed. Now that I knew the truth about the patent, about the very real reason we could be targeted for sabotage, I had no doubt Giovanni was right. I'd seen a person trying to distract me and scare me, with roaring success. There was no need to fear anything otherworldly or fanciful was at play when the truth was even more frightening.

Someone of flesh and blood was to blame. Someone wanted us to suffer.

And the girl had to be involved. Perhaps even Piero. Why else would they have pretended not to know each other? Where was she now? She had to have heard the noises.

"Buona," I murmured.

Giovanni looked at me. "What?"

"It's Buona."

"Don't be stupid, she's just a girl." He shook his head, lips pursing. "She's got nothing to do with it."

I watched him, searching his face, his body, for something I couldn't put a name to.

It's there, if I could just remember.

"It's more likely that driver or one of the workers I've hired. All of them bastardi. Just out for money."

Wouldn't Leonardo have said the same thing about him?

Giovanni started to pace across the mill floor, stomping out the lingering flames, kicking away the useless wooden debris. Our future in fragments.

We would lose it all. Would we even have a home when the child came? Would Giovanni face jail time for defaulting? What would I do, when I had no occupation, no skills beyond what I'd learned at the sweets shop?

My heart couldn't find its rhythm and started skipping about in search of it, taking my breath along with it. I tried to focus on Giovanni's shape as he moved, but my eyes shifted around the mill, unable to settle on anything.

The silence grew and deepened. I tried to put voice to all of those questions, but it took too much effort.

"It'll have to be the oak trees, then," Giovanni suddenly said. "I'll have to sell them all. There's no other choice."

My mind clutched at his words, piecing together their slippery syllables. The oak trees up the mountain, that's what he meant.

But without them, he'd never get the mill working. These debts would never allow us to afford the investment of purchasing more trees. Or had I misunderstood that too?

Giovanni was nodding to himself, his steps already less frantic, his hands less tightly clenched. "Those trees might be enough to get me out of this mess."

The trees would save him, then. I felt a tickling need to laugh.

And I wanted to go home.

I eased myself up, wincing at the cuts I had on my hands and feet. It took me a moment to remember why I had them and why I was so terribly cold. My mind felt as thick as Mother's taffy.

I walked out of the mill, blinking. Which way was I supposed to go? Was it that path to our house or would it take me to the sweets shop?

I blinked, shaking my head. I felt my mind screeching like a nudged needle on a record, out of a groove and back on its track.

This was my home. There was no sweets shop anymore.

"Careful," I said to myself.

"Sibilla!"

Buona was running toward me, skidding just once on the ice but managing to stay upright. She clutched her coat around her, tucking something into its folds as she ran.

I didn't want to talk to her, not now that I knew what she had been doing. Despite whatever Giovanni said, I knew she was involved. I started toward the house.

"Are you all right?" she called out.

"I'm fine."

She ran after me. I could hear her panting at my back. "What happened? What was that crash?"

"Oh, is this really necessary, all of this pretending?"

She grabbed my arm, bringing me to a halt me and making me turn to look at her. She searched my face. "What are you talking about?"

"Just stop it. I know what you're doing." I lifted a hand before she could speak. "Don't even mention making me tea because I know you're putting things in it. I saw you with those flowers."

She shook her head. "Sibilla, wait, you don't understand—"

"I'm pretty sure I do," I said. "I'm tired of everyone lying to me."

Before I could stop it, a shiver racked my entire frame.

The girl looked down at the wet slippers on my feet, her eyes widening slightly. With a sigh, she slid her coat off and swung it around my shoulders before I could move away. "You'll catch your death out here like this. I'll light the fire in your room, but you have to put on some socks as soon as possible and get into bed."

"I don't want anything from you."

"Sibilla, this is ridiculous."

But I turned away as if she'd not spoken and ran the last length to the house and up the stairs. I'd had enough of lies. From everyone.

It was as I reached the music room that I felt a bulge pressing against my hip. Frowning, I reached into the coat. There was something inside the lining. I patted the edges until I found a cleverly disguised button and I unhooked it, revealing a pocket. Inside it were an empty flask and two apple cores.

The image of Buona as she'd run to me returned. How she'd hidden what she carried in the cloak. She'd been fully dressed, even wearing her boots, and she'd not come from inside the villa, but from behind it. There'd been no slamming door, no footsteps racing down the stairs.

She'd been out of the house when it had all happened, taking food and drink into the woods.

There could be no question now that the girl was involved. There was also no question that Giovanni would never believe me.

We'd welcomed our own destruction right into our home.

I GRIPPED THE BOWL OF polenta tighter as I stopped at the doorway to the large sala, the biting smell of something akin to bile making me groan. I should have known the smell would still be there.

I forced myself to breathe through my mouth, but it did no good. I couldn't eat in this room. I would have liked to sit in there and pretend nothing was wrong, but I couldn't.

I'd caught the first trace of the odor yesterday, and Buona had first assured me that she couldn't smell anything and then, when she'd seen I'd not believed her, no matter how many times she repeated the lie, that it would be gone by today. She would clean the entire room, she'd said. But of course, she'd been lying. Whatever their strategy was, whether to scare us off or harm us, this was part of it, I was certain.

Giovanni, for his part, smelled nothing, saw nothing, did nothing. He was allowing it all to happen right in front of him, and I didn't know how to make him realize what was going on around us. He had brought it all upon us with his lies and cheating, and now he was too blind to see Buona's role in it.

I walked to the music room with my bowl and closed the door behind me.

The fire was still crackling but it had grown weaker. I hesitated in front of it, taking in the dwindling stack of firewood next to it, and sighed. I'd wait a bit before feeding it.

I turned on the radio, welcoming the now usual static, and sat at the piano bench, my child pressed carefully against the edge of the keys. I made myself take a few bites of the polenta. For the past couple of days, my appetite had abandoned me almost entirely, but I knew I had to feed myself to remain strong for the upcoming birth.

It'd not been easy, though.

Now that Buona knew I suspected her teas and refused to drink them, I couldn't be certain she wasn't adding her plants to my meals. How could I trust her to serve me stews or roasted meats or crostate? No, now I only allowed foods that I could *see* had nothing strange cooked into them. If the polenta had had even a bit of parsley, I wouldn't have touched it. I'd not risk my child's life when I was so close to holding him in my arms.

And my caution was working, for I felt better than I had in months. I hardly needed sleep. A good thing, too, because that pitiful recording of horse cries continued night after night and I couldn't do as Giovanni did. I couldn't just ignore it or pretend I couldn't hear them. So I sat at my piano for hours each night, drowning out its voice with my mother's waltz and the radio's hiss until dawn came and I could rest in one of the armchairs for a bit. The recording tended to begin again around midmorning and then again later in the afternoon, but here and there I could peck at rest if I needed to.

With my free hand, I tapped lightly on the keys. I smiled at the rough calluses I was getting on the pads of my fingers. Mother would have been happy to see me practicing for so many hours.

The front door slammed shut.

I winced.

"Sibilla!" Giovanni screamed.

My spoon clattered against the bowl. I held my breath.

His stomping footsteps raced toward the music room and I wanted to leave, just slip out the window and flee to the woods, but my muscles refused to obey.

Giovanni swung the door open, sending it crashing against the wall, and came at me.

I gasped as he dragged me out of the bench, the bowl in my hands falling and shattering on the floor while I tried to find my feet.

"You useless, stupid woman!" He dug his nails into my arms and shook me. "Do you find it amusing to lie to me? Is it something you enjoy?"

I wanted to speak but my voice had done what the rest of me hadn't been able to.

"Stop it!" Buona yelled and was all at once there, her arms tangling with mine and Giovanni's, her hands yanking on his. "Have you lost your mind? Let her go!"

She dug her own nails into his skin and he did release me then, with a gasp of pain.

I scrambled back until I could tuck myself into the nearest corner and wrapped my arms around my child.

"What was the point of it?" Giovanni hissed. He swerved around Buona and drew closer to me again. "Why would you do something like that?"

The girl's trousers brushed my legs. "What are you talking about? Something like what?"

"Like telling me we have hectares of healthy, beautiful oak trees when that's nothing but a lie."

I looked up and met his gaze. I'd never seen such rage in it, and not only could I not grasp why it was directed at me but why it was there at all. Nothing he said was making any sense.

"We do have them, Giovanni. I saw them."

The taut stillness of an animal about to strike crossed his face a moment before Buona gripped his arm with both of her hands. His fist made it only halfway to my face.

The movement dislodged something inside me.

I couldn't feel the wool under my hands where they pressed over my stomach anymore or the trembling legs that were making the rest of the dress twitch. I could have been a statue or air.

Giovanni shook Buona off with a shout and kicked one of the armchairs, tipping it backward. "There are no trees. There are just dead stumps!"

"Buona saw them too."

Had I only thought the words or had I actually said them? I didn't know if I'd even opened my mouth.

But I must have, for Giovanni spun to look at the two of us. His lips rose from his teeth in a snarl. "Have you both gone mad? I've just been up there. I've seen it with my own eyes."

"Sibilla—" Buona began.

"There isn't anything except for dead trees!"

The girl turned to me, a deep frown cutting down her forehead. "Your husband is right. I didn't see any trees when we went up to the mountaintop. There were only stumps."

I shook my head. "You were with me and we both saw them. We even talked about how beautiful it all was."

"Except I never mentioned the trees, Sibilla. I thought you meant the view."

I seemed to plunge back into my body all at once. It was like falling through a frozen river's surface.

"No. You're the one who's lying," I said.

"It's the truth. There's been a blight on the oak trees in the area for a long time," she said. "My father used to tell me all kinds of stories about it, how there'd been trouble with the ones on this property, even before his own father's time. They fell ill, I think, and infected the surrounding forests."

"Of course they did." Giovanni's bark of laughter tried to draw blood. "Isn't that just my luck?"

Buona placed her hand on my arm. "I'm sorry but there was nothing up there except for poison parsley and a few other herbs. I didn't realize you thought otherwise."

I pulled my arm away. She was lying to me, doing her best to confuse me from the truth. I could even understand it because I knew she was working to sabotage us, but Giovanni, why was he lying, too? Why was he doing this? Had she gotten to him?

She has. I saw it happen.

I stepped away from Buona and walked to my husband. "I know the truth. The trees are up there. You're just saying whatever she's told you to say, and I don't know why."

I saw the disgust in his face as he searched my features. "I am rather tired of the mad wife routine. Are you so stupid to not realize we are ruined, Sibilla? Without those trees, we have nothing, not even enough money to buy the food we need to get through the winter."

There was a crackle of electricity from the cables above us and a whinny from the forest as he stepped closer, grabbing my arm. I flinched and dropped my gaze.

"We can't even sell this place, for no one wants a mill that doesn't work, land that is good for nothing, and a river that won't stop collecting dead animals. We have no options, no future, and you've decided it's the perfect time to start imagining things." He shoved me away. "I don't know why I married you when all you've brought me is problems. I should have left you in that sweets shop."

"You can't imagine how lovely it is to see you."

The horse on the recording cried out again. Oh, they'd hiked up the volume terribly loud today. I pressed my hands to my ears, feeling tears spilling down my cheeks. I could hardly stand it.

"Here, have some of mine."

"Sibilla," Buona said.

I hurried to the only protection I had.

As I placed my hands on the piano keys, I heard the girl and Giovanni saying something that I couldn't make out over the panicked animal. But I didn't care. This was the only thing that mattered.

They left the room at the same time that I began to play.

But this time a melody other than the waltz leaped from my fingers, something that took me a moment to recognize. A piece I hadn't played since . . . when had that been?

Since that dinner, the one Giovanni's assistant and his wife had attended.

Oh, I'd forgotten I'd played for them, sipping prosecco and laughing with Leonardo in between pieces, accompanying his own rather melodic voice in one of the more popular dance hall tunes. How pleasant that entire evening had been. Well, until—

My mind snapped shut over the next part of the memory. But my heart raced, drowning out even the recording, because there was something here that had reminded me of that night enough for my fingers to settle on that melody.

I looked at the door through which Giovanni and the girl had left. Yes, the memory had left a trace in the air, like perfume.

Easing myself up from the bench, I tapped lightly to the door, following that trail. Though the animal's cries were still raw in the air and I was sure they would cover whatever noises I might make, I couldn't help wincing at the creak in the floorboards near the door.

I shifted just enough to see out into the corridor.

Buona and Giovanni stood together at the arch leading to the courtyard. They were so close I couldn't tell if they were touching or not, but my husband was almost leaning over her. There was nothing casual about their faces, their stance.

I'd seen this before.

"No, I can't do that." Giovanni whispered. "It'll have to wait."

Buona shook her head with violence. "It can't wait. Don't you realize that?" she said. "It has to be now or—"

Giovanni lifted a hand to stop her next words. He paused, listening for a moment before bringing a finger to his lips. He nodded in my direction. "Sibilla?"

Wincing, I took a step back. I tasted blood and realized I'd bitten into my lip.

"Is everything all right?" His steps started toward me. "Why did you stop playing?"

"I-I'm tired. I want to rest a bit."

I took a deep breath and forced myself to walk out into the corridor, passing my husband without a look. Buona hurried to my side and tried to take my arm, but I shook her off and continued to the bedroom.

A low burning rage had settled in my chest.

It was easy to see it all now, every corner of the treachery that Buona and the trespassers had planned. To ruin Giovanni and destroy me by taking what was mine. My health, my home, my husband. And they'd try to take my child too. I was certain.

I met Buona's eyes as I turned to close the door behind me.

Well, I'd not let them. I would rip this girl out of our lives.

I would find a way.

MADDALENA
1596

MY SHOES CLICKED AGAINST THE stone of the colonnade as I walked its length for what felt like the millionth time. Where were they? They'd said they'd be here in the morning, and it was practically afternoon.

I clutched at my hands. It wasn't difficult to suspect that the massaro had lied to Florindo and didn't actually intend on sending any of his *sbirri* to help us. The man hadn't even allowed my husband into his home, after all, but had made Florindo speak of the thievery that we'd fallen prey to without allowing him out of our carriage. I supposed if I'd been the one to go request his help, he'd have sicced his hounds on me.

The irritation I'd felt when Florindo had returned and told me everything surged up again. The massaro sending his subordinates instead of coming himself to handle matters for a family of our ranking was an affront. It was not done. And I didn't believe for one moment that he was leaving the region with his wife and child this very morning, as he'd claimed.

The mill's wheel creaked, pulling on my attention.

I turned to look at the few men still carrying sacks of the new grain into the area we'd prepared for its storage. Dry and off the ground and large enough to hold the rest of it, when we managed to purchase it later this week. As soon as the sbirri left, if they came at all, Florindo would have to send a note to the lender to let him know the workers had cleared the boulders and that the oak trees were now accessible for his inspection. We could afford no more delays.

Laughter drew my eyes back to the path leading out of the property. Two men on horseback approached. Finally.

I hurried to the front door and opened it just as Giacomo lunged, scopperel raised like a lance at Ugo. The blue and red pinwheeled end struck my youngest in the stomach and he made a show of clutching at it as he swooned, gasping and gurling, while his siblings and Florindo clapped. Even Giusto was smiling.

The moment she saw me in the doorway, Marcellina made a quick motion to Francesco and Vincenzo and they pulled up the blankets they had allowed to fall to the vestibule floor. Willful beings, my children. But at least the twins had remained in the armchairs I'd had brought out, resting. A wise decision, for they knew very well I would have had them march up the stairs back to bed if they'd done otherwise. Until it was completely eradicated, an illness like the bloody flux was always waiting for a chance to claw its way back to roaring strength.

"Florindo, they're here," I said.

He nodded and started toward me, tapping the convalescent twins' heads as he passed and mouthing the word "behave" at them.

I could feel his nerves when he gave my arm a squeeze and walked out of the villa. He waited until the men had ridden right up to the stairs before raising a hand in greeting, one which neither of the sbirri returned. Not the best of beginnings.

"Messer Caparalia," one of them said, pulling on his horse's reins as Florindo made his way down the steps, "we were told you had concerns about trespassers."

Were they not planning on dismounting? Would they force my husband to speak up at them?

Florindo seemed to follow the path of my thoughts because he came to a stop a few steps off the ground. Level with the men. We'd been married for decades and his astuteness still managed to catch me by surprise.

"Yes, that is what I told the massaro," he said, "but, as I also told him, it has not only been trespassing."

"What else, then, messer?" The man's voice was without inflection. Certainly without a hint of interest.

"Intruders, a group which includes a man we employed named Antonio, have destroyed personal effects of my wife's. And, our most pressing concern, they've stolen lumber from our oak forest. Please," he said and motioned for them to descend, "if you'd follow me, I can show you exactly what the problem is."

"That won't be necessary," the man said. "The visit is really just a formality, messer, because there's nothing we can do to help."

What nonsense was this, now? I grasped my skirts and started down to join Florindo.

"I don't understand," he said.

"It's quite simple. There's no way to prove who has been stealing something like lumber. I assume there are no markings on the trees that might differentiate the ones on your property from someone else's?"

"No, but—"

"Then even if we scour the region for piles of oak, we will not be able to charge anyone with theft, for we won't know its provenance."

I felt all of me ruffle up. This was too much.

"Messers," I said, "that is a frightfully simplistic way of looking at things. No one is requesting you search the area for our lumber. We are asking that you help us catch the culprits in *flagrante delicto*, as it were. Surely that is not beyond your capabilities."

The sbirri exchanged a look. The one who'd been silent so far sighed and looked at me. I recognized him then. He'd been at my cena, sitting at the table to our left. I remembered the white scar on his cheek. "You suspect they'll be back, then?"

"Yes, of course. If you'd do as my husband suggested, as it is your duty to do, you would see the tools they've left behind, the logs they still have to bring down the mountain. You may even get a sense of who could be working with Antonio to accomplish such a horrid thing."

The man shook his head. "We are too busy this morning, madonna."

"Afternoon," I said. "You've arrived late."

"Exactly my point. There's too much to do with half the region abandoning their homes because of the flooding and the illness." He lifted an eyebrow. "I'm sure you know about all of that."

I felt my stomach dip as if I'd just dropped from a great height. They blamed us, too, like everyone else.

They'd not help us.

"Then perhaps you could order a couple of sbirri to keep watch at night," Florindo said. "That would be enough to frighten the people responsible and keep our property safe."

"No," the first man said. "I'm afraid that is impossible, as well, messer. We've had losses in our own ranks and do not have the number of men needed to handle private complaints."

It was my husband's turn to flare up with irritation. "Robbery tends to be a private complaint. Would you say the same thing if the massaro's property had been stolen? The chancellor's?"

"But it wasn't."

This was pointless. They'd not come to do anything but smirk at our circumstances.

"And Antonio?" Florindo said. "Will you not at least do something about him?"

The first man shrugged. "Do you have proof that he is involved? Did you actually witness him doing any of the things you claim?"

If I hadn't felt like screaming my throat to ribbons, I might have laughed. Because I realized now that even if we had seen him, elbow deep in my jewelry box or swinging one of the axes at a tree himself, these men would never have believed us. No one in the region would have.

"Come, sposo," I said, and touched Florindo's arm. "They will not help us."

"But what are we supposed to do? Just allow them to keep robbing us and destroying our property?"

The first man shrugged again before tugging on the horse's reins, turning the beast in anticipation of departure. "Perhaps you should return to Genova, where you belong." He made a sound in the back of his throat and the horse started forward. "It would be the best thing for everyone."

The other sbirro followed, tossing only one more look over his shoulder at us before cantering off. Like someone had flung oil into flames, rage blazed within me. I'd had enough.

This was a land of laws, wasn't it? We were as deserving of protection under those laws as anyone else.

"I won't accept this," I said and turned, racing up the steps.

"What are you going to do?" Florindo called after me.

"I'm going to see the chancellor again and he will have to listen. Someone has to take some responsibility!"

I had the first servant I came across fetch the carriage, and after a beat of hesitation, the two flasks of tonic I had left. It wouldn't hurt to try to help Silvia once more. Perhaps her husband had thought better about her health now that he knew she was with child.

Yes, logic had to prevail even here.

But as the carriage struggled with the muddy road, taking me once more to the chancellor's villa, the certainty, the blaze in my thoughts began to fade. If he refused to help us, what would we do? Anyone would be able to do as they pleased on our land without fear of consequences. How long would it take for that information to spread, for us to become the target of all manner of violence?

My hands shook as I knocked on the door and waited through an even deeper silence than I'd experienced yesterday morning. My skin tingled with the stillness of the place. Seconds passed, then a minute, and no one approached. I knocked again.

Only silence met me.

Something was wrong here, I felt it like a film clinging to my skin. I did hesitate for a moment, but if there was a chance I could get the chancellor to see me, to help us, I would take it.

Pressing my handkerchief to my nose and mouth, I gripped the handle, expecting the cough of a lock but not hearing it. I pushed the door open.

"Scusatemi," I called as I walked inside. "Is there anyone?"

Once more, I waited to hear rushing steps, to see a breathless servant ready with apologies, but no one came. And I couldn't waste any more time.

I followed the path I'd taken yesterday, my heels too loud against the villa's pulsing silence, my heart almost matching them. Every door I passed, I expected someone to come through it, I prayed someone would, but they remained closed. The hallways remained empty.

Of people, at least.

As I walked deeper into the house, it was difficult not to notice the rats that had found their presence through the grand hallways unimpeded and had grown bold. I had to walk around a chittering group of them as they lapped up the remains of a puddle I didn't care to investigate too closely.

But the smell that grew with each step I took was the worst thing. A mixture of rotten food and unemptied chamber pots. Of bile. It cut through the rose water with ease and it carried a tinge of something beyond illness in it. It was a smell that would linger.

Santissima Madre, how had this happened? How had this household buckled so rapidly?

If Silvia was strong enough, she needed to leave the villa. She'd never find health within these infested walls.

At last, I saw a set of marble stairs that were grand enough to belong in the sections of the villa that the owners would use. I started up, keeping my hands from the smooth banister. Thinking of the fire I'd have to request from my servants so that I could burn every stitch of clothing I wore.

The sound of a door opening made me suck in a rose-tinted breath.

"Silvia? Salvatore?" I said, hurrying down one of the passages toward the sound. "It's Maddalena Caparalia. I'm sorry for the intrusion, but I need your assistance."

I turned a corner just as the same servant from yesterday stepped out of one of the many doors. He struggled to keep hold of a deep bowl and a few washing cloths.

"Madonna, you can't be here."

"It's urgent that I see the chancellor. It's . . ." The words scattered and I grabbed at them at random. "We're in danger of losing everything and not even the massaro is listening. Could you let him know I'm here?"

"It won't be possible, madonna."

"But we have no one to turn to. We're all alone." I shook my head. "I don't even have to bother the chancellor. Perhaps, if she's feeling any better, I could at least talk to Silvia. She can intercede for us." And I could give her the tonics without anyone knowing. "Is she in there?"

I started for that door.

"No, madonna—"

But I was already slipping into room, sighing with relief at the sight of the gaping windows, curtains swaying in the cleansing breeze. This was what the entire house needed. Fresh air.

I crossed the private sitting room and stopped only long enough to tap lightly on the bedroom door before stepping inside. It was unseemly to walk in like this, but this could be the only chance I had.

"Forgive my barging in this way, Silvia."

Oh, but I wasn't intruding. Instead, I was too late.

Silvia lay pale and still in her dressing gown, hands folded in prayer on her chest. The silver cross she held gleamed in the afternoon light that rippled through the gentle movement of the curtains. She hadn't been dead long, but she was dead, nonetheless.

"The doctors bled her again and she was much too weak to withstand it," the servant said from behind me.

I squeezed my eyes shut. Salvatore should have listened to me.

And I should have pushed harder to see her.

"The chancellor ordered me not to even speak with you if you came, madonna, to have you thrown out if you walked in. I'm afraid he won't help you, even though . . . even though I know you tried to save his wife." He exhaled sharply. "She spoke well of you, madonna."

I glanced at him, blinking away the first few tears. He looked a shade paler than yesterday, his face tinged with yellow. "She was a friend, the only one I had in the area."

He nodded. "Madonna Cestarello was a generous and gentle person, always welcoming, and she will be missed greatly." He cleared his own tears from his voice. "But you really must go, madonna. The chancellor cannot find you here."

He started to turn away.

"One moment," I said, fighting against the fist of grief in my throat as I reached into my satchel. "You are ill."

"No . . . I . . ."

"I recognized the symptoms yesterday and you look worse today. Here." I held out the two flasks. "I don't have any more, but these doses will go a long way in clearing the flux from your body."

"No, madonna, I couldn't."

"Please. Why suffer through the illness when help is right here?" I held his gaze. "Let me help you. I couldn't do it for Silvia but I can do it for you."

Something in him shifted, for all at once he looked older and so tired I didn't think he'd be able to remain upright. He was more ill than he'd appeared.

Lowering his eyes, he gave me the smallest of nods.

I handed him the flasks. "Half in the morning and the other half at night, and drink plenty of water but only that which you boil."

"Thank you, madonna."

"And leave this place. Tell the others to do the same. The current condition of the house can only breed sickness."

"There are no others, madonna. Everyone who didn't die left days ago. Besides the chancellor, of course."

I frowned. The poor man had been dealing with this on his own?

"But I must stay to see to Madonna Cestarello's burial preparations," he continued. "I won't leave without seeing her laid to rest."

I would have liked to place a hand on his arm, offer him some gesture of comfort, but I dared not. He was too ill and my children too vulnerable. "Drink the tonics and boil all water."

"Yes, madonna."

With a last look at Silvia, I made myself turn away. There was nothing more I could do here.

The chancellor wouldn't accept my condolences even if I managed to get him to see me, and I couldn't bear the thought of another argument. Of having more cruel words flung at me and my family. Not today.

"You did all you could, Maddalena," Florindo said.

I forced myself to nod despite my own doubts on the matter, gripping the balustrade tightly, and stared out at the expanse of our land. The night was tight around us, stars and moon folded in clouds, the first tendrils of mist creating a haze around the flickering oil lamp resting at the top of the colonnade stairs.

"It's just the injustice of it, sposo. That's what eats away at me. She was not yet thirty and she was so very happy." I sighed. "None of this would have happened if that atrocious young man hadn't spread lies through the countryside."

But I wasn't even certain of that. Was that where it had really started? Or had it been at the cena where I'd made my first enemies? Or even earlier, on the day we'd arrived?

It was all an entangled chaos of events. Though I supposed everything was.

Florindo wove his fingers through mine and squeezed.

Blinking away tears that were entirely useless, I looked over at the two men standing at the door of the mill. They sat in the glow of their own lamp, twisting cords of hemp into rope.

"Are they reliable?" I said.

"Entirely. Ilario, whom you've met, and Nino, are the two best workers I have. I would trust them with my life."

And that wasn't too removed from what we were asking from them, for if anything happened to that grain . . . no, it was too distressing to even think about.

"I don't see Giacomo. Where did he go?" Florindo said, frowning. "He was right there a moment ago."

"He went into the mill. I'm certain he imagines I'll forget he's out here if I can't see him, that we'll go inside to retire, leaving him free to keep guard alongside the men."

He'd been trying to convince me of this through the entirety of our cena, urging his father onto his side as well, somehow thinking that Florindo would have considered such a preposterous idea any more than I.

He chuckled. "He should know better by now."

"Yes, he really sh—" I narrowed my eyes. Something was moving out there. "What is that?"

"What?"

I opened my mouth but the words vanished as a figure, no, two figures, shaped out of the night itself slipped from the shadows. They raced toward the sitting men. I had just enough time to gasp before one of the shapes swung something against Nino's head, the man dropping from his chair, crumpling to the earth with nothing more than a grunt.

Ilario leaped to his feet.

There was a rush of air from somewhere beside me and then two hands were shoving me forward, onto the stairs. I yelped, the heels of my shoes slipping against the marble, the force of the strike ripping my hands from the balustrade. I felt myself tip forward as a shape darted past me.

"Maddalena!" Florindo shouted, lunging.

His fingers latched on to the lace around my neckline and he pulled, the fabric groaning in protest but holding. He gripped my arms and pulled me back, against his chest.

A scream rose from below us, from the mill, and it was now Ilario who folded to the ground with a gut-twisting crack.

I could feel Florindo's shouts rumbling against me as he called for help, but none of it really touched me now, because Giacomo appeared at the mill's entrance.

He'd run out at Ilario's screams and he stood there, in front of those figures. I held my breath.

A gust of laughter dark with mockery swept through the night.

Then the figures started running, back the way they'd come, back into the trees, and our son gave chase.

"No," I said. "Giacomo!"

He didn't look at me, didn't stop or even slow, but raced right into the woods, right out of my sight.

I was careening down the steps before Florindo realized what was happening. My heart was trying to crack my chest open, Ilario's pain-soaked shrieks, my husband's calls, all of it muffled by fear.

They'd kill him. If he caught up with them, if he confronted them as he was bound to do, I would never see him with life again.

Every fear I'd ever had was compressed into this one horror. I plunged into the forest.

"Giacomo!" His name flew from me, wind-stolen, pine branches snapping at my face. The darkness was smothering. "Giacomo!"

I followed his voice like I had when he'd been an infant, trailing through the dark of the house to reach him before his wet nurse did, pressing him to my breast despite every cold glance the woman, heavy with milk, flung my way.

I could see him now, my brown-eyed cherub.

This wasn't happening.

"Please, Dio, please," I murmured and shoved branches aside, feet stumbling over rocks and roots. I heard a snapping and crashing behind me, and I knew Florindo was nearby but I felt more alone than I'd ever felt. Searching for my son through a lightless night.

"Giacomo!"

There was a laugh from somewhere ahead of me. "Your mamma is here, boy. Go hide behind her skirts before it's too late."

It was Antonio's voice.

"Leave us alone!" Giacomo shouted. "You have no right to do this!"

"Come say that a bit closer, boy, or are you as much of a coward as you look?"

My son made a sound of pure rage and there was the crunch of branches and dried leaves. Holding my breath, I raced toward the noise, my gaze digging into the darkness, but I couldn't see anything.

A metallic snap echoed through the woods.

Giacomo's first agonized scream could have been a hammer to my knees. My legs stopped on their own, refusing to take me farther, and I began to shake under the onslaught of a drenching cold sweat.

"That is unfortunate. What now, boy? Have you learned your lesson or do you need another one?"

Giacomo screamed again.

And I was just standing here, uselessly.

"Stop!" I called, ripping myself out of my paralysis like ripping a plant from the earth and running once more toward the violence. "Leave him alone!"

Antonio laughed again and the sound was all at once close. Too close.

A hand latched around my wrist and squeezed, fingernails cutting into my skin. "Or what, madonna? What do you plan to do to me?" He drew closer, until I could feel his breath on my face. "Who exactly do you think you are, woman?"

Ahead of me, Giacomo's raw scream split in two and I heard the clatter of a falling body.

A growl clawed its way out of my throat and I shoved my elbow into Antonio's side, rushing forward, all of me leaping toward my now silent child. But he pulled on my arm and swung me to the side with ease. My back slammed against a tree trunk and I groaned as the pain rippled through me.

"Oh, you'll learn your place soon enough," Antonio said, releasing my wrist. "You all will."

Through the furious pounding in my head, I heard him move away and start walking deeper into the woods. In seconds, the crunch of his steps faded, silence falling like a weight on me.

"Giacomo," I whispered.

My legs quivered as I lurched forward and forced them to obey me, to lead me to my firstborn.

The tip of my foot struck something heavy.

Holding my breath, I bent and touched it, my hand jerking back at the chilled metal that it found under my fingers.

"Maddalena!"

"I'm here." I squinted against the blackness and traced the shape of what was in front of me. It was large and solid. Had I seen anything of this size the last time I'd been in the woods?

My shaking fingers trailed up and brushed against warm wetness. Its viscosity made my temples start to pound but I continued up.

The metal, narrowing to points, ended in flesh whose very feel I recognized. Iron teeth were buried in Giacomo's calf.

"Florindo," I called, or tried to because my throat was filled with sand-like fear. "Florindo, he's here."

I knelt beside my son and scrambled up his body until I found his chest, the rise and fall of it wrenching a sob from my own. My hands clenched around his tunic.

"Maddalena, where are you?"

"I found him! He's injured but alive."

Florindo hurtled through nearby branches and then he was there, his silhouette a shade darker than the night.

"Is he all right? What happened?"

"It's an animal trap. He lost consciousness."

"They led him right to it."

I tightened my grip on my son. Antonio had provoked him, taunting him forward. The trespassers had placed this trap here. "Yes."

I felt the flare of Florindo's rage as it met mine. I half expected the pine trees around us to catch fire under the force of it.

"We need to release his foot," he said, kneeling on the opposite side of our son.

"How?"

I saw him shuffle, the shadow of his hand wiping at his face. "I think we have to pull down on both sides of the trap, at the same time, to release the springs. But I'm . . . I don't know for certain."

I heard what he was thinking in the tremor in his voice: that any of the men he'd been acquainted with in Genova, those who had tossed invitations for hunting parties at him for years and which he'd always declined, would have known what to do. "I can't stalk and kill animals for sport, Maddalena. It's brutal," he'd always said.

But brutality was what we now faced.

Beneath my hands, Giacomo began trembling. The loss of blood and the pain were pummeling his thin frame.

I gripped Florindo's arm. "We have to try. We need to get him back to the house, quickly."

He took a deep, shuddering breath and shifted, placing his hands on the trap. "Can you find the top of the jaw, the one on your side?"

I touched the teeth wet with my son's blood and followed them up, feeling the contours of the metal monstrosity. "Yes, I have it."

"We have to push both sides away from his leg."

I could feel his eyes on me.

There was no time to hesitate and think about what could go wrong if that wasn't how the trap was sprung. "I'm ready, sposo."

"On three, then, yes?"

"Yes."

"One." I heard him swallow. "Two."

My entire body tensed.

"Three."

I pulled on the metal jaw with every bit of strength I had and then stole more from the air itself. Something in my arm twinged in protest as the trap screeched with a voice full of rust, but I would have torn myself to strips of flesh if it'd been necessary.

It began to open.

"It's working, Maddalena. Keep pushing!"

Grunting, I pressed down. More and then more.

The spring clinking into place as the trap opened wide was one of the most beautiful sounds I'd ever heard. Without allowing myself more than a breath, I gripped my son's mangled leg and shifted it away from all of those steel teeth. My hands were already slick with his blood.

"He's free," I said.

Florindo leaped to his feet and hurried to my side. I felt him slide his hands under our son's arms and legs, lifting him as if he were an infant again, fallen asleep far from his bed.

I held Giacomo's injured leg so that it would not bounce with the movement as we started off back to the house at as near a run as either of us dared, for we didn't know what was broken or shattered. What could be further destroyed by the jostling of terrified parents.

"They set this up, all of it. They goaded him," I said. "They were looking for violence, to hurt as many as possible."

"Creatures from the very bowels of hell," he murmured.

Giacomo stirred in his arms, letting out a whimper that at once began tipping over into a wail.

"We're taking you home, amore. You'll be all right." I gripped one of his hands. "Just hold on a bit more."

"I sent for the doctor, Giacomo," Florindo said. "He'll be on his way to the house by now, too, and he'll help you."

The same doctor who had bled Silvia to death. I gritted my teeth and tried to shake that thought from my mind. Tomorrow, I'd have a servant fetch another physician, from Torino or Alessandria, but for tonight, the man stewed in superstition would have to do. Neither my husband nor I would allow him any absurdities.

Florindo stumbled over something in his path and Giacomo let out a howl. He tried to reach down to his leg, grasping for it like he could piece the bones and flesh back together, but I stopped him.

"Mamma," he cried, clutching at my hand.

He didn't sound fourteen but four, and I could have eaten the people who had done this to him whole. "I know, amore. It's just a bit more and then I can give you something for the pain."

Finally, the glowing oil of the lamps cut through the darkness.

"There!" one of shapes waiting for us said, pointing our way.

Flames bobbed toward us, servants appearing and reaching out for Giacomo, muttering among each other, women rushing off to boil water without requiring a word from me. It was all a flurry of perfect activity that I knew I should have been part of, but couldn't be, for I didn't know how to separate myself from our suffering child.

We took him to the kitchen and Florindo and I eased him down onto one of the kneading tables, but still I couldn't release his hand. He was breathing rapidly and his wide eyes, glowing with fear, couldn't find a place to land on.

A groan drew my gaze across the room, to where Ilario lay on another table, his face crumpled with pain as he clutched at his own mangled leg.

"And the other man, Nino, what happened to him?" I said to one of the women stoking the hearth's fire. Her name slipped away from me.

"He's all right, madonna. He received a blow to the head, but he's already conscious."

I sighed with relief. There had been no deaths, then. Not tonight.

But there was plenty of pain, and that was something I could remedy. "Do you know where my cucinetta is?"

The woman nodded.

"Would you please fetch a glass bottle that has 'Poppy Pods' written on it?"

"Of course, madonna."

"Thank you."

She hurried off and I turned back to Giacomo, who was biting his lips to keep from screaming as one of the men carefully cut off the left leg of his breeches. For the first time, I took in his wound.

The trap had locked onto his ankle and calf and had twisted the foot as it clamped shut. There was the white gleam of bone jutting through skin, puncture marks already puffing up in purples and blacks as blood pooled on the table and dripped down to the floor.

"The doctor will need to set it, Mona Maddalena," Giusto said beside me. "The other man's leg, too, and the wounds will have to be kept clean, but I saw plenty of these injuries when I assisted my father. Do not fear, mona. They can be remedied."

Words like candle-glow in the darkest night.

I placed a hand on his arm. "Thank you, Giusto."

With the slam of a door, the head steward rushed into the kitchen, still becloaked, smelling of winter air. He strode toward Florindo and me. "The doctor has fallen ill with the flux," he said, panting. "He cannot come to help."

My husband stepped away from our son. "Does he not have an assistant he can send?"

"No, messer. He says the entire household is ill, including the son who helps him."

"Santa Madre," I hissed and tightened my grip on Giacomo's hand. He was the nearest physician in the area. Even if we sent the steward out right this minute in search of another in the somewhat closer cities of Acqui Terme or Novi Ligure, it would all take too long. At least three hours, and likely much more.

"What do we do, Maddalena?" Florindo said.

I shook my head.

"Mona," Giusto said, softly, "if you'll permit me, I can try to help. I can try to shift the bones and then splint and bandage the wounds. At least so that they're not out in the open like this."

I looked up at him. I should perhaps have felt reluctance at the offer, and I probably would have if anyone else had made it, but Giusto had known and cared for my son since the boy was five. He'd not endanger his well-being any more than I would. If he suspected he was doing him more ill than good, he'd stop.

With one glance at Florindo, I nodded. "Please try. With Ilario, as well, if he agrees."

Giusto bowed his head. "Then I'll need a few things, bandages of some kind, the purest alcohol available, and something to use as splints for their legs. Anything rigid will work. In a bind, my father always used sticks."

Florindo motioned to the steward, who set off at once to fetch them.

The woman I'd sent to my cucinetta almost crashed into him as she returned with the bottle full of dry, bulbous pods, which she held up to me. As Giusto crossed the room to speak with Ilario and the servants began gathering the supplies required, including a small demijohn of grappa that the cuoco provided, I uncorked the bottle and reached inside for two medium-sized bulbs.

"Place these in four fingers' breadth of water and let it all boil," I said to the woman, whose name came to me in a clap of sound—Assunta. "When it is ready, strain it and serve Ilario a quarter of a cup of the liquid and my son an eighth. No more than that."

"Yes, madonna."

Assunta made to turn but I stopped her. "Actually, bring me the drinks first."

It was better never to take the potency of poppy seeds for granted.

She bowed and headed to do as I'd told her.

Giusto was back at my side, strips of clean linen hanging from his arm. "We're ready to begin, I think, mona."

I swallowed, willing the water and poppy pods to boil as quickly as they could. "Yes."

Giacomo hissed as the first cloth soaked in the grappa touched his calf. His leg jerked away from the pain, which only managed to send him howling again as his ankle's bare knob of bone shifted against ruptured skin.

"Scusatemi, Messer Giacomo, but we need to clean the wound." Giusto pressed his lips so tightly they disappeared from his face and wrung the newly soaked cloth until a splash of grappa covered the calf.

My son's eyes fluttered. Yes, unconsciousness would be better.

But the next of the ministrations sent him screaming once more. And then again. Next to me Florindo flinched at each of our son's cries, for they felt like lashes of a whip against our skin.

"The tea is almost ready, madonna," Assunta said, from where she stood by a small cauldron.

"Good." I held tighter to my son with one hand and wiped my tears away with the other.

From across the room, Ilario's contained cries told me he was receiving the same treatment, the same liquid scorching of flesh.

Assunta was all at once by my side with two cups. I took the one that had the most tonic in it, closed my eyes, and listened past the whimpers and cries of pain around me, past all of the human noises. The slow voice of the poppy swirled up like steam. I nodded at its sedate words and handed it back to Assunta before taking up the other cup, the one meant for Giacomo. It was a bit more potent than I'd expected, but the plant's voice recommended the deeper sleep for his injury.

"Please give that one to Ilario," I said and Assunta obeyed without wasting a moment. I'd have to remember to reward her diligence when this was all over.

"Giacomo, amore," I said, stroking his damp hair. "I need you to drink this, all right? It's for the pain."

I blew on the liquid and then helped him lift his head. I pressed the cup to his lips.

He grimaced at the bitterness but drank it all in one trusting gulp. In a moment he'd begin feeling the effects, the soporific weight of the poppy.

"Mona," Giusto said, lowering his voice and wiping at the sheen of sweat on his forehead, "I have to shift the bone in his ankle now, before I splint it. I'm afraid he'll have to be held down."

I looked at my child and already saw the slackness of sleep beginning to fall over his features, the tight grasp of pain loosening its hold. But even the poppy wouldn't be potent enough to mask the grinding of rearranged bones.

I stepped away from the table and pulled on Florindo's arm so that he'd do the same. We'd be useless trying to hold our child down as he struggled against what was about to befall him. "Do what you need to do, Giusto."

He nodded and motioned to four of the larger men who had been helping with the cutting of bandages. With a few soft words, he positioned them around the table, urging them to take hold of Giacomo's arms and healthy leg, one of them to weigh down the thigh of his injured one.

My poor child.

"Tomorrow morning," Florindo began next to me, his words almost inaudible against the pounding of my heart, "I'll take as many men as I can up to the mountain. We'll wait for the trespassers all day if we have to, but we'll end this, sposa. They will not harm our children again."

I fixed my eyes on the blood that was spreading across the center of the kitchen and kept them there as our son began to scream once more.

The memory of another, smaller pool of blood leaped into my mind then. Francesco's, settling on mud and shattered glass on the morning we'd arrived. And then another, blood bright against the white of chamber pots.

A cold breath raced down my spine.

For it almost seemed as if fate had laid claim to one of our children's lives from the moment we'd stepped on this land. And fate had a habit of getting what it desired.

SIBILLA
1933

IT WAS STILL SNOWING. The small, undefined powdery flakes that had begun falling this afternoon had thickened and were clearly visible now in the light of the lamp at my side. I pulled the wool blanket tighter around my shoulders and glanced past the piano and the radio at the fireplace. The flames had weakened already.

I grabbed hold of one of the armchairs and dragged it closer to the fire, wood scraping against wood. Giovanni had spent the entire afternoon pulling two more horse carcasses from the river and hadn't bothered to fetch more firewood.

My child stretched inside me, making me wince and smile at the same time. He'd been racing through the day today, and it didn't appear as if the night would calm him. Not that I could blame him. The last thing I, too, wanted was to lie still while treachery went on all around me.

"Soon, amore," I said. "In just two or three weeks, you'll be here in my arms."

A winter's child.

I frowned at the memory of that morning with Buona, the pleasantness of our conversation, all the kindness she had shown me. It had just been an act to earn my trust. An act someone as thirsty for companionship as I had fallen for easily.

"She'll be gone before you get here," I murmured, laying a hand on my stomach. "I won't let her come near you."

How I'd manage that, I wasn't sure yet, not with Giovanni against me. But once I did, everything would be back as it was. Giovanni would break loose from the spell the girl had cast on him and he could stop pretending the oaks were gone. He could focus on selling them and paying what he owed, allowing him to call the carabinieri and lift us from ruin. It would take longer to get the sawmill working, but we'd be fine. For my part, I would do my best to forget his confusion and disloyalty. He wasn't truly to blame. Buona had managed to trick both of us.

The child shifted right beneath my hands. I smiled at the strange fluttering sensation.

"How insistent you are today." I slid the fabric of my slip up and placed my hand on my bare skin. "I'm right here, see? You're not alone."

I tried to recognize what I was feeling through the layers that separated us, an elbow or a knee? A hand?

He kicked out and I exhaled sharply. "A bit more gently, amore."

But he did it again, with even more force this time. It bent me over, a gasp leaping from me as the pain came again and then again. He was kicking at me.

"Stop, child, please."

But he didn't, and the strength behind the next strike vibrated against my palm. I could feel the shape of what had just touched me.

Something was wrong with it.

I pulled the slip up and watched my flesh rippling as the child moved, like he was readying himself for another hit.

It came quickly but it wasn't the viciousness of the blow that made me clasp a hand to my mouth.

What pressed against the inside of my skin was not a hand or a foot but a small hoof. The child's leg stretched and the hoof pushed forward, as if it wanted to kick its way right out of me. The silhouette had nothing human in it.

Bile rose up my throat, the back of my tongue stiffening, and I grabbed the first thing I could find, an old flower vase, before the bit of food I'd eaten spilled out of me. My eyes burned.

"Oh, Santissima Madre," I gasped. "Please."

But I didn't know which words to use to articulate my plea. A plea for what?

I looked down at my stomach again, the room pulsing darker and brighter, darker and brighter, with each of my heartbeats. The movement had stopped, the being within me had receded. But the image of what I'd seen had not, and I doubted it ever would.

What did I have inside me?

I smothered a sob with my hands and felt the days and weeks and months of expectation shatter against me. I would birth a monstrosity, an abomination.

It was this place, Buona, her teas, the carcasses, it had all seeped into my womb and warped my child into something unspeakable. They had stolen my perfect son from me.

I made to cradle my stomach, but my hands jerked back as if scorched.

In the pounding silence of the horrid night, a door clicked open. The light footsteps that followed, the muffled sound of bare feet, came from Buona's room and hurried down the passage, toward the courtyard.

She was creeping outside again. Hadn't everything she'd done been enough? What betrayal was she planning now? What else would she steal from me?

The rage that I'd felt earlier roared inside me and propelled me across the room. I slammed the door open, ignoring the snap of wayward electricity against my hands and bringing one of the sconces crashing to the floor in my wake, and lunged out into the corridor.

"Sibilla?"

I hurried toward the girl, the tears on my cheeks crackling dry in the burning heat of my anger. A quick glance told me I'd been right. She *was* bare of feet, her shoes clutched in her hands along with a heavy blanket, her coat all buttoned up. Here was my chance to prove the truth to my husband.

"Giovanni!" I called out.

At my shout, a shadow in the corner of the hall jerked. I flicked my gaze to it for just long enough to see that it was the black form I'd seen in the mill. It held its hands curled into claws at its side, but this time I knew it was just one of the intruders and I wouldn't be cowed or distracted. In fact, I welcomed it, for it would let me show my husband what Buona was doing under his very nose.

"Giovanni!"

"You should be sleeping, Sibilla," Buona said. "You need to rest."

I walked closer, stepping into a pool of cool moonlight, my eyes shifting rapidly between her and the shadowed intruder, and she took a slight step back. "Where are you going?"

"Just outside for a moment. I wanted some fresh air."

The ease with which she lied. "You have a window you can open in your room and it's snowing."

"That's why I have a blanket, so I can watch it for a bit. It's soothing."

"You do realize you're barefoot. Why would you walk the house without shoes? Is that also soothing?"

She frowned. "I didn't want to wake you by stomping about."

At least that had the ring of truth in it. I watched her for a moment, her grip tightening around her shoes, her eyes flicking from me to the floor and back. Cunning laced every one of her stares, each one of her words. There wasn't anything kind or innocent about her, nothing that made her worthy of her name.

"You may have Giovanni fooled, but I know exactly what you've been doing," I said. "I know who you've been helping. Or do you want to deny that, too?"

Her head snapped up, and this time she couldn't disguise the fear in her face.

"You've been lying all of this time and I trusted you." The tears began again. My arm jerked toward the shadow. "How could you let them into the house? You've ruined everything."

"Sibilla," Giovanni said from behind me, his voice dark with sleep, "you don't think we've had enough of your nonsense today? Go to bed."

"No, I will not. Look, she's trying to sneak out! I've been trying to tell you she's been working against us from the start and here's proof. She's even allowed one of—"

The intruder was gone. There was no one in the shadows.

"It was here. It was right there," I said.

"You're hysterical."

I turned to face him. I caught his frown and the swift glance from me to Buona, the sleep and irritation evaporating from his features in a blink.

"I'm not hysterical." I shook my head, a hand hovering over my stomach as even more tears spilled. "You don't know the things she's done. What she's allowed."

Giovanni swallowed. His breathing had sped up and his fingers had a slight tremble to them. "You're—you're right, I don't. Why don't we go into the bedroom and you can tell me everything?"

"You have to call the carabinieri."

His jaw tightened but he nodded. "And I will, tomorrow morning. It's too late now."

"You have to look for the other intruder, then. He's in here somewhere."

I heard Buona start to speak, but Giovanni stopped her with a single look.

"As soon as we lock the girl in her room and you tell me what you've seen, I'll begin doing just that."

I held his gaze. He sounded sincere enough, but it had all been too easy. Nothing was ever easy with Giovanni. "You're just humoring me. You don't really believe a word I said."

His exhaled, the tendons in his forearms shifting as he clenched his hands. "The truth is that I don't know what to believe, Sibilla, because you still haven't told me what's been happening." He walked closer to me, reached for my hand. "That's why I want to have a calm conversation and go over everything clearly. That sounds like a reasonable plan, doesn't it?"

His tone made my teeth grind together. He sounded like he was trying to keep a creature of the woods from bolting. Or biting.

Before I could do anything, he took a step forward and latched his hand around my wrist.

"Just give it here, Sibilla."

With a frown, I looked down and saw him pry open my hand, releasing the piece of jagged glass I clutched. A piece of the sconce that had fallen and shattered. I shook my head as blood trickled to the floor. When had I grabbed it? I had no memory of it.

Giovanni tossed the glass across the courtyard, where it further cracked, but didn't release my wrist. Instead, he tightened his grip.

I pulled to get loose but he tugged me forward, taking hold of my other arm.

"Stop it," I said.

"This is for your own good," he said and started dragging me. "You're not yourself."

"No! Let me go!" I tried to plant my legs but the tiles were too slick, my house slippers easily giving way to Giovanni's strength.

"Help me, would you?" Giovanni called to Buona.

The girl ran toward me, and I could only howl as she took hold of one of my arms. I bent my legs and pulled down with every bit of strength I had, trying to drag the two of them to the floor, tip them off balance. Anything that would give me the moment I needed to escape.

"Sibilla, you'll hurt the child," Buona said, fighting to remain upright.

As if she cared one bit.

I dug my nails into her shoulders, making her hiss, but she held on as Giovanni gave me one violent pull.

The force of it made my feet slip from under me and I fell forward, their grip on my arms the only thing that kept me from hitting my stomach against the floor. Even so, something in my side stretched beyond its limit. I gasped at the swift pain.

Giovanni forced me up again and released a hand for just long enough to slap me.

Once.

The blow burned against my skin. It rang through my bones like a note through a tuning fork and brought all of me to a stop.

"That's enough," he said. "If you keep struggling, I'll do it again. I won't stand any more of this nonsense in my house."

I could feel all of me was shaking one instant, and the next, I had lost my body again. When Giovanni dragged me forward, I sensed my legs in a muffled manner, as if there were layers and layers between me and the movement that he was forcing.

Something was wrong with my vision as well, for I was watching myself be taken to the music room from somewhere over my left shoulder. I knew I should have felt panic, rage, something at this betrayal and viciousness, but I was a vast blackness. Filled with nothing but echoes, like a porcelain figurine.

Giovanni led me into the room and forced me down onto one of the armchairs near the weak fire. The lamps winked under a surge of electric buzzing.

"Stay with her," he said, looking at Buona. "I don't think she can climb out the window in her condition, but I'm not in the mood to chase her across the woods."

"And what we talked about—" she started.

"I already gave you an answer."

"But this changes things."

Giovanni shook his head and strode to the door. "I've had enough of all of this for tonight. You have the other key to this room?"

She nodded.

They'd planned this, then. They'd been waiting for a moment to do it and, like the fool I was, I had given it to them.

"Don't let her do anything stupid," he said and left the room. The lock clicked into place.

Buona sighed, running a hand across her forehead. There was blood on one of her shoulders, likely from my injured palm. She murmured something I couldn't catch and walked to the fireplace, adding a log to the starving flames.

A tingling sensation was returning to my feet and the dullest hint of an ache crept up on my side, but the rest of me could have been smudged away like a charcoal drawing and nothing would have changed. I didn't think I would have felt it if Buona stuck one of my hands into the flames.

"I am sorry, Sibilla," she said. She pulled the other armchair closer to the fire and to me. "None of this should have gone as it did. You're not hurt, apart from your hand?"

I said nothing.

"I can bandage it up. Let me see."

I met her eyes. "I don't want a single thing from you."

She opened her mouth to say something else, to spew some lie at me, perhaps even to gloat, but I turned away, toward the fire.

She had won. I was a prisoner in my own home, just as she and whoever she was in league with had planned from the start.

I'd allowed her to burrow herself in, even into my womb, and now it was much too late to pry her out.

Then the thought struck me like a blow: if I couldn't remove her, I'd remove myself. And her own treachery would give me the opportunity I needed to do exactly that.

I HEARD THE GIRL STAND, but I kept my eyes closed, my breathing as deep and steady as I'd forced it to be for the past half hour.

If I'd needed any more proof of her deception, this would have provided more than enough of it. I'd stopped her from going outside earlier, from taking food to the intruder she was helping, and so she needed to do it now despite the instructions Giovanni had given her to watch me.

This would be my chance.

Buona tapped lightly across the room, stopping every few seconds to make certain I'd not woken. My heart raced at the click of the lock and the creak as she attempted to open the door as softly as possible, but I remained still. Even as she stepped out of the room, locking me in once more, I didn't dare twitch a finger.

I waited for silence.

And then I pushed myself off the chair, tucking the blanket on my lap under my arm and grabbing the one Buona had left behind before hurrying to one of the windows. The one I knew, from a morning of cleaning, opened without too much difficulty.

I tugged at the handle until it gave. Cold air sliced at me, but I didn't allow myself to think of my flimsy slippers or my threadbare housedress. I needed to make it to the cave leading up to the oaks and wait there for morning, when I could look for help without fear of tripping over my own feet. The blankets I carried would be enough to keep me from freezing in the few hours left of night.

Giovanni's words rang in my ears as I gave a hop, just high enough to be able to sit on the edge of the window. Even without pregnancy weighing me down, I'd never been particularly agile, I knew that, but I also wasn't an invalid. This time, he'd underestimated me.

Not just this time.

I swung my legs out into the night and felt for the ground. I bit back a hiss when the cold, crunching denseness of snow met my feet instead of the bare earth I expected. Had it really snowed this much? My toes were already soaked.

Unless I wanted to wake Giovanni while trying to find proper shoes, there was nothing for it but to continue, wet slippers or not.

I hopped down with a wince and wrapped the two blankets around me before starting off down the side of the house, toward the kitchen courtyard and the woods beyond.

The moonlight was a pale sliver, just enough to let me see a few steps in front of my pluming breath. In the forest, not even this light would reach me.

"It doesn't matter. I'll manage," I whispered. "I have to."

My hands went to cradle my stomach before I remembered the hooves. The corruption I carried. I wiped away the beginning of furious tears and hurried on.

The silhouette of the ancient dovecote appeared even sooner than I expected, and I exhaled in relief because the house was still silent behind me. I'd have enough time to slip into the forest. Every extra second before Buona discovered me missing would help me disappear. If I had to, if they came looking in the cave, I'd hide up among the oaks themselves.

I was mere steps from the collapsed stone wall when the dark figure appeared. It slid from the shadow of a tree, its lurching steps silent in the snow, the hulking shape of it blocking my path in moments.

I stopped, swallowing down the jolt of fear. I had to get past the intruder.

"Let me through," I said. "I don't care what you're planning on doing or who you work for. I just want to leave."

The figure remained silent.

My hands trembled as I clutched the blankets tighter around me, feeling the pulse of each second I wasted.

I shifted, ready to go around the man even if I had to climb over pieces of fallen stones, and he jerked to the side, blocking my way once more.

"But you told me to get out! That's what I'm doing."

The man made a wet click in the back of his throat. I tried to see his face, see if I could make out his features, his expression, but he had to be wearing a hood or a mask because peering into that darkness revealed nothing.

The slight trembling I'd felt grew under the pressing silence. The man's eyes were locked on me—I could feel them, his stare heavy.

"Let me pass."

He started making a grinding sound. Was it his teeth? But it was so loud he'd have to be cracking them under that force and the sound was almost... mechanical.

A shout came from the house. I had no time left.

I started forward, ready to lunge past the intruder, but I wasn't quick enough. The man swung his arm so rapidly I only heard the whistle of it and I gasped as something sharp sliced into my arm.

Just go. Run.

I darted to the side, and this time the man's weapon tore into my back, the pain of it knocking all breath from me. With a moan, I stumbled forward, but the next cut, into my thigh, dropped me to my knees.

"It's too late," he said. The words came as if from jaws that had been fused together.

"Please." I pressed a shaking hand to my bleeding thigh. The snow in front of me faded out and then back in with each of my heartbeats.

That grinding began again.

"Sibilla!"

The man was right; it was too late, for a pair of hands now clutched at my arms, pulling me up.

"He's there," I said. My teeth chattered.

"Stop it. There's no one," Giovanni said, his hands tighter than Buona's as they latched on to me. "What have you done to yourself?"

I didn't even bother to look behind me when they began dragging me away, back to the prison they'd made of my home.

"You're so foolish, Sibilla," Giovanni hissed.

And, considering everything, I had to agree with him on that.

BUONA STEPPED INTO THE ROOM as I began playing again. The tray she carried jangled as she set it down to lock the door behind her, making my teeth grind together. She made to turn the dial on the radio but I banged my hands down on the keys. I bit my lips to keep from flinching at the pain in my arm.

"I just want to find you a station with music playing," she said.

"Leave it." The static was soothing, unchanging and steady. It allowed me to get as close to sleep as I was managing these days.

With a sigh, she brought the tray toward the piano. "Are you sure you do not want some of the stew I made? Or the roasted potatoes from last night?"

I didn't even look at her.

"At least let me bring you a bit of wine, as the doctor prescribed."

"No." I took the glass of sugar water and the plate of bread she held out to me. Hunger wasn't something I felt much of any longer, but the sweetened water would take away some of the trembling that had started since I'd been caged.

"You and your child need more than that." She shook her head. "You need a real meal."

She must have thought me very foolish indeed if she expected me to trust her with my meals. And besides, even if I were willing to take that risk, I was finding it difficult to stomach anything but sweet water and plain bread. The creature I had within me refused all else.

I took a sip and followed Buona's movements as she walked to the fireplace and added a log to the fire, kneeling to worry the embers with the poker. With a sigh, she sat back on her heels.

Her gaze fixed on the flames that only just managed to keep away the chill from the deepening winter.

A quick shove to unbalance her and I could grab the keys in her trouser pocket. Yes, and then? With my injured thigh, I'd not be quick enough to unlock the door before she reached me.

Buona stood and I looked away, biting into the bread.

"Sibilla, your husband is destroying himself chopping down pine trees," she said. "He's spent hours out there already today, and it's still snowing rather heavily." She turned to me. "Perhaps you could say something to him before he falls ill. Ask him to sit with you for a bit, out of the cold."

I shook my head.

I didn't want to see him.

I was tired of hearing the same refrain from him as I'd heard for the past couple of days, of the supposed missing trees, of how we'd not make it through the winter, of how he needed someone to offer him support and comfort, and of how he did *not* need a child right now, or a wife who was always hysterical. As if he were trying to excuse his choice of turning to Buona.

He kept lying about everything, and I couldn't stand it any longer. It wasn't enough to keep me captive, but I had to forgive and fuss over his actions as well?

The recording of the horse's cries began again, undimmed by the boards that now shuttered the windows, and I took another sip of the water before turning back to the piano.

The now constant screaming was wearing on me, mostly because I couldn't convince my captors to allow me access to the piano or even the radio at night. Humming in the bedroom where they forced me to retire each evening wasn't nearly as effective, and it took much more out of me. If they would just let me play through the night, things would be easier.

"Why not try another piece of music?" Buona said, drawing nearer. "I'm sure there are other beautiful ones."

"No." I barked out the word. "This is the only one that stops it."

"Stops what?"

I kept my silence. I shouldn't have said anything at all. There was no point to it, for they both still pretended they didn't hear the recording.

"Sibilla, stops what?"

I exhaled sharply and was about to tell her to leave me be when a kick in my stomach robbed me of breath. My lips tightened with the pain.

"Are you all right?"

As if she cared.

I breathed slowly, feeling the being inside me shift about, almost seeing the floating hooves ready to strike me again at any moment. Bile rose to my mouth. I wanted it out.

"You must be excited about seeing the baby soon," Buona said. Her voice was too bright, like false jewels. "Have you thought of a name yet?"

"No."

She nodded. "Some women wait until the child is born and manages to survive the first few weeks. My own mother didn't name me until the day of my baptism, and even then, she refused to call me anything but *bebè* until months later. To avoid tempting fate or the devil, or something of the sort. No reason to take any risks, I suppose."

I turned to look at her fully, my hands clenched away from my bulging midsection.

"I'm not going to name it at all, because it is not my child."

She frowned and searched my face. "What do you mean?"

"You know exactly what I mean. You did it to me."

Buona's cheeks lost a shade of color. "Sibilla, I didn't do anything to you."

I scoffed.

"I would never harm you or your child."

"I've already told you it is not my child."

She opened her mouth to speak, but a knock cut off her words.

I turned to look at the girl, who stood, locked in place, as a murmur came from behind the door. It was a man's voice, I could tell that much, but it wasn't Giovanni's.

The radio's hiss filled the room as the seconds passed and neither of us moved.

And then the voice said one word, clearly: "Buona."

The girl gave a jolt like someone had flung boiling water on her. "No," she said as she spun around. "You can't be here. Not now."

She hurried to the door, her hand sliding into her trouser pocket. This was my chance.

I rose quickly, leaving the being inside me to manage the rush of movement as best it could, and waited for the girl to use the key. I walked closer. Ready to rush past whoever or whatever stood behind that door to get away from Giovanni and her and this place. And if the intruder and his blade appeared . . . I'd run even faster.

"No, you have to go back," Buona said, turning the key.

The lock clicked open.

I didn't allow myself a breath of hesitation. I rushed at her and shoved her aside.

She yelped as she lost her balance, her flaying arms grabbing hold of the small table by the door and sending it crashing alongside her.

I didn't stay to watch, I didn't pause to see who had called her, but ran.

"Sibilla!"

A man in a blue cap had already darted ahead of me, racing down the corridor. The trespasser from all those days ago and, I suddenly realized, probably the same one who'd played at shadows to scare me. As I took the corner, I saw him yank the front door open and disappear into the afternoon in a moment.

I winced as the bed slippers I'd not bothered to take off this morning skidded against the stone floors as I hurtled across the courtyard in his wake. I gripped the arches, running from one to the other to keep from falling, cursing at myself for my stupidity, but there was the door. Open in front of me. All I had to do was go through it and keep running until I found a house, one other than Piero's. It would take Buona a minute or two to get to Giovanni, wherever he was in the woods, giving me more time to get ahead before they gave chase or ran for the telephone. I could do this.

Steps rang out behind me. Too close. "Stop!"

I lunged for the door and raced outside.

Something hard rammed my side just as my slippers landed on the slush of snow that had collected by the entrance.

"You don't know what you're doing!" Buona said and pushed me again as she ran past me.

The soles of my feet, now soaked, slid under the force of her blow. I gasped as I lost my footing and the weight of my body sent me careening across the layer of ice the snow had concealed.

To the very edge of the colonnade.

I slammed into the low balustrade and dug my fingernails into the stone to keep from tumbling over it. I felt one of my nails snap off at the root but the pain never reached me because my eyes were locked on the long fall beneath me.

I had seen this view before.

The blanket of snow in the abyss below.

Leonardo smiled at us from across our dining table as he lifted the wineglass. "To our future," he said. Next to him, his wife did the same. She tipped her golden-locked head in my direction and then turned to Giovanni.

Their eyes met.

I couldn't swallow the sip of wine I'd taken.

Panting, I gripped down on the balustrade. "Stop," I said.

Knowing it wouldn't.

"I wonder where Emilia and Giovanni have disappeared to," Leonardo said, sitting back in the chair and sipping the last of his wine. "They've truly missed a concert worthy of any stage, Sibilla."

"You're too kind. I'm afraid I tend to bore Giovanni with my playing." I rose from the piano, a strange, fever-like nervousness in my limbs. "I'll go fetch them so we can have coffee with the exquisite amaretti biscuits you've brought."

I left the room and walked to the kitchen, the only reasonable place in our small home where they could have waited out the music. In their soft voices there was something that stopped me from calling out.

I looked in.

Giovanni and Emilia stood much too close to one another, her hand on his arm, her gaze holding his in an almost physical grip.

"Please," I said.

But there was no pleading with the red, all of that red my memory held, which fell over me now like a shroud.

I GRIPPED THE TIN LUNCH *pail tighter and chided myself for leaving my gloves at the house. Giovanni was right; I was always forgetting something. Even last week, for the dinner we'd had with Leonardo and his wife, I'd forgotten to buy the bread Giovanni had specifically asked for.*

I would have to start making a list to check before stepping over our threshold.

"Yes, and I'm sure I'll forget where I've put that, too," I muttered.

Stomping my feet lightly to keep the cold from my toes, I waited for a car to pass and crossed the street. A man tipped his hat at me and I nodded in acknowledgment, though I felt my cheeks warm. For I couldn't imagine what he thought of seeing a young woman in my condition crossing one of the less well-lit parts of Torino on her own once evening had fallen.

I hurried on.

The glow from streetlamps made it more difficult to see anything but the silhouette of the sawmill in front of me, the black mass of the building still making me feel as if I were falling backward every time I looked up at it. I still couldn't quite grasp the size of it, even after having strolled down this same street every day with Giovanni while we'd gone out. I smiled at the memory of those walks, or thought I did, because the cold had numbed my lips.

I passed by the main entrance to the mill, trying not to flinch at the honk of a horn somewhere behind me, and continued down to the back one, the one that was left open when people were still working after hours.

Nerves bubbled up in my stomach. I looked down at the lunch pail holding a simple cena of bread, cheese, salami, and wine.

Giovanni was not one for surprises, but this couldn't possibly bother him, could it? He could continue with his work on the patent while we ate. We didn't have to talk, and I wouldn't distract him. I wouldn't even ask to turn on the radio. He'd been working so terribly hard lately, missing meals to ensure we had a better future, that it seemed the very least I could do was to bring him a bit of domestic cheer.

"If he doesn't like it, I can just leave him the food, give him a kiss, and go home," I murmured, taking the side street that led to the snow-covered yard and to the warehouse.

I hurried past the piles and piles of logs waiting for the saw and pulled the back door open. The darkness of the building pressed against me at once, and I waited for my eyes to adjust before moving.

"Because we don't need an unpleasant fall," I said, rubbing a hand against the child that seemed to be growing by the hour. There were still three months before she was born, for I was certain it would be a girl, and I didn't know how I'd accommodate her if she kept up this pace.

"I suppose we'll manage, won't we?"

At least our doctor was pleased with the progress we'd made.

Once I could see the outlines of walls and doors and machinery, I started down the series of interlocked hallways to reach the stairs that would take me to the third floor. Not the easiest of climbs in my condition, and one that left me puffing in what Giovanni would have said was without question unladylike, but no one was watching. I leaned against the wall for a moment to catch my breath, to straighten my skirt, to brush back the hair I'd curled just this morning, wishing I'd touched some gel to it before leaving the house. To look presentable.

The murmur of Giovanni's voice came from the only room where the light was on. Likely Leonardo had remained behind to help him.

Oh, I should have added more food to the lunch pail. How silly of me not to think of it.

I smiled at the thought of all three of us sitting together, even to a threadbare meal. Leonardo was always so kind.

Perhaps he'd even encourage Giovanni to show me a bit of the plans, which until now my husband had not wanted to bore me with.

I walked as softly as I could manage down the short corridor to his office. I wanted to see their looks of surprise as I stepped into the room, lunch pail in hand.

"You can't imagine how lovely it is to see you," Giovanni said. "It's been an absolute horror at home."

My hand froze, midway to pushing on the half-opened door.

"I can't get her to speak of anything but the child."

"That's normal, isn't it?"

It took me a second to recognize the voice.

"I don't know, but I can hardly stand it. Sometimes I'm afraid I'll throttle her just to get a few moments of silence."

"That's rather unkind," Emilia said, but I could hear the laughter in her words.

A chill descended on me, though my face was afire.

"The truth is often unkind."

I heard the tap of heels as someone walked across the room.

"Won't you offer a girl a bit of something to drink?"

"I'm afraid I have a shortage of glasses." The trickle of pouring liquid. "Here, have some of mine."

I made myself lean forward just enough to peer into the room, when what I really wanted was to disintegrate.

All I could see from this angle was a deep-red coat that rested on the chair in front of Giovanni's desk, one made of a velvet so fine I could feel its softness under my fingertips. Light danced along its fibers.

"And your present? Do you like it?"

The warmth in Giovanni's voice brought on the first tears.

"You know very well I do. The color is exquisite."

"Then where is the gratitude?"

A shift of clothing and I couldn't stop myself, I leaned forward until I could see them. Emilia was sitting on my husband's lap, her arms wrapped around his neck, his face turned up to hers like he was facing the summer sun.

"I am grateful, signore," she murmured.

"It's ingegnere."

Her laughter sparkled as golden as her hair. She leaned forward and kissed him.

I turned around, my arms and legs shaking so violently I had to cling to the wall as I forced myself to walk back the way I'd come. The lunch pail scraped against the bricks, the bottle of wine and the glasses I'd brought because I knew Giovanni didn't have more than one in his office tapping against each other.

He didn't love me. Not a bit.

The thought was a whirlpool that took everything down with it.

The disgust in his voice when he'd spoken of me sent waves of hot shame through my body.

He didn't want the child, or me, and he would abandon us both when a good enough opportunity presented itself. I could see that now. And then what would we do?

We had no one and nothing.

My mother was in a casket. My newly married father hadn't bothered to invite me to his wedding, and if he'd received my letter telling him of my pregnancy, he'd given no indication of it. The few friends I'd had before marriage had drifted further away with each invitation Giovanni had told me to turn down. A bore, all of them, he had said.

And I, too, was a bore. A nuisance he wanted to throttle.

My ribs seemed to turn to stone. Was I still walking?

The darkness of the corridor grew thicker and the stairs were not where they should have been. I couldn't remember if I'd made the right turn or any turn at all.

The lunch pail slipped from a hand I couldn't feel anymore, its contents spilling, glass shattering.

I left it and stumbled forward.

What should I do now? How could I go home and lie down in the bed we shared? Should I pretend nothing had happened and wait for my husband to unstitch me from his life? But how would I pretend when all I would be able to see was that red coat, those pale hands in my husband's hair?

A sob ripped through my lips before I even felt it, so that I had to press them tightly to contain the worst of it.

"Is someone there?" Giovanni called from much too far away.

The child inside me shifted in protest as I started running, my shoulder scraping against the wall of a passage I didn't recognize. I could almost see myself from above, a panicked mare running blindly through a forest of black corridors, plunging ahead with nothing but fear rattling through her head.

"Who's there?"

I blinked and found myself outside all at once.

I stood on the edge of a platform I'd seen many times from below. There were a few guardrails, but none in front of me.

I looked down. Far below me, there was just snow.

The chaos I'd felt a moment ago was gone, having broken like a fever, leaving behind only the residue of tears on my cheeks. I felt a stillness I'd perhaps never experienced before, not standing beside my mother as she stirred a vat of chocolate, or even sitting with her at the piano. Absolute peace at being certain of what I was going to do. I wrapped my arms around my child.

"We'll be all right," I said. "You don't have to worry."

I didn't turn at the gasp that came from behind me, but instead took a step forward.

And fell.

My eyes opened and closed and opened again to a woman with gold for hair. Something was wrong with my chest, for I couldn't draw breath. My mouth was filled with liquid metal.

Voices and footsteps.

And then the cruelest curtain of red falling over me, tangling me in its folds until there was but darkness.

MADDALENA
1596

"**Y**OU MUST PROMISE ME YOU'LL be careful," I said.

Florindo lifted himself onto Spuma's back with a grunt, and the animal started to turn in circles before he had managed to slip his other foot into the stirrup.

Mad creature.

I pulled on the reins and it snorted at me but came to a stop. I didn't know why he was taking the damned beast when all it would do was create more problems.

"Of course, I'll be careful, sposa." He motioned to one of the men nearby, who handed him the only true weapon we possessed, a musket that Florindo had fired just once on the day that he'd bought it twenty-odd years ago. The blast had almost made him drop it.

I'd watched last night, as we'd sat by Giacomo's bed, how he'd taken it apart and cleaned it, his lips pinched as if he'd taken a sip of something impossibly sour.

If it came to it, would he be able to fire?

Ugo left my side and started walking up to the horse to get a better look at the musket, and I pulled him back, away from the reach of Spuma's hooves.

"Mamma," he said. "I want to see it. Why can't I go with Father?"

"Because I say you can't, child. He can show you later how the musket works, but you're staying here with me and your siblings for now. Don't you want to help me with Giacomo and Ilario?"

His forehead knotted and he shook his head.

"That's not very kind of you. You won't help me even if I let you choose the poppy pods to boil? I need a good eye for the task."

He said nothing but at least the frown disappeared. He slumped back to my side.

"You will send one of the servants for me when the doctor arrives?" Florindo said. "I'll leave a watch up at the mountain and come help."

I nodded. "But it won't be for hours yet."

The steward had left in the carriage as soon as dawn had arrived, so it was likely he wouldn't be back until well into the afternoon with whatever physician he was able to find. Until then, the most I could do was provide Giacomo and Ilario sanctuary from the pain.

"Give him a kiss from me when he wakes," Florindo said.

"I will, sposo."

He pulled on the reins and forced Spuma to turn.

The six workers he was taking with him wisely gave the beast a wide berth and waited until they were out of biting and kicking range before starting after my husband.

It seemed rumors of the animal's temperament had spread as rapidly as everything did in these parts.

"Oh, Maddalena," Florindo said, turning in the saddle, "I hate to burden you with more, but if you have time, could you check on the couple of men I've left working in the mill? Just every so often to make certain they know what they are doing?"

As if he needed to ask. "Of course."

He gave me a smile so fragile I could have blown it away, and then continued on. The group of them headed down the dirt road toward the side path to the forest.

Although Florindo himself had removed the animal trap, red with our son's blood, this morning and hadn't found any others in the area, I couldn't stop a fresh surge of worry. The thought of anyone else getting hurt, even that white insanity on hooves, made me bite at my lips. If only I'd had time to make protective sachets . . .

Sighing, I watched the men until the pine trees hid them.

I turned and started back to the colonnade. "Come, Ugo. Let's go see how your brother and Ilario are."

Once I looked in on them, I'd go up to the cucinetta to start those sachets and see if I had the herbs I needed to put together a balm for the wounds. The doctor would surely recommend washing them with wine, but I'd always seen better, quicker healing with the application of certain herbs. Without an apothecary nearby, my choices were limited, but I should still have goldenseal in my reserves. I could add that to a crushed garlic and black walnut base that would work marvelously to stave off pus.

There was silence behind me where none should have been. Ugo did nothing quietly.

I glanced over my shoulder to see what had caught his attention enough to keep him from coming after me. Just in time to see him darting into the woods.

"Ugo!"

But he had already disappeared.

"No," I said and started after him, my heart already trying to leap out of my throat. "Not again. Ugo, stop!"

But he didn't answer and I couldn't see him.

This had to be a nightmare. I couldn't possibly be running once again into the forest chasing after one of my children. Not after last night's horrors.

"They'll all spend the rest of the day in their rooms," I hissed. "I've had enough of this disobedience."

In every branch that snapped under my feet, I heard the metallic clank of iron jaws, in every groan of the wind against the trees, the beginning of a scream.

I followed the path that Florindo and the men had made, racing right to the entrance to the mountain, but saw no sign of Ugo. If he had chased after his father, he had to have gone in. There was no other option.

Voices echoed all along the walls and tangled together as I entered the cave and headed for the stone stairs. They were a knot of sounds, and I couldn't tell to whom they belonged or what they were saying. Panting, I forced myself to stop and listen for my son's piping voice but didn't hear it.

Was he up there or was he still in the woods?

I took the steps at a run.

A pile of manure lay in the center of one of them, and even in my scramble to get to the top I had to shake my head at Florindo. He couldn't have tied Spuma to one of the trees outside? He had to drag it up the mountain to make everything more difficult for everyone?

The closer I got to the opening, the more I began to be able to pick apart the voices I heard. Florindo and a couple of the men, those I knew.

And then there was another, one I'd hoped not to hear again outside of a podestà's court.

Antonio's.

My legs found a reserve of swiftness, and I leaped up the last few steps in an instant.

This field was empty of people, and I could hear the real distance of the voices now that the echoes were gone. They came from much farther down, from where I'd seen the remaining oaks the first time we'd come up here.

It all looked more violent in daylight as I followed the path of chutes down, all raw tree pulp and splintered bark, my eyes searching for a darting boy in between the sawdust and stumps. A boy who didn't appear.

The voices were closer now.

The first thing I saw as I crested the small hill separating the fields was Spuma, almost glowing in the morning sun. On him was Ugo. He sat in front of his father, who had his arms wrapped around him, and he didn't have a single scrape on him.

I exhaled, feeling the relief spreading down to my toes.

Florindo looked at me, drawing the eyes of the group of seven people who were not supposed to be there.

Antonio lifted an eyebrow. "Will the entire family be joining us, then?"

Insolent boy.

I crossed the distance between me and my loved ones and dared Spuma's wrath as I came to stand beside the animal, reaching up to touch Ugo's knee, eyes casting about for injuries I might have missed. He'd have his punishment for his willful disobedience once we were back at the villa, but for now, all I felt was a marrow-deep gratitude that he was unharmed and in his father's arms. Safe.

"How touching," Antonio said. "Although I can't imagine why you wouldn't want to be rid of at least one of those imps you have."

"You will watch your tongue," Florindo said.

One of the men beside Antonio, whom I realized now was the missing dove-keeper, snorted. He tapped the axe he carried against his leg.

"I will not, and they are horrors," Antonio said. "I rather thought I was doing you both a favor by bringing the illness into the villa. Thinning the herd with a few pails of raw water."

I sucked in a breath. A buzz filled my ears as blood rushed up to my head.

He had done that to my twins. He had placed them in mortal danger.

I'd had quite enough.

Of everything.

I strode forward until I was within striking range and slapped him. The clap of it multiplied across the hills and valleys all around us.

The dove-keeper and the other men surged forward, but I refused to take a single step in retreat. The workers Florindo had brought with him also drew closer, flanking me, although if they carried blades or any other weapons, I hadn't seen them.

"You spiteful, fiendish creature," I hissed. "I'll see you thrown in a cell where you'll rot for the rest of your life, you mark what I say. And the same applies to the rest of you."

"I don't think so," another of the trespassers said.

His face was familiar. Yes, he'd been one of the men I'd met on the day we'd arrived, one of the ones who had helped carry my father's alchemical tools up to the cucinetta.

"Look around you, woman," he said.

He motioned to the webs of ropes wrapped around stumps and felled trees, the chutes already holding freshly cut logs. A large oak at the edge of the mountain had a wedge of wood missing from it, an axe still lodged in the bark. It was a few strikes away from being pulled down with the help of the rope tied around its trunk, the other end hanging in hasty, wide loops around the branch of another tree.

That was how they'd kept us from hearing the trees falling, then. By lowering them slowly to the ground.

"We're here," he continued, "taking what we want, as we have been for weeks, and no one besides a few half-starved workers have offered you their help."

"And no one will."

I turned to look at the new voice and saw the leader of the group of men the children and I had encountered in the woods the day of the sowing. The other three were beside him.

They'd all been involved.

"No one will help a sorcerer. A *strega*."

"How dare you!" Florindo boomed. Ugo flinched in his arms.

I almost reached for him, to bring him down beside me, but I didn't want him within range of these monsters' grasps. He was safer with the barrier of Spuma's temperament between him and them.

"You will not speak to my wife in that manner!"

The trespassers laughed. All of them except for Antonio, who just watched us, arms crossed over his chest.

"We'll speak as we please," he said. "Not a one of us is in your employ any longer. And really, I can't imagine why you think you have the right to be acting so high above us. You're practically destitute, or have you forgotten? All your servants know it, and I made certain everyone else in the region does too. You can expect no more loans, no more help. I told you last night you'd learn your place."

"Seems like even your devil's work has its limits," the dove-keeper said. He spat in my direction.

The men behind me shouted in protest, and I had to halt Florindo with a raised hand. This couldn't slip out of our control.

"Get off our land," I said between clenched teeth. My face was so hot I expected to feel flesh melting off.

"Or what, strega? How will you have us thrown out? With those weaponless men beside you or with one of your enchantments? And if you do manage it, how will you keep us out? Your own ungodliness has poisoned the chancellor against you, and neither the massaro nor his sbirri will help, for they're very much on our side."

"Side? There is no side," I said. "You are on our land, trespassing. You are in the wrong."

Antonio's mouth twisted in disgust. He glanced from me to Florindo, shaking his head. "You continue to accuse us of trespassing, when it was you who took our land."

"What nonsense is this?" Florindo said.

"You didn't bother to learn the history of the place you bought or cared to think of the lives that you destroyed when you did so. And so now you face the consequences of that indifference."

I glanced at my husband, but the confusion was as easy to read on his face as I was certain it was on mine.

"What are you talking about?" I said.

"If you had bothered to ask, you would have known that the people who used to live on this land had done so for generations. Our family." Antonio motioned with an arm to the men around him. "We farmed it and milled it, we were born on it, our ancestors died on it. Our family built the stone steps you climbed up to get here and helped plant half the trees you see before you. And we hoped someday to purchase it from the nobleman who took half of our work in payment for allowing us to live and work on it."

"But instead," the dove-keeper said, "he decided to sell the property to those willing to pay much more than we ever could have. Do you know, he gave us three days to leave the land? Our home? Do you have any idea what it's like to be ripped from the only place you've ever known, from your livelihood? To have no one listen as you ask for some legal recourse?"

Despite myself, I could feel their despair, the anger they carried. It was like sawdust in my mouth. "A perfidious action, to be sure, but one you cannot blame us for."

Antonio's top lip lifted in a snarl. "And tearing down the home our great-grandfather built with his own hands, constructing your villa on its bones, we can't blame you for that, either?"

I frowned and looked up at Florindo once more. I hadn't known there'd been a house on the land.

He shook his head. "No, I'm afraid you can't lay even that blame at our feet. We bought the property fairly, to do with as we please. I am sorry the house was destroyed, and of course what that nobleman did was barbaric, but it doesn't change anything."

"It was our home!" the boy spat out. "All of this was!"

"And now it is ours." Florindo sighed. "By law."

One of the other brothers, the leader of the group we'd encountered in the woods, nodded.

"Yes, and we've made sure that the same law that failed us, fails you too. We want you torn from this land just as we were. When we take the rest of our oaks, your debts will accomplish that."

My teeth gritted, the granule of reluctant sympathy I'd felt growing now dissolving in the bile of his words.

"We've seen who you are, all of these men have seen you, too," I said. "We'll go to the massaro and tell him everything."

Antonio scoffed. "The massaro knows who we are. We're paying him a portion of what we make off this lumber to keep quiet, so I assure you he is well aware of our names."

Santa Madre.

"And most of his sbirri have known us since childhood, so they won't help strangers like you over us. They wouldn't have done so even before learning that you dabble with unholy forces, but they certainly won't now that they know."

My hands were clenched so tightly they shook.

Ugo shifted on the horse, the first notes of bored fussing reaching me, and I all at once wanted nothing more than to grab him and take him back home, away from the mountain.

I forced myself to remain still. I couldn't leave Florindo alone with this.

"You've made it all much too easy for us." Antonio shrugged. "You let us into your home, you gave us access to everything, including your children. You expected servants, so that is all you saw in us. No threat at all. For people who seem to think you're so superior to us, you are damned foolish."

"That's enough," one of the men behind me said.

The dove-keeper turned to look at him. "You're a traitor, you know? You're just like us and you bow and scrape to these people who'd take your very blood if they needed it. You should all be on this side, with us."

There was a rumble of low voices.

"You attacked Ilario and Nino and a boy of fourteen to get your way," another man said. "Who are you to talk of morality?"

"We are taking what is ours. What is right and fair. If anyone tries to stop us, they will be met with resistance," Antonio said.

"Right and fair?" It was my turn to curl a lip in disgust. "You brought disease into our home, threatening the lives of everyone in the villa. You destroyed our dam—"

"Our dam," he said. "Our family built it. My brothers and I used to help our father maintain it. Just as we maintained the mill and the fields and the forest and everything else you've taken for granted since you arrived."

No, I wouldn't be lectured by this boy or his brothers. Not when they'd felt no compunction at putting lives at risk. "We'll go higher for help, then. To the podestà of the region, and we'll get his assistance in removing you."

But even as I said the words, I realized how hollow they were. The podestà would ask the massaro to confirm the problem, to provide information and the support of his sbirri. Which he'd never do.

Antonio watched me stumble upon that thought.

"You have no recourses," he said. "We'll continue to take the trees, and if you try to prevent us in any way, all of this will get much worse. What you've experienced until now will seem a mere nuisance to what we can do."

The dove-keeper tapped the axe against his side again. "And I imagine you really wouldn't want to do anything that puts your children at risk. You'd do well to remember that thanks to our brother, we know precisely where they sleep."

The words were lashes. They burned into me.

I heard Florindo's sharp inhale.

"Have you lost your senses!" one of the workers shouted. "You don't threaten to hurt children over a patch of land. It's madness."

"This has all gone too far," another one said, stepping past me.

"What are you going to do, then?" the dove-keeper said. "Come on, traitor. Show us."

The rumble of male anger shook against the tree trunks, the voices knotting once again as the shouts multiplied. The laughter of the dove-keeper joined with his brothers' taunting calls, which they flung at the workers with jeering smiles. Only Antonio held his silence.

"Enough!" Florindo yelled, but not even his voice could cut through the chorus of rage.

Ugo's first whimpers pulled me back to the horse's side, the animal snorting at my sudden movement, its honeyed eyes flicking from man to man as its nostrils flared. Its flanks had started to shake.

One the workers picked up a branch to the laughter of the dove-keeper, who swung his axe forward, lightly. As he would a toy.

This would be out of our hands in seconds if we didn't do something.

"Damn it all, stop!" Florindo shouted.

But the roar of voices just grew and spilled over the mountain.

I saw Florindo bring the musket forward from where it hung against his back, pointing it up at the sky as he wrapped the horse's reins around his forearm, and my heart's beating became as frantic as my thoughts. I grabbed for Spuma's rein rings, feeling the scrape and pinch of the animal's teeth as it nipped at me, and restrained its head as much as I could manage.

The beast neighed in anger.

"Cover your ears, Ugo!"

The musket shot rattled through my bones.

Spuma shrieked, its hot breath against my hands, and jerked forward, trying to rear up or kick or do anything that might set it loose. I held on to it, fighting for my footing, as Ugo's wails began. The scent of gunpowder burned into my nose and eyes.

Boulders of silence crashed down on the group.

"This is unacceptable," Florindo boomed, his face mottled with red. "Are we no better than beasts? We will have civility here!"

He shifted on Spuma, unwinding the reins from his arm and handing them to me as he started to dismount.

I opened my mouth to tell him to bring Ugo down with him, but the musket's voice was still ringing in my ears and then he was already on the ground, already walking away from the horse.

"Mamma," Ugo whimpered.

But I couldn't control the beast and help him down at the same time.

"Grab on to the saddle," I told him. "I have a hold of Spuma, I promise. Everything with be all right."

He sniffed and wiped at the tears on his cheeks but obeyed. His small hands tightened around the leather.

"We will not accept another threat from you," Florindo said, walking toward the seven trespassers, the musket at his side still pointing at the sky. "Leave our property."

"I don't think you've understood," Antonio said, shaking his head. "Unless you plan on somehow shooting each one of us and dealing with the consequences of murder, nothing is going to change. You have no say in this. We will take all the trees and you'll have no choice but to leave."

The boy radiated hate.

How could I not have seen it? I, who claimed to be so perceptive. How could I have ever allowed him into our home?

Florindo took a step toward him and the dove-keeper moved to block his path. The other brothers shifted to stand closer to their youngest sibling.

My husband slipped the musket back over his shoulder and lifted his hands, palms up. "Please. I'm not going to shoot any of you. But we have to be able to resolve this. We can think through it and find a solution, one that doesn't involve violence."

One of the brothers, with a scar running down the side of his nose, who had been silent until now, stepped closer, his eyes level with Florindo's. "Go back to your villa. Go on. Enjoy it while you still have it."

"This is absur—"

The man shoved Florindo back a step.

I held my breath and the entire mountain seemed to do the same. For the first time since we'd met, I didn't know how my husband would react.

He blinked and remained still, watching the man's growing sneer, their barely contained laughter in his face.

The tension made the hairs on the back of my neck prickle up.

Moving much more rapidly than I would have imagined, Florindo made the wrong choice. He shoved him back.

Gran Dio.

The man smiled and grabbed Florindo by his tunic, one sharp wrench more than enough to toss him off balance. My husband fell with a grunt.

"No, stop," I said, but my voice had lost most of its strength.

The man snorted and stepped closer without glancing at me. He kicked out at the musket, jerking it away from Florindo's reach. "You're too soft, old man. Too many years of doing nothing, I gather."

The men helping us rushed forward, shouts of protest leaping from their mouths as they tried to push their way to Florindo, but the trespassers blocked them with ease, holding axes and shovels and anything else they'd had at hand. Even Antonio had grabbed a pitchfork bent with age and rust.

"Leave him be," one of workers said.

"I don't see why we should."

"It's not a fair fight."

"I've not seen much fairness in my life, have you?"

Florindo tried to shift away, shuffling backward on his elbows, but the scarred man moved with him. He shoved my husband back down, pushing at his chest with a muddy boot.

"Enough!" I shouted.

Ugo let out a wail and Spuma whinnied tightly, a trembling thread of sound, as it tasted the same sulfur of fear in the air that had filled my mouth. I tightened my grip on the animal's reins.

"Stop this!"

The scarred trespasser did look up at me now and smiled again before cocking his leg back.

"Haven't you realized it yet? We don't take orders from you," he said and kicked Florindo in the ribs.

Ugo screamed.

My husband curled into himself with a groan and I realized now that I could have committed murder. I was capable of it. If I'd had the musket in my hands, I would have fired it. And not at the sky.

Racing footsteps pulled my eyes from Florindo's prone figure to the two men who had just appeared on the hill separating the fields.

"What is happening?" one of them said, panting. "We heard the musket shot from the mill and—"

His gaze landed on my husband. Eyes widening, he looked at me, at the other workers, at the trespassers. It was now that one of our men leaped forward, taking advantage of the instant of distraction to break past the dove-keeper, running toward Florindo.

He just wasn't fast enough.

The thud of the axe as it crunched into bone brought bile up my throat, but it was the scream of distilled pain that bent me over and emptied my stomach.

The man fell.

One look was enough to see his knee was gone, shattered into bone shards.

The mountaintop lit up with screams once again. The workers picked up rocks and sticks and started hurling them at the trespassers as the injured man fell onto his back, gasping, his body starting to shake under the force of the pain. Florindo shifted forward and reached for him, but the scarred man kicked him back again. And then again.

I felt each blow as if it'd been directed at me.

"Papà!" Ugo shrieked.

I looked up at my son, the empty words of comfort that were already on my lips slipping from me as I saw Spuma rear up on its hind legs. Its high scream smothered all other sounds as it kicked at the sky. I felt myself unable to gaze away from the beast's vicious dance, hooves obscuring the very sun, covering me in shadows.

Ugo let out a cry and one of his hands slid from the oiled leather.

I blinked. This was no time for stupidity.

I yanked on the reins with everything I had in me and bent, feeling my knees brush the dirt in the effort. The horse tossed its head, snorting, its nose flaring as it tried to shake me off. It kicked out with its front legs and I just managed to sidestep a blow to the chest that would have cracked open my ribs.

"Spuma, stop!"

But there was no reaching the animal. I could see it in the glowing white of its eyes. Even when I pulled it down to the ground again, its teeth clanked, in fear or rage or both, attempting to reach my hands and my face. I'd not be able to hold the beast for much longer. I needed to get my son off its back.

I searched around me for anyone who could help me, but there was no one to call on. No one who didn't also need help. Then we'd do it ourselves.

"Ugo, listen to me," I said, looking up at my sobbing child. "I need you to jump to the ground. I know it's high and you're frightened, but you need to get off Spuma."

"Papà," he said.

"I know. We'll go help him as soon as you're safe."

And back in the villa. Because even if I had to drag him through the entire forest, I'd get him inside and away from these people before I would return to help. I knew Florindo well enough to realize it was the action he himself would have urged me to take. Yet, despite that knowledge, I didn't dare look behind me at my husband. I didn't know what I'd see and I couldn't lose focus now. Spuma let out another piercing whinny and tried to rear up again. I groaned and pulled on the reins, wanting nothing more than to hit the animal into unconsciousness.

"Ugo, there's no time. You have to jump! Now—"

A sound needled into my mind.

It pulled all my attention away from the violence around me and tugged it down, deep, into the raw roots of my being.

A furious ringing.

The sudden and brutal need to cry sank its teeth into me, tearing at me in that terribly familiar way. It pulled me back to my eight-year-old self, dissolving to tears at the sight of my cousin or watching that Barbary pirate ship nearing the coast, carrying my brother's death in its plague-tainted hold.

The certainty of what was coming.

The scrape of bare grindstones, clouds of flour dust haloing the simple light of a spark.

The mill.

When the explosion came an infinite second later, it shook the mountain, the sound darker and more powerful than thunder, than the dam breaking, than anything I'd ever heard before. It snuffed out everything else.

Except for fear.

Spuma lunged forward with a throat-tearing scream.

With a gasp, I pulled on the reins, digging my feet into the dirt as I spun under the animal's force, but the leather whipped out of my hands, sending me to the ground as the horse bolted. With my son on its back.

"No!"

"Mamma!"

The beast raced past the workers and trespassers, the men leaping out of the way, its hooves stomping by Florindo before he could force his broken body to grab the dragging reins.

Even its whinnying shrieks, which were trying to shatter the sky, couldn't drown out Ugo's calls for me.

I leaped to my feet and ran. Stumbling over my skirts but somehow remaining upright, I darted past the men, whose bodies still thrummed with the explosion.

"Stop!" I screamed. "Spuma, stop!"

It was useless.

The horse was a panicked arrow of white plunging through the oaks, their branches snapping over Ugo. He had one arm up to block the worst of the blows from his head and he was shifting about on the saddle. If he fell now, he could land on anything, and at that speed . . .

"Hold on to the saddle! Use both hands!"

But Spuma's wild whinnying swallowed my voice.

There were steps and shouts behind me, but I didn't know what the men were saying and I didn't care. The only thing that mattered was in front of me, my son's small body whipped by branches.

Fabric tore as my dress caught in splintered bark. The pull of it sent me against the side of a wooden chute and my leg hit it with a crunch, one that I hardly felt because only now did I realize what lay ahead: the half-cut oak I'd seen earlier, the rest of the rope wrapped around its trunk, swinging loosely across the horse's path to hang from another tree. Beyond it, the mountain, coming to an end.

Spuma had to stop. The barrier of rope would spook it, force it to retreat or rear back. There was no alternative. There just wasn't.

"Santa Madre, per favore," I muttered and found I couldn't run anymore. The overpowering trembling in my legs had forced me to an abrupt stop. I clutched my hands in prayer, in supplication, in anything that might urge those hooves to slow.

But no one was listening.

Spuma raced right into the rope and dragged Ugo through the loose coils of it that hung from the branch, which now scraped across his face. The heavy loops fell onto him, tangling him with the horse.

Spuma gave another scream and galloped on, its powerful chest now pulling on the rope, tautening it. The oak it was tied to creaked and the wedge the trespassers had cut into its trunk began to splinter under the horse's force.

Another pull did it. I gasped as the tree tipped forward.

The oak crashed down in a storm of cracking branches, the crown of it listing off the side of the mountain. The horse let out a piercing whinny and sped up in a fresh surge of fright.

There was just nowhere left for it to go.

"Mamma!"

Ugo's golden hair rippled as he turned to look for me.

My arms flew out as if I could erase the distance and grasp my child. But if I had unholy powers, I couldn't find them, and fate did have a habit of getting what it desired.

Spuma's white shape glowed in the sun as it ran out of land and disappeared in a twist of limbs and rope.

The snap ricocheted across the entire mountain, rebounding against me, knocking the scream I'd not realized I'd been hurtling from my throat.

And then I was at the edge of the mountain, my legs folding under me. Hands digging into the dirt to keep them from tearing at my flesh. Staring down at my son's lifeless body as he swung from the tangle of rope around his neck, his small feet tapping lightly against the rocks and ivy.

SIBILLA
1933

THE PAIN WAS IMMEDIATE, A thunderclap of it that struck me down. A flood of hot liquid splashed down to the snow beneath me.

I let out a cry as pressure began at my sides and rippled inward, a hardness wrapping around my abdomen like the tightest of corsets, squeezing all breath from me. My legs trembled.

No, not now.

I gripped the balustrade and let out a low moan.

"Sibilla?"

Buona's light footsteps raced up the steps and she appeared on the colonnade again. I felt her gaze rake through me, taking in the wetness beneath me and the pain that was hardly allowing me to breathe. She hesitated, and her hands tightened around her apron as she looked out across the land. I saw the moment she made the decision, turning away from the path the man in the blue cap had taken.

"We need to get you inside," she said and started toward me.

"Don't come near me!" I said. "Don't you dare touch me!"

Another wave of pain, red and hot, swept across me, and I gasped under its force.

Despite my words, Buona hurried to my side and tried to take my arm, but I pushed her away. I wouldn't make it that easy for her to be rid of me. All she would have to do was shove me again, perhaps down the steps, and it'd be over. I'd be out of the way just as she'd obviously wanted since she'd arrived. No, I'd not give her the opportunity.

I forced myself to move. I wanted to race down the stairs, but I knew I'd not make it past the mill because this creature inside me wanted out, and there was no stopping it. I could feel it. It would kick its way through me if I tried to leave.

Bending under the pressure around my midsection, I stumbled back inside.

I'll never make it out again. That was my only chance and it's gone.

Buona tried to herd me toward the bedroom, but I hissed at her and went to the music room instead.

The next surge of pain burned the inside of my eyelids sun-red, and Giovanni's dark silhouette pressed against it, the paper cutout of a man by a hospital bed. All wringing hands and well-earned guilt stamped on his posture. How kind and thoughtful I'd thought him to be, not daring to leave my side for days at a time after my "accident." How devoted.

How stupid of me.

But this time he'd not get away with it. Not him. Nor Buona.

"Sibilla, do you want to sit down?" Buona said. "Are you sure you don't want to go to the bed?"

"Leave me be," I spat out at her.

I walked across the room, the movement easing some of the tightness, some of the brightness from my eyes.

Giovanni and the bedside faded.

"I'm going to call—"

A sizzling sound, like lit sparklers, stopped Buona's words and pulled my gaze to the corner of the room. The collection of electrical wires high on the wall gave a jerk, as if something heavy had tangled in the center of it, yanking cables from their circuits.

"Watch out!" Buona said, grabbing my hand and tugging me back as a raw, live wire swung my way.

A shape crackled into sight. The silhouette of a body, snapping and popping with light as it dangled from the wires. Its feet tapped against the wall, burning it black, before disappearing.

Santissima Madre.

The radio whined down to silence.

"*Merda*, there goes the power," Buona said.

"How did you do that?" I gasped. "That's not possible."

"Pay attention, Sibilla." She pulled on my arm again. "I'll have to fetch Piero and tell him to go for the doctor. Don't move from this room and don't go near those wires while I call your husband back from wherever he is so he can stay with you."

I tore my gaze from the wall and shook my head.

"Well, I can't just leave you alone," she said.

"Go." I wiped at the sweat trailing down the side of my face. "I don't need you."

The girl frowned, her eyes fixed on me.

"Go!"

But she didn't move.

And then another bright wave of pain swept me under. I gripped the armchair as my knees softened, my jaws clenching tightly at the feeling that someone, something, was kicking at my spine.

"It's happening too quickly," Buona said, coming closer again. "The gaps between the pain should be longer. This isn't normal."

Of course it wasn't. There was nothing normal about the hooved creature inside me.

Tears burned down my face. This was all too much.

I squeezed my eyes shut and there we were again, silhouettes of Giovanni and me, my arm in his as he helped me out of the hospital bed. His head turned, watching my face as he handed me a bag of marzapane. How I'd smiled and thanked him for the gift, cooing over his patient understanding and forgiveness. How he'd let me do so without a blush.

In the forest, the horse shrieked.

"I don't think there's time to fetch the doctor." Her voice came as if through layers of cloth. "I don't even think there's time for me to go find your husband."

I bit my lips against the spreading pain and felt myself sway, the room darkening for a breath.

Buona's hands were on my arm. "You need to lie down."

I groaned, leaning against her despite myself, my entire body trembling enough for my teeth to chatter. "I'm not leaving the room," I gasped out.

She exhaled. "Fine." Her grip on my arm was gone and then she was pulling the cushions from the two armchairs, placing them on the floor next to the fireplace before racing out of the room.

"I don't want to do this," I murmured. "I want to leave."

I winced at another shriek from the forest. It sounded closer, as if the horse had leaped out of the recording and was now galloping toward this very room. "I don't want to see Giovanni again. Or Emilia."

I frowned. No, not Emilia. It was the other one, wasn't it?

Buona.

The girl ran back into the room with a bedsheet and towels draped over her arm, an iron pot hanging from the other.

Buona placed the pot in a corner of the fireplace, where the flames were burning brightest, and then draped the bedsheet on the floor, over the cushions.

She motioned for me as the pressure began again and I found myself kneeling, my hands gripping the bedsheet as I rocked under the muscular current of pain. It pummeled me, ripping me from myself.

I drifted out onto a patch of cool darkness. Everything easing. Although I could hear a voice calling me, I ignored it and let it remain distant, there, with the worst of the pain.

"Sibilla."

Someone was shaking me.

Why couldn't I just be left alone?

"You need to stay conscious, Sibilla. Can you hear me? You need to come back."

More shaking, and now the voice was pulling me, returning me to the bright heat of pain. I opened my eyes.

Golden hair hovered above me, glowing in the fire's light. I'd known it. I'd known she was waiting here, somewhere, ready to show herself when I was most vulnerable.

"Emilia," I said.

"It's Buona, Sibilla. You know me. Come, have a sip of wine."

She shifted and the gold tarnished and it was the girl who was there, bringing a glass to my lips. I tried to turn my head away, but she held it in place with her other hand.

"You need more strength to continue," she said. "You're weak as a puppy. Drink."

I did as she said because I had no other choice, and the wine was the sweetest thing I'd ever tasted. I wanted to gulp it down, but the pain allowed me just three sips before starting again, and this time something had changed. The pressure had settled low and heavy. There was a finality to it that my entire body recognized.

"I think it's time," I gasped. "It wants to get out."

I heard the ruffling of clothing as Buona lifted my wool dress and pulled down my slip.

"You'll have to push now," the girl said. "You're as ready as you're bound to be."

I let out a strangled sob.

"Don't fret, Sibilla. I've helped dozens of goats do this and I'm sure it's no different."

It didn't matter because it was happening, now, whether I was ready or not, whether Buona knew what she was doing or not.

On the next crest of pain, I did what my body was demanding of me and bore down.

"That's good!" Buona said. "Keep pushing!"

A ringing started in my ears, but no, that wasn't right. It wasn't in my ears or even in my head. It was coming from a distance, the sound of bells. Someone was ringing bells.

With a cry, I pushed again, using the next wave of pressure, and burning blades seemed to be tearing at me.

"I can't do it!" I said.

"Yes, of course you can, and you will."

And she was right, for my body had slipped out of all of my control, reins snatched from my hands as it galloped ahead with what it needed to do.

I pushed through flames over and over again.

Screams ripped out of me, and I could hear them race and crash through the entire property, but they seemed to warp by the second, so that it was no longer my voice shattering itself against the trees and the mountainside. The voice of another woman, *that* other woman, shrieking her pain.

"One more, Sibilla, just one," Buona said.

I stole a breath and pushed once more.

Like a taut thread, the pain stretched until it could not sustain itself any longer and then snapped.

"Oh!" Buona said.

I gasped at the sudden and overwhelming relief, my arms and legs shaking and then collapsing like a marionette's limbs, my back and head and chest soaked with sweat.

It was over. This horridness, at least, was finished.

I allowed my eyes to flutter shut for a moment as I let Buona deal with the cord, breathing deeply, reveling in the calm, the stillness I felt throughout all of me. For the first time in months, my body was my own. There'd be no more kicking hooves.

And I realized the tranquility wasn't just within me, either.

Outside, the horse's cries and the ringing bells had stopped.

With a small coo, the girl stood and wrapped a towel around the creature I'd birthed before she began to gently rub it. It didn't cry, as infants were meant to do, but instead let out a snorting cough and a mewl.

"You were right," Buona said, smiling. "It's a boy."

I turned away. It might have been male, but I knew it was not a boy and so did she.

I listened to her walk to the fireplace and drag out the iron pot.

"We'll just give you a quick warm wash, winter child. Leave you glowing for your mother and then I'm rather certain you would like your first meal."

My lips twisted at the thought.

"Oh, he's perfect, Sibilla."

I turned to look at her once again. "You don't need to keep lying."

"What do you mean?" The towel in her arms moved in all manner of odd angles as she wiped at what it contained.

"That . . . thing is not perfect. It's an abomination."

Buona frowned, shaking her head. "You're wrong. He's a beautiful child, look."

She walked toward me. I tried to shift away, but my exhausted body was not fast enough to move before she knelt beside me.

"Look at your winter child." She chuckled. "A proper one, too, born in a snowfall."

Mottled, bruised pink was the first thing I saw, a scrunch of wet, swollen features that resembled a newborn's but were not. A black patch of coarse hair covered the crown of its head. An arm moved out of the towel's confines and there was a small dark hoof where a hand should have been. I'd known it would be there, I'd expected it, and still I felt a bitter wave of nausea at its sight. I winced as I pulled myself up, using my elbows and my forearms because the muscles in my stomach refused to cooperate.

"Give it here," I said and reached for the towel.

Buona hesitated, her hands tightening for an instant, but she did what I said.

Deep watery eyes looked up at me as I brought the bundle closer, hooves clopping together as the creature shifted. I pulled the towel away from its body.

It was a small thing, not the rosy, porcelain-skinned cherub that it should have been, and its splotched pink flesh was taking on an edge of gray even as I watched. Its legs, too, ended in hooves. The ones that had kicked out at me with such anger.

Yet I saw no anger in it now. It was just defenseless and pitiful, shifting against my hands.

What could it possibly do to me?

I brushed its cheek with my fingertips, watching it watch my movements. It was softer than I expected. Warmer.

And then it opened its mouth, folds coming into its face as it scrunched up its features in the prelude to a cry.

The sound that came out of it chilled the sweat covering my body. I'd been wrong. It could still hurt me.

It was a whinny.

"Oh, Dio," I said.

Buona chuckled. "He's probably just hungry."

The cry hitched up and a snort came into it, a horrid puff of air that made my hands shake. Its hooves clicked together, its mouth widening as it shrieked with the same panic I'd been hearing since we'd arrived at the mill.

I couldn't bear it. Not when it was right here, coming from something that had been inside me.

"Stop," I said. I shook the bundle lightly to try to snap the sound in two, but the movement just made it louder.

"Sibilla," Buona said.

"Please, stop," I said.

But the creature kicked out, hitting the air with its four hooves, and kept up its piercing shriek.

My heart's beating was painful as I clapped a hand against its mouth. I expected the sharp nip of teeth, but there was just warm wetness.

"Sibilla!" Buona said. She lunged forward and grasped at the bundle, trying to rip it from my hands.

But I held on, because I knew if she took it, she'd allow it to continue, and then the crying would never end. Neither the radio nor Mother's waltz would be able to drown it out. I could feel the growing power in the screams—they would seep into everything.

"Let me have him," Buona said. "I'll take him into another room so you don't have to hear him."

I almost laughed. As if a door and some walls could keep that horrid sound at bay.

I pressed my hand harder against the creature's mouth, trying to muffle the shrieks. All I wanted was for it to be quiet. If it would just stop making that noise I could think and decide—

"Stop, Sibilla!"

The girl leaned into me, pushing an elbow into my chest as she tried to pull the bundle toward her. I felt my grip slip. My hand slid from the being's mouth and the sound surged through the room. Buona began to stand, readying to give herself the leverage she needed to take the creature with her, and I did the first thing I could think of. I shoved my shoulder into her.

She tipped backward, releasing the bundle, the ragged hem of her trouser ripping where it'd caught under her shoe. She grunted as her head struck the wooden edge of the armchair and she landed with a clatter of limbs. She made no attempt to move or stand.

The creature gulped in a breath and renewed its cry.

"Enough, please!"

But it wouldn't obey. Its screeching tore at my mind, I could feel it scraping my thoughts to strips. I had to stop it. Had to.

I pulled the towel over the creature, trying to at least muffle the sound. Small hooves struck at my hand through the fabric as I pressed down, willing it to silence.

"Just be quiet," I said, closing my eyes. "For a few minutes, that's all. Give me some peace."

It felt like hours, but the noise did begin to weaken and then, finally, it stopped altogether. The hooves settled. Stillness descended on the room like the warmest, heaviest of blankets. I exhaled and felt the knots in my muscles starting to dissolve.

That was all I'd wanted.

I shifted the bundle from my arms and placed it on the floor, pulling the towel away from the creature's face so that it could breathe untroubled as it slept. Once it woke again, I'd have to think of how I would feed it, for I'd not be latching it on to my breast. The mere thought of those hooves kicking at my bare flesh made me wince.

The room tilted as I made to stand and I had to stop and wait for the pinpricks of darkness to fade from my eyes before I could continue. My legs shook, thighs aching like I'd run through all of Torino, but they held me as I crossed to the piano and eased my sore body down onto the bench. I placed my hands on the keys but did not press down, for I was loathe to break the silence so dearly won, even for music. I just wanted to remain in this moment, alone and safe, for as long as I could.

I started the waltz without making a sound. Nothing ached or stung any longer. Everything was just fine.

The gunshot in the woods jolted a real chord from my hands.

Behind me, I heard Buona beginning to stir.

The small refuge of silence I'd managed to create cracked around me.

"Sibilla?" the girl said.

I remained as I was, trying to delay the moment when I'd be dragged back to noise and pain and lies and to whatever that gunshot meant.

"Where's the child?"

I sighed and motioned to where it lay. "It's sleeping. Don't wake it up."

Clothes rustled as the girl began to crawl to the bundle I'd left on the floor. I could see her from the corner of my eye as she pulled the creature into her arms, touching its face, grabbing one of its hooves, pressing a hand to its chest, each movement growing more frantic.

"What did you do?" she said, much too loudly.

What a stupid girl. She'd get it screaming again if she kept that up. "I told you it's sleeping, leave it be."

She shook her head, clutching at the creature. "He's dead, Sibilla. You killed him!"

Dio, I was so tired of the lies. What was the point of any of them now, but especially of one like this one?

I heard rapid footsteps in the corridor, heading toward the music room, and all of me bristled. The last person in this world I wanted to see right now was the liar I'd married.

I could still hear how he'd spoken of me to Emilia. The laughter they'd shared at my expense.

Had anything he'd ever told me been true? Had he ever loved me at all, at least at the start, or had I just been the perfect dull-enough woman to cook his meals and keep his home while he did as he pleased?

"Keep him out," I said to Buona. "He's not welcome in here."

But the girl remained where she was and then it was too late, for Giovanni was at the doorway. His pistol rested against his thigh.

"This door should be closed and locked, Buona," he said as he walked inside. He glanced at me and then at the girl, a frown marring his forehead as he took in the stained bedsheet on the floor, the iron pot. "What's happened?"

Buona let out a sob, drawing my husband to her.

Giovanni made a strange, strangled sound I'd never heard before. I swallowed, for I could imagine what he was seeing. I'd had weeks to grow as used to the idea as I could manage and the sight of that creature had still brought waves of nausea.

But at least he wasn't pretending not to notice its unholy deformities like Buona. A small blessing.

"Oh, Gran Dio," he said. "What is this monstrosity? Sibilla, what did you do?"

"I didn't do anything," I said. Of course he'd blame me for it. "It was this place and that girl."

"No!" Buona said. "I didn't do this!"

I shifted on the piano bench until I could see both of them fully. "Really? You're going to deny that you were plying me with concoctions of who knows what plants? Making me ill, twisting the child in my womb into something unspeakable?"

The girl blinked, sending tears down her face. "Sibilla, the teas I made for you were just to calm you. You were hearing things that weren't there and becoming so overwrought with everything that I feared for you and the child. It was nothing but bugleherb and—"

Her eyes widened as her gaze landed on something hanging from Giovanni's woolen coat pocket. She snatched it.

"Where did you get this?" Buona held up a blue cap. A splotch of dark red stained an entire side of it.

"One of the trespassers," he said, his voice a husk. He still had the bundle in his arms, and his face had lost so much color, I expected his legs to buckle at any moment. "I saw him in the woods."

"But why is there blood on it?" she said, her voice breathy with fear.

"I-I called for him and he started running. I fired a warning shot into the sky and he tripped. Fell and hit his head."

"No," Buona gasped. "Where is he? Is he alive?"

Giovanni's eyes narrowed. "Why do you care?"

"Answer me!"

"He's dead."

Buona groaned as if she'd received a blow.

For the first time, I saw the suspicion that had been weighing me down for weeks cross Giovanni's face.

"Who was that man to you?" he said.

But the girl didn't look at him, starting across the room instead, darting toward the door. As sure-footed and quick as she was, Giovanni blocked her path with a violent ease I knew too well. The bundle shifted in his arms. My entire body tensed, awaiting the renewed whinnying, the snorting. But the creature slept on.

"Girl, you need to answer, this instant," Giovanni said.

Buona tried to go around him, but he shifted, taking a step forward so that she was forced to retreat. She pressed the bloodied cap to her chest with a sob.

"Who was he?"

She shook her head, her fingers squeezing into the wool, staining themselves with red.

Giovanni gripped her arm. "Who was he, Buona?"

"My brother!" she yelled. "He was my brother!"

I frowned.

"Your brother was one of the trespassers?" Giovanni said. "He helped in sabotaging the mill?"

She yanked her arm away. "No, of course he didn't. He was innocent, he didn't have anything to do with that."

"Oh, yes, so innocent he was running around our land, freely knocking on this room's very door," I said. "I tried to warn you. I did tell you she was involved."

"No! He didn't do anything, I swear it. And neither did I." She shook her head once more. "He isn't . . . wasn't well. He was born different, easily confused, but he would never have done something like that. He was so gentle." Her voice cracked and she pressed a hand to her mouth.

I scoffed. Were we really supposed to believe that? "What was he doing wandering about here, then? Traipsing through our property as if he owned it?"

"It wasn't his fault. I brought him with me on the day I arrived. I couldn't leave him alone because he doesn—didn't know how to care for himself. So I hid him in the old stables." She wiped at her eyes. "I needed the job and you wouldn't have given it to me if I'd told you about him."

Giovanni ran a trembling hand through his hair, moving the bundle again. My teeth gritted together.

"Will you put that creature down?" I said. "You'll wake it and I can't bear its noise."

He flinched and turned to look at me, frowning, his eyes searching my features as if he had not the slightest idea of who he was looking at. I would have liked to claw that expression off his face. He had no right to it.

"Put it down," I said.

He pinched his lips together but, for once, he did as I said and laid the bundle down on the nearest armchair.

Buona took the opportunity to lunge for the door again, but she wasn't quick enough. He gripped her arm before she could cross the threshold and pulled her back.

"Enough," he said. "You're not going anywhere until you tell us exactly what's been going on here."

"I've already told you! I hid my brother and kept him quiet through the day so that no one would see him." She turned to look at me. "I did it with that same tea I gave you, Sibilla. I didn't harm anybody. Please, I just want to see him."

Did she really expect help from me, after everything she had done? "And Piero? How is he involved?"

"Piero?" she said.

"Why did you pretend not to know him? What was that whispered conversation all about the day he came to visit?"

She shrugged and gave a shuddering sigh. "He knew about my brother and he wanted me to tell you, that's all. And I should have. I should have told you that day that you followed him into the woods, Sibilla, but I didn't know how. I'd already been hiding him for so long by then . . ."

I chuckled. I couldn't help myself. She was quite the little actress, but she'd not fool me again. "You're a liar."

Giovanni turned to me. "Sibilla—"

"She might have you in the grip of her charms but I can see right through her lies."

"Her charms? What in Heaven's name are you talking about?"

No, he'd not do this to me again. Try to convince me I hadn't seen what I'd seen. "I heard the two of you talking, and in a very private manner.

Buona telling you that it couldn't wait any longer. Insisting that it, what-ever it was, had to be now."

"Oh, Sibilla." The girl took a step toward me, her hands held out as if in supplication. Her face gleamed with tears. "I was asking him to call the doctor again. You weren't well, you're still not, and you needed to be watched."

The truth came to me all at once, hitting me with such force that I felt myself recoil, my back hitting the piano.

I understood now why they kept pretending, why Giovanni was going along with her treachery. He'd even said the words himself.

How had it taken me so long to realize it?

It had been a lie, all of it. Cleverly planned.

Who had it been who had told me about Dottore Lupponi's letter, a letter I did not see? Who had pushed me to find the "truth"? What evidence did I have of what Giovanni had claimed about the patent?

They'd arranged everything between the two of them. There were no trespassers. There was just them. Even this nonsense with the brother had to be staged, to confuse me even more.

"That's been your plan all along," I said, turning to Giovanni. "The mad wife, locked safely and conveniently out of the way."

His face twisted under his deepening frown.

"The entire charade of the horse, of the oaks. The broken mill parts." I scoffed. "You've probably been planning this since the ordeal with Emilia, when I became too troublesome for you." I almost smiled at the way he winced. "And now this place, so removed from everything, has given you the perfect opportunity to put the plan to work. Have your wife committed and you're free to do as you please. You even found a pretty and eager witness to all of my madness."

Buona tried to get closer to me, but I stood and she took a step back. The room swayed so that I had to grip the piano to steady myself. "She can help you with that creature now, too, so you don't need me for anything at all."

My breath caught as another thought slammed into me. If they'd man-aged to deceive me with the rest, they could have also found a way to do so with the child. But no, they couldn't have done such a thing, could they? Would they have been so vicious?

I started toward the bundle.

"What are you doing?" Giovanni said and now he came to stand in my path.

"I need to see what's in there."

"No, Sibilla."

My eyes widened. That was all the confirmation I needed.

It had been the two of them, then, they'd tricked me into thinking there was something wrong with my son. That he had hooves and made inhuman sounds and I'd fallen for it. Gran Dio, they'd made me feel disgust at his birth. All to ensure no one would ever find me sane.

There were no depths to which they wouldn't sink to get what they desired. I looked from one to the other, shaking my head. "But how did you do it? How did the two of you manage something like that?"

"You need to calm yourself," Giovanni said. "You're overwrought. No one did anything."

"You'll forgive me if I don't take you at your word," I said. I stepped past him.

He grabbed both my arms and pulled me back. "Stop."

"Get your hands off me." I jerked forward, trying to get loose, but his grip just tightened. "Let me see! He's my child."

"Grab the baby," Giovanni said and Buona moved to do just that.

No, I couldn't let her. She would take my son where I'd not find him. I'd never see him again.

"Don't touch him."

Her eyes flicked to me, yet she didn't stop.

"Buona!" I kicked out, trying to find some leverage that would help me rip free of Giovanni's grip, but my wet slippers slid on the wood. My hands became fists that could strike nothing.

"Leave him! Don't you dare touch him!"

"It's for the best," Buona said, grabbing the child. "Truly."

"Give him to me! He's mine!"

Giovanni spun me so that I could no longer see what was happening, gripping my forearms. "Sibilla, enough. It'll do no one any good for you to see it. The child is dead."

"Liar!" I tried to reach his face, claw at it with my bare hands until he released me, until he couldn't cry the false tears I saw glittering in his eyes, until he couldn't tell me any more lies. But he held on.

"You're not well," he said, his voice breaking. "I don't know what I'm going to do with you."

I felt a growl rumbling in my chest. "You'll do nothing with me! I don't want you near me or my child, do you understand? You've taken enough of my life."

Golden hair blazed across my mind.

My head felt as if it would crack open. Rage, a kind I'd never felt before, made my very blood impossible to stand as it burned through my veins.

"Do you have any idea how much I hate you?" I said. "You're a liar. You've caused all of this, you've destroyed my life, and now you're taking another child from me! You've taken all of them, everything from me!"

Giovanni let out a sob. He shook with it, but he didn't release me.

"Please," he murmured. "Sibilla, I am sorry."

I spat in his face.

"Signora, is everything all right? I heard a gunshot."

It was Piero's voice, coming from somewhere in the house.

Behind me, Buona gasped. From the corner of my eye, I saw her quick shape as she ran past us, once again toward the door, clutching my son to her chest.

"Fetch the carabinieri, Piero!" she said.

"No, stop," Giovanni said, releasing me, turning toward her.

"They're both mad!" Buona shouted. "They killed my brother and their child!"

I didn't see when Giovanni pulled the pistol from his belt.

"Stop!" he called again, but the girl didn't listen.

The shot rang out as her hand touched the doorframe and she lurched forward, stumbling out into the corridor like someone had shoved her. Her legs held her for just a few seconds more, her head turning, her eyes meeting mine one last time.

She still gripped the child in her arms as she fell.

Footsteps thundered down the corridor and Piero appeared at the door, gaze locked on the girl's body.

"What—?"

The next shot knocked the words from his mouth. He gasped, a gurgling, wet sound. Blood bloomed across his chest as his legs slid from under him.

My breathing was ragged in my ears. I scrambled backward. My feet slipped on something, the soiled bedsheet or the cushions, and I felt myself falling, knees landing with a thud against the wood. I started to shake as all of me fought against what I'd just seen, unable to grasp onto anything except the pure animal need to run. But there was no way out except past Giovanni. And I couldn't leave my son.

The shots still lingered in the air as Giovanni lowered the pistol against his thigh. He shuddered. Even from the back, I could see him panting.

I pressed my lips together to keep from screaming.

"You have to know I didn't want any of this to happen," he finally said, voice splintering. He turned to look at me and his face was contorted under the weight of his tears. "I didn't have any plans to be rid of you, as you claimed. None of this was a trick. I know you don't believe me, but I wanted us to be happy here, to have a new start and raise a child together. I thought we deserved it, after everything that happened, but nothing has worked in this cursed place. Not the slightest thing. And now it's too late."

He walked closer and knelt in front of me and for an instant I saw the young man I had fallen in love with that morning in the sweets shop, staring out as if through the bars of a cage. Just for an instant.

Behind him, in the doorway, the familiar black figure slipped into view. It dug its claws into the wooden frame as the grinding of its teeth filled the room.

Giovanni tried to smile but his lips wouldn't obey him. "You don't have to worry though. I promise you we'll be all right. And this is one promise I can keep."

The figure jerked forward.

I squeezed my eyes shut, wrapping my arms around myself, and painted the image of my mother's piano keys across the black expanse of my mind.

Something cold pressed against the center of my forehead.

I played the first chord of the waltz.

MADDALENA
1596

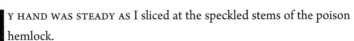

M Y HAND WAS STEADY AS I sliced at the speckled stems of the poison hemlock.

The few candles I'd bothered to light flung the shadows of my movement against the high walls of the empty kitchen. I'd never seen it this still before, this empty of activity, with the only sounds my careful chopping and the gurgling of the stew in the hearth. The memory of the day my children had come racing through the room, my hand in Ugo's, tried to rise, but I shoved it back. No good would come of remembering that.

I scraped the white, lacy flowers off their stalks and made a small pile of them. I would add all of the plant to the stew, including the roots, for potency equaled speed and that was crucial. I'd not let them suffer more than was absolutely unavoidable. In all of this horror, that was at least the one thing I was certain of: Ugo had not suffered. His death had been instantaneous.

The sound of his cracking neck whipped through the kitchen. It was a fist to the stomach.

I had to bend over, the knife clattering onto the cutting board, as I forced myself to breathe. I'd lost count of how many times that sound had doubled me over already just this evening, always painful and always a surprise.

"Only a little while longer," I whispered. "And then it'll be over."

I yanked myself back from the maw of grief.

I couldn't allow myself to disappear into it now, as I had for that entire first day and night. The neighbor of madness, it had been a blinding and greedy creature, consuming everything in its path, the rest of my children's names, all sounds except for Spuma's shrieks, the feel of anything but Ugo's soft hair when the men who had lifted him back up the mountain had handed him to me.

Shame roiled in my stomach as I thought of the way I'd left everything for Florindo to handle as I'd sunk into that grief like a stone in a river. I'd not allowed him his own mourning as he dealt all alone with the doctor and Giacomo's leg, with our other children, with the knowledge that we were entirely ruined.

Our future, lost.

We'd not be able to pay back any of the loans, of course, not a one. Not with a mill shattered by the explosion. The trees might as well not have existed and even the dam had started cracking again, though whether it was from sabotage or faulty construction, I didn't know. Or care. As things stood, we'd be destitute in a week or two. The massaro would not delay galloping to our villa, then, to escort us off the land that would no longer belong to us. And yet, what did any of that matter when weighed against the small body resting now in one of the sale, candlelight and cyclamens keeping vigil until he could be buried?

I made myself straighten and take up the knife again.

The solution to it all had come to me yesterday, with the dawn, just when I'd thought my mind would shred apart like my grandmother's tablecloth. I could feel now the same calming warmth falling over me that I'd felt then as I'd watched the reddening sky and gripped on to the thought that all this suffering did not have to last long. I had the tools to make everything all right. I could protect us from the pain of the loss and from the future racing toward us.

And that was exactly what I would do.

The only regret I had was Giusto, for he loved the children and would mourn them. But that couldn't be helped.

The low, dark voice of the hemlock pulled at me again, issuing another of the many warnings it had given me since I'd snipped it from the forest and placed it on the cutting board.

"Yes, I know," I said. "Thank you. But I do need you now."

"Who are you talking to, Mamma?"

I turned to Marcellina, who stood at the doorway, and made myself smile. "Just the herbs, amore."

She walked toward me. She looked thinner than she had been just two days ago and her eyes were swollen from crying. "Where are Martino and the other servants?"

"I gave them a night to themselves," I said. "They deserve a bit of a rest after all of this. Besides, I wanted to have a meal together, just the seve—" I exhaled. "The six of us. It won't be anything fancy, mind, only a stew. But what do you think about using the unicorn plates?"

Her eyes widened. "Really?"

My smile ached. What a silly, cruel thing, to have always been so careful with that majolica set when I could have granted Marcellina the pleasure of seeing it more often. Would a chipped plate have made a difference to anyone, to anything?

"Would you fetch me a few sprigs of rosemary from that pot?" I said and motioned across the room.

Marcellina did as I asked, picking them with care and pressing them to her nose as she walked back to me. As she handed them over, her gaze landed on the stalks splattered with purple, on the pile of white flowers. She looked up at me, frowning.

I held my breath and her eyes.

Something crossed her face, and as well as I knew my daughter, I didn't know what I was seeing. She watched me with the same intensity with which she'd stared at my herbarium back in Genova, but no expression crossed her face. Her thoughts remained hers.

I opened my mouth without a real idea of what I was going to say, but she looked away, down at her hands.

"Do you need more help?" she said. "Or can I go find the twins?"

I swallowed. "You go on. I just have to add this to the pot and let it cook for a while."

She nodded and started to turn.

"Wait." I pulled her back, into my arms, and pressed a kiss to the top of her head. "You know I love you so much it burns, right?"

Her head moved against my chest.

"Good." I released her and smiled despite the tears I felt rising. "All right, go, find your brothers."

I watched her leave, wishing I could have at least seen a shadow of who she would have been if we'd never come here, if things hadn't happened exactly as they had.

I shook my head to tear the hope right out of it—for that would, *could*, never happen—and finished slicing the hemlock along with the rest of the herbs. I kept my mind poised over a great, bright nothingness, allowing the mechanism of movement but nothing else.

When everything was ready, I pushed the herbs off the cutting board and into the stew pot. It had an hour or two left to simmer.

Bene. Because I still had one more thing I needed to do.

I walked out of the kitchen and headed down the courtyard, out to the colonnade one final time. My heart beat just a bit faster as I started down the stairs, descending slowly, stepping right into the mud that was starting to congeal with the chill.

I looked at the land all around me, at the dark mill, the pine tree forest, the mountain, and its oaks beyond it. Everything that had caused us so much harm.

"Well, I have some harm of my own to bestow," I murmured. "Let us see if I am the strega everyone seems to think I am. If I have the power to deal some of the justice we were denied."

Clenching my hands, I dipped into myself, diving down and down through the years, past the barricades of decorum and normalcy I'd built for myself, into all of that which my mother had urged me to keep silent about. I clutched onto that pure, smothering need to cry that I'd first felt when I'd seen death embracing my cousin, and made no attempt to hold it back. Any of it. Not this time.

From all around me rose voices. Those of seeds waiting for spring, of frozen roots and trampled leaves, of weeds that held on, green, through the chill, and I pulled on it all, on every voice, on every bit of hope and suffering and strength I had at my reach. I took it all.

Gorged as a leech, I looked at the mill.

"This is what is yours, then: endless destruction. Your wood will rot and crack and you will never escape the explosion that took my child."

A rope fraying, a man lunging for its end as a wooden part hung suspended in the dusty air for a moment before crashing to the floor. Shattering.

A coil of swirling blackness appeared before me and I exhaled as I felt it pull at my strength. I offered no resistance. I fed it.

I brought up the image of the torrent as it had been on the night of the flood. Feral.

"For you, I grant you waters filled with death and no dam that will ever last, for you will never again be anything but mad."

Water and rocks crashing through wooden planks, sweeping a man under their force. Bloated deer carcasses squelching out of a black mouth.

The blackness grew. Deepening.

The mountain came next.

"Your oaks will sicken and die. Hemlock will rise like a scourge from their rotting roots, multiplying, covering the land until it is dry as a husk."

A field of stumps drowned in white flowers, a tree on its side trapped in ivy and moss, its bark black with years.

And then the family. The trespassers who had so arrogantly walked in and out of our home.

I called Antonio's face to my mind and held it there, pinned in place like an insect.

"Oh, and you." I breathed, feeling my skin tingle with anger or power or both. "Those with a single drop of your family's blood in their veins will summon their death if they step foot on this land. This place will be their end just as it was ours. I swear that."

A man falling in the forest, head striking stone. A bloodied blue cap. A girl clutching at a child as her chest blossomed with red.

The dark form before me churned and continued to grow, finding its shape, becoming large enough to block my view of the mill.

The claws at its side curled and my hands echoed them, fingernails digging into my palms under the oncoming wave of tears. I ground my teeth together, forcing the words to come.

"Yes. This land will remember it all. It will carry the memory of what has happened like a stain that will never wash off. It will pulse through it like a plucked lute string. You will never forget me or mine or what you have stolen from us."

A young woman's face, all tussled curls and bright eyes, filled my mind. I felt myself hesitate, the words on my lips weakening as I saw her cradling her stomach.

My son's golden hair flared bright enough to blind me. I squeezed my hands tighter. I would have my destruction.

"No one who lives here will ever be safe again," I hissed. "I swear it."

My palms were wet, my fingers slick, and I looked down. Perfect half-moons oozed red.

Smiling through my rage and lifting my gaze once more to the lurching darkness I'd created, I held my hands out, drops of blood dripping, falling to the mud below. Seeming to sizzle as they met the silent, horrified land.

1934

THE MAN SWIPED AT A COBWEB. One of the women must have missed it yesterday.

Not that a cobweb was bound to draw much attention to itself when there were entire sections of plaster crumbling down every time he slammed a door too roughly, but he had been hired to prepare the property and that was a responsibility he wouldn't shirk. Even if he had to pluck spiders out one at a time.

Wiping his hands against his trousers, he peered into the kitchen. Clean, bare. Just as the new owners had requested.

The man still didn't quite understand how the property had passed on to the hands of the couple who would be arriving in three days. From Milano, of all places. An arrangement, a scandal of some kind. Something to do with a stolen patent, if he wasn't mistaken. But it was all very peculiar.

Then again, everything about this place was peculiar.

He walked down the corridor to the music room, or at least that was what he'd gotten into the habit of calling it, for the piano had been there.

Though he supposed he could have as easily called it the blood room. He sighed at the dull stains on the wooden boards.

He and the local women he'd hired had tried their best, but there was just so much any of them could do against all that red. Even the piano, which he'd been loath to toss out and had taken to his own home, still had traces of it on its keys, which nothing could remove. From the rumors that had spread through Ovada, the man, the perpetrator of the crimes, had fallen against it when he'd shot himself, coming to rest on the bench, hands held out to his wife.

And then there were the claw marks on the doorframe.

His gaze lingered over a set of deep gouges on the wood, much too high for any animal to have made. He and the local women had tried to hide them, but every bit of wood paste they applied cracked right off. Like they refused to be covered up.

Not for the first time since he'd taken on this task, he felt the hairs on his arms rise.

Why anyone would want to come live in a place like this, he didn't know. Yes, he'd heard the new owner had aspirations of putting the mill back to work, but he was bringing his wife along with him and this was no place for a woman.

Still, it wasn't any of his concern. He had done what he'd been hired to do and cleared the house of all traces of the previous owners. He'd even had the astoundingly shoddy electrical work ripped out. The villa was as bare as a newborn. The only thing that remained was the stone table in the largest sala, which was impossible to so much as shift. If the new owner—an ingegnere Pisani, if he remembered correctly—wanted it removed, he'd have to hire people to take a sledgehammer to it. It seemed a shame, for it was very old and had likely seen its share of extraordinary meals, but it wasn't any of his concern.

The man crossed the courtyard and walked to the door, stepping out onto the colonnade. The summer sun blazed down on the villa, the torrent talking to itself as birds sang in clashing choruses. Despite the heat, there was a slight breeze that smelled of pine and of something darker but not unpleasant.

Even he had to admit it was rather lovely like this, out here.

He took the heavy iron key from his vest pocket and began pulling the door closed.

Somewhere in the forest, a horse cried out. Likely from a nearby farm, lost.

It was as the door clicked into place, in that second, that he heard the piano, the lilting first chords of a waltz.

The piano that was no longer in the music room because it was in his home.

His skin prickled as a gust of winter air tried to push him back, off balance. He shoved the key into the lock at the center of the puffed angel face and turned it before racing down the steps.

He kept waiting for the coldest of hands to grip his arms. To pull him back.

No.

No matter how enticing it might sometimes look, there was something wrong with the place. He'd known it from the moment he'd first seen it and he was not one to ignore his instincts. No one should live here.

He, for one, would make certain he never stepped foot on the land again.

And that piano would be firewood.

ACKNOWLEDGMENTS

I WANT TO THANK MY MOTHER, in more ways than one. From an early age, she introduced me to the beauty that horror can offer, the stark cruelty of Quiroga and the insistent violence of Poe, feeding what has become an obsession with what awaits full darkness. She also knew I'd be a writer, even before I did, buying me notebooks "just in case" and setting up writing areas for me that I didn't know what to do with . . . until I did. Her efforts and support have earned her hours of listening to me work through plot knots, pacing concerns, I-don't-have-a-title woes, and so much more. #SorryNotSorry.

I also want to thank my sister, for her unwavering, pom-pom shaking support despite being an absolute wimp when it comes to all things horror.

Thanks to my dad for all his work bringing our mill back to habitable conditions. If I need electricity to power my laptop in the middle of the forest, I know you'll rig something up.

A big thanks to Mauro Molinari for always being there to help.

Another huge thanks to Helga for her sharp eye, and Bill and Sue for believing in the novel. I am forever grateful to the entire CamCat team.

Edur, thank you for the company throughout that long winter. If I try outdoor writing again in minus-degree weather, a horn to the solar plexus will likely snap me out of it.

And to my home, the solitary watermill in Molare sitting at the edge of the Bosco del Cavallo. Without you and your oak forest, this book would not exist.

ABOUT THE AUTHOR

BORN IN URUGUAY TO LATINO and Italian parents and having lived in Miami, Florida, for twenty-three years, Valentina Cano Repetto has now made her home in the secluded watermill in Northern Italy that inspired this novel. When not writing, you can find her searching for wild herbs or cuddling with her dozen goats.

If you enjoyed
Valentina Cano Repetto's *Sanctuary*,
consider leaving a review
to help our authors.

And check out
Megaera Lorenz's *The Shabti*.

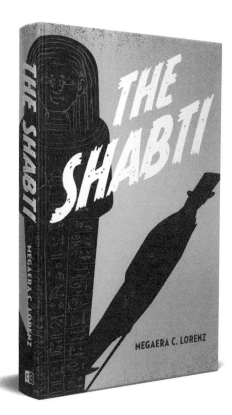

CHAPTER ONE

DASHIEL QUICKE SAT AT THE CENTER of the stage, his head bowed, a shimmering stream of ectoplasm flowing from his open mouth. As the ethereal discharge cascaded over his lap, it seemed to borrow its own luminescence from the white-hot arc lamps that blazed overhead. Perspiration prickled his scalp and soaked his shirt collar, but he welcomed the punishing heat of the lights. He'd spent enough time working under the cover of darkness. He was a man with precious little left to hide.

The watchful eyes of his audience bored into him. The atmosphere was thick with their morbid curiosity. Even at a demonstration like this one, Dashiel didn't shy away from theatrics. If tonight's crowd of gawkers took nothing else from the experience, they would at least leave entertained. His shoulders heaved and he swayed in his seat as the ectoplasm continued to unfurl, pooling on the floor at his feet in a filmy heap. His hands, resting on his knees with the palms facing up, twitched spasmodically.

Someone in the audience let out a low whistle. Another onlooker, seated closer to the stage, groaned in disgust.

"Holy cats, mister," said a voice from somewhere in the middle seats. "How much of that stuff you got in there?" A handful of the speaker's neighbors broke out in raucous laughter.

Dashiel pulled the tail end of the ectoplasm out of his mouth, then rose to his feet and moved to the edge of the stage. He held it aloft in front of him, spreading it out wide between his hands. The ends trailed down on either side of him, sweeping up dust and grime from the battered floorboards as he walked.

"I hope you're all duly impressed by what you've seen here tonight, ladies and gentlemen," he said. "Your average Spiritualist would tell you that it's impossible to produce ectoplasm under these conditions. It's sensitive stuff. Disintegrates under full light, you see. The theory has it that light disrupts the ectenic force that the spirits use to manifest it out of the medium's body.

"What they won't tell you is that it's made of common cheesecloth. Or muslin, if you're the type of medium who likes to live large and spring for the good stuff. It doesn't really matter which one you use, though. Either one looks mighty impressive if you've got a dark séance room and a strong will to believe.

"They're both just about infinitely compressible—perfect for hiding in tight spaces, away from the prying eyes and hands of doubters and debunkers. And to answer your question, young man," he added, smiling in the direction of his heckler, "unless the fellow at the general store shorted me, it's exactly three yards."

Satisfied that everyone had gotten a good look at the ectoplasm, Dashiel walked back to the center of the stage. Like most campus theaters where he had performed, this one was a humble affair. It held enough seats for about two hundred spectators. Only a battered chalkboard sign outside the front entrance served to announce his performance that evening. Paint splatters, scuffs, and the faded remnants of spike marks from past theatrical productions marred the dark floorboards of the stage, which creaked beneath his feet with every step.

"My spiritual instrument is speaking to me again," he said. With nimble fingers, he wound up the trailing ribbon of muslin ectoplasm as he spoke. The length of cloth vanished within seconds into a bundle small enough to fit between his cheek and his gums. "I'm receiving a very strong impression. The spirits have a gift for someone who is here in the theater tonight."

Someone in the audience snickered. Dashiel blithely ignored them. He tossed the roll of muslin onto the rickety table that stood at the center of the stage, where it joined several other tools of his trade—a dented tin trumpet decorated with bands of phosphorescent paint, a stack of cards inscribed with forged spirit messages, and a fluffy drift of white chiffon veils. He turned his attention to the audience, squinting at them past the glare of the footlights and the bluish fog of cigarette smoke that hung low and heavy in the air beyond the stage.

The spring had been a cold and dreary one, and that always meant good business. The house wasn't packed, but there was still a decent crowd. Except for a lone middle-aged gentleman in brown tweeds seated in the front row, the audience was overwhelmingly youthful. Bored college boys and girls filled most of the seats, their dreams of necking with their sweethearts under the mellow April moon dashed by the chilly weather. So far, they had reacted to his routine with rowdy enthusiasm.

"Is there," Dashiel asked, pressing his fingers to his temples, "a Professor Hermann Goschalk among us?"

It came as no surprise to Dashiel when the man in the tweed suit rose to his feet. He clutched his hat to his chest and cleared his throat, glancing around as if he expected some other fellow to step up at any second and identify himself as the person in question.

"Um, I beg your pardon," he said at last. "That's my name. Do you mean . . . me?"

Dashiel smiled. "Unless there is more than one Hermann Goschalk in the audience, then I think I must. Join me on stage, if you please, sir."

Professor Goschalk made his way to the stage, accompanied by scattered applause, whoops, and whistles. In Dashiel's experience, there were few things that a collegiate audience liked better than the prospect of a faculty member making a spectacle of himself on stage, and this crowd proved to be no exception. The professor didn't seem to mind. He trotted up the steps and stood smiling shyly at Dashiel like a starstruck kid meeting a matinée idol.

"Hello!" he said.

"Good evening, Professor," said Dashiel, with a brief bow. "Please, be seated." The professor nodded, blinking owlishly under the blazing lights, and took a seat in one of the two folding chairs that stood in the middle of the stage beside the table.

Hermann Goschalk was a little gray mouse of a man, about fifty years old. Dashiel guessed that his well-worn suit was at least half as old as its wearer. His rumpled brown hair was generously streaked with silver, and he had large, uncommonly expressive hazel eyes—an excellent asset in a sitter. The more demonstrative the face, the greater the sympathetic response that the unwitting shill would arouse in the audience.

"Thank you," said Dashiel. He sat down in the other chair and fixed the professor with a penetrating gaze. "Before we proceed, I hope you don't mind if I ask you a few questions, just to get my bearings. I want to be absolutely sure I do have the right Hermann Goschalk, after all."

"Of course!"

"Wonderful. Now, stop me if I'm mistaken in any detail. You are a member of the faculty here at Dupris University, a professor of Ancient Studies, specializing in the language and civilization of the ancient Egyptians. Is that right?"

"Yes, that's absolutely correct," said Goschalk, with an enthusiastic nod.

"Very good." Dashiel inclined his head and squeezed his eyes shut for a moment, as if trying to draw his next morsel of information from some deep and inscrutable well of hidden knowledge. "Is it true that you used to keep a black cat in your younger days, back when you worked as an assistant druggist at that pharmacy in—"

"Milwaukee, yes!" Professor Goschalk's astonished expression couldn't have been more perfect if he'd rehearsed it. "Good heavens, you even know about old Tybalt?"

"I do," said Dashiel, nodding solemnly. "He must have been quite the beloved companion."

The professor chuckled. "Oh, he was a terrible little yungatsh! He'd lie there in the windowsill soaking up the sun and hissing at anybody who dared to get too close. Did a fine job keeping the store free of mice, though." He smiled fondly. "Papa always said a pharmacy without a cat was a pharmacy without a soul."

"Ah yes, that's right. He was the drugstore cat. Your father owned the pharmacy, and he was hoping you'd carry on the family business. But you longed for greater things. You decided to pursue a degree in Egyptology. Once you completed your studies, you came to work here . . . about fifteen years ago."

"Gracious, yes! But how on Earth did you know all these things?"

"Before a second ago, I knew hardly any of it," said Dashiel. "All I knew was that you once worked in a pharmacy and had a black cat. Just enough detail to impress you—and get you talking. It wasn't too hard to put the rest together from there." He winked and patted the professor on the shoulder. "I daresay you'd be a plum customer in the séance room, Professor Goschalk."

Goschalk gaped at him. "Well, I'll be a son of a gun!" he said. A ripple of laughter erupted from the audience.

"Thank you, Professor, you've been very obliging," Dashiel went on. "But if you don't mind me taking just a little more of your time, there's one more thing I'd like to ask you before I let you go. At this moment, the spirits are telling me that you recently lost something of great sentimental value. Is that true?"

The professor nodded. "As a matter of fact, I have. Gosh, how uncanny! It was a cabinet card of my mother. I've kept it on my office desk for years, but I noticed it was gone not two weeks ago. I can't imagine what could have happened to it."

"That is too bad. But perhaps we can help you find it again." Dashiel rose and moved to stand behind Professor Goschalk, resting his hands lightly on the man's shoulders. He gazed out at the audience and spoke in a booming, authoritative tone. "Ladies and gentlemen, you are about to witness one of the most powerful forms of mediumistic manifestation. But I must ask for your help in amplifying the potency of our connection to the spirit realm. Please, raise your voices in a hymn of praise."

He nodded to the elderly organ player stationed at stage right. She curtly returned his nod, then began to grind out a shaky but serviceable rendition of "From the Other Shore."

Three or four voices in the audience piped up with gusto, while a handful of others mumbled along uncertainly.

It was hardly the sort of performance he would have gotten from his regular Sunday evening congregation back at Camp Walburton, but it would have to do.

Dashiel let his eyes flutter closed and allowed his head to loll back as if he were falling into a trance.

"Dear ones who have passed beyond the veil," he intoned above the drone of the organ, "we beseech thee to reunite this gentleman with his lost portrait of his beloved mother. Keep singing, ladies and gentlemen! I am sensing a vibration from the other side. The spirits are with us!" He raised his arms in a dramatic, sweeping gesture, and as he did so, an object tumbled into Professor Goschalk's lap.

"Oh!" said the professor.

"Oooh!" echoed the audience.

Dashiel lowered his arms, letting his hands come to rest on the back of Goschalk's chair. He nodded again to the organist, who stopped playing. "Thank you, Mrs. Englebert. Please, Professor Goschalk," he said, "tell us what you have just received."

Goschalk pulled a pair of wire-rimmed glasses from the inner pocket of his jacket and slipped them on. Slowly, he picked up the item in his lap and squinted at it. He turned in his seat and blinked up at Dashiel in amazement.

"Why . . . it's my photograph!"

"The same cabinet card of your mother that used to sit on your desk?"

"The very same, down to the faded spot in the corner. Oh, that is magnificent. Absolutely phenomenal!"

Dashiel bowed and smiled graciously as the audience burst into whistles and hearty applause.

"Thank you, Professor. Ladies and gentlemen, what you have just seen is known in the spook business as an *apport*. Impressive, yes? But of course, like everything else I have demonstrated this evening, a complete hoax. I hope you'll forgive me, Professor, when I explain that this photograph was stolen from your desk, in broad daylight, by one of my own personal agents—someone who is, what's more, entirely corporeal and very much alive."

"I'll be damned!" said Goschalk, his eyes more saucerlike than ever.

"It was a simple matter for me to obtain a list of the names of people who bought advance tickets for tonight's demonstration. Having selected your name from the list, I sent my young assistant to gather some basic intelligence. Your students and colleagues were happy to share a few choice tidbits of information with someone who, they assumed, was a prospective pupil in the Ancient Studies program.

"That's how I learned of your position in the department, your time as an assistant druggist, and yes—even old Tybalt. As for your photograph, all that my accomplice had to do was to pay a brief visit to your office, posing as a student with a rather vexing academic question. When you got up to consult one of your books, he quietly purloined the cabinet card from your desk. Thank you, Professor. You may return to your seat."

Professor Goschalk rose, clutching hat and photograph, and toddled off the stage, still looking delightfully befuddled. Dashiel was conscious of a pang of wistfulness.

Had he still been in the business of fleecing the rich and bereaved, this was exactly the sap he would have wanted front and center at every service.

A STINGING WIND HAD PICKED up by the time Dashiel wrapped up his act and wandered out of the theater. He turned up his collar and huddled against the wall by the side entrance, debating whether to hail a cab or brave the walk back to the modest room he had rented a few blocks away. Absently, he drew one of the last two cigarettes from the crumpled packet in his coat pocket and placed it between his lips.

"Those things are terrible for you, you know," said a good-natured voice from the shadows.

Dashiel turned, slowly and deliberately, doing his best not to look alarmed. He'd managed to make himself a number of enemies over the past few years, what with one thing and another, and he didn't relish being crept up on in dark alleys. When he saw that it was only the little professor from his demonstration, his shoulders slumped with relief.

"So my doctor tells me," he answered with a wry smile. "But you can only ask a man to give up so many vices at once." He slipped the unlit cigarette back into the package and put it away.

Professor Goschalk chuckled. "I suppose that's true," he said, looking very much like a man who had no particular experience with vices, much less giving them up. "That was all very impressive, by the way, Mr. Quicke. Very impressive. If you hadn't explained how it was done, I wonder if you wouldn't have made a believer out of me."

"Well, if I had, you would've been in good company, Professor," Dashiel assured him. "I've hoodwinked everyone from medical doctors to bishops."

"I shouldn't wonder! Please, call me Hermann." He extended a hand, and Dashiel gave it a firm shake.

"Dashiel. It's a pleasure."

Hermann's fingertips lingered on Dashiel's for a moment as the handshake ended, and his brow furrowed with sympathy. "Oh, gosh, your hands are like ice! It is awfully cold, isn't it? Well, this is what passes for spring here in Illinois, I'm afraid. Do you have far to go? I can give you a lift."

"That's very kind of you. I'm just over on 58th and Crestview."

Hermann beamed, and Dashiel realized that he was handsome, in his understated way. He wasn't sure how it had escaped his notice before. "Perfect!" Hermann said. "There's a nice little diner on Crestview. Please, let me treat you to dinner. Unless you have other plans, of course."

"No plans," Dashiel admitted with a hint of wariness. In his experience, this sort of amiable generosity tended to come with strings attached. However, the ex-medium business wasn't a lucrative one, and he was in no position to balk at the offer of a free meal. Besides, it had been a while since he'd dined with anyone socially, and the notion appealed to him. "Dinner sounds swell."

⸻

"YOU MUST BE QUITE THE regular here," said Dashiel. They'd been hailed with a chorus of friendly greetings the moment they stepped into the Nite Owl Diner, one of those sleek little modern establishments that looked like a converted railcar. They sat across from each other in a cozy booth, lit by the yellowish glow of an incandescent bulb hanging overhead.

"I suppose I do come here a lot," Hermann said, looking a little sheepish. "But their tongue sandwiches are truly the gnat's whiskers, especially after a late evening marking papers."

With Hermann's hearty encouragement, Dashiel had ordered a dinner of roast lamb, buttered corn, and whipped potatoes that seemed extravagant by his recent standard of living. Coils of fragrant, shimmering steam wafted invitingly from the plate. He willed himself to take small bites, resisting the urge to scarf it all down.

"This lamb goes down easy, too," he said. "Much obliged, by the way."

"Not at all!"

Dashiel took a sip of coffee before going on, in a carefully casual tone, "So, the missus doesn't mind all those late evenings at the office, eh?" He was still casing the man, like one of his marks. In the old days, he would have gone home and written up a nice little file after a social tête-à-tête like this. Personal information, no matter how trivial, was a medium's true stock-in-trade, and old habits died hard.

"Oh, there's no missus," said Hermann, his cheeks pinkening. "I suppose I'm what you'd call a confirmed bachelor. No, it's just me and Horatio."

Dashiel raised his eyebrows questioningly. "Horatio?"

"My cat."

"Ah."

"Didn't the spirits tell you all this?" Hermann asked, blinking innocently. "Oh, don't mind me, I'm just making fun. What about you? Do you have any family?"

"Just my sister, back in Tampa. But I haven't heard from her in some time."

"Ah," said Hermann. "A Florida man."

"That I am. Born and raised in Tarpon Springs. My work took me all over, though. Before I left the business, I spent several years at one of the big Spiritualist camps in Indiana. But you heard about that at my demonstration."

Hermann nodded. "You mentioned an accomplice before. The person who purloined my photograph. Do you always work with a partner?"

"Oh, no. That was just a kid I hired for a couple of bucks to do the job for me before the act. These days, I'm on my own." He hoped this answer would be enough to satisfy Hermann's curiosity. The evening had been pleasant so far, and he had no desire to sour the mood by discussing the details of his former working arrangements.

Hermann scraped some horseradish sauce over a slice of bread, lost in thought. When he spoke again, Dashiel was relieved that he had moved on to a different subject. "What I can't understand," he said, "is why you decided to give it all up. As good as you are, you must have made a mint!"

"And how," Dashiel agreed, a little wistfully. "But I suppose even the most vestigial conscience starts to get a bit inflamed when you're bilking little old ladies out of their inheritance day in and day out. I just plain got sick of it."

"Hmm. And now you've made it your life's mission to expose all that fraud and humbuggery to the world. It's kind of poetical, don't you think?" Hermann leaned forward, his big hazel eyes shining with enthusiasm. "I mean, who better to uncover a hoax than someone who knows exactly how it's done? All those parapsychologists and ghost-hunters and whatnot must have nothing on someone with your experience!"

"Oh, certainly."

"Which reminds me," he went on, a little more hesitantly. "If it's not too much of an imposition, I was wondering if you might help me with something."

Ah, there it is. As always, the ulterior motive. Dashiel felt a sting of disappointment. He'd found himself enjoying Hermann's company for its own sake. Still, whatever he wanted, maybe it would pay something. "Oh? What did you have in mind?"

"It's—well, I feel a bit silly actually saying it," said Hermann, looking abashed. "But you see, in addition to being a professor here at Dupris, I'm also the curator of our modest collection of Egyptian antiquities. Sometimes I keep very late hours in the research archive upstairs from the museum, and lately, I've been noticing some, er, very strange activity in the building at night."

"Strange activity," repeated Dashiel, narrowing his eyes. "As in . . .?"

Hermann fiddled with his fork. "Oh, you know. Weird noises. Things moving around when they ought not to. And, um, the bleeding walls. That sort of thing."

"The bleeding what?"

"I've tried to ignore it, but it's become more and more bothersome lately. I've had to stop bringing Horatio to work with me because it unsettles him, you see. The students have been asking after him, and I can't very well explain all this to them, can I? I mean, what would I say? And I know this is going to sound a bit peculiar, especially to you. But I just can't shake the feeling that it's, you know." He glanced around before continuing, dropping his voice to a conspiratorial whisper. "The real McCoy."

Dashiel set down his silverware and sat back, nonplussed. "Hermann, I must confess, I'm surprised," he said. "And a little disappointed. I thought you understood that the whole point of my demonstration this evening was to show that all that spirit stuff is bunkum."

"Of course, of course," said Hermann, now blushing fiercely. "But just because most mediumship is bunk doesn't necessarily mean that there's absolutely no such thing as spirits, does it? Anyway, whatever I'm experiencing, if it is a hoax—"

"I assure you, it is."

"Yes, well, if it is, why, I bet you'd sniff it out quicker than I could say Jack Robinson. You must know all the tricks."

"I suppose you do have a point there," Dashiel conceded.

"I'm sure you're right, of course. Only, if you'd just come and take a look, it would surely set my mind at ease. And, naturally, I'd compensate you for your time . . ."

He looked so comically earnest and plaintive that Dashiel had to fight back a bemused laugh. "All right, all right," he said, dabbing his mouth with his napkin to hide his amusement. "You've piqued my curiosity. I was planning to spend another day or two in town anyway. Shall I drop by tomorrow morning?"

"Oh, you're a mensch!" said Hermann, beaming with gratitude. "Tomorrow morning would be perfect."

DURING HIS NEARLY TWENTY YEARS in the medium business, Dashiel had met many people whom he would generously describe as "eccentric." Hermann Goschalk, he mused, was certainly an odd one, but there was something different about him that Dashiel struggled to put his finger on.

It didn't surprise him to encounter a well-educated man who believed in spooks. Even the brightest were not immune to true-believer syndrome if believing in something—no matter how patently ridiculous it might be—

filled the right need in their souls. But Hermann's game seemed different. For one thing, he wasn't in mourning for anyone, as far as Dashiel knew, nor did he come across as especially spiritual. He seemed to regard his purported visitors from the other side as little more than an interesting nuisance.

He briefly entertained the idea that Hermann might be trying to pull a hoax on him, but that seemed unlikely. He had developed an excellent nose for fraud, and he detected none of the characteristic stink about Professor Goschalk.

Still, something about the situation made him uneasy. He passed a restless night in his drafty room in the boardinghouse on Crestview, which was not helped by the fact his bed felt like an unevenly laid pile of bricks.

The next morning, he rose early. He trimmed his already impeccable mustache, pomaded his dark hair, and donned an old but crisply pressed suit. He dithered for several minutes over whether to bring his cane before stubbornly deciding against it. It didn't take long for him to regret his choice. By the time he'd arrived at the Wexler Building, where Hermann's office was located, his leg was throbbing.

Cursing his pride, he hobbled for the lift.

Hermann's office was on the third floor. When Dashiel arrived and stepped out of the lift, a secretary who looked like a rumpled and world-weary Janet Gaynor poked her head out of a door just down the hall.

"Are you Quicke?" she asked, squinting blearily at him.

He tipped his hat. "Guilty as charged, I'm afraid."

"Oh, thank God. Professor Goschalk's been asking about you every two minutes since he got in."

Dashiel glanced at his watch, perplexed. It was only just past eight o'clock; he was certain the building would have still been locked if he'd arrived any earlier. Aside from the somnolent secretary, the only other sign of life he'd seen there was an elderly janitor pushing a dust mop around in the lobby.

"Well! You can tell him that his lonesome hours are over." He smiled and spread his arms grandly. "I'm here."

The secretary rolled her eyes and disappeared back into the office. A moment later, she re-emerged. "Okay, go on in. Room 302, around the corner and to your left."

Hermann was waiting outside his office door when Dashiel rounded the corner. "You're here!" he said, bouncing jovially on the balls of his feet. "Wonderful! Won't you come in? I'll have Agnes bring you coffee and a Danish."

"Good morning, Hermann. You're too kind."

As Dashiel approached, Hermann's grin faded. "Oh, gosh," he exclaimed, "you're limping!"

"Not to worry," said Dashiel smoothly. "It's an old injury. Flares up sometimes when the weather gets cold."

"Oh, I see. Did you serve in the war?"

"Lord, no. You flatter me. I was far too old for the draft. And even if they had called me up, I'm sure I would have found a way to slither out of it."

Hermann frowned and nodded sympathetically. "Well, I wouldn't blame you. Awful mess, that war."

"Why don't you tell me about your ghost?" Dashiel urged, eager to change the subject.

"Of course!" said Hermann, lighting up again. "But I really think it'd be better if I showed you. Take a load off for a moment, then we'll head downstairs."

Hermann's office was a cluttered affair, packed so densely with bookshelves that there was hardly any space to turn around. A sturdy wooden desk stood in the middle of it all, lit by a sunny window. Books, piles of papers, and framed pictures obscured most of the surface of the desk. Replicas of Egyptian objects crowded the windowsill, along with a potted geranium that boasted numerous clusters of bright red blossoms. Hermann moved a stack of papers off of one of the two chairs by the desk and graciously invited Dashiel to sit. Having wolfed down the promised coffee and Danish, Dashiel accompanied Hermann back down to the ground floor. Most of the action took place, Hermann explained, in the gallery, although the thing would also put in occasional appearances in the archives upstairs. The gallery lay behind a pair of ostentatious Gothic-style oak doors, which were currently closed to the public. Hermann produced a big brass key and unlocked them, ushering Dashiel inside. The Egyptian collection was confined to a single room, but it was a large one, with a lofty ceiling and several bright, expansive windows.

When they entered, a tall, dark-skinned fellow of about seventy, dressed in a security guard's uniform, strolled over to greet them. It was clearly the end of his shift. He carried a tin lunch pail, and his coat was slung over his arm. "Morning, gentlemen," he said, touching the brim of his hat.

"Oh, Clarence!" Hermann beamed. "Just the man I wanted to see. Clarence, this is Mr. Dashiel Quicke. He's here to investigate our little . . . disturbances."

Clarence raised an eyebrow. "How do you do, Mr. Quicke? You a rat-catcher, by any chance?"

"Well, in a manner of speaking, I suppose."

"He's an expert in the realm of occult phenomena," said Hermann, dropping his voice to a stage whisper as he spoke the last two words. "Clarence is our night guard," he went on, turning back to Dashiel. "So far, he's the only other person besides me who's witnessed any of the happenings around here. Other than Horatio, of course."

"Really!" said Dashiel, looking dutifully impressed.

"Come on, now, Professor," said Clarence, with the indulgent expression of a man who had had this conversation several times before. "Like I told you, I did hear—"

"And see!"

"—and see, yes—some sort of little critter skittering around in the gallery. But frankly, I think that kitty-cat of yours would be a better man for this particular job than any spirit hunter or what have you. No offense, Mr. Quicke."

Hermann's eyes widened in dismay.

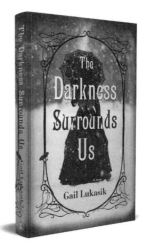
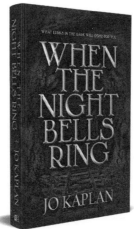

CamCat
Books

VISIT US ONLINE FOR MORE BOOKS TO LIVE IN:
CAMCATBOOKS.COM

SIGN UP FOR CAMCAT'S FICTION NEWSLETTER FOR
COVER REVEALS, EBOOK DEALS, AND MORE EXCLUSIVE CONTENT.

CamCatBooks   @CamCatBooks   @CamCat_Books   @CamCatBooks